Lynne Pemberton was born in Newcastle. She had a highly successful career as a model before she met her husband and became involved in running a group of luxury hotels in the West Indies. Her previous novels are the bestselling *Platinum Coast* and *Eclipse*. She divides her time between Barbados and London.

'A pacey read . . . that keeps you turning the pages to the end.'   *OK!*

'One for the holiday suitcase.'   *Tatler*

'A rising star in the blockbuster firmament.'
                    Observer

LYNNE PEMBERTON

SLEEPING WITH GHOSTS

HarperCollins*Publishers*

This novel is entirely a work of fiction.
The names, characters and incidents portrayed in it
are the work of the author's imagination. Any resemblance to
actual persons, living or dead, events or localities is
entirely coincidental.

HarperCollins*Publishers*
77–85 Fulham Palace Road,
Hammersmith, London w6 8jb

This paperback edition 1997
1 3 5 7 9 8 6 4 2

First published in Great Britain by
HarperCollins*Publishers* 1996

ISBN 0 649941 4

Set in Aldus by
Rowland Phototypesetting Ltd,
Bury St Edmunds, Suffolk

Printed and bound in Great Britain by
Caledonian International Book Manufacturing Ltd, Glasgow

This book is for my mother.
I love you very much.

Acknowledgements

I wish to thank Matthias Kunheim and Martin Summers for their generous help and suggestions on this book. Mark Weitzman from the Simon Wiesenthal Centre for his assistance. Henry Aron and Dr Henry Spooner and Gerald and Merill Powell for the use of Barn Acre. A big thank you to Heather Bell for her expert legal counsel and Jonathan Lloyd, my literary agent, whose help from conception to publication has been immeasurable. Finally, special thanks to my husband, Mike, for his constant support.

Chapter One

'SS *Oberführer* Klaus Von Trellenberg was your grand-father.' Stunned into silence, Kathryn felt an impulse to laugh. But Aunt Ingrid's face was stern.

In the same impartial tone, the revelation was repeated, the words exploding like shards of broken glass that shattered the stillness.

'SS *Oberführer* Klaus Von Trellenberg was your grand-father.'

Kathryn felt her jaw drop and couldn't stop it. The shock induced a faint trembling and she drew in a long breath as her aunt continued.

'Freda refused to discuss the past. It never happened, she buried it, her childhood in Germany, the war, everything that had gone before 1945 ceased to exist. She reinvented herself, erasing her Prussian past to embrace a new identity here. I think she almost believed she was English.' A harsh guttural sound tinged her voice with bitterness. 'I never understood Freda, we were total strangers; how we ever sprang from the same womb is beyond me.'

'Is this why you wanted to see me, to tell me that my grandfather was a Nazi?' Kathryn sneered. 'Is this some kind of joke? My mother's father an SS officer? It's ridiculous! Her father was Kurt Hessler, a factory worker killed on active duty in 1943. He was *your* father too, Ingrid, you

1

should know.' Kathryn tried to contain the hint of fear entering her voice. 'And your mother died of tuberculosis before the war.' The doubt in Kathryn's words begged to be assuaged. *'Didn't she?'*

Ingrid was shaking her head, eyes narrowing to thin slits full of derision, and Kathryn felt a strong urge to slap her aunt's face.

'Your grandmother was a Prussian aristocrat. She died in Berlin at the close of the war. She killed herself.' Ingrid's mind drifted back to a cold January in 1945. The memory of that night, repressed for so long, flooded her mind; so lucid it startled her, and she squeezed her eyes tightly shut. Yet the image had come to life, moving through her head like the jerky silent movies she had watched so avidly as a child. She saw herself sitting on the edge of her bed in the Von Trellenberg house in Berlin. She was shivering not from cold, but from fear, and she knew she must get down to the cellar quickly. With hands clamped to her ears, to shut out the terrible sound of bombs dropping all around, she remembered calling first for Freda, then her mother, as she ran out of her bedroom and down the long hall towards her mother's room. Up till this moment the memory had always been in black and white, and now for some reason it was a vivid colour.

Her mother was dressed in an emerald green taffeta ball gown; her limp body looked like that of a rag doll hanging from the makeshift gallows erected from a bedpost and library ladders.

The sound of the air raid faded to nothing as Ingrid's screams, and the hammering of her own heart, filled her ears. Luize Von Trellenberg was wearing matching green silk shoes, one of which hung precariously from her big toe, the other had fallen to the floor. With a shudder, Ingrid remembered tripping over that shoe as she stumbled out of the room. She also remembered banging her head, and thought how strange it was that she should recall this now – after fifty years. She remained lost in thought as Kathryn spoke again.

'Are you trying to tell me that it was all lies: my mother's childhood in Cologne; her parents; the house where she was born, and grew up; the house that was bombed to the ground? Answer me, Ingrid, was it all lies?'

Ingrid forced herself to concentrate on the beautiful face of her niece, not beautiful at the moment actually, she noted, but contorted with outrage. Still she did not reply.

'Do you really expect me to believe that my mother's entire past life has been a complete fabrication, and that this Von Trellenberg person, this Nazi, was my grandfather?'

Kathryn's tone reeked of dissent and Ingrid sprang to her defence. 'Your grandfather was an aristocrat, he was a wonderful man, well respected, much loved; you have Von Trellenberg blood, you should be proud. Your great-grandfather Ernst was a national hero, a highly decorated general in the First World War.' Her speech slowed down, dropping pitch, and she emphasized each word distinctly as if speaking to a child, or someone who didn't understand the language. 'Your mother was born in our country Schloss, near Mühlhausen in East Germany, and Joachim and I were born at 42 Regerstrasse, our house in Berlin. We are aristocrats, born into great wealth and privilege; we had nannies, servants, private tutors, and we lived in grand houses, surrounded by beautiful things. If it hadn't

3

been for the war, we would have . . .' Ingrid stopped abruptly and dropped her head.

When she lifted it again, Kathryn was certain her aunt was going to cry. Yet beyond the thin film of tears, there was something else: a burning resentment. And Kathryn had to resist the urge to remind her aunt that it was Germany who had started the war.

Ingrid stared for several minutes at Kathryn as if she was invisible. Her voice when she continued had returned to an even tone. 'Your mother chose to deny her past; but now that she is dead, I wanted you to know, to understand. Even your father had no idea, he was told the same as everyone else.'

Shifting uncomfortably in her hard wooden chair, Kathryn tried to make sense of what the old woman opposite had just disclosed. After a few moments she rose, and pulling herself up to her full height of five foot ten, covered the few steps that separated them.

'I *can't* believe what you're telling me, Aunt Ingrid. It seems so unreal, like something out of a movie, or the sort of story that makes fascinating reading in the Sunday supplements and only ever happens to other people.'

Kathryn loomed above her aunt who sat bolt upright in the centre of a small sofa, tiny hands clasped tightly in her lap, seemingly oblivious to Kathryn's bewilderment.

'You look just like your grandfather, Kathryn; in fact you're the image of his mother, Eva. She was very beautiful, you have the same flawless skin, and honey-coloured hair.'

Silence so loud it was deafening filled the small room.

4

An icy chill ran up Kathryn's spine, and her blood went cold.

'Anyway, I shouldn't worry about your grandfather now; he died in active service, on 10th November 1944. Suddenly distracted, Ingrid looked past Kathryn towards the bay window overlooking the front garden. 'I must prune the roses this afternoon. I've got a beautiful display, don't you think?'

Following her aunt's eyes to the cluttered foliage, Kathryn tried to pick out the rose bushes in the dense and gaudy profusion of untidy bedding plants virtually covering the tiny front garden. Forcing her voice to respond evenly, and thinking how incongruous it was to be discussing an English garden in the same breath as World War Two, and the Nazis, she said, 'Magnificent, Aunt Ingrid. Mother always said you had green fingers.'

At this Ingrid reached forward, startling Kathryn as she grabbed her bare forearm. Her hand, callused by years of hard work, bit into the flesh as she forced her niece down on to the sofa next to her, so close their thighs touched. Kathryn recoiled from the smell of stale fish in the old woman's breath when she spoke.

'I can't believe your mother ever said anything good about me. Freda hated me. I was the favourite you see, but she thought she was. Oh yes, Freda deluded herself all her life, always so vain and insolent, even as a child, kissing and cuddling *Vater*. But I knew it was me he preferred, even though she was prettier. I was musical, I played the piano and the violin; my father adored music, he had ambitions for me to become a concert pianist. Father always told me that I was talented, and that I would go far.'

5

Kathryn thought ironically that had Von Trellenberg lived, he would have been disappointed to see exactly how far his younger daughter had gone. Married at eighteen to a brutal man who had systematically abused her and her son Stefan, one night Ingrid had retaliated – puncturing Karl Wenzel's lung with a carving knife. He had survived, but only just, and afraid to face his wrath, Ingrid had fled to join her sister in England. Kathryn would never forget her own childish excitement at the prospect of her aunt and cousin coming to live at Fallowfields. She had anticipated fun and laughter to evict the numbing silence that had taken up residence after her father and mother had divorced.

Instead her hopes had given way to bitter disappointment: Ingrid turned out to be surly and bad-tempered, whilst her son Stefan, who at fourteen was two years older than Kathryn, was sullen and menacing in his quiet cunning.

With a pang of contrition, Kathryn recalled her delight when, eighteen months later, Ingrid and Stefan had moved out. Ingrid, at Freda's insistence, had found a job as a seamstress at a shop in the small town of Cranleigh. With grudging reluctance, Freda had then bought her a cottage on the outskirts of the town and, having done so, felt no more obligation to the younger sister she had always detested.

Last week, at her mother's funeral was the first time Kathryn had seen her Aunt Ingrid for fifteen years. She had aged beyond recognition: an old woman standing alone in the church vestibule, leaning heavily on a walking stick, her face framed by a shock of white hair that could have been momentarily mistaken for a hat. It wasn't until this figure was joined by a tall, good-looking young man that Kathryn knew it was her Aunt Ingrid. She would never forget Cousin Stefan's penetrating midnight blue eyes; his gaze had terrified her when she was twelve, and it was still chilling twenty-two years later.

Ingrid began to rock to and fro, gazing unblinking into space. With a sense of shock, Kathryn stared into the liquid depths of her vacant eyes thinking about something her father used to say to her mother. *'Your sister's not all there.'* As a child, Kathryn had always wondered what piece was missing. With increasing unease, she chose her next words carefully.

'You and Freda changed your name to ''Hessler'' – why?'

A hush followed, then Ingrid uttered a soft moan and answered. 'It was Freda's idea. She said it was best to assume new identities in order to make a fresh start, because it would be simpler.' Ingrid could hear her sister's voice as clearly as if it were yesterday: *We must reinvent ourselves; the children of Nazis will be ostracized and made to suffer, like the Jews. It's for the best, Ingrid, believe me . . .*

'When the war ended, I was only sixteen. But Freda was eighteen and very strong-willed; all she could think or talk about was how she intended to leave Germany and start afresh. She was very attractive, in a sultry sort of way; everyone told her she looked like Marlene Dietrich, but I could never see it. Before she met Richard, your father, she was sleeping with an American officer. I can't remember what he was called now, it was one of those ridiculous American names like ''Chuck'' or ''Brad''. He was working in the office for relocation of refugees. It was all such a mess after the war: misplaced people with no homes, nowhere to go. Anyway, this officer issued false papers for Freda and myself. I wanted to tear them up when Freda told me with triumph that she'd used not only her body to bribe the American, but also a necklace belonging to our mother. A beautiful old piece, that had been handed down through several generations. It was set with over a hundred baguettes, and a fifteen-carat flawless pear-shaped diamond. God knows what a necklace like that would be worth today!'

Ingrid was so preoccupied with her story she didn't hear Kathryn's sharp intake of breath, nor did she notice her look of profound shock as she tried hard to absorb what her aunt was telling her.

Kathryn had always known her mother was determined, but to prostitute herself? She found it hard to accept she would stoop so low. There were a million and one questions racing around her head, but she kept quiet and allowed Ingrid to continue without interruption.

'I will never forget the very first time I saw the necklace. I must have been about four or five. My mother was dressed for a state occasion, and I whispered to my nanny that Mama looked like a princess. My mother leaned forward to kiss me, and I stretched on tiptoe to touch the tip of the diamond drop gleaming against her bare neck. Her perfume filled my nostrils as she whispered in my ear, "This necklace will belong to you one day, my little Ingy."

'So you can imagine, the thought of some loud American woman, strutting around in a seventeenth-century Von Trellenberg heirloom, made me feel physically sick. But Freda merely pooh-poohed my protests, insisting that desperate means required desperate measures, and that if we were to go forward we had to forget the past. Then Freda got sick, and as usual got lucky, meeting your father like she did during her stay in hospital.'

Ingrid felt the old familiar stab of jealousy as she recalled her elder sister's excitement at falling in love with the handsome English doctor, Richard de Moubray, who had asked her to marry him.

'I begged Freda to take me with her to England, to a new life, but she was so full of herself and so madly in love with your father that the last thing she wanted was a sister to worry about. She thought I would be a burden.' Pausing for a moment, eyes beginning to dart from side to side as if searching for something she had lost, Ingrid's voice became ragged and disjointed as she muttered incoherently under her breath in German.

Kathryn watched the old woman in morbid fascination as she resumed her account. 'I was wretched after the war, a helpless young girl, barely sixteen, a child. I had lost my family, and everything I held dear. For a while I hated my mother for committing suicide, I was very angry and I blamed *her* for leaving me. Only later, after I had found and read her letters, did I realize how desperate and how very sick she was in the last months of her life. Her adored son Joachim had died of gunshot wounds in a French field hospital in 1944, two weeks before his twenty-first birthday. Four months later her beloved Klaus suddenly stopped writing, and in the ensuing weeks all contact between them ceased. She tried without success to locate him. She was certain that he had deserted Germany, and his family, for ever – afraid of recriminations because of his Nazi connections. The vast country estate was requisitioned by the government, a fortune in antiques and art were looted by the Russians, I believe she even sold her priceless Fabergé egg collection. We lost everything.'

Ingrid's lids fluttered then closed as if to shut out the memory. She began to pick manically at the tattered remains of a fringed cushion near her lap, a dark blue tangle of veins clearly visible under her papery skin. 'Freda left not long after that and I was left stranded in that huge empty house. I hid most of the time, afraid to go out; the Russians were everywhere. I had no money or food, I was alone, except for the ghosts. At one point, I thought I was going insane, and if I hadn't met Karl Lang when I did, I might have done so. Or joined my poor mother. I must admit, in the long, dark nights, I thought about ending it many times, anything would have been preferable to that terrible fear.'

A lump formed in the back of Kathryn's throat and she swallowed with difficulty. The face next to her, loose and dulled with age, had suddenly reverted to that of a frightened young girl, alone in Berlin amidst the chaos of defeat. It filled her with an unexpected sympathy for this desolate old woman, who had lost her entire family in the space of a few months. It also confirmed what she had always suspected about her own mother. Freda had been a cold, callous creature, unable to love, or even show compassion to her own sister.

'I'm sorry,' Kathryn said kindly. She knew it sounded lame, but could think of nothing else to offer. Gently she placed a hand on Ingrid's lap, but the old woman pulled back from her touch.

'It's over now, thank God; all over a long, long time ago,

so long I sometimes imagine that none of it ever really happened or that I dreamt it all.'

A snuffling, followed by a scratching noise, momentarily distracted them both; they looked towards the sound, made by a West Highland Terrier, pushing his wet nose around the door.

'Come, Sasha!' Ingrid called affectionately. The dog's ears pricked up instantly and he trotted towards her, leaping on to the sofa to settle in her lap. Ingrid patted the dog's head, brightening a little. 'Well, I have a new life now,' waving a hand around the shabby room. 'My pretty cottage, and my garden.'

'Are you sure my father never knew the truth?' Kathryn asked.

Ingrid shook her head. 'As far as I know, Freda told him the same as she told you, and everyone else: that she was Freda Hessler, born in Cologne, you know the rest.'

Kathryn took a deep breath, knowing how important the next question was. 'OK, now about my grandfather . . .' She was surprised her voice sounded so calm. 'Was Klaus Von Trellenberg one of those despicable Nazi monsters?' Kathryn felt her mouth dry up, as she watched a muscle in Ingrid's jaw twitch uncontrollably.

The old woman began to shake and Sasha growled softly. 'My father was an officer, an *SS Oberführer*. He was an aristocrat, a highly respected man and a good German, who served his leader and his country with loyalty and integrity.'

Kathryn persisted, her sense of outrage and shock spurring her to confront the question uppermost in her mind. 'You haven't answered my question, Aunt Ingrid. Was he

11

guilty of war crimes? I need to know.' Kathryn was almost shouting. She was also tempted to grab her aunt by the scruff of her slack neck, and wring the truth out of her. *Shit, the old witch is so controlled*, she thought, and in that instant was reminded of her own mother Freda, always calm in crisis, so damn cool, when all around were reeling.

'Ingrid, look at me please.' Kathryn ordered.

Her aunt obliged, but her eyes were dead.

'I accept that this man, this Nazi, Von Trellenberg, was my maternal grandfather. If he was a war criminal, I have to come to terms with that.' She spat the words out as if eager to be free of them. 'For God's sake, Ingrid, I deserve to know; because if he was, it would help explain a lot of things I never understood about my mother.'

Ingrid stood up. She was a few inches shorter than Kathryn, but her back was ram-rod straight, and her thick hair rising from the top of her head like a white busby brought her almost level with her niece. She faced Kathryn, her eyes openly hostile. 'I want you to go now, please, I've got a lot to do.'

Kathryn was furious. 'That's great, Ingrid, thanks a lot! I don't see you for countless years, then my mother dies, and you drag me down here to tell me all about her secret past. Well, I've listened to your revelations patiently, and I don't mind admitting I'm deeply shocked. Who wouldn't be? It's a lot to take in all at once.' Bright spots danced at the corner of Kathryn's eyes, and she was vaguely aware of a dull ache in her left temple.

When her aunt did not answer, Kathryn added, 'Listen, I can easily find out the truth by researching the archives in Washington or Germany, so don't lie to me, Ingrid.'

Screwing her eyes tightly shut, Ingrid dropped her voice to a hoarse whisper. 'I refuse to discuss my father further. Klaus Von Trellenberg is dead; let him rest in peace.'

The hot sun streaming through the car window was very warm, heating her bare arms, but it couldn't penetrate the cold numbing horror inside. The letters 'SS' and all the horror they conveyed kept leaping into her head, accompanied by a multitude of images from films: jackbooted Nazis, with merciless eyes and arrogant poise, wretched hordes of men, women and children herded on to trains for their journey to genocide.

Holding the wheel very tight, her knuckles bone white, she forced herself to erase the picture of a Jewish child in a red coat. It was a scene from *Schindler's List*; the child's face had remained with her for weeks after she had seen the film, and now it returned to haunt her once more.

Turning left off the main road, she drove up a narrow dirt track stopping at Northfields Farm. Kathryn read the name on the gate several times in an attempt to calm her nerves; then, letting her head drop on to the back of the driver's seat, she began to shake, an uncontrollable quaking that terrified her. She stumbled out of her car, walked up to the gate and, leaning against it, gazed across a deep meadow where cows were grazing. From a clump of trees to the left she could hear the faint gurgle of a stream, the grass smelt fresh from a shower earlier and the sun was sparkling on new puddles. A large cow, the biggest of the herd, ambled slowly towards the gate, stopping a few feet from where Kathryn stood. Out of eyes the colour of dark chocolate, the animal surveyed her with mild curiosity. The intense pounding in her head started to abate, and with it the panic she had experienced earlier gradually subsided.

Kathryn stood very still for several minutes. The dull drone of insects in the hedgerows and the muted rumble of a tractor in the far distance were the only sounds breaking the stillness of the hot afternoon. She lifted her eyes to a cloudless blue sky and watched a lone wood pigeon swoop low to peck in the long grass behind the cow, who flicked her long tail angrily several times until the bird took flight.

Kathryn felt a comforting return to normality. She had no idea how long she had been there, and was surprised when she returned to her car, to see that it was ten past two. She had been standing by the gate for over half an hour and was going to be late for a two-thirty appointment in Westerham.

As she turned the key in the ignition and drove off, she thought about Ingrid's insistence at her mother's funeral, and during three subsequent telephone calls, that it was of the utmost importance they should meet. Kathryn wished she had listened to her first impulse, which was to refuse. She had never liked her Aunt Ingrid, and knew that the feeling was mutual. *Ingrid is probably content*, thought Kathryn with a smile, *now that she's off-loaded fifty years of repressed emotions on to me.*

Kathryn imagined her aunt standing in the same place she had left her, next to the shabby sofa, surrounded by tired furniture, and faded fabric. Alone, except for Sasha, in her dark cottage; alone with her memories, and echoes from the past.

'Von Trellenberg,' Kathryn muttered the name under her

breath, then elaborated, 'Klaus Von Trellenberg, aristocrat, Nazi SS officer. *Shit*,' she swore, then again louder, 'Shit!This is like something out of a bad movie.' She swerved to overtake a lorry, slamming on her brakes to avoid colliding with an oncoming car. With the sound of its horn blaring in her ears, she slowed down, forcing herself to concentrate on her driving.

Over and over, Kathryn told herself that her grandfather was dead, or so Ingrid had said. It all happened long before she was born, she reminded herself, and there was no evidence that Klaus Von Trellenberg had committed any crime, well none that she knew of; yet the grim reality that he had been a high-ranking SS officer remained, and with it an isolated fragment of fear.

Why had Ingrid wanted to put her in the picture, Kathryn wondered. Was there some good reason apart from the fact that she was a bitter old woman with a twisted sense of duty, who simply thought her niece should know the truth? Or was it a final act of revenge on the sister Ingrid had always detested? Kathryn toyed with the hope that Ingrid had lost her mind and that the entire revelation suggested the ramblings of senility.

She clung so hard to this hope that she almost missed the turning to Fallowfields, the house where she had been born, and had lived for the first eighteen years of her life. Her thoughts drifted back down the winding pathway to her childhood, cosseted in rural English country life with Freda, the mother who had baked cakes for church fêtes, taken her to the pony club, and watched her compete in local gymkhanas. Freda, who had grown prize-winning flowers, and had been a pillar of Kent society. With a short laugh Kathryn imagined the face of Mrs June Burrows, her late mother's closest friend and chairman of the local townswomen's guild, if she told her at the next committee meeting that Freda de Moubray's father had been an SS officer.

When Kathryn pulled up in front of the house, she saw a young man poised in the act of ringing the doorbell. Stepping out of her car, she walked towards him, fixing a bright, determined smile on her face, recalling something her ex-husband Tony had said to her the first night they'd met. 'If you're smiling, the whole world will think you're winning.' The thought made her smile widen, as she held out her hand in greeting.

'You must be Mr Grant, the estate agent?' Kathryn stood in front of him. 'Sorry I'm late.'

The man nodded, coal-black eyes peering from behind the half-moon spectacles decorating his thin, white face.

It hadn't been a particularly good morning for Oliver Grant. In fact it had not started well, and had got progressively worse. His car had broken down, the train had been late, he had lost an important sale an hour earlier, and now he had been standing in the hot sun for the last fifteen minutes positive the next client was not at home. His voice, when he eventually found it, was deliberately clipped.

'Are you—'

'Kathryn de Moubray,' she supplied, walking smartly past him. 'Please come in.'

Oliver rejoined her in the hall, where he held out a long thin hand, the parchment colour of its skin broken by a clump of densely black hair. 'Oliver Grant of Brinkforth and Sons.'

16

Kathryn smiled politely again, her unusual dark, almost charcoal-grey, eyes shining.

Bloody attractive girl, Oliver thought, *and about to come into some money.* He decided to be nice, *Turn on the charm, old boy*, he told himself, *you never know your luck.* 'OK, Miss de Moubray, to work. First I need the dimensions of all the rooms.'

'Follow me,' Kathryn invited, leading the way down the gloomy hall.

Their feet made little sound on the carpeted floor, dark brown and threadbare in several places. The walls were decorated in a sombre beige-and-tan striped wallpaper, with a faded floral border at the skirting and a dado. Grant scribbled notes, muttering encouraging comments under his breath, as they entered the dining room.

'We always ate in here before my father left,' Kathryn explained. 'Of course after that, my mother ate less and less.'

She stopped speaking abruptly, her attention diverted to a watercolour on the wall behind the estate agent. It depicted a fishing village in Provence. Her father had bought it from a street vendor on their first family holiday in France.

'I really have no idea why my mother kept that horrible painting.' The comment held a hint of apology.

Glancing at the watercolour, the estate agent was forced to agree. It was dreadful, but he thought better than to pursue the subject so he changed it.

'Fallowfields is typical of most houses built in this area during the twenties. Red brick, and timber façade, three to four beds, a couple of acres. Three reception rooms,

17

substantial kitchen, inglenook fireplace. A good solid family house.'

This was delivered in estate-agent speak. If he had been completely honest, which he wasn't because it didn't come with the job, he would've said that he found the mock Tudor architecture extremely ugly, the rooms dark and pokey, and decorated with morgue-like taste. The owner had obviously hated colour; one shade of dull brown was mixed with another shade of duller brown.

As if reading his mind, Kathryn announced with emotion, 'I hate this house.'

This statement appeared to surprise the estate agent. 'I must admit it's not exactly to my taste either; I'm more of a period sort of chap myself, if you know what I mean.'

Kathryn was scanning the room, gazing on the Spartan effects, and shabby decor, with obvious distaste. 'I've taken a few personal items, the rest of the furniture you can sell.'

She saw that his eyes had followed hers and settled on a photograph of her mother taken when Freda had first come to England, a distinct look of uncertainty on her unsmiling face. 'My mother was German you know,' Kathryn provided.

'Uh huh,' Oliver nodded slowly, his face adopting a 'Well, that answers everything' sort of look. His glasses slipped an inch down his nose, he pushed them firmly back into place before saying, 'I heard about your mother's tragic car crash. Nasty business. I'm sorry.'

Her eyes did not waver from Freda's photograph when she said, matter-of-fact, 'My mother died a long time ago, so don't be.'

A short nervous cough covered the estate agent's embarrassment. He averted his gaze.

'Come along, Mr Grant, we're not finished yet,' she said in a brighter voice.

Following her out of the living room, he trudged up a narrow staircase. He fixed his eyes on the smooth orb of her left buttock; it was the closest one to him, the panty line clearly visible beneath her tight denim jeans. He wondered if she wore lacy, see-through panties – the type he ogled in magazines. By the time they had reached the top of the stairs he was contemplating asking Kathryn if she was busy next Saturday. It was the annual dinner dance at his cricket club. Oliver was certain she would enjoy it, he always did.

Kathryn inclined her head towards an open door directly in front of them. 'That's the master bedroom, not very apt in this case, since there hasn't been a master in there for a very long time.' Having said this, she left him to measure up, before stepping alone into the room next door.

This bedroom looked exactly the same as the day she had left home. There was a crack in the face of the old Dohrmann alarm clock, one of the few remaining possessions her mother had brought with her from Germany. And the rosebud-pink patterned wallpaper which Kathryn had always hated had started to peel around a damp patch above the bed. But otherwise nothing had changed, and she was reminded of another time, long ago, but not forgotten.

Kathryn squeezed her eyes tightly shut as the demons, for ever hovering on the edge of her consciousness, began to invade. A shutter in her memory clicked, and Richard de Moubray's face appeared. Not for the first time Kathryn thought how strange it was that every time she visualized her father, she saw only his face, never his body; he always looked sad, and the image was always in black and white. Even after almost twenty-five years, however much she tried to imagine him looking happy and at ease, he always wore the same expression he had worn the day he had left home.

'I love you very much, Kathryn, but I won't be living with you any longer. I'm leaving to live with someone else; you will be staying with Mummy, but we'll see each other often, and I promise you will still be my little princess.'

It was the last time he ever called her his 'little princess', and after that day she had not seen him for exactly eight months, five days, six hours and twenty-four minutes. She knew; she had ticked the days off her calendar when she was nine years old.

Kathryn had lost count of the times she had stood in exactly the same spot, running and rerunning the little scene in her head, certain that it must have been something she had said, or done, that had made her daddy leave.

Slowly her eyes opened and she blinked to clear the thin film of moisture blurring her vision. Each season viewed from this bedroom window had brought with it vivid memories, painful in their clarity. With tinkling childish laughter pealing in her ears, she recalled her seventh birthday.

Her father walking towards her, carrying something . . . He is smiling, the special smile, the one he has for her, and her alone. She is running across the lawn, long blonde hair streaming from her upturned face, rapt in childish wonderment; her screams of delight mingle with the playful yelps of her birthday present – a golden Labrador puppy.

Shaking her head to disperse the memory, Kathryn stepped back from the window to sit on the edge of her old bed. With the flat of her hand, she stroked the quilted counterpane, her fingers lovingly resting on a small scatter cushion propped up against the pine headboard. She traced the border of an embroidered primrose; it was lopsided and the bright yellow petals had faded to a dull cream. A hint of a smile flickered across her face as she cast her mind back to the kindly Mrs Crowther, her needlework teacher, who had helped her with the embroidery. A painstaking task for a twelve-year-old who was neither patient nor a natural needlewoman.

Brimming with pride, she had brought the finished article home from school to sit on her bed next to Rumple, the one-eyed teddy she'd had for as long as she could remember. The smile slipped from her face as, with a pang, Kathryn recalled her shock on finding Rumple gone, and her stinging indignation towards her mother for having thrown her beloved companion away. It was as if her childhood had departed with Rumple, he who had shared her dreams, been party to her innermost secrets, and comforted her when her heart ached.

Oliver Grant's voice cut sharply through her reverie.

'I'll send a photographer over tomorrow, so by early next week, we'll have all the details ready to send out.'

Standing up, Kathryn said, 'The sooner the better as far as I'm concerned.' She was suddenly seized with the familiar urge to get out of Fallowfields. The house had always been oppressive, but for some reason without her mother it was worse.

Following Kathryn downstairs, after taking the dimensions of her old bedroom, Oliver's gaze roamed up and down the back of her legs, coming to rest once more on her backside. He fantasized about her bending over his bed wearing nothing but a black G-string. He blushed a little as he felt his erection rise and with his briefcase in front of his groin, he stopped at the front door.

'Well, I think that just about wraps it up for now,' he said. 'I have a meeting with the surveyor tomorrow, and I also intend to do a full inventory of the contents. It's amazing what turns up hidden away in attics and cellars; sometimes old people die and leave a fortune in antiques – actually only a couple of weeks ago . . .'

The estate agent looked animated for the first time, and Kathryn suspected he was about to embark on a long boring monologue of his occupational experiences. She interrupted his flow.

'I'm sure you've got lots of fascinating anecdotes to relate, Mr Grant, but I've got to get back to London for an important meeting, and to be honest I'm late now.'

Her clipped tone, followed by a curt glance at her watch, were not lost on the estate agent, who, looking a little miffed, clamped his mouth shut and hovered on the doorstep.

Kathryn held out her hand. 'I want a quick sale, Mr Grant, and I don't mind dropping the price, if that's what it takes.'

Taking her hand, he responded, 'You can rest assured,

Miss de Moubray, I'm sure I'll get you the asking price *and* a quick sale. Trust me.'

There wasn't an estate agent on the face of the earth she would have trusted, but her face softened and she could not resist a wry smile as Oliver Grant accelerated into his full sales pitch.

'You are in good hands with Brinkforth and Sons; we have a few potential clients who spring immediately to mind for this highly desirable residence. I know that houses like Fallowfields do not stay on the market long.'

Kathryn nodded, and watched him walk to his car. She then stepped back into the house, closing the door quietly behind her. She leaned against it, letting out a long sigh, thinking how relieved she would be when Fallowfields was sold. She gazed around the dreary hall, and as usual she was conscious of the all-prevailing sadness that seemed to seep out of the very walls. Whispering echoes caressed her ears: her mother's heels clicking on the wooden floor, as they had done at exactly the same time every weekday morning; her voice urging Kathryn to hurry or she would be late. *Yes*, she would be very happy to be done with Fallowfields.

Kathryn picked up the mail from the hall table. She stuffed it into her shoulder bag before running up the stairs two at a time to close an open window which she had spotted on her arrival. She was panting as she reached the landing. Hesitating on the threshold of her mother's bedroom she tried to recall the last time she had been in there. Five, six years, maybe longer, she couldn't remember exactly, all she did know was that she dreaded going inside, and had to force herself to open the door. She spotted the open window, and kept her eyes fixed on it as she crossed the room. She willed herself not to think of the night she had run in here as a terrified five-year-old in need of a cuddle and soothing voice after a disturbing nightmare. Instead she had been greeted by her father, naked and gleaming with sweat, frantically moving up and down and grunting like some crazed animal. It was only after she moved to the side of the bed that she realized her mother was under him, her face buried deep in the pillow.

As Kathryn had watched in silence, hardly daring to breathe, Freda had lifted her head slightly, turning to face her daughter. Their eyes had met, and in that split second Kathryn thought her mother was going to die.

Now, standing very still in the middle of the room, she was transported back to that time; she could still feel the rising panic, and the fur tickling the roof of her mouth as she had bitten down hard on top of her teddy's head, before screaming at her father to stop hurting Mummy.

Kathryn stretched forward to close the window. Having done so, she turned to leave, swearing as she stubbed her big toe on the bedside chair. She stooped to rub it, her eyes drawn to a loose floorboard under the bed. It was sticking up at an angle, a couple of inches from where she knelt. The wood was rotting, pitted with tiny holes. Fixed with a single nail, it moved easily and her heart missed a beat when she saw something glinting in the small cavity below. When she slid her hand down to pull out a box, she thought of all the stories she'd heard about hiding money under the bed. The box was about ten inches in length, and six inches high; it was made of silver and tortoiseshell, and very beautiful.

Kathryn stood the fine object on the dressing table, thinking how incongruous it looked amidst the functional hairbrush, comb, and assorted plain wooden boxes her mother had used. She dusted the lid with the flat of her hand, her index finger tracing the intricately carved flowers and leaves decorating the lid. It was locked, but she was gripped by the most weird sensation. It was as if the inanimate object was speaking to her. *Open me, please*, the box seemed to beg. Kathryn looked around the room for something to break the lock.

In the dressing-table drawer she found a pair of nail scissors. After several attempts the tiny silver lock opened with a sharp crack. Panting slightly from a mixture of exertion and anticipation, she lifted the lid at last. It was, as she expected, a jewel case, and in perfect condition. There were three different-sized compartments, all intact, and the dark purple lining looked as good as new. It contained no jewellery apart from a silver crucifix Kathryn had worn for her confirmation. The chain was tied around a bundle of photographs and letters, and the cross, blackened with age, hung from a ragged blue ribbon. Carefully she untied the bundle, and sorting through the photographs found to her surprise that most were of herself, in different stages of development from birth up to university graduation. There were a few of her parents; one on their wedding day, and another taken on a holiday in Wales a few years later. Her father looked detached, in stark contrast to his wife's serene expression. There was a sealed brown envelope, the padded sort used for sending fragile mail. It contained a wad of money. Kathryn quickly counted three thousand pounds in used fifty- and twenty-pound notes.

She was about to replace the memorabilia, when she noticed another tiny hinge on the inside of the lid. Running her index finger around the edge, she could feel a thin ridge and a moment later her finger encountered a spring catch. She pressed it, jumping as a panel dropped open and a photograph frame fell out, landing face down with a dull clang.

Squinting to read the faded writing scrawled across the back, she lifted the frame closer to her eyes. It read, 'Von Trellenberg family, Schloss Bischofstell Mühlhausen, 30th July 1936.'

It was a group shot, the family bunched together in a wide doorway under a coat of arms set in stone. Her eyes rested on the face of a little girl, about nine years old; her heart missing a beat at the angelic features framed by a mass of platinum curls. Kathryn was certain that if the photograph was in colour, the child's eyes would be a bright periwinkle blue. She knew because they were her mother's eyes. There was another younger child in the photograph, smaller and very plain. Kathryn assumed by the shape of the high domed forehead and long nose that it was Ingrid. This child was squirming shyly behind the left leg of her mother, who appeared to be trying in vain to push her daughter forward and smile herself at the same time. A young boy of about ten Kathryn guessed to be her Uncle Joachim. He was standing tall and very upright, sunlight glinting off the top of his golden crown. His small upturned face was radiant in admiration as he looked at his father dressed in the uniform of a German SS officer.

Kathryn shivered in spite of the heat, there was something obscene in the young boy's look. She felt a sudden tightness in her chest, and drawing in a shaky breath, her hands tightened their grip on the photograph. She would have dropped it if the urge to keep staring were not so great. Klaus Von Trellenberg's face was almost a mirror image of her own. Beads of cold sweat popped out across her brow, and the back of her neck felt suddenly very icy. She threw the frame down, breaking the glass, breathing deeply, willing herself to stay calm. For God's sake, why did she have to *look* like him? Was it not bad enough that she had a Nazi for a grandfather? But to be the spitting image! Then out loud she yelled, 'Why, Mother, *why* didn't you tell me? Why did I have to find out now, when you're not around to explain it? There's so much I need to know.'

Fighting back angry tears, Kathryn stuffed everything back into the box, and carrying it close to her chest she strode out of the room and downstairs, not stopping until she reached the front door. Stepping outside, she slammed the door shut for what she hoped would be the last time. As she turned the key in the lock, she glanced up at the wooden sign hanging above her head. It had a crack running through the centre and age had worn away some of the gold lettering. It now read, ' al ow i lds'.

With slow precise movements Kathryn walked back towards her car, past a scarlet blanket of poppies, and herbaceous borders thickly stocked with a glorious summer display. Stooping to pick a stephanotis, she held the flower close to her nose, inhaling the fragrant scent. A picture of her mother in vivid Technicolor popped into her mind. Freda in a battered straw hat, bent double, her gloved hand working furiously in the soil; then a fond memory of her mother's excitement after winning her first prize at a local flower show.

A cloud covered the sun, and with it the image darkened. Freda's expression had changed, devoid of emotion, clearly indifferent to the news of Kathryn's First in English from Edinburgh University. Blinking back tears of profound regret, Kathryn wished, as she had so many times in the past, that she had been able to reach her mother. They had been like strangers, uncomfortable in each other's company. Freda had never been able to acknowledge her daughter's considerable achievements. Resentment had taken the place of pride and Kathryn knew her own successes had burnt inside Freda like a white hot coal. For a long time she had searched for something, anything, to bind them as mother and daughter; but she was sure, with the certainty of feminine intuition, that her mother had firmly locked the door to her soul the day her father had left, if not before.

Had Klaus Von Trellenberg been guilty of hideous crimes during the war, perhaps genocide? Kathryn wondered if that was why her mother had been so distant; had she been burdened with a terrible secret? They were both dead now, and Kathryn doubted she would ever know the truth, yet she found it impossible not to care.

The flower slipped from her hand, she watched it flutter gently to the ground before slipping inside her car. Putting her foot down hard on the accelerator, she roared forward, tyres churning up the gravel drive.

Before turning out on to the road, Kathryn allowed herself one last fleeting glance in her rear-view mirror, but the house was obscured in a cloud of dust.

Chapter Two

'This time I really believe we've got him.'

Mark Grossman studied the sensitive face of the man seated on the opposite side of his desk. The deep-set eyes lit with an expectant gleam had taken on a golden hue and looked lighter than their usual amber. His mouth opened as if to speak, but closed as Mark continued.

'Our sources tell us that he's been spotted in the West Indies. An eye-witness account which, as you know, can be totally unreliable, but we've checked this one out thoroughly. It seems, if you'll excuse the expression, kosher.'

Mark blinked several times, his head ached, and there was a gritty sensation behind his eyes.

'You look tired, Mark,' Adam commented

'Yeah, I feel lousy. I'm wrecked. My schedule has been, to put it mildly, a little tight. Argentina two days ago, back in Manhattan for a meeting, then five hours later, I jumped on a flight to Israel. I arrived in town at six a.m. this morning on the red eye from Tel Aviv. I don't know if I need a crap or a haircut.'

Adam grinned, 'Both probably.' Then lowering his voice said, 'So our little Nazi friend is holed up in the West Indies. It's a hell of a long way from his last known address.'

'Not as far as you might think. Boats ply from South

America through the Indies constantly, there are lots of small craft skippered by dubious captains who would not be adverse to taking on an unusual fare. Come on, Adam, think about it. Who would question a retired European living in the West Indies when there are literally thousands of them? The ex-pat brigade: the English with their gin and tonics, and the Yanks with their ridiculous cocktails.'

'You're right, anyway who cares how he got there; more important, we know he's there. And he's still alive.'

Mark nodded. 'If our sources are correct, he has a rare form of bone cancer. Two weeks ago he went to the local hospital in St Lucia for a scan. Unfortunately for our suspect, an American doctor Ben Weitzman happened to be on a lecturing tour in the West Indies. Dr Weitzman, who is a bone cancer specialist, was asked to take a look at him. Ben Weitzman's mother is a Holocaust survivor, you may have met her brother – Nathan Drey?'

Adam shook his head. 'His name doesn't ring a bell.'

Mark went on, 'Nathan died a couple of years ago. He worked for the Centre when I joined in 1979.'

Mark blinked. *Seventeen years*. It seemed like yesterday. He had been twenty-six, a child of Holocaust survivors, and an ardent recruit to an organization he felt needed young blood, and new ideas. He had desperately wanted to rid the Horowitz Centre of its old image. An image he knew many people shared: that of embittered Jews, tormented by their time spent in the camps, obsessed with psychopathic cat-and-mouse games of hunting down anyone who had even a slight connection with the Nazis.

Mark Grossman, now Head of Intelligence, felt he had

achieved his objective in some small measure, and hoped that the Centre was now recognized throughout the world for spreading an important message. Man's inhumanity to man could not be ignored, and racial bigotry had to be addressed and punished, to ensure that what happened in Germany before, and during, World War Two never happened again.

Adam was speaking, intruding on his thoughts. 'You were telling me about Nathan?'

'Sorry, yes, I was miles away, thinking about when I first met Nathan. He was a good man, if a little fanatical, I suppose if you've lived through four years of Auschwitz, it kinda makes you that way. He helped to capture Eichmann, and for years he worked night and day on Von Trellenberg. Nathan was like a dog with a bone, he left no stone unturned. I would often come into the office in the early morning, to find him slumped over his desk sleeping. He'd been there all night. He was the one who tracked down Von Trellenberg in Bolivia in 1958. Nathan thought he had him then, but he was double-crossed by some local Argentine creep. Anyway both Klaus and the Argentine guy disappeared without trace. But Nathan had managed to get a couple of photographs of the man he thought was Klaus, and Nathan's sister Anna positively identified him as Von Trellenberg. Anna and Nathan Drey were both born in Berlin. She was a celebrated concert pianist and composer before the war. Von Trellenberg knew her. Apparently he and his father had attended several of her concerts. She was interned in Bergen Belsen in 1943, and claims to have seen Von Trellenberg visiting the camp at least three times.

31

'Anyway, to get back to the current situation, the man with bone cancer claims to be Dutch. Says his name is Van Beukering, from Rotterdam. Yet when questioned about Holland, he became very agitated and eager to leave. Then when Dr Ben Weitzman asked him where he was born, he reeled off a street name in Amsterdam, instead of Rotterdam. Weitzman then made an appointment to see him a few days later. First he called me here, and I arranged for his mother and one of my colleagues to fly to St Lucia. This Van Beukering didn't turn up for the appointment. Ben's tried to contact Van Beukering's own doctor, but he's on vacation overseas and we've been unable to locate him. The man gave a false address to the hospital, and so far we've hit a brick wall with all our enquiries.' Mark sighed. '*Nobody* on St Lucia seems to have seen or heard of this guy. Meanwhile he's disappeared into thin—'

'Did Dr Weitzman see his hand?' Adam interrupted.

Mark nodded, unable to contain the rising excitement in his voice. '*Yes*. Apparently that was the first thing he noticed; the third finger on his left hand was severed at the knuckle.'

Adam banged the top of the desk with his clenched fist. 'That's him! You've got him, Mark.'

'Well, it isn't absolutely positive yet, but I feel we've got enough to continue investigating. This is the closest we've come since Argentina.'

Adam, his fist still clenched in a tight ball, stood up and began to pace the small office. He was wearing what he always wore: jeans. Today they were black, teamed with a white shirt made by Bernie Katz in the finest lawn cotton, the same shirt-maker his father had used before him. And a pair of tan hide cowboy boots, custom-made from a firm in Houston. Mark could not recall ever having seen him in anything else and was, as always, struck by the image of an ageing rock star, rather than the reality of a successful international art dealer.

When Adam finally stopped pacing, he stood in front of Mark and said, 'Argentina was close, I really thought you had the bastard then.'

A nerve began to tremor uncontrollably in Mark's left temple. He massaged it with his forefinger, also thinking of the last time they had come this close to the man he had been hunting all these years. It had been in 1987, in a remote hill village close to the town of Santa Rosa, in Argentina.

Mark would never forget that night.

The sky was bigger than he could ever have imagined, and blacker, although rashed with stars. The frenzied animal screams breaking the stillness had caused his heart to race, and then came the wild tangerine glow – so bright it had hurt his eyes, lighting up the sky like a huge glowing torch that he thought would burn for ever. The stench of charred flesh in the burnt-out remains of the ranch would remain with him for the rest of his life. As would the despair he'd felt when he'd learnt that the bodies had all been local farm hands.

Mark stood up. He had pale eyes and pale skin, and an unruly thatch of thick, black hair. He ran his hands down the front of his crumpled navy blue suit and, straightening his tie, he listened intently to Adam's next words.

'I want to be there when you get him, Mark.'

'*If* we get him. The bird has probably flown by now.'

'He's ill, he's dying; he's unlikely to be making any long journeys. No, I think he's there in St Lucia. Hiding out somewhere. I'd love to go down there myself, I'm sure I could hunt him out of his fucking rat-hole.'

Mark Grossman shook his head, like a father to an errant son. He had a deep affection for Adam Krantz, and for his late father Benjamin who had been a patron of the Centre for many years. But Adam's ambition was just not professional and it was more than his job was worth to allow it.

'You know I can't have that, Adam. Just supposing it is him – you know the procedure: we've got no official authority in the West Indies; we have to make an application to the St Lucian government for a warrant for his arrest and extradition. The local police resent intruders and can be very uncooperative. You're too emotionally involved in all this; that could impair your judgement; you might take the law into your own hands. I don't want to risk that liability. Von Trellenberg is a big fish, we can't afford to screw up.'

'Look, I promise to be a good boy, do exactly what I'm told, no screw-ups. I've always wanted to go to the West Indies and I'm due for a vacation. Come on, Mark,' he pushed. 'You owe me.'

Mark sighed and, turning away, he scanned the floor-to-ceiling wall of books in front of him, without seeing one title. Adam was right: he did owe him. Adam had helped a lot in the past, and not only with money. He had invested time and commitment.

Neither man spoke for several seconds.

Mark finally broke the silence. 'You're right, the Centre

owes you and your father a lot. So now you're calling in your dues; is that how it is? You're putting me on the spot, man. I thought we were friends.'

'We are, Mark, that's why I feel I can ask. You know how important this is to me. I understand your position, but I'm begging you as a patron and a good friend to bend the rules for me just a little.'

The two men faced each other. Adam, although not unusually tall at five foot ten, towered above the diminutive Mark – who now relented. 'If it is him, and we make a formal arrest, I'll see what I can do.'

Adam smiled, then quickly composed himself, but not before the other man had seen a hint of triumph in his face. Mark rubbed the tip of his long nose saying cautiously, 'I make no formal promises. Who knows, this man may not even be Von Trellenberg.'

'How many other eighty-two-year-old Europeans with a severed finger can there be living in obscurity in the West Indies?'

Mark shrugged, his face impassive. 'You know me, Adam, ever sceptical, it goes with the job.'

'Yeah, I appreciate that. I know you've had your fair share of false alarms.'

'Who doesn't . . .' Mark looked resigned, then added on a brighter note, 'I'll keep you up to date with developments as and when they occur, and now you really will have to excuse me. I've got to fly down to Washington and be back in time for dinner with the family. That is if I still have a wife and kids, I've forgotten what Victoria looks like.'

Adam gripped his hand firmly in farewell. 'I feel very

confident, Mark. Good vibes, you know what I mean? I really think that this time we've got the son-of-a-bitch!'

Adam left Mark's office five minutes later, stepping on to First Ave and into glorious June sunshine. The light, blindingly bright, danced across acres of Manhattan glass, soaring into the china blue sky. A light breeze ruffled his dark hair as he hailed a taxi, asking for 76th and Madison.

Upper eastside was gridlocked, so he got out at the corner of 74th, strolling the two blocks to his art gallery. 'Morning, Lenny,' he waved to the street vendor, on the corner of 76th.

Lenny waved back. 'It's going to be a hot one, Mr Krantz, they say in the high eighties.'

'You'll sell more Cokes then.'

'I wish I was selling on the beach in Bermuda!'

'And I wish I was there with you,' Adam smiled before walking on.

He stopped outside his shop, admiring the recently completed sign above the door: 'Krantz Fine Art'. The gilded calligraphy had taken over a week to paint by hand and in Adam's opinion looked much better than the previous 'Krantz Gallery' sign his father had designed in the early fifties. Benjamin had stubbornly refused to change it – insisting that his clients came to him not because of a fancy shop-front, but because he had a fine reputation as a dealer of the utmost integrity.

The gallery was cool, and there was a sense of calm in the hushed surroundings. At the sound of the doorbell, Joanne, Adam's PA, peered from behind a pile of canvases.

'Morning, Mr Krantz,' she greeted him with a warm smile.

'Morning, Joanne,' he returned, walking past her into a small office at the rear of the gallery. 'Any mail?'

'Tell me a time when there *isn't* any mail!' Joanne said, joining him. 'The usual circulars, bills, invitations, etc. And this.' She picked up a letter from the top of the pile and handed it to him.

Adam's eyes flicked briefly over the correspondence; a small nerve at the corner of his mouth twitched as he protested, 'Some people never give up! How many more times do I have to tell this schmuck that I do *not* want to sell the Renoir.' He screwed the letter into a tight ball and dropped it into the bin. 'Write to this creep, tell him if he doesn't stop bothering me I intend to take legal action for harassment.'

Joanne fished the offending letter out of the bin, and began to unfold it. 'We may need this as evidence,' she said practically.

'Did Lynda Hamilton get back to you on the Degas etchings?' Adam asked.

Joanne nodded. 'Yep, she promised to call with a decision before close of play today and, before I forget, she invited you to a party next weekend at her house in Southampton. Sounds like a very smart bash.' The last sentence was accompanied by a high-pitched whistle.

Adam leaned against the side of a desk. The expression on his face said it all. 'Make sure you tell her I'm busy next weekend.'

Joanne chuckled. 'Ms Hamilton is going to be mighty pissed, I think she wants more than your etchings.'

'That's the trouble, so do I. Lynda's too old for me.'

'Come on, Adam, she's only a couple of years older than me, and that ain't too old.' The retort was hotly defensive.

'Lynda Hamilton is at least ten years older than you, Joanne; she's in her mid-fifties. She's been under the knife several times.'

'You sure?' Joanne looked surprised, then before waiting for a reply said, 'Well, she looks great for over fifty. Listen, if that's what cosmetic surgery does for you, I'm going to start saving right now for my first lift.'

'Don't ever do it! All you'll look like is an older woman who's had surgery; it's grotesque. Besides all that, Lynda Hamilton isn't my type.'

'Too rich, or just too available? Which is it?'

Adam's warm eyes twinkled with amusement. 'You, Joanne, are just *too* nosey.' He emphasized the 'too' while touching the end of her nose.

Joanne blushed, dropping her eyes, raising them a moment later to watch Adam walk to his own office. He left the interconnecting door ajar and she sat down behind her desk, thinking that if she had wanted to be really pushy, she would have asked him just who was his type. Jennifer, his estranged wife? Elegant, cold, and more interested in money, and acquisitions than him. Or a certain Miss Daryl Harper, with her baby-face? *Shit-face* more like, Joanne thought as she pictured the archetypal spoilt playgirl, hell-bent on spending Daddy's hard-earned cash in as short a time as possible and who, in Joanne's opinion, was far too young, and not good enough for her boss.

Joanne's mind wandered back to 29th January 1985: her first day working for Adam Krantz. It had been bitterly cold, with temperatures way below zero. She would never forget the cute way he had helped her out of her coat, warming her frozen hands in his own. Nor would she, or could she, ever forget the day a year later when she had bought a valuable Cézanne that Adam had previously rejected as a fake. Wildly excited he had swept her out to the Four Seasons Restaurant, for a celebratory supper. That night outside her apartment, Adam had held her very tight and thanked her, then to her astonishment he had kissed her full on the mouth before saying goodnight. With her heart fluttering, she had stood very still watching him walk to the end of her street, where he hailed a cab. Her eyes did not move until the tail-lights were out of sight. Later with her heart still fluttering, she had fantasized about making love to Adam Krantz. And she still did, though not as often now, by shutting her eyes tightly, opening her legs, and allowing her husband to slip silently into her body.

Adam sat down behind his desk; his palms spread flat, he moved them slowly across the smooth maple wood surface, thinking how much he loved fine things. The early nineteenth-century English antique desk gave him great pleasure, as did the breakfront bookcase – English again, but slightly earlier than the desk – and a pair of eighteenth-century French chairs. A set of Lautrec etchings and a large Pissarro landscape filled one wall and the remaining space was painted with a blue wash. When he had decorated his office two years previously Joanne had described the colour as 'Wedgwood', but it looked paler to Adam, more like the colour of very faded denim. The large room, pristine and sparingly furnished, was a testament to his dislike of clutter.

Joanne jotted something down on her notepad and, without looking up, called through the open door. 'Remember you've got to call Martin Beck at Sotheby's, and Alain Turquin in Paris about the Manet.'

Adam picked up a pencil from a selection stacked in a Tiffany silver box, a gift from his mother for his fortieth birthday last year. He jotted both names on a pad, even as Joanne's voice drifted through once more. 'And don't forget you've got to pick Calvin up today, and whilst I'm on the subject, it's his seventeenth birthday in two weeks.'

Adam looked exasperated. 'Give me a break, Joanne, I do know my only son's birthday.'

'OK, OK.' She raised her hand as if to ward off a blow. She was tempted to remind him, that she *had* reminded him of all of his family occasions for the last ten years. 'Keep your shirt on, Mr Krantz. You know me, just being efficient.'

His tone softened. 'I'm picking him up at four this afternoon. I've decided to drive myself, so I plan on leaving here around two.'

Joanne appeared in the doorway. 'No problem, it's pretty quiet here on Friday afternoons usually; anyway, there isn't much ever happens around this place that I can't take care of.'

Adam raised both hands. 'What on earth would I do without you?'

'Well, don't forget I told you I need a vacation. I haven't been away for a couple of years, and these old bones could do with a dose of sun.'

Adam was dismissive. 'Did nobody ever tell you too much sun is bad for the skin?'

'It's worse than not enough, and I haven't had any.' She planted both hands on her wide hips, and fixed what she hoped was an appealing smile on her mobile face. 'A week in Maui, David got us a deal.'

Adam looked up and she sensed his irritation. Her instinct was confirmed by his next announcement.

'Maui sucks, ask anyone. Unfriendly natives trying to rip off unsuspecting American tourists. Anyway, it's the rainy season, there's no sun, you and David are better off staying in New York.'

Joanne pulled a long face and in a plaintive voice said, 'But I've *always* wanted to go to Maui. It's a great deal, eighteen hundred dollars all inclusive.'

Adam leaned back in his chair. 'David got it cheap 'cause it's the wrong time of year. Like I said, go in the winter.' His tone was dismissive.

Undeterred, Joanne persisted. 'Come on, Adam, give me a break; hell, I'm whacked and I need a vacation. If I don't get one, you're not going to get the hundred and fifty per cent input I give to this business.'

'When?' Adam asked.

'Next week?' Her eyebrows rose, accompanied by a pleading expression that filled Adam with guilt. He knew he was lucky to have Joanne. She had majored in Art History, and had worked as a restorer for six years. She had a catalogue in her head of every art collector and artist from Albani to Zoffany, and could spot a forgery a mile away, but more important she tolerated his unpredictable personality with consummate patience. In truth she was his right hand and he would be lost without her. He made a mental note to book a vacation in Maui for Joanne and her husband, just as soon as this thing in the West Indies was over.

Adam rubbed his hand across his face and sighed. 'You're right, Joanne, you do need a vacation. You and me both, but I think I've got to go away next week. On business,' he added quickly. 'I'm not sure yet, so can we talk about it later?' He looked and sounded genuinely sorry.

The smile slipped from Joanne's face, her tone changing to one of resignation. 'OK, you're the boss; but I've got to let David know before the end of the week, or he'll divorce me.'

'He'd be mad to do that.' Adam was smiling warmly.

'Yeah, right. But you know men, never appreciate what they got, till they don't have it no more.'

'Point taken, Jo. I promise to let you know just as soon as I know. Now can we get some work done around here. First and foremost, call Lynda Hamilton and get me out of that party. Tell her I've got to go to—'

'Maui?' Joanne offered. Then before he could reply, she added, 'Don't you think you should consider the sale of the Degas, Adam? One little-bitty party ain't going to kill you, sometimes in life we all have to make a few small sacrifices.'

'Sacrifices for what?' Only half listening, he racked his fingers through his shoulder-length hair whilst thinking about that trim he kept promising himself.

'Money, you know, like sixty-five thousand dollars' worth of sacrifice, the profit from which pays my wages for—?'

'A month,' he finished for her.

'I wish,' she said, raising bushy black eyebrows that met

at the ridge of her nose. Adam had often wondered why she didn't pluck them but had always been too polite to ask.

'Joanne, believe me when I say *no* amount of money would induce me.' He sighed heavily, running the back of his hand across the dark stubble on his jaw, remembering that he had forgotten to shave that morning. 'Come on, you know as well as I do that it's not just the party. Lynda's bony ass could be studded with twenty-carat diamonds and she could want to buy an entire collection of Impressionists . . . but I absolutely refuse to get laid by her.'

There had been a multiple pile-up on Route 87, and traffic was at a standstill. Adam, stuck on the George Washington Bridge, looked at his watch and cursed. The drive upstate to Albany took at least two hours on a clear road.

He arrived at his son's school after five, over an hour late. Sprinting up the wide stone steps leading to the entrance to Highclare Academy, he could see the back of Calvin's head framed in the open window, his dark crown shining like polished jet.

Calvin turned when his father entered the hall.

'Sorry I'm late, Cal, but there was a hold-up on the New York Interstate. It was chaotic.'

There was no welcoming smile for Adam, nor did his son move towards him when he said, 'It's OK, Dad. I'm used to it, you're always late.'

'*Always!* Come on, that's not fair.'

Calvin looped a lock of wayward hair behind his left ear. His sapphire blue eyes, almost exactly the same shade as his mother's, challenged Adam, reminding him of Jennifer

43

when she was angry. 'OK, I'll give you *sometimes*.'

Adam stepped forward to touch his son's arm, changed his mind and cuffed him playfully around the chin instead. Pulling a ridiculously long face, he said, 'No smile for your old pop?'

Calvin started to grin, his bad temper melting like butter in the sun. He could never stay annoyed with his father for long.

Gently Adam hugged Calvin towards him. 'It's great to see you, Cal; how have you been?' He ruffled his son's long hair.

'It's great to see you, Dad; I've missed you.' It felt good to hold his father close. Calvin wanted to savour the moment, enjoying the slight prickle of Adam's stubble and the faintly acid smell of lime, and something else he didn't recognize.

After a few seconds Adam relaxed his embrace then, holding Calvin at arm's length, he looked him up and down in appreciation. 'Wow! You've grown in the last month, nearly as tall as me. And man, what a great tan! You look like you spent the last few weeks at the beach.'

'I wish,' Calvin grinned. 'Misspent time playing ball.'

'Oh, yeah, how's it going? Sorry I missed the last match, I was in Europe. Your mom said you were great, and that you made captain.' Adam patted his son on the back, he was beaming with pride. 'Congratulations, Cal; you put your dad to shame, I can barely hit the ball.'

Warmed by his father's approval, the sullen expression Calvin had worn earlier was replaced by a radiant smile.

Adam wrapped an arm around Calvin's shoulder. 'Come on then, son; let's hit the road.'

Arm in arm they walked to the car. Calvin peered inside.

'No driver today, Dad?' he asked, opening the passenger door.

'Nope, I felt like being alone, lots of stuff on my mind. It seemed like a good opportunity to sort it out.'

Cal searched his father's face. 'And have you?'

'Sort of,' Adam said, jumping into the driving seat. He turned on the ignition staring straight ahead. Calvin recognized that distant look and knew better than to pry. His mother had warned him that his father had a dark side that he revealed to no one. Calvin suspected that this had been part of the problem in their marriage. He had broached the subject with his mother once, but Jennifer had been subtly evasive.

'Anyway, tell me about you, Calvin. How's school? Your mother tells me you got great grades. She also told me you want to leave.'

From the corner of his eye, Calvin studied his father's reaction as he repeated what he had been practising for days. 'Highclare has been great for me; I've enjoyed it, well most of it. After you guys split, I felt a bit lost, and being away at school with lots of others in a similar position helped a lot.' He was staring into the middle distance. 'It was pretty hard at first, Dad, I just wanted it to be, well, how it was before; you know, happy families, and all that stuff.' There was no bitterness in his voice, just regret.

Adam gave his son a long glance. Calvin's angular jaw jutted forward in what Adam knew was a defiant gesture, his mouth was taut. But a few seconds later, his bottom lip had begun to quiver ever so slightly and he squinted as sunlight suddenly flooded his eyes. He shut them, but not before Adam had seen the thin film of unshed tears.

Adam felt the boy's pain like never before, realizing for the first time that he'd been so selfishly obsessed with his own hurt, he'd failed to recognize his son's. Reproaching himself, he was filled with a deep remorse, and the compulsion to make amends.

'Believe me, Calvin, when I say that I know how hard it must have been for you; all kids want their parents to be together, whatever the cost. They don't understand that it's not always possible. I don't need to tell you that your mother is a strong-willed lady, and once she gets her mind set on something there's no turning her.'

'Would you have her back now, Dad?'

The unexpected question caught Adam off guard. 'Why do you ask?'

'Just something she said last time I was home.'

'Yeah, go on.' Adam was curious.

'A song came on the radio and she got a kind of funny look on her face, you know, wistful, and her voice sounded different, kinda foggy. She said, "This was the first song I ever danced to, with your father." When the record ended, she turned to face me. Her eyes were full of tears, and I thought she was going to cry. Then she said, "I loved him very much."'

Adam knew the song. '"I'm not in Love" by 10CC?'

Calvin nodded, 'That's the one.'

'Next time you see your mother, ask her what song reminds her of Jordan Tanner.' Adam's anger altered his handsome face and his son was sorry he had brought the subject up. They travelled in stony silence for the next few minutes, until Calvin broke it.

'I think you should know that I don't want to go to

46

Harvard next year, Dad. I don't want to be a smart-ass lawyer. I want to go to Art College.'

This revelation did not surprise Adam who asked, 'Is your mother aware of this?'

'Yep, but you know her as well as I do, she's a snob and all she cares about is what her fancy friends think. Harvard Law School is the ultimate as far as she's concerned. She has this vision of art students with long hair, hanging out and doing drugs. Not the clean-cut Wasp image she has in mind for me! But I don't want to do that preppy scene, and I hate the thought of being part of a hot-shot law firm. Most of the lawyers I've met at Grandma's are creeps.' Calvin spoke with the angry conviction of a headstrong sixteen-year-old determined to have his own way.

Adam agreed wholeheartedly. 'You're right about lawyers; most of 'em are assholes, give or take a couple, one of whom is my best friend. I never thought for one second Law School was right for you, Cal. You've got talent, real talent, and I would love you to be an artist. My greatest regret in life is that I can't paint. That's why I hang out in an art gallery for a living, you know, getting it all second-hand.' Adam slid his hand across the car seat, covering Calvin's, he squeezed gently. 'You've got my support, son. If Art College is what you really want, and it makes you happy, fine by me. Your Grandfather Krantz would have been proud, he would have encouraged you every inch of the way.'

Calvin breathed a huge sigh of relief. 'You'll back me then, Dad, when it comes to the showdown?'

An image of Jennifer's enraged face drifted before Adam's eyes. He blinked to clear it from his vision and

47

said in a voice he hoped sounded reassuring and positive, 'I'm absolutely certain that between us we can make your mother see sense.' He increased the pressure on his son's hand.

'Gee thanks, Dad! I knew I could rely on you.'

That night Adam went with Calvin to Lusardi's, an Italian restaurant he'd been taking him to since he was old enough to walk. Over *linguine pesto* they reminisced about Calvin's thirteenth birthday party, spent in the same restaurant. The teenager had got very drunk on Chianti, it was a memorable first.

Afterwards, back at Adam's apartment on Central Park West, on Calvin's insistence they played a selection of his all-time favourite blues artists. The boy whistled and snapped his fingers in tune with the music, commenting that he been the only kid in the neighbourhood to be lulled to sleep by John Lee Hooker, Robert Cray and Wolf Man Jack, instead of the usual nursery rhymes. Adam chuckled to himself thinking how much he loved being like this, just the two of them together. Later they shared a couple of beers, whilst watching a late-night TV movie in the small den that had once been Calvin's playroom.

Halfway through the movie Calvin fell asleep. Careful not to wake him Adam switched off the television, then bending down he extracted the half-empty beer can from his son's grip. Straightening up, he stood very still for a long time, gazing with admiration at his son's body sprawled across the sofa. Calvin was lean and tanned, and toned from hours on the playing field. And Adam was suddenly filled with an indescribable rush of pride and wonder at the fact that he had somehow created this undeniably handsome young man. All the hackneyed parent-and-child clichés sprang to mind. Adam plumped for 'the best investment I've ever made'.

Briskly he walked down the hall, past the kitchen into the living room. It was a vast space with large floor-to-ceiling windows filling one wall, whilst pictures filled every other available square inch – including the bathrooms and the back of the kitchen door. Adam had never particularly liked the apartment, but now as he looked around he realized he hated it. It was more like a gallery than a home.

'It's got no soul,' he muttered, pouring Scotch into a tumbler and lighting a Marlboro Red, thinking of the months Jennifer had spent decorating the interior with her camp interior designer friend, 'Jovi' or 'Javi', some stupid name he couldn't remember. Rolling the whisky around the glass, he listened to the ice clinking while finally deciding that the apartment was a monument to his wife: monochromatic, ultra chic and seriously expensive.

Crossing the room he stood next to the window. It was an exceptionally clear night. The dark sky high above Central Park was wild with stars, gold and white lights twinkling like scattered jewels above and below his eyrie on the twenty-second floor. It reminded him of another night five years ago when he and Jennifer had moved in. Memories of the hours of frenzied unpacking flooded back; hanging pictures in great excitement, and eating Chinese take-aways sitting on packing boxes, drinking Cristal champagne out of hastily washed mugs. Yes, it had been a night similar to this one and they had made love on the floor in exactly the same spot where he now stood. Afterwards, he recalled his bare soles had pressed against the side of a suitcase as he had lain, still deeply embedded in her softness. Adam had been awed by the look of radiance on Jennifer's face: the serene afterglow when desire has recently departed and love remains.

Turning abruptly away from the window, and the memory, Adam finished his drink, then poured himself another before leaving the room. Padding quietly down the hallway, he passed his favourite painting, a Renoir he had acquired at his first auction. He had been a year older than Calvin, almost eighteen at the time.

During his Spring break he had been invited to accompany Benjamin Krantz, his father, and a world-renowned art dealer to a sale of French Impressionist art at Sotheby's in London. Encouraged by his father, Adam had entered the bidding, acquiring the painting for three thousand dollars below the estimate. Adam would never forget the thrill he'd experienced when the hammer had come down, with the auctioneer's shout of 'Sold' ringing in his ears, or his excitement when the painting had arrived at the Krantz Gallery on Madison Ave along with several others his father had purchased. Benjamin had given him the picture and Adam's life-long love of fine art had begun.

His stockinged feet made no sound on the thick pile carpet when he entered his study. Adam knew this room like the back of his hand and easily negotiated his way in the dark. Sitting down, he flicked a switch, illuminating the desk-top. Taking a key out of a drawer, he used it to open another drawer to his left. Lifting out a box file, he began to riffle through the assorted papers. It took him a few minutes to find what he wanted.

Holding the old newspaper cutting under the strong spotlight, he drank deeply of his whisky whilst staring into the arrogant face of Klaus Von Trellenberg standing next to Heinrich Himmler at a Nazi party rally in 1939. Adam narrowed his eyes in hatred, and allowed a cruel smile to distort his generous mouth.

'I'm going to get you this time, you son-of-a-bitch.'

He was still smiling as he crushed the paper into a tiny ball in the palm of his hand.

Chapter Three

Kathryn was very cold. She could not feel her hands and feet, and when she opened her mouth to speak no words came, in fact she was unable to make any sound at all. She was completely naked, and her body looked different. Not quite like her own. It was very thin, and totally hairless. Slowly she parted her legs and to her horror saw that she was covered in open sores.

She was alone in a small room, it was about ten foot square, there were no windows or doors, and the walls were painted white, perfect new snow white. There were no lights, yet it was glaringly bright. It felt like being inside a large floodlit cardboard box. She looked up when she heard the voice, which seemed to be floating out of the ceiling. It was a soothing sound; like a caress it washed over her, and she wondered why she felt afraid.

'Kathryn, Kathryn, it's so good to meet you at long last.'

She pulled her legs into her body to cover her nakedness, dropping her head to her knees. She began to shake, her whole body jerking uncontrollably as the voice got louder.

'Kathryn, it's your Grandfather Klaus; look at me, Kathryn, please.'

She was afraid to look, but the voice kept insisting, and eventually she raised her head, opening her eyes wide. A disembodied head floated in front of her face. It was covered in a black mask, resembling the type worn by executioners in the Middle Ages. Her mouth opened to scream, but no sound came, and still the voice kept on.

'I've come to save you, Kathryn. I love you, I want to take you home to Germany with me, where you belong.'

The hideous mask came closer. She tried to cover her face, but her limbs were paralysed. The head was an inch from her now. She wanted to close her eyes, but her eyelids refused to move. She could feel hot breath on her cheek; it smelt strangely sweet, like boiling sugar.

The death mask moved up and down, the voice repeating, *'I love you, Kathryn, your grandfather loves you. I'm going to take you to Germany, you'll be safe there.'*

She could no longer feel her heart beating and thought that perhaps she was dead. Then, suddenly the mask was stuck to her face like glue, the lips fatty and very wet. They began to suck at her, first at her mouth, then at her nose – sucking harder and harder. She struggled to breathe as she felt her whole face being suctioned into the huge gaping gash until she was gasping for air.

Her heart was banging, when a minute later she woke up. The bedclothes were tangled around her head, and for a split second she wasn't sure where she was. Pulling the sheets off, she sat bolt upright in bed. Her palms were clammy and her hair stuck to her head, soaking wet.

Kathryn took a few deep breaths, she stayed very still until her breathing returned to normal. This was the second time she'd had the dream since her Aunt Ingrid had told her about Klaus Von Trellenberg less than a week ago. She closed her eyes again, willing herself not to think of him. But she could feel her lids twitching as with nagging consistency the cold repetitive voice in her head kept banging on: *Klaus Von Trellenberg, Klaus Von Trellenberg.* Then her grandfather's face, as it had appeared in the photograph, materialized in her head. But instead of wearing the arrogant half smile, he was laughing. She could hear him. The sound rose to a hysterical screech, pealing in her ears.

With the flat of her hand, Kathryn wiped small pearls of perspiration from her brow and the back of her neck. Sweat rolled down her temples and she experienced a return to the unreality of the day she had learnt about her unwanted SS connections.

The thought of her mother's father as the archetypal Nazi, a cold-blooded psychopath on an indiscriminate killing spree, made her feel physically sick. Suddenly she began to cry. Kathryn realized it was the first time she had cried since Freda's death. With a sense of shame she buried her face deep in the pillow, admitting to herself that she had never loved her. In fact she conceded there were many times when she had *hated* her. Hated her resentment, her hostility, and her lack of communication. *Was it such a terrible crime to dislike your own mother?* Until now she had thought so, and had berated herself for not trying harder. But after what Ingrid had revealed, it seemed easier to accept that her mother had been impossible to love.

Kathryn spent the remainder of the night wide awake. It seemed interminably long, and she was pleased when dawn broke with a roll of thunder, heralding the start of a storm that was to last all day. Unable to face food, she made herself a pot of strong coffee and was just pouring her third cup when the telephone rang. She glanced at the clock in the hall, wondering who could be calling her at seven-thirty a.m.

It was Emily de Moubray, her father's second wife.

'Good morning, Kathryn! I do hope I haven't woken you, but I wanted to catch you before you left for the office. I can never get through to you there. You're such a busy girl these days.' Emily sounded infuriatingly breezy.

'Hi, Emily. How are you?'

'Since you only spoke to me yesterday, I doubt there's much change,' she giggled.

Kathryn bit her bottom lip, suppressing the rising irritation that Emily frequently engendered in her.

'I'm calling because your father can't make supper next week. Would it be possible for us to come up to town *this* Saturday? Sorry to mess you around like this, Kathryn, but he has to attend an important lecture on Friday the eighteenth. He only found out about it last night. Frank Kamer, the doctor he's working with on the cancer vaccine, is over from America and has agreed to speak. The lecture will be followed by a dinner – you know, the same old boring surgeons' do.'

Since she had never been invited to any of her father's lectures or functions, Kathryn did *not* know, and was tempted to remind Emily that she had not shared her father's life since she was nine. She bit back the recrimination, afraid to sound bitter or, worse, a martyr. She had no time for whining self-pity. Yet she had to resist the urge to ask why her father could not speak to her, himself. Anyway she knew the reply would be the same as usual, delivered in a brisk defensive manner. *You are aware how busy your father is, Kathryn. I try not to bother him with mundane matters.*

'If you can't make it, Kathryn, I'm sure your father will understand, but don't forget we won't be back in England for at least a year.' Emily sounded rather pleased by this prospect.

'Well, I *was* supposed to be going to a big society wedding, but I'll have to cancel.'

'Oh dear, never mind, I'm sure there'll be others.' Kathryn felt her hackles rise at Emily's dismissive tone. 'We'll be in town at lunchtime. I have some shopping to do, so perhaps you could amuse your father for the afternoon.' Not waiting for Kathryn to respond she said, 'And please, Kathryn, something simple – you know how he loathes fancy food. The last time you made that rich creamy sauce he felt most unwell for days.'

Kathryn was seething. On the occasion referred to, she had spent hours shopping and preparing a meal she knew her father had loved. He had even called her the following day to compliment her on the best dinner he'd had in years. So she had to bite back an acerbic retort. Past experience had taught her that agreeing with Emily, or simply saying nothing, was infinitely easier than any other course. But it was at such times that she wondered anew what her father saw in this sanctimonious and frivolous woman, who was neither intelligent nor amusing.

Tony Mitchell, her former husband, had suggested once – after Kathryn had been complaining hotly about her stepmother – 'She's a lot younger than your father, good for the old man's ego and his libido. The quiet ones, still waters and all that; she's probably dynamite between the sheets.'

Kathryn had grimaced. The thought of Emily in the throes of passionate lovemaking with her father was so repulsive, she'd had to push it firmly out of her mind.

Now she could not suppress her irritation for a moment longer. 'OK, Em, I get the message; I won't cook at all. I'll book a restaurant, then we can all have exactly what we want.'

'No need to get tetchy with me, Kathryn, and don't call me *Em*, you know how I detest it; anyway, don't you think it much better that I say, rather than you spending a ridiculous amount of—'

Kathryn interrupted. 'I've got to go, I've got a breakfast meeting. Like you said, I'm a busy girl! I'll see you both on Saturday, my place at noon.' She put the telephone down, without saying goodbye, then sipped her coffee whilst imagining Emily making a point of seeking her father out, wherever he was, to inform him in her high-pitched, sing-song voice that his daughter had slammed the phone down on her, and that the older Kathryn got the ruder she became. Kathryn had long ceased to care what Emily thought of her, but she accepted with a sharp pang, that she did care very much about her father's approval. Climbing the stairs to her bedroom, she could not help wondering how he would react to Ingrid's revelations. As she showered and dressed she decided to tell him everything on Saturday afternoon.

Half an hour later she left the house. With her mind in a fog, she climbed into her car, throwing her coat on to the back seat. It was raining hard when she pulled into the multi-storey car park in Brewer Street. She donned her mackintosh, realizing at the same time that she'd forgotten her umbrella. With the collar of her coat up tight to her ears, and using the *Daily Telegraph* to cover her head, she ran across Golden Square into number forty-six.

Kathryn shared the lift with Roger Thompson, a junior accountant. They chatted about the weather, before alighting on the fourth floor and walking together through the double glass doors that led to Trident Productions. Kathryn smiled at Helen the receptionist who was busy making coffee.

The girl held up a cup. 'Want one?'

'No thanks, I've had four already this morning. I'm all caffeined out.'

Kathryn walked down a long corridor interspersed with doors. She stopped at the last door but one, experiencing the familiar quick thrill, as she read the brass nameplate. 'Kathryn de Moubray, Producer.' It was only four months since her promotion, and she was still waiting for the euphoria to wear off. 'You've worked bloody hard for it,' her boss Rod Franks had said at the time. Rod was not generous with his praise, and she knew he was right: she *had* worked hard, damned hard, but it still felt good to be rewarded. The achievement made all the long hours, and the self-sacrifice, worthwhile.

Kathryn crossed the room, her feet making little sound on the thick carpet. She had chosen the office interiors herself and wished, now, that she had gone for the more traditional oak desk and bookcase that she had liked originally, instead of being talked into the smoke-grey and chrome furniture Rod had favoured. 'Too macho,' someone had said, adding that it was a dyke's office. She hung her coat up and, running her fingers through her recently bobbed hair, sat down behind her desk and began to write a list of things she had to do. At the top of the list she put, 'Fax Steve Fisher in Washington. Ask him to research Von Trellenberg in archives.' Then she followed it with, 'Call Bob Conran re pilot for Girls in the Red.' When her direct line rang, she continued writing as she picked up the phone.

It was Jack McGowan. 'Good morning, Kathryn, how are you on this hideous Monday morning?' Without waiting for her reply, he went on, 'Don't you think we should be somewhere, *any*where else, than London in this bloody rain? It's been pissing down for weeks! How about we slip down to my house in the South of France, it's wonderful in June, we can sip chilled rosé on the terrace, and watch the sun set . . .'

'I'm in the middle of a big job; you know that, Jack. I can't just schlepp off to the Med at the drop of a hat.' The word 'hat' jolted her into saying, 'Speaking of which, I'm afraid I can't make the wedding on Saturday. I'm really sorry, but my father wants to see me.'

'Well, tell him you've got a prior engagement.' His tone implied there was nothing more to say.

Kathryn drummed her short fingernails on top of her desk. 'I *am* sorry, Jack. But he's leaving for a lecture tour of the States soon. He's only going to be in London for one day. I have to see him, we've got a lot of things to sort out. I need to discuss my mother's estate, and all that stuff, you understand don't you?'

Jack did not. 'Can't you see him on Friday? I could send a car for you first thing Saturday morning. You could still make the wedding, it doesn't start until midday. Call your father now, tell him it's a case of life and death; he's

59

a doctor, he'll appreciate that. Tell him you've got to work on an important project all weekend, tell him *anything*!'

'I'll tell him the truth, Jack,' she interrupted tersely. 'That's not difficult for me,' she added, intimating that deceit came easily to Jack McGowan.

'Business is about *avoiding* the truth, playing the game, Kathryn. Come on, you know that as well as I do.'

She chose to ignore this remark. 'I'm not sure if he can make it on Friday, but I suppose I could ask.' Kathryn was merely placating him; she was secretly pleased to get out of what she suspected would be a posh but boring wedding.

Encouraged by her hesitation, Jack said, 'Now when are you going to get another opportunity to wear that fabulous hat?'

She was smiling. 'Ascot?' she ventured. 'Ladies' Day, perhaps?'

His voice dropped an octave. 'I would prefer you to wear it this weekend. First for the wedding, then later for me, with nothing else but high heels, and that special smile. You know the one you wear when I—'

She interrupted with, 'Shame on you, Mr McGowan!'

'I'll be totally inconsolable if I have to spend the weekend alone,' he told her.

Kathryn also lowered her voice. 'Since when have you ever done that, Jack? Oh and by the way, I'd love to wear the hat and heels, specially for you. If not this weekend then some time in the near future.'

His loud expulsion of breath was followed by, '*This* weekend, Kathryn.'

'I'll let you know by Thursday when we're going to the

Buchanans for drinks. That will give you twenty-four hours to find a replacement.'

The humour had left his voice when he said, 'There is none.'

Reluctant to confront his disappointment any longer, she made an excuse to terminate the conversation. 'My other line's ringing, I've got to go. I'll call you later.'

She replaced the telephone thinking about Jack McGowan. He was either in love with her or, alternatively, deeply in lust. Not entirely sure of her own feelings, which fluctuated from heady infatuation to irritation at his possessive need to control, she was left uncertain and confused. When she punched out Bob Conran's telephone number her thoughts were still with Jack. They had met at a cocktail party two years previously when she'd found him overpowering and far too egotistical for her taste. She had refused to have dinner with him, making the excuse that she never went out with married men. Then at a film premiere eighteen months later, she had bumped into him again. She had been with her boss Rod, head of Trident, an independent film company responsible for more than one hundred and sixty hours of television production each year. Rod had given her the low-down on Jack McGowan.

Born in Aberdeen to a Scottish father and English mother. Powerful industrialist. Oil-rig machinery. One of the top five hundred richest men in the country. A true-blue Thatcherite, heavily tipped for a knighthood in 1982 and 1983, when he was pouring money into the Tory party, and had billions of pounds' worth of export contracts littering his desk. Notoriously ruthless, yet a great philanthropist, and patron of the arts. Several much publicized run-ins with the press, and one particular nasty libel case in the mid-seventies involving insider dealing on the stock market. A brief affair last year with the soprano Anna Cavelli had culminated in the break-up of his twenty-eight-year marriage; although he and his wife had no plans to divorce. He'd had a daughter who'd died of a drugs overdose at twenty-two, and there was an adopted son from his wife's first marriage.

Jack had made a beeline for Kathryn at the post-screening party, persuading her to leave the teeming milieu, and join him for a quiet supper at Harry's Bar. She had agreed reluctantly and, to her surprise, she'd had a wonderful evening. Subsequent outings had followed, and Kathryn had been forced to revise her first impressions of Jack McGowan. Though not entirely wrong, they were greatly diluted by her discovery of his ironic sense of humour, and irrepressible charm. She recalled in detail the first time they had made love, the encounter had left her overwhelmed. Formidable he might be to his business opponents, but in bed Jack had proved gentle, and sensitive to her every need.

Bob Conran's deep voice broke into her thoughts as he answered her call, and instantly she forgot about Jack as she began to discuss the development of the Girls in the Red project. Bob was dashing out to a meeting and could only spare her a few minutes. He suggested lunch the following day. Kathryn consulted her diary, and they agreed to meet at Le Caprice at one. The light on her intercom was flashing as she replaced the telephone. It was her secretary, Sally. 'Mr Franks wants to see you asap. A word of warning, he's on the warpath about something.'

Kathryn had a good idea what it was. 'Thanks for the

tip, Sally; I'm on my way.' She clicked the intercom switch off, and headed for Rod Franks's office. Kathryn waited on the threshold for a few moments, thinking about her boss. She had known Rod for ten years, and worked for him for six. He was highly talented, hot-tempered, and great at what he did. He had started out at sixteen, as a runner for a small film company, and had come up through the ranks. Ten years before, at thirty-five, Rod and his life-long friend Neville Morgan had started Trident, but Neville had died of Aids two years ago. Rod was a tough bastard, there was no denying that, but Kathryn understood him, at least most of the time. She also respected his enormous talent, and shrewd intellect. He in turn admired her tenacity, her creative flair, and her ability to get things done; but more important, they shared a mutual passion for the business. Both were totally committed to producing good, aspiring constantly to 'great' television.

When she entered his spacious office, Rod was next to the window, his back to her. Rod had style, she had to give him that, his office reflected it. Very chic, very minimalist, very nineties. Blond wood-panelled floors, beneath blonder panelled walls. A David Hockney painting and a huge vivid splash of Miró the only colour in the room. *Less is more*, Rod was fond of saying; if you got it right, as he so often did, she was forced to agree.

On her third footstep he turned, he was dressed in a dark blue lightweight Paul Smith suit and a collarless white cotton shirt. His dark hair was slicked back with gel, it glistened in the overhead spotlight. Wasting no time on pleasantries he said, 'Did you know that Sue Chandler was pitching *our* idea, about the black heiress, to Ryan Messum

63

at Fox?' And when Kathryn nodded, he added, 'Well why the hell didn't you tell me? I could have stopped her.'

'If you recall, Rod, the story was *my* idea originally. I told her about it the night before she left Trident. I thought she needed a break, after the shabby way you got rid of her.'

'Look, darling, I'm the one who needs a break around here. Sue screwed up on two major productions. *Women.*' He slapped a hand to his forehead, and took a step towards Kathryn. 'The next time you decide to give away great ideas that, I might add, are already in development, ask me. OK?'

'OK, Rod, it wasn't such a great idea anyway. Girls in the Red is far better.'

'It was so lousy, I heard Messum almost kissed that fucking bitch's ass when she pitched it to him.'

Kathryn couldn't help grinning. 'Can you imagine Ryan Messum kissing *anyone's* ass?'

In spite of himself Rod began to smile. 'No. The only thing Messum would be likely to kiss is his own reflection, or that yappy Jack Russell he takes everywhere with him.'

He sat down behind his desk and indicated a chair opposite. 'You're right, Kathy. Girls in the Red *is* a much better project.' He was the only person apart from her father who ever called her 'Kathy'. 'How's it coming?'

'It's coming; we're on schedule. Tim got some great footage in Leningrad and Moscow. And I'm having lunch with Bob tomorrow to finalize the script.'

'Good, tell Bob he owes me lunch, too. In fact he owes me several.' Rod formed a fist. 'He's as tight as a fish's backside.'

Kathryn winked. 'Have you tried one lately?'

Rod grinned. 'Leave my sex life out of this.' His telephone rang, he picked it up, pressing the hold button, then pointing at her with the same finger. 'I'm not finished with you yet. Can you dig out your high-heeled sneakers and red dress for a book launch tomorrow night at the Groucho? It's the new Collins publication by that guy Stuart.'

She knew the book. '*Beyond Madness*, by Nick Stuart?'

'That's the one, I optioned it this morning.'

Kathryn stood up. 'It's a great book, but I'm not certain it will adapt well.'

Rod pressed the hold button again. 'Nigel, great to hear from you. Listen, I've got an amazing, too-good-to-miss idea for a documentary about the culling of rhinos in Tanzania.'

Kathryn turned to leave.

'Hold on, Nigel.' Rod looked at her expectantly.

She nodded her acceptance to the Groucho do, already dreading the noisy, shoulder-to-shoulder, cocktail party in Soho. She was halfway across the office when she heard Rod fling a final remark at her.

'I want you to meet the author, Kathy. Apparently he's very tricky, so you need to use every ounce of your irresistible charm.'

Kathryn stopped at the door. 'If the stories about Nick Stuart are true, I think *your* charm might work better.'

She could hear Rod chuckling as she left the room.

Kathryn arrived at her flat in Notting Hill at ten past six. She had exactly forty-five minutes, to shower, wash her hair, change and get to Jack McGowan's house in

Hampstead for seven. She decided it wasn't possible; planning her apology, she listened to her messages on the answering machine.

Bleep: *Hi, Kathryn. Steve Fisher here. Thanks for the fax. Rod Franks is obviously as truculent as ever. Good to see that things don't change. I've got some hot-off-the-press gen on your Nazi. Give me a call on 202 657 8826. Ciao.*

Bleep: *Kathryn, Bob Conran. Sorry but I'll have to change our lunch date. If you get in before seven call me, if not I'll speak to you at the office tomorrow morning.*

'Damn you, Bob! You *promised* to deliver the script.'

Bleep: *This is Oliver Grant from Brinkforth and Sons. It's four-thirty on Thursday 10th June. We have a firm offer on the table for Fallowfields; I would like to discuss it with you, please call at your earliest convenience.* There was a short pause then, *By the way I have forwarded the mail from Fallowfields to your present address.* Bleep.

There was no time to digest this news now and instead Kathryn punched out Steve Fisher's number in Washington. She got a nasty nasal voice asking if she wanted to leave a message on his voice mail.

'Steve, it's Kathryn. It's six-fifteen London time. I'm racing now, going to a drinks party. I'll call you when I get home. If I miss you, fax the info to my office asap. Thanks for working on it so quickly. Hope you're well, and still enjoying life on Capitol Hill.'

She was undressing as she ran upstairs, and within twenty minutes, she had showered and was wearing an ankle-length simple black sheath, with matching high heels; her unwashed hair gelled back from her face.

On the drive out to North London, she planned what she would say to her father on Saturday. The death of her mother, and the unwelcome knowledge about Freda's past life would have to be addressed. She imagined his reaction: one of initial shock, then suppressed emotion, followed by a complete refusal to discuss it.

When she pulled up in front of Jack McGowan's house in Hampstead, a quick glance at the car clock told her she was only ten minutes late. *Not bad going*, she congratulated herself, cutting the ignition and grabbing her jacket from the back seat.

Jack's housekeeper, Mrs Peacock, opened the door. Kathryn heard a familiar deep voice as soon as she stepped into the hall.

'I don't care what Nadia Foreman says; she may be a brilliant lawyer but remember, Paul, she's not God and we can't afford any adverse publicity right now. The contract with the Saudis is almost in the bag.'

Kathryn handed her jacket to Mrs Peacock, thinking – as she always did – that anyone less like her name would be hard to find. Mrs Peacock was brown. Everything about her was expressed in varying degrees of the colour. From her mouse brown hair; to her ashen, liver-spotted skin; dull muddy eyes; and muted beige clothes. Kathryn accepted her offer of a drink, choosing a glass of mineral water, and popped her head around the open door to Jack's study. He was standing next to his desk, one hand holding the telephone, the other writing something on a pad next to it. He had his back to her. She waited for a couple of minutes listening to his steady voice, the soft Scottish intonation still evident in certain words.

'I don't give a damn if she likes it or not, she's got to do it or look for a job elsewhere. There are plenty more budding young lawyers where she came from, Paul, remind her of that. And while you're at it, remind her of the spin-off and perks this contract will give her, not to mention the existing perks she is currently enjoying with the chief executive.'

Kathryn assumed Jack was talking to Paul Rowland. She had met Paul a couple of times and liked what she had seen. For a chief executive he had an awkward boyish sort of charm, with a shyness that she had found extremely appealing. Not that shy she conceded; he was obviously having an affair with Nadia Foreman. The sultry, aggressive lawyer Nadia, and Paul Rowland, seemed an incongruous couple to her. She hadn't met Paul's wife Christine, but Jack had mentioned that she was a bossy overpowering woman. If she found out, she would probably kill him.

Silently Kathryn backed out, almost bumping into the Peacock, who was carrying a tray bearing a Perrier water and a bowl of cashew nuts. With her broad back, the house-keeper held open the door to the drawing room, giving her usual disapproving glare. Kathryn took her drink, and looking directly at Mrs Peacock she began to smile. *Why let the old dragon bother me?* She was still smiling, when she stepped inside the room.

It was a big square, with high ceilings and huge picture windows front and back. It could have been beautiful, if it wasn't so cluttered and dark. It had been built in the late eighteen-nineties, when Hampstead was a garden suburb. Jack had bought it in 1978. In her opinion it had been decorated with lots of new money, and bad taste. But then who determined 'taste'? Kathryn mused. And who was she to be so critical? Rod had once said to her, *There's no such thing as good or bad taste, merely taste* – after a particularly scathing comment she had passed on the decor in her father's house.

Jack's voice rose, but she could no longer make out what he was saying. A minute later she heard footsteps in the hall followed by, 'Mrs Peacock, get me a gin and tonic.'

Paul Rowland is getting soft in his old age, Jack was thinking as he stood in front of the large mirror in the hall. If he screwed up on this one, he would have to seriously think about getting rid of him, get in some new blood. He brushed a few imaginary specks of dust from the collar of his dress suit, adjusted his bow tie with fastidious neatness, then cracking his knuckles one by one, in a stage whisper he spoke to his reflection. 'Not bad for an old boy of almost fifty-eight.'

He thought about Paul again. Jack hoped Paul *would* pull this deal off and come out smelling of roses. He liked him, and he trusted him. Paul had been with KJM for twenty-four years. He could remember him as a fresh-faced eighteen-year-old, making the tea.

Mrs Peacock approached with a beaming smile, breaking his train of thought. He accepted his gin and afforded himself one last glance in the mirror before walking into the drawing room.

Kathryn was standing in front of the window at the south side of the house. From here, she had a view down the deep close-cut lawn. It was bordered by untidy flowerbeds, and ended in a high brick wall, clad with dying ivy. Jack hated

69

gardening. *Gardens are a bloody nuisance. They cost a fortune to plant and maintain, and we only get to appreciate them for a few days a year.* She had heard his opinion several times. It was raining hard, small puddles were beginning to form on the uneven surface of the circular paved terrace. She watched the water bounce off the top of the white wrought-iron table they had eaten off in last week's sunshine. It looked desolate now.

Hearing the chink of ice in Jack's glass, she turned to greet him. 'Hi, Jack, old Peacock let me in.' She pulled a long face. 'I'm convinced that old bitch hates me. I'm sure she's in love with you, and after you and your wife split up she was convinced she'd get you.'

Jack looked genuinely surprised. 'You're not serious are you? Peacock in love, it's ridiculous!'

Not wanting to discuss the widowed housekeeper any longer, Kathryn said, 'Why not? You're a very attractive man.'

Also eager to change the subject, he beamed, his cosmetically altered smile flashing white and even. Standing very close to her, he murmured, 'You look beautiful, Kathryn.'

Aware of his alert, aquamarine eyes wandering admiringly over her statuesque body, warming to his admiration, she moved deliberately to expose one long leg from inside her dress. It was slit to mid-thigh.

He liked the way her dark honey hair, slicked back from her face, accentuated her strong jaw and high cheekbones. She was wearing a pair of diamond drop earrings he had bought her for her thirty-fourth birthday the previous month. Bending forward to plant a kiss, he felt her perfume fill his nostrils. It was a new fragrance, sweeter than the musk-based one she usually wore. He wasn't sure he liked it.

'New perfume?'

'Mm, you like?' She held out a bare arm.

'Not sure yet.' He kissed the inside of her wrist. 'It might grow on me.' He straightened up then looking at her closely said, 'You're a little pale tonight, Kathryn, are you all right?'

Unable to tell him the real reason, she used an excuse. 'I'm fine, just working too hard I suppose.' In fact she had spent the entire day debating with herself whether or not to tell Jack about Klaus Von Trellenberg. This evening on her way to his house she had finally decided not to. The more she talked about it, the more real it would become; far better to pretend it had never happened. No one else could connect her to Trellenberg. Yet in her own mind she could not erase the reoccurring image of her grandfather dressed in SS uniform. She wondered with dread if it would always be there.

'You could do with a holiday,' Jack was saying, but Kathryn was staring into space, a faraway expression on her face. '*Kathryn*, did you hear me?' He clicked his fingers in front of her glazed eyes.

She shook her head. 'Sorry, Jack, did you say something?'

'I said you need a rest, a holiday.'

'Try telling Rod Franks that!'

Jack made no comment, and went on as if she hadn't spoken. It was a habit she was positive he was unaware of, but that did not stop her irritation.

'I've got to go to Singapore in a few weeks' time . . . Why don't I extend my stay and we'll do a bit of island-hopping: Phuket, Ko Samui, Bali. Only yesterday I heard about a wonderful tented hotel, somewhere in Indonesia. How about it?' Jack urged, taking a sip of gin and tonic.

'I'm not sure if I can get the time off work. We're just about to start a new series for Channel Four, and you know what a stickler Rod is . . .'

'Tell Rod you need a break. I'll buy you your own bloody production company if he sacks you.'

There was no doubt in Kathryn's mind that Jack meant what he said. If she didn't stop him, he would be buying her expensive gifts constantly. Gently she said, 'That's not the answer, Jack; you can't go through life buying everything and everybody.'

'Why not? It's worked so far!' He lifted his glass. His pupils were like tiny black icebergs, gleaming over the rim. He winked and grinned.

She inclined her head a little, a soft blush colouring her skin. Under the sophisticated façade Kathryn wore so easily, there was a fragile vulnerability. Jack found it highly provocative, and would have liked to make love to her there and then. His mind ran riot with erotic imaginings in which her long dress bunched up around her waist, and one full breast lay exposed – his tongue tracing the nipple, erect and puckered; her naked backside, rounded and hard, pressed against the rain-spattered window. He felt an erection stirring, and marvelled afresh at how Kathryn had managed to revitalize his flagging libido. Nothing like a surge of testosterone to make a man feel good, he thought with a self-satisfied grin on his face.

'What are you thinking, Jack? All of a sudden you look very pleased with yourself.'

'I was thinking how lucky I am to have a woman like you, and how easy it would be for that same woman to make an old man very happy. Two weeks in the Far East, not too much to ask is it?'

'No, Jack, it's not too much to ask, and it's a lovely thought. I know I would have a wonderful time, and you would spoil me rotten, but not right now. I've got a lot on at the moment. Later in the year perhaps.'

Shrewdly Jack detected that her voice held no promise, yet it did not deter him from saying, 'I could never spoil you enough, Kathryn, well certainly not sufficiently to make you rotten. The offer is open, think about it; I won't be asking anyone else.'

'OK, Jack, thanks.'

'Talking about asking someone else, have you spoken to your father about this weekend?'

Reluctantly she lied. 'Yes I have, he can't get down to London until Saturday. He's been working with a doctor from America who's developed a cancer vaccine. The doctor is over here from California and my father has to entertain him.' With pangs of regret and resentment, Kathryn thought back to all the times she had needed her father and he had been too busy working to be there for her. 'His work is very important, all consuming you might say.'

Jack detected the bitterness in this last sentence, and felt a surge of sympathy. He had enjoyed a rare closeness with his own father, and had looked forward to a loving intimate relationship with his only daughter. It still hurt like hell

73

to think about Laraine. Jack stared hard at Kathryn but it was his daughter's face he saw. She was laughing, she had laughed a lot as a child and he missed that more than anything else. She had worn her hair swept back in a long ponytail from her petite pretty face. Yes, she had been pretty and he wanted to remember her like that; not the way she'd looked at the end. Had she lived she would have been two years younger than Kathryn was now. *How could Richard de Moubray neglect his beautiful daughter?* Jack surmised that the man was not only a fool, but also a bloody selfish one.

'I'm sorry about the wedding, Jack.'

His face fell. 'I'm sorry too.'

Feeling guilty, and slightly rattled, she gave his arm a pinch. 'Come on, cheer up, there'll be other weekends.'

Jack did not reply but she noticed a subtle change in his body language; he stiffened and his free hand clenched tight.

Kathryn felt bad about lying to him, and even more so about not wanting to spend the weekend with him. Jack was so good to her, too good; his doting indulgence she sometimes found claustrophobic.

'Listen, Jack, I've said I'm sorry. Let's not make a big deal of this. I'm sure you'll have a better time than me anyway. I've got to listen to that dreadful Emily all evening. Believe me it's a fate worse than death.' She decided to make amends by saying, 'How about you come over to my place for brunch on Sunday? Scrambled eggs and salmon; you can bring the champagne?'

This suggestion seemed to cheer him up, it produced a smile at least. 'I'd love to. I'll need cheering up after the

Foster-Ward wedding. I'll drive back to London first thing Sunday morning.'

She stepped up to him, playfully pinching his arm. 'That's settled then, and now don't you think we should go ... The Buchanans' party's going to be over before we get there.'

The envelope from Brinkforths was the first thing Kathryn saw when she padded downstairs the following morning. It contained four letters, and a compliment slip. There was a reply to an application her mother had made about an advanced floristry course, plus an electricity bill, and a telephone bill. She scanned the list of charges, astonished by three overseas calls amounting to over three hundred and fifty pounds. Kathryn was certain British Telecom must have made a mistake: Freda had hardly ever used the phone, she'd had very few people to call. She made a mental note to call BT when she got to the office.

The last letter was addressed to 'FREDA' in capital letters with no surname. The big looped scrawl almost filled the entire front of the small blue envelope, and part of the address had been spelt incorrectly. Tearing it open, Kathryn felt her heart miss a beat when she saw that it was written in German. Struggling with her schoolgirl grasp of the language, she began to read.

My dearest child,
  I cannot begin to express how much your letter has meant to me. After all these years, to know you are alive has brought great joy and a sense of purpose that I believed was lost from my life. I can't

*tell you how many hours I have spent looking at
your photographs. It fills me with . . .* Kathryn could
not read the next few words and made a mental note
to buy a German dictionary, but she surprised herself
by translating the next paragraph easily . . . *How I
wish things could have been different, Freda, but
we are all mere victims of fate. Mine dictated by
circumstances and history, as you know only too
well. I lost faith with that madman who wasted so
many lives and brought our beloved country to her
knees.*

*The memory of your face I will take with me to
my death, which I know will not be long; months,
weeks, who can be sure with cancer. I have . . .* she
had to skip the next word . . . *my welcome on this
earth and await my end with no fear, only a mixture
of profound relief and anticipation. I will be with
your mother once more. If I don't write again, you
will know why. Don't forget what I told you, and your
promise to me, Freda. It is all up to you now. I love
you, have always loved you, and always will.*

Kathryn shuddered, recalling the voice in her nightmares.
The letter was not signed, and she couldn't make out the
postmark. Riffling through her kitchen drawers, she
eventually found a tiny magnifying glass that had come
out of a Christmas cracker the previous year. Using one
eye, she read the postmark again: *2nd June, St Lucia, West
Indies.*

Chapter Four

'I'm absolutely adamant: Calvin is *not* going to Art School. Have you seen some of the students? I doubt they can string an articulate sentence together. Probably too high on dope.'

It crossed Adam's mind that the students were there to paint and not to be articulate, but he kept quiet. When Jennifer was in a determined mood, she became totally unreasonable. Past experience had taught him that arguing back invariably made her much worse.

She uncrossed her long, willowy legs and Adam was afforded a brief glimpse of stocking top and a millimetre of black lace. They were sitting in his apartment, facing each other on opposite sofas, like military opponents. Jennifer tossed her head defiantly, a gesture he knew well. It was one of the things he had noticed the first time he had met her. Her dark auburn hair had been longer then, swinging across her shoulders like a slick of russet gloss paint. Two weeks after they had split up, she had cut it and he had to admit she suited it short. The style gave her face a boyish quality, and today, wearing very little make-up and with her creamy skin tanned from twelve days' vacation in Hawaii, Jennifer looked much younger than thirty-eight. She reminded Adam of a wary colt; fresh, bold and very beautiful.

'Not all art students are as you describe. In fact, I can name two kids who've just graduated and who look more like budding stockbrokers than aspiring Andy Warhols. And I don't need to remind you about Luke, Matt and Kelly Bronson's son, who got expelled from *Yale* last year for taking drugs.' He spread his hands wide. 'So it doesn't necessarily follow . . .'

'OK, OK, Adam. I'm sure there are exceptions; we can all pull examples out of the bag if we choose, but that's not the point.'

'Well, what is? Correct me if I'm wrong, Jennifer, but didn't you kick up a storm at a very similar age? Your father told me that he almost went berserk when you took up modelling instead of a business course at Vassar. He still thinks to this day that you would have made a brilliant lawyer.'

'He's a stubborn old fool!'

'*Stubborn*, I'll give you, Jennifer. *Old*, yes; if you call seventy-four "old". But a *fool*? Come on, Richard Carmichael is nobody's fool.'

With a wave of her hand, she snarled through clenched teeth. 'I didn't come here to discuss my father, you always were good at changing the subject when it suits you.' She began twisting the diamond ring she was wearing on her wedding finger.

Adam raised his eyebrows. 'New ring?'

'Yes, I'm engaged.' He felt his stomach contract into a tight knot, followed by a searing pain, as if someone had just injected boiling water into his gut. The reaction made him want to throttle Jennifer, this woman whom he had loved with a passion. Sitting now on his sofa, in an apartment they had shared, she looked so poised and in control. And she was armed with the ability to wound him, so painfully, with a few simple words.

He could hear the contempt creeping into his voice, but was unable to contain it. 'How can you be engaged to marry when you're still married to me?' Not waiting for her reply, he went on, 'So Jordan Tanner has bought you a ring, *big deal*. I wouldn't get carried away if I were you, Jennifer. If his past record is anything to go by, he seems to get through women like most men get through—'

'Shut up, Adam, or try and say something original. We are engaged to be married when my divorce comes through; anyway, I came here to talk about our son's future, not to hear you run Jordan down.'

'Yeah, yeah, you're right; sorry. Old wounds, you know how it is.'

Jennifer lowered her eyes, concealing the flash of guilt his words had produced. She did know how it was for him.

'Does Cal know you're engaged?'

When she looked up to speak, some of the cool edge had left her voice. 'No, not yet, we're going to tell him next leave-out weekend. Jordan's planning a trip to his place upstate.' She paused, 'You know, to help find the right moment. I shouldn't worry, he's very fond of Calvin.'

Adam doubted there was a 'right moment' and he knew, without a shadow of doubt, Calvin did not reciprocate Jordan Tanner's affection. 'Cal still harbours hopes of you and me getting back together, so I really don't know how he's going to take the happy news.'

Adam shifted in his seat, pulling a cushion out from

behind his back. Jennifer stood up to her full five foot eight, stretched, and with both hands on her narrow hips walked across the room, not stopping until she came to the bookcase on the far wall. Picking up an ashtray, she walked back towards him. Adam watched her slow feline movements, they had always aroused him. She lit a cigarette, the smoke rising in front of her face, and she looked at him through slanted eyes.

His hair, normally flowing on to his shoulders, was caught in an untidy ponytail – several strands had strayed and were curling into his neck. The top three buttons of his shirt were open and his initials could be seen, hand embroidered in pale blue, on the inside collar. Jennifer recalled the first time she had kissed that neck; she had noticed the monogram and thought it very chic.

Adam stretched his left leg, worn denim pulling taut across his upper thigh. His jeans rode up to reveal an inch of calf, thick black hair curling over the rim of his tan cowboy boot.

God, you're an attractive son-of-a-bitch, his wife thought to herself, fighting an overwhelming urge to touch him. She had never stopped wanting him. No man had ever physically satisfied her like Adam Krantz. There was a warmth between her legs as her mind ran rampant with thoughts of him inside her, his mouth on her body, hot and hungry, like a starving animal on a feeding frenzy. Inhaling smoke deeply, she was scrutinizing his face.

'And how do *you* feel about the idea of us getting back together, Adam?' There was something in the way she narrowed her eyes to slits that gave her the distinct look of a cat. An alley cat, Adam thought, realizing with a surge of anger that it was exactly the way she had looked on that afternoon, eighteen months ago, when he had arrived back from London two days earlier than anticipated.

He hadn't called home but had called Joanne to make a reservation for dinner at the Manhattan Ocean Club, one of Jennifer's favourite restaurants. The scene remained like a stage set in his head: always in vivid colour – every word, movement, nuance, in excruciating detail. Jennifer was bent over his desk, her blue skirt hiked up around her waist, both legs were spread wide apart, a pair of white lace panties hung from one ankle. Her left breast was exposed; the nipple, puckered and dark, seemed unusually large. There was one gold button missing from her white Chanel blouse – the one he had bought her in Paris on vacation the previous year. As she strained forward, hold-ing the edge of the desk, her abundant hair fanned across his open diary.

Jordan Tanner, his trousers gathered around his ankles, was gripping her hips and there were pink marks on her smooth skin where his fingers had been. His open shirt flapped against his naked thighs as he moved rhythmically in and out of her body.

Stunned into silence, Adam had watched them from the open door of his study – the Hermès carrier bag containing a scarf and belt for Jennifer dangling from his grip. He had felt strangely detached, like watching a film, and at one point even wanted to laugh. Hardly daring to breathe, he had listened to Jennifer's moans, and Jordan's increasing grunts as his thrusting approached ejaculation. Adam would never forget their faces which had turned towards

*him in shock when he had spoken very quietly, in a voice
that he didn't recognize as his own. 'I do hope Jordan is
wearing a condom, Jennifer; you really don't know where
he's been.'*

'I asked you a question, Adam.'

A thin spiral of smoke curled into the air between
them.

'Us? I don't think it would ever work.' His mouth tightened. 'Too much water under the bridge. You must understand I can't get this vision of you shacked up with that
senseless creep Jordan Tanner out of my mind. I mean if
a beautiful woman like you has to get laid behind her
husband's back, I really think there are—'

'Stop it, *stop* it, please!' Jennifer was shaking, and
it pleased him to see her robbed of her cool composure.
'We've been through this before, it's all totally negative
stuff.'

'Oh *negative*, is it? I don't think saying what one really
thinks can ever be negative, Jennifer.'

Ignoring this reasoning, she ground her cigarette out
viciously into the bottom of the ashtray, the calm voice of
her therapist whispering in her ears, *'Guilt is negative. You
must be positive. Do not under any circumstances take on
your husband's guilt. He will, if you allow him, try to
make you feel responsible for everything that's gone wrong
in your relationship; most men do.'*

Composing her features into a smile that, to Adam, resembled a sneer, she said, 'I really would like Cal to go to
Harvard, Adam. He's very bright, it's a great university
and can offer him everything. Think of the people he'll
meet, the cream of society, how can you deny him that

82

opportunity? I would really appreciate it if you didn't fight me on this one.'

'I think Calvin has a mind of his own, Jennifer. You know as well as I do that he's headstrong, and if he wants to go to Art School – he will. I don't think I'll have to fight, this is something he wants real bad. The kid's got a gift, real talent; think about him for once, and not yourself.'

Jennifer stood up, her expression unreadable. 'You're right, Calvin *is* strong-willed. He takes after you in that respect, you always were a stubborn bastard, and so secretive. I really don't know what I hoped to achieve by coming here. Jordan warned me that you would deliberately try to oppose me.'

'Did he now? I suggest you tell Jordan Tanner to come over here and say that to me personally if he dares. The little asshole may be brave enough to make a pass at my wife, then get laid, but he's scared shitless to face me.'

Jennifer glared like a wild predatory cat. 'Damn you, Adam Krantz! You know why I had to seek the comforts of another man, you were never around.' She strode towards the door, grabbing her jacket from the back of a nearby chair. 'Don't worry, I'll see myself out. And mark my words, I'm determined no son of mine is going to Art School, to end up like you, trying to sell a few meagre paintings and struggling to survive. I'm certain that if your father hadn't died and left you everything, you'd still be struggling.'

'Thanks, Jennifer, you always did have a special knack of making me feel great.'

'It's the truth, and you know it.'

Adam sprang to his feet, blocking her way to the door. 'Money isn't the be-all and end-all of *everyone's* existence. Need I remind you of our early years together, how we laughed and loved in my basement in Greenwich. At that time we had very little, so how come we were so happy?'

They both fell silent, remembrance of pleasures past evident on their faces.

'That was a long time ago, Adam, I don't even want to think that far back. Like you said earlier, *too much water* . . . I need to think about what's happening right now, and I want the best for my son.'

'*Our* son, Jennifer, or were there other dalliances I know nothing about?'

Her right hand rose, poised in midair as if to strike him, but something held her back. She dropped it down by her side. 'Please step aside. I've nothing more to say to you; except, believe me, you've both got a fight on your hands.'

Hopelessly he stepped to one side, but warned, 'Be careful, Jennifer, you'll lose him.'

His words fell on deaf ears, Jennifer was already out of the door, slamming it so hard it rattled the hinges.

Five minutes after his wife had left, Adam put on some old jazz records and started to drink. He usually restricted himself to a couple of Scotch and sodas, but tonight he felt like getting thoroughly smashed. *Had* he neglected Jennifer? The question nagged at him: was he to blame for her blatant love affair with Tanner? Dropping two ice cubes into a large tumbler, he filled it to the top with whisky and drained the glass. Staring into the bottom, he concluded that Jennifer was probably right. He refilled, thinking back over his eighteen-year marriage.

He'd always tried to divide his time equally between his family, his work, and his search for the man responsible for the murder of his late father's family. But now he knew he had failed to balance all three. The promise he had made to his father twelve years ago had become an obsession. Jennifer understood that; he had not.

Adam sat down on the sofa still warm from Jennifer, the words she had uttered so passionately after his father's funeral, resounding loud in his head. '*Your father is dead, Adam; for all you know this German guy is dead also. And even if he is still alive, when you eventually get to him, he'll be too old and senile to stand trial. For God's sake forget it. Let them all go, they're your father's ghosts not yours. Your life is here and now, with Calvin and me. We need you.*'

Images of his wife flooded into his mind. He tried to banish them, but they refused to be exiled: Jennifer on their wedding day, a vision in white lace and tulle; then on honeymoon, alighting from a *vaporetto* at San Marco in Venice, laughing at his stumbling Italian. A smile creased his face as a picture of Jennifer in the last stages of pregnancy entered his mind, her huge belly suspended above long skinny legs had put him in mind of a red-headed stork, albeit a beautiful one.

You're a glutton for punishment he told himself as he visualized her the day they had met in his father's gallery. She had accompanied her father, a collector of Dutch art. Whilst old Benjamin and Richard Carmichael had discussed a Rembrandt, Adam had observed Jennifer, tall and slim, dressed in a simple silk shift. It had been obvious to him she was not wearing a bra. As she leaned forward to study the paintings, he had been unable to keep his eyes off her small, perfectly formed breasts, straining against the sensuous fabric.

Aware of his scrutiny and enjoying the effect she was creating, she had played the coquette. They had both giggled afterwards, when he had admitted that for him it was lust at first sight.

The first time they had made love would stay with him for ever. Her skin was the colour and texture of alabaster, her pubis a slightly darker shade of auburn than her hair. She had recently returned from a vacation in the South of France, and he recalled admiring her all-over tan, and listening to her stories of nudist beaches and discotheques under the stars.

Adam had thought Jennifer very sophisticated and worldly, even though she was three years younger than him. He could hear her voice as clearly as if it were yesterday, telling him he was her drug – she was addicted to him, and she wanted him to go on making love to her for the rest of her life . . .

'Goddamn it, Jenny baby; what happened?' he whispered into his glass. She was an affliction that was going to take a long time, and a lot of treatment before remission, and at this moment Adam wasn't sure if it was a complete cure he really wanted.

He tried to think back over the years. Deep down, Adam knew that it wasn't only his promise to his father that had rankled with his wife. It was something more subtle. His ambition had never matched hers. Whatever she got or however much he gave her, it was never enough: Jennifer always had to have more. 'You should have licked more ass, that's where you've gone wrong all your life,' he muttered into his half-empty glass, as he crossed the room to get the bottle of Johnnie Walker. 'You could never get up those tight rich butts.'

With the bottle swinging in his right hand, he sat down again in the same position. The voice of Ella Fitzgerald singing 'Long Ago and Far Away' seemed poignantly apt as the alcohol slipped down his throat, and oblivion rose like an old friend to enfold him in a warm, protective glow. Dropping his head against the back of the sofa, Adam closed his eyes. The bottle slipped from his relaxed fingers, whisky soaking the Indian rug. He didn't even notice, his mind had strayed to the last weekend he had spent with his father in his home in Connecticut ten days before his death.

That was when it had all begun. 15th March 1984. Adam would never forget the date, it was imprinted on his mind like Calvin's birth, the day he was married, his father's death, and all the other important days of his life.

It had been the kind of day advertisers always use to promote Alpine ski vacations: crisp, clean, 'feel good' weather. A thin blanket of frost covered the closely cut lawn, smooth and gleaming like freshly piped icing sugar. Adam and his father had walked together down the twisting stone pathways, through the carefully tended gardens, wintry sun warming the backs of their heads. Benjamin was taking a long time to recover from a bad bout of pneumonia, a recurring problem for most of his life. Adam had sensed his father was critically ill, but he'd had no idea his death was imminent. The older man had clung to his son, using him like a crutch. His talk was of family: his wife Helen's green fingers; Calvin's artistic leanings; and his daughter Janet's baby boy.

It wasn't until they'd stopped to sit on a small wooden bench that Benjamin had broached the subject most on his mind.

'I'm dying, Adam, not long to go now; and believe me when I say that I have no fear, only sadness. I don't *want* to go, damn it. All this talk about life after death, and how wonderful it is! I'm certain it's a load of baloney – how can anything be better than this?'

'Don't talk like that, Dad, you're going to be fine.' Yet even in his reassurance, Adam was aware of a strong sense of foreboding. The brightness had left his father's eyes; it scared him, and made him recall something his best friend Nick had said when he'd lost his mother. *The light had left her eyes, man, it was like watching the remnants of a dying flame. Then nothing.*

Adam surveyed the tall pergola opposite dripping with wisteria, then looked past that to a huge birch tree, tall and strong, its trunk wreathed in an icy shroud, soaring upwards as if to touch the sun. He tried not to think about his father dying, it was hard to imagine not being able to talk to him ever again.

'I'm not worried about your mother. Helen is as strong as an ox. We've talked in great depth, she's resigned and prepared. I know she'll cope.'

Personally, Adam didn't think anyone was ever prepared for the absolute finality of death, but he said nothing as his father went on.

'Helen's family are known for their longevity, so she will, no doubt, outlast you and your sister.' Benjamin chuckled, a

88

spark of his old self had returned; then, as if to thwart his good humour, he began to cough, fighting for breath, his body heaving with the effort of trying to speak through a throat thick with phlegm.

'Don't try to talk, Dad,' Adam said, holding him very close. The old man's bones, as sharp as knives, cut through the thin fabric of his shirt, yet he was loath to release his hold, for what he instinctively knew might be the last time.

'Damned old age, it robs you of everything! The old pecker died a long time ago, and now the ravaged body is about to join it. Thank God my mind hasn't been ransacked, I can still beat your mother at chess any day of the week, but then she was never much good anyway. How about you and I have a game later?'

Benjamin squeezed his son's hand and Adam, feeling a wave of sadness at his father's feeble grip, said, 'I'd really like that, Dad. If you feel up to it.'

A comfortable silence settled, broken after a few moments by Benjamin. 'I have something very important to ask you, Adam. I've been thinking about it for some time now and have come to a decision. Your mother would go mad if she knew – she's told me to let sleeping dogs lie – so I would be obliged if you didn't tell her, at least not while I'm still kicking.'

'Sure, Dad, what is it?'

'Before I ask, I want you to feel free to refuse. I don't want you to feel in the least bit obligated to me ... you know, the old man's deathbed wish, all that stuff and nonsense.'

He paused and drew in a long ragged breath. 'In 1948 I met a man called Simon Horowitz; we became friends, and

I've been funding and working very closely with the Horowitz Centre ever since. My main objective has been to find a German called Klaus Von Trellenberg. He was responsible for the extermination of my family.'

As Benjamin stared ahead, his forlorn expression changed to a strange tortured scowl that seemed alien on his usually benign face. For a second Adam was certain his father was about to cry. He had only seen him do so once, at a wedding. But that was different, they had been tears of joy.

All at once, though, Benjamin's features reverted back to their accustomed geniality and his voice gathered strength as he continued. 'My father Joseph Krantz was a brilliant businessman, who founded his own bank at the age of thirty-two. He was a generous philanthropist, and a great host, renowned for his wit and creative intellect. Joseph knew how to love and was loved in return. He wasn't a practising Jew and married out of the faith to my mother who was a typical Aryan from a distinguished upper-class German family. We children were not considered Jewish, and I think that deluded my father into a false sense of security. That and the fact that he had many friends within government ... As early as 1934, my mother foresaw the danger and tried to persuade him to leave Germany. But he wouldn't listen and when he eventually did it was too late – *much* too late.' Benjamin coughed, breathing deeply and rasping into his handkerchief, his body jerking spasmodically.

The spectacle made Adam's stomach lurch and he watched silently as the old man spat into the handkerchief, covering the spots of blood with his hand.

'I don't even know where my father died,' Benjamin

continued. 'I know my brother Aaron tried to escape, and lost his life in the attempt. I found out after the war that my sister, Anna, was sent to Treblinka. She was only twelve. I was more fortunate. I would have perished, no doubt, but for my mother's foresight in taking me to relatives in Paris, then on to Marseilles where we gained a passage to America. The poor woman believed that my father and the rest of the family were following a few weeks later.' Benjamin sighed, blinking back tears.

'We arrived in New York on a freezing February day in 1938. I was small for my age and looked younger than fifteen. My mother had been sick on the voyage and I spent most of the time at sea caring for her. She was very frail and I struggled to support her down the gangplank. Yet every day she somehow found the strength to go to the port, where we spent long hours watching the ships from Europe dock. I can still feel the bitter wind biting into my flesh through the meagre protection of my thin coat. But our hopes dwindled as we searched the endless stream of strange faces for a familiar one. Until one day we did not go to the port, and my mother told me in a voice I hardly recognized as hers that the storm clouds over Europe had eventually broken, and the war had begun. I remember being bewildered, asking if that meant my father, brother and Anna were no longer going to join us in America.'

He drew in a long even breath. 'Timing, that's the very essence of life: good and bad timing. After the war I went back to Berlin in 1948. It was a devastated, raddled city; still recovering from defeat. I went to the house where I was born, and where I lived until 1937. It had been bombed and very little remained. I remember standing very still, my

91

back against the drawing-room wall. It was very strange: all I could recall was my father telling me it was time for bed. Yet I could hear laughter, assorted laughter: my mother's tinkling and sweet; my sister's quiet mirth; my brother's rare jocular outbursts; and booming above all the rest, resounding through the charred remains of my childhood, my father's warm humour.

'It was a blustery October day and I left the house to wander aimlessly down Podbielski Allee, where I played as a child. And for the first time, I cried. Boy did I cry, like a baby! And I never returned. I traced our former house-keeper, Eva Gurtner, who told me about Klaus Von Trellenberg: of how after my mother and I left, he came to the house several times. She showed him into my father's study and the two men talked privately, for many hours. Before the war Klaus's father was one of *my* father's closest friends. They shared a love of fine art, and music. Ernst Von Trellenberg would often come to our house in Berlin for supper parties, and I have a vague recollection of a handsome young Klaus sometimes coming with him.

'Early in 1939, Eva had been forced to affiliate over a Protocol. This was a document to record Jewish assets that were to be confiscated. In my father's case, his art collection. The Protocol was typed up in his presence, but he wasn't given a copy. According to Eva, it was carried out on the orders of Klaus Von Trellenberg – who was also present.

'When, in early March 1941, my family mysteriously disappeared, Eva was dismissed by the SS and the house was locked up. Before her dismissal, she packed all my father's personal papers into a suitcase, thinking that he might return for them. She gave me the case and in it I found a key to a bank vault in Switzerland, where my father had stored twenty very important paintings. Old masters. He must have got them out of Germany before the Protocol. They enabled me to start my business in New York. He also left a will bequeathing his entire art collection to his male heirs. There are approximately one hundred and eighty-five paintings still missing. It's a priceless collection.'

Adam was shocked to hear of this; he'd had no idea. But Benjamin hadn't finished yet.

'Before you say anything, Adam, let me finish. I want *you* to continue my patronage of the Centre. What your mother refers to as my "obsession", I prefer to call a "pact". One that I made with myself and God a long time ago. I believe Von Trellenberg stole my father's art collection. Find one, and you might find the other.'

Chapter Five

'Tell me about the dreams, Kathryn.' As Dr Gillman surveyed Kathryn intently, she noted that she had reverted back to the nervous fiddling with her hair and cuticles, something she had stopped doing the last time she had seen her. Dr Gillman glanced down at her file, that had been six weeks previously.

'The dreams, well actually they're more like *nightmares*, started the day my mother's sister told me my maternal grandfather was a Nazi, an officer in the SS.'

Dr Gillman made a couple of notes, speaking as she wrote. 'Is he dead now?'

Kathryn hesitated. 'I'm not sure. Aunt Ingrid told me he died during the war, but *I* believe he's still alive.'

The doctor raised her head, focusing her eyes directly on Kathryn, who returned her searching with a completely open look.

'What makes you think your grandfather is still alive, Kathryn?'

'I found a letter from him, it was sent to my mother but she died before she could read it.'

Patricia Gillman was surprised yet her face remained impassive. 'You didn't tell me your mother had died.'

The doctor's soft voice always had the effect of transporting Kathryn back to her childhood. She supposed it was because it reminded her of Dorothy Ferguson's slightly accented Welsh. Miss Ferguson had been her English teacher, she had introduced her to poetry. Kathryn had spent many long summer days in the dense wooded coppice close to her home, reading until the light faded, strolling home in the balmy dusk with the resonant voices of Dylan Thomas and Sylvia Plath ringing in her ears.

'I'm sorry about your mother, Kathryn. When did she die?' Dr Gillman asked.

'She died three weeks ago; I don't want to talk about it.'

'As you wish, but you must realize that by suppressing your emotions towards your mother, you may be causing them to manifest themselves in the dreams.' She paused.

Kathryn bent her head. 'I know, but I find it very painful at the moment. The problem is I don't miss her. I don't even feel bad about that, I feel worse about the fact that I didn't love her.'

'Did she love you?'

Kathryn shook her head. 'She stopped loving, I think, when she lost my father.'

'We can only love, if we are shown love, Kathryn. And you are not a lesser being if you are not loved. Sometimes, parents find the dependence of children a huge burden. They even resent the child for robbing them of their own independence. If they themselves had a dysfunctional childhood, it's very difficult to give what they never received. Your father's rejection and your mother's lack of demonstrative love damaged you severely. You must not feel any guilt for not loving, it's not your fault. It's impossible for any of us to control how we feel, but we can control how to deal with those feelings. Now please describe the last dream you had.'

Kathryn cleared her throat. 'I've had several, they're usually very similar. All harrowing. I'm emaciated, covered in open wounds and weeping sores. Sometimes I'm outside in a vast open space, no trees, no buildings, or any form of life; it's like some huge nuclear wasteland. Then there's another more recent version where I'm in a box-like room. It's very bright. There are no doors or windows, and I'm alone and very cold. In both cases I'm visited by a disembodied head, covered in a black executioner's mask. The head has holes for the eyes, nose and mouth. The eyes are the most terrifying part, they're the same as mine.' She shuddered.

'And the mouth, a bright red slash, speaks to me in a soft soothing voice telling me he's my grandfather, he loves me, and has come to take me to Germany, to safety. Then it kisses me, sucking me into the horrible wet hole.' Kathryn stuffed her hand in her own mouth and began to bite her nails.

Dr Gillman made more notes, then placed her pen neatly next to a photograph of her husband who, Kathryn thought, looked at least ten years younger than the doctor.

'It's a very interesting dream, Kathryn. I'm not a dream therapist, but I know enough to see that your preoccupation with family, your father and older men is once more manifesting itself in your subconscious. Do you remember when you first came to me, you had been having very lucid dreams about your father? You were embarrassed to admit that in one of them he came to you in bed, and stroked your naked body, and that you were loath to wake up to find yourself alone.' Patricia Gillman doubted the existence of this Von Trellenberg character. She suspected he was a figment of Kathryn's imagination. Or perhaps he *had* existed, but she was certain he was not still alive.

The doctor decided to change the subject for a moment. 'How is your relationship with Jack McGowan progressing?'

'Not bad.'

'What's that supposed to mean, Kathryn?'

'Well, it means exactly what I said. Hit and miss, up and down; you know, not bad, not great, sometimes OK. Jack is a really sweet man. He's generous to a fault, more so than anyone I've ever known, and I know he genuinely cares for me. He's indulgent and patient, like a doting father, but sometimes I feel I'm drowning in his adoration. He makes too many demands on me emotionally, demands I can't meet. Jack's in love with me, and I'm not in love with him – although I do like him a lot. Sometimes I feel like I'm using him, and that in turn makes me feel bad.'

'*Bad*, how? Guilty bad, or resentful bad?'

There was no hesitation from Kathryn when she said, 'Definitely guilty bad. I want to give him what he's prepared to give me, you see, in terms of commitment. Yet I feel I'm always letting him down, giving him less than he deserves.'

Dr Gillman leaned back in her chair. 'You are to a degree, but *is* that so bad? We all use each other sometimes; why not be loved for a change? It will build your self-esteem. I personally think Jack is very good for you. He's a stabilizing influence. The support system you have so far lacked. He's the daddy you've always wanted, and you are in some ways the daughter he lost. You may not be in love with Jack, but are you absolutely sure you could cope with the sort of vulnerability that intense and passionate love brings? Think back to your marriage.'

Kathryn cast her mind back to the first two years with her husband Tony, then the trauma and near nervous breakdown after the relationship had totally collapsed.

'You're terrified of rejection, and you always blame yourself when it happens. We all have to confront rejection, but we balance it with approval and self-esteem. Until you learn how to deal with it reasonably, you are far better to stay in the close comfort of a relationship with a man like Jack McGowan.'

'I came here to talk about my nightmares, Dr Gillman; not Jack.'

The doctor ignored her patient's rising irritation. It was common with Kathryn who, she knew, much preferred to keep her emotions suppressed. When confronted she often reacted with anger.

'I believe your dreams are a direct consequence of your mother's death. The revelation about her father being a Nazi has given you an excuse for her distance, resentment, and lack of affection. If you can believe she was the daughter of a psychopathic monster, it will make it easier to accept her lack of love for you.'

Kathryn glanced at the clock on the wall, her hour was almost up. 'Thanks, Dr Gillman,' she said standing up.

The doctor rose, holding out her hand. 'My pleasure, Kathryn. I would like to see you next week, particularly if the dreams persist.'

'I can't make next week, doctor. I'm going away.'

Patricia Gillman could not control a slight quizzical arching of her neatly plucked brows, but refrained from asking Kathryn where she was going. It was none of her business. Then she smiled warmly at Kathryn's next words.

'I know exactly what I'm going to do. You guys call it acting positively, being in control.' Kathryn had gripped the doctor's hand firmly.

'Come and see me when you get back from wherever it is you are going. And good luck, Kathryn, I do hope you find what you're searching for.'

'I hope so too, and thanks for everything, Dr Gillman.'

When she turned the key in her front door, Kathryn could hear the telephone ringing. It stopped as she reached it. *Damn!* She hated it when that happened. She usually left her answering machine on, but this morning she'd forgotten. After a late night with Rod at the Groucho, she had overslept, and been late for her eight-thirty appointment with Dr Gillman.

Kathryn was tired, dog-tired, she yawned and rubbed the back of her neck. The Deception job was killing her. Bradley, her new assistant, was not only wet behind the ears, but also brain dead. If he didn't shape up soon she was going to have to fire him.

Kicking off her shoes, she left them in the middle of the hall before wandering into the kitchen. As she made a mug of tea she tried to ignore the dirty breakfast dishes piled up in the sink, reproaching herself for being untidy, and cursing her daily for getting the flu.

Kathryn considered what Dr Gillman had said this morning. The doc was right; she had to stop feeling guilty about every damn thing, and get on with her life. That had been the problem with her marriage to Tony: she had blamed herself for all of *his* shit; taken on all of *his* problems and made them her own. She poured boiling water on to a tea bag, pressing the bag with the back of a spoon before scooping it out and into the sink.

'If I had known then, what I know now,' she muttered, then added, 'Or if I'd gone to a shrink earlier.' Kathryn wasn't even sure after a year in therapy if she was any better, she just understood her problems better.

The tea was piping hot, it burnt her lips and the back of her throat. Cupping the mug, she cast her mind back twelve years to the night she had met Tony Mitchell. She had gone to Pam Wakeley's dinner party. She hadn't wanted to go, but Pam had insisted, promising her a wonderful dinner companion who was to die for. Kathryn had met a few of Pam's unattached men before, she wouldn't have caught a cold for any one of them, let alone died. But this one was different. Tony Mitchell was drop dead beautiful. Recently divorced, he had rugged good looks that wore an air of wounded melancholy which she had found irresistible. He was some years older than her, and she had thought him very mature and sophisticated. How wrong could she be: Tony was a child.

That night they had made love on her sofa, and again the following morning in the shower, and less than an hour later standing up against the kitchen sink as she had cleared away the breakfast dishes. Up to that point Kathryn's sexual encounters had been restricted to a long and boring engagement to a childhood sweetheart, and a few one-night stands with fellow students at Edinburgh University.

The only other time she had come close to anything as

intense had been when she was nineteen, on holiday in the South of France.

Kathryn had been invited to stay with her best friend from University, Tanis Colefax. The wealthy Colefax family had rented a very chic villa near Grasse for the month of August. Nicholas Sheen, an American writer and an old friend of Roger Colefax, had joined the house-party for the last week. From the first moment she had clapped eyes on the forty-five-year-old, Kathryn had been smitten. Sheen, possessed of a laconic wit and lazy Southern charm, coupled with deep blue eyes, and long greying hair, had captivated both Kathryn and Tanis. They had giggled, returning his focused stares across the dinner table with blushing enthusiasm. But it was Kathryn he wanted, and she had proved a willing partner. Now she recalled with a secret smile their frenzied lovemaking in Nick's room while the rest of the house slept.

Tony Mitchell had stimulated her in the same way as Nick Sheen and foolishly she had confused lust with love. Within a week of meeting Tony she was hopelessly involved with him. They were married twelve weeks later. Tony had his first affair exactly ten weeks to the day after they were married. She found out three years later, and then only by chance. 'Why do I unearth all of this when I've been shrink-wrapped?' she whispered to herself and pushed the painful memory out of her mind, concentrating instead on the present and Jack McGowan.

What was it about Jack that fascinated? Was it that he was the archetypal father figure, who was there for her unconditionally? Or was it something more complex, as her therapist implied when she talked about Jack? That she needed to be needed, had to make men love her. Somewhere deep in her subconscious the doctor's voice nagged from several sessions ago. *'You are pursuing not only a father, but a father who is also a lover. It's a complex combination and Jack will have a lot to live up to.'*

But what Gillman had said about using Jack had hit home in a way that Kathryn was reluctant to admit. Yes, he was wealthy and supportive, a good companion and a skilful, attentive lover. But at the end of the day she was not in love with him. Why not just enjoy Jack? Accept the father–daughter relationship? Why keep searching for more, when it could be good like that? The questions nagged. Why does it have to be so bloody complicated, Kathryn thought as she picked up a property magazine, and wandered into the living room. Sliding down into the sofa she flicked through the glossy pages, her eyes drawn to a three-bedroom house in Upper Cheyne Row, Chelsea. The lease on her flat was due to expire in three months. Until last week she had been considering renting it again, and had adamantly refused a loan from Jack. But the sale of Fallowfields, expected to fetch at least a quarter of a million pounds, placed her in a different position. Kathryn dropped her head on the back of the sofa, her eyelids fluttered, then closed. She had not slept well ever since the day she had found out about Von Trellenberg; she decided to take a sleeping pill later, obliterate the nightmares; no death mask tonight to disturb her sleep, she hoped.

Her eyelids shot open on the first ring of the telephone. Kathryn picked it up, hearing her father say her name.

'Kathryn, is that you?'

'Hi, Dad, how are you?' She hated the forced bright intonation she affected every time she spoke to him, it was as if she was trying too hard to be nice. *God, it was sick-making*. There was a long pause. 'Dad, are you still there?'

'Yes, Kathy, I'm here and I'm fine; but Emily is very ill. She hasn't been well for some time now. Aching joints, tingling in her hands, unaccountable lethargy. I kept putting it down to menopause.'

Kathryn held back from retorting that Emily had seemed fine when she spoke to her a couple of days ago, and that she was a hypochondriac who had used illness to cover her laziness for years. She was pleased she'd refrained from saying so when she heard her father's next words.

'I'm afraid she's got MS, we had it confirmed yesterday.'

'Oh Dad, I'm so sorry.'

There was another pause then in a grave voice he said, 'I don't think I need go into details as to how crippling the disease can be, and it's obviously going to affect our lives profoundly.'

She had heard her father's sigh. 'How is Emily taking the news?'

'Not well, not well at all, she's totally distraught, inconsolable actually.'

'I'll come down to Wiltshire, if you'd like me to, Dad.' She held her breath, hoping that in his hour of need, he would need her.

'Emily doesn't want to see anyone at the moment. I really think it would upset her to have anyone else around. I have to be here for her at all times. I've cancelled my trip

103

to the States and postponed several lectures. Emily needs constant emotional support, I can't deny her that.'

'I understand, Dad,' Kathryn said, biting her lower lip, struggling with a potent mixture of emotions. Inwardly she berated herself. Instead of feeling sympathy for Emily, she was consumed with resentment towards her rival, who always won her father's attention.

'Obviously we won't be coming up to London now. I'll be in touch, Kathryn, perhaps we can meet up when Emily's feeling a little better.'

'Don't worry about me, Dad, you've got your hands full. Oh and by the way, Fallowfields is under contract, if it goes through, I'm going to take a much needed holiday, so I may be away for a while.'

'A holiday will do you good, Kathy, you work too damn hard.'

'I wonder *where* I got my work ethic from, Dr de Moubray?' If she could have seen her father, she would have been pleased to see his warm smile.

'My work, I admit, has been my passion.'

Along with Emily, Kathryn thought with bitterness. She would like to have said as much. But from a very young age, her inherent perception had taught her that her father hated confrontation, and she had learnt to say only what she knew he wanted to hear. Old habits die hard she thought, and berated herself for not being honest with him. 'I'll call you soon, Dad. Meanwhile take care, and don't forget to look after yourself, you're going to need all your strength to care for Emily.'

'I realize that and to be honest, Kathryn, I'm not sure—' He stopped speaking abruptly. 'I'll have to go, Emily's shouting for me.' He sounded agitated, and for the first time in her life Kathryn felt sorry for her father. Emily Jane de Moubray at the peak of health was a self-centred, demanding bitch. God only knew what she would be like with a terminal illness.

'Bye, Dad.' She tried to sound optimistic. 'I'm sure it's going to be fine.'

'I hope so, Kathryn. I'll be in touch.'

Thoughtfully she replaced the telephone, and jumped when it rang a second later.

'That was quick, you must have been literally sitting on the phone,' Steve Fisher said, his deep voice bubbling with humour.

'Hi, Steve, how are you?'

'I'm fine, sorry I didn't get back to you sooner but I've been out of town for a couple of days. Anyway I've got some news for you.'

'Fire away, I'm all ears.'

'Your Nazi, according to the Washington Archives, was born in Bremen in 1912. He was an active Fascist and joined the party in 1934, a few months after the Night of The Long Knives. At that point he was an *SS Obersturmbannführer*, married with two daughters and one son. No trace of the family, all believed dead or missing. Last recorded on active duty late 1944.'

Steve stopped speaking, and she heard the rustle of paper. 'Does it say what he did during the war?' Kathryn asked.

'Yes. In 1939 he was promoted to *Oberführer* and in September of the same year was assigned to the Reich Central Office for Jewish Emigration under the command of Reinhard Heydrich. After Heydrich was assassinated by the Czech resistance in 1942, your man was assigned to the office of the Interior Minister – Heinrich Himmler – who was, I'm sure you're aware, in ultimate command of the Nazi racial extermination plan. Von Trellenberg was originally believed to have committed suicide two years later, but was spotted in South America, by an eye witness, in 1958, and then again as recently as 1987.'

He might still be alive. Kathryn began to shake, she held on to the telephone with both hands.

'Kathryn, you still there?'

She took a deep breath. 'I'm still here, Steve. Is there anything else?'

'The usual party records, military background, all that stuff. I'll photostat it all and send it over, if you like.'

'I'd appreciate that, Steve.'

'I hope I get an acknowledgement for my research in the credits; no listen, better still, you owe me dinner next time you're in Washington.'

'You're on for both, and thanks.'

'Think nothing of it, call me any time.'

'I'd rather call you Steve,' she quipped, surprised she could think of anything even mildly amusing when the frightening images of her grandfather were tearing through her head once more.

As she replaced the telephone for the second time, she was filled with a strange sense of isolation. She now understood why her mother had been so desperate to get out of Germany. Freda's father was a living, breathing monster, and that same monster was also a part of herself. A small part but a part, no less. Her stomach felt empty, then it began to ache with a pain akin to the gnawing of hunger. Von Trellenberg was still out there somewhere, she suddenly felt certain of that. Steve had said he'd been spotted in 1987. That was less than ten years ago.

It was then she began to feel very cold, but only from the neck down, her head was hot. Though familiar, the sensation was nonetheless terrifying. She was eight the first time it happened. Kathryn would never forget the late February day when the world seemed to come to a halt under a granite sky, untouched, fresh, as if it had never been inhabited. She had sneaked out of the house at dawn, giggling when the next door neighbour's tabby, his tail frozen poker straight, had brushed against her legs, racing past her into the warmth.

Gliding across the ice, she had practised her routine for her forthcoming skating competition. The cawing of a crow in the far distance was the only sound to break the stillness. Then she had been aware of another sound: a loud cracking. At first Kathryn thought it was a branch snapping. Then her own screams had filled her ears as her body jack-knifed and the freezing chasm swallowed her. Frantically pawing the slippery surface to find a grip, she had felt her heart stop beating, convinced she was going to die, when minutes later the park keeper had hauled her out.

The next time had been just as frightening. She was standing on the doorstep of Fallowfields watching the tail-lights of her father's car gradually fade into the distance the night he left home. That time her head had throbbed mercilessly, she had shivered uncontrollably and it had been days before the icy chill thawed.

The last time was on the day that she had gone to pick

up her baby daughter from the intensive care unit. The coldness started as soon as Kathryn glimpsed the controlled sympathy in Sister Pearson's eyes, and she knew her baby was dead.

Don't think about Charlotte. Kathryn willed the memory to go away, but it refused. *Charlotte*: it was such a beautiful name and she was a beautiful baby. Perfect in every way, golden skin, golden hair, violet-coloured eyes, the eyes of an angel. She couldn't remember the last time she had allowed herself to think about her, she hadn't even told Dr Gillman about her daughter. And now with all this trauma, this family shit, she was losing her grip, losing her hard-fought-for control.

Moving trance-like across the hall, Kathryn opened a cupboard door and pulled out the jewellery box she had found in her mother's bedroom. Lifting the lid, she took out the frame that contained the photograph of the Von Trellenberg family. Holding it close to her chest, she walked slowly to the kitchen, her heart bumping against the glass. With deliberate precision she took the photograph out of the frame then, lighting the gas hob, she thrust the image face down over the naked flame. Shocked by how calm she felt, Kathryn stood very still until it had burnt to ashes. Finally, leaning forward, she blew the dust into the air, not stopping until every particle was completely dispelled.

In the same zombie-like state, she took a bottle of white wine from the fridge, then climbed the stairs to her bedroom. She peeled off her clothes, leaving them where they fell. Taking two sleeping pills, she washed them down with the Chardonnay.

'Now enter my dreams at your peril, Von Trellenberg,' she challenged, falling on to the bed. 'You fucking bastard,' she muttered to herself, squeezing her eyes tightly shut as two tears rolled out.

Ten minutes later Kathryn fell into an exhausted drug-induced sleep. She woke at dawn, with what she supposed must be a migraine. She had never had one before, but decided this was no normal headache. Her throat was bone dry, and her mouth felt like the inside of a woollen mitten. She just made it to the bathroom before she was sick; violently, head-hammeringly sick. With her face hanging over the toilet bowl, Kathryn consoled herself with, *At least I didn't dream about Von Trellenberg.*

'I don't think I can let you go. There's a lot of pre-production work involved in this new series and Brad, as you well know, is still the new kid on the block. He's going to need your help every inch of the way.'

What Rod said made sense, and Kathryn knew she was wrong to insist on taking leave at such a crucial time. But she also knew she had to do something about Von Trellenberg and the nightmares.

They had stopped for a week, but three nights ago had started again. She fought a rising nausea as her thoughts returned to last night, when she had woken shaking and in the grip of a cold sweat. Kathryn had thought she was going mad. She had tried to contact Dr Gillman but she was on leave. The dream, though similar to the others, had been much the worst so far.

An inmate of a concentration camp, emaciated, lice-ridden, and very close to death, she was called to the house of the commandant, where she was forced to strip. Trying in vain to cover her nakedness, she'd had to endure the attentions of the commandant. Prodding her with a long stick, he had demanded that she dance for him. Shouting and begging him to stop, she'd become aware of something else entering the room. And she knew before even turning round that it was the masked head. It had grown much bigger, and was now huge, the size of an elephant's head.

Rod's firm voice thankfully intruded on her unwelcome memories. 'You can take time off *after* this production, Kathryn; go away for a long break. But right now it's impossible. Come on, you know how difficult it is at the moment.'

She sighed. 'One week, Rod, that's all. This is very important to me.'

'Is jet-setting with your wealthy boyfriend more important than an eight-part Channel Four series? This could be the big breakthrough for Trident, we can't afford to screw up.'

Kathryn began to pace the floor in front of Rod's desk. 'I know all that, Rod, and I think you know that I would never let you down. How about if I told you that I'm going away with Jack, that I've stumbled upon something that could turn into a brilliant documentary, something very exciting for Trident.'

The anger left Rod's eyes for a second, to be replaced by curiosity. A lock of hair fell into his eyes, he pushed it back impatiently. 'Go on, excite me.'

Placing both hands on the top of his desk, she leaned forwards. She was wearing a thin silk vest under a linen jacket and Rod could see the outline of her large breasts.

It didn't stimulate him, Rod preferred his women to be men.

'Ex-Nazi war criminal hiding out in the Caribbean, dying of cancer, sends a letter, has a secret he wants to impart.' She stopped, to see if her words had had the desired impact. Rod had an inscrutable face, but she noticed that his nearly black eyes had narrowed. One hand was rubbing his jaw, something he always did when he was even mildly interested. Encouraged, Kathryn continued. 'I have information as to his whereabouts. Steve Fisher dug up some info from the Washington Archives. I may be on to something really big.'

'How is Steve these days? I haven't heard from him in years.'

'He's great, loves the job at the *Washington Post*.'

Rod grinned. 'Yeah, all that high-powered politics shit would suit Fisher down to the ground. So you've got a harebrained story? Sounds far-fetched to me, these Nazis are so old now they're all either senile or suffering from Alzheimer's. Convenient disease for the bastards. Tell me, what made you decide to go on a Nazi hunt?'

Kathryn lied. But she was not good at it, and she stumbled over her words. 'After my mother's death, my Aunt Ingrid, that's my mother's sister, gave me a letter; well, she didn't actually give it to me, I came across it in her house. Anyway, it was from a friend of hers in Munich. This friend—' she plucked a Germanic-sounding name out of thin air, '—Eva Hoffman – said in the letter that she had always thought her father was dead, but had just discovered he was alive. Her father happened to be Klaus Von Trellenberg, a Nazi and a wanted war criminal, so I did a bit of research and came up with enough information to investigate. Trust me, Rod, this could be the story of the decade.'

'Spare me the bullshit, Kathryn. I've been listening to the story of the decade, for decades.'

'This is different.'

'They *all* are.' Rod raised his voice.

Aware that he was losing patience, she tried one last shot. 'Look, I'll work overtime with Bradley, night and day if necessary. I promise to get the job out on time. Come on, Rod, give me a break. Have I ever let you down before?'

Rod dropped his eyes and began to write something on a pad in front of him.

'Can you get all the storyboards for Deception ready to roll before you go?'

With her mind racing, she calculated the amount of work. 'That's a tall order, it's a couple of weeks' work at least, but I'll try.'

He shrugged; pointing his pen in her direction, he clicked the ball in and out. 'You'll have to do more than *try*. Get the storyboards ready; then, and only then, you can go on your Nazi hunt. That's the deal.'

Dear Jack, she deleted 'Dear', and typed 'Dearest' instead. *When you receive this fax I'll be en route to the West Indies. It's a long story, so I won't bore you with it now. I'll be away for a couple of weeks, so unfortunately I can't join you in Bangkok. When you get there, give my love to the Oriental and stay away from Pat Pong! I'm sorry I wasn't at home when you called yesterday, but I got your fax. It was very sweet. And it seems like you're man-*

aging to have some fun in between business meetings.

Well, that's all for now, Jack. Take care.

She signed the fax longhand, *'All my love, Kathryn',* reread it, then sent it to the Regent Hotel in Singapore where Jack was staying.

As the fax transmission ended, the doorbell rang. A quick glance out of the window confirmed that it was her taxi. Kathryn opened the door. 'Taxi to Heathrow for Miss de Moubray?' She nodded, handing the cabbie her suitcase.

As the cab pulled away from the kerb, the driver said, 'Hope you're not going to France or Spain, love, the bloody air-traffic boys are on strike again, long delays expected.'

'No, I'm going to the West Indies.'

'Struth, it's OK for some, got room for me in yer suit-case?' The cab driver was grinning, but she was deadly serious when she replied.

'Sorry, this is one trip I've got to make alone.'

Chapter Six

'Taxi, missy!' 'Taxi here!' The two young men were playfully vying for Kathryn's attention, when she emerged from the customs hall at Hewanerra Airport, St Lucia. They were quickly joined by another three, all haggling for business.

'Ah got good clean taxi, lady, air conditioning no extra.'

Then another voice louder than the rest, 'Ah don charge fer no air conditioning.'

'He don charge, 'cause he don have!' This statement uttered by a long skinny youth produced a peal of raucous laughter.

Confused, she let her eyes dart from one to the other, eventually resting them on an older face towering above the rest. The body attached to the face stepped forward and, lifting her heavy suitcase as easily as if it were an empty paper bag, said, 'My name is Luke Vernan, don take no notice of these guys, ah can take you anywhere you want to go, in reel style.'

The man called Luke had big mobile features and a shaven head, smooth and gleaming like polished mahogany. The skinny youth let out a long low whistle, shouting to him, *'Kute nom-la!'*

Kathryn did not understand the patois, but assumed from

the boy's sardonic tone and challenging body language that whatever he had said was intended to provoke. Luke ignored him, still focusing his attention on Kathryn. 'Where you going, miss?'

Kathryn looked at the slip of paper in her hand. 'Ledera Hotel, in Soufrière.'

'That will be 250 EC, plus eight dollars extra for air conditioning.'

Luke's car was a nineteen-seventies dark red Chevrolet. The back seat was covered in faux leopard print, faded and rubbed bare in places. It smelt of damp and a slightly pungent odour which Kathryn identified as rum.

'So you on holiday?' Luke asked as they left the airport, turning on to an extremely wide road.

'Yes.'

'First time in St Lucia?'

'Yes, I've been to Barbados, and Jamaica before, but never St Lucia.'

'You going to need a guide then. Nobody knows the island like Luke Vernan, as lived here all ma life, am nearing fifty-five, and ah got ten kids.'

Kathryn was smiling. 'You've been busy, Luke.'

This produced a wide grin. 'Yeah mon, as bin busy with six women.' He swore as the back wheels hit something on the road. 'Got ya!' Luke yelled next. 'Dem pesty cats, roaming wild, I git one most every day, sometimes two.'

Peering past a tattered furry mascot and through the film of grime covering the back window, Kathryn saw the small inert body of a cat in the middle of the road. Its hind legs jerked a couple of times then were still.

'You hot, missy?'

As Luke asked, she felt a rivulet of perspiration trickle between her breasts. 'Yes, roasting alive, what happened to the air conditioning?'

'Well see, miss, it's on, but ah don think it's working none too good.' He began to fiddle with the controls on the dashboard.

'I don't think it's working none at all!' Kathryn said. 'And by the way, why is it extra?'

Luke wound the window down. 'Air conditioning take up a lot of gas, miss, so we have to charge extra. Extra gas, extra dollars.'

Too tired to ask the obvious question of why that did not apply in other parts of the world, she changed the subject. 'So, tell me, Luke, what is the main source of economy here in St Lucia?'

'Banana, cacao, some coffee and tourism; but banana not so good as when I was a young boy – they selling bananas in South America cheaper, so lots of folk get laid off de plantations.'

They were passing through a small village. Kathryn opened her window to get a better view of the rum shops, their dimly lit interiors displaying a few half-empty bottles stacked higgledy-piggledy on uneven wooden shelves. Luke braked suddenly, throwing her forward. A dog, so thin she could see its entire rib cage, stood in the middle of the road. Luke blew his horn and swerved. Shouting abuse at the world in general, he pulled up at a set of lights, ignoring an old woman who stuck her head through the side window, at the back. Her withered lips dragged back from the tooth-less gaping hole in her grizzled face and Kathryn shrank against the back seat as a bruised fruit was thrust under her nose.

'Fresh pawpaw,' the vendor clacked, clutching the fruit in her claw-like grip as if her life depended on it.

Vigorously shaking her head, Kathryn could not help thinking that the woman would have been perfectly cast as one of the witches in *Macbeth*. She was thankful when the car turned sharply to the left, beginning to climb a steep hill out of the village.

'Look, there's de banana . . .' Luke pointed to the densely packed banana trees lining both sides of the road. There was a brisk breeze and the leaves, some three foot in length, were flapping up and down like huge fans. The long stems bore thick batches of bananas. Some were bagged up in blue polythene, obviously ready for picking.

They passed a youth hitching a lift, he shouted something in patois. Luke replied by sticking his middle finger into the air. The exchange prompted Kathryn to ask, 'Is there much crime in St Lucia?'

'Some. Crackheads and gasos mostly, from St Vincent and Jamaica, come in illegally to git to the tourists. But ah don have much trouble, not with mah friend here.' The taxi driver fumbled with one hand in the waistband of his trousers. Kathryn stifled a cry as he pulled out a small handgun.

'Don be scared,' Luke said, opening the barrel and flicking four bullets on to the passenger seat next to him. He thrust the gun over his shoulder. 'Go on, take a look.'

The gun was much heavier than she had anticipated, the steel barrel cooling her sweaty palm. After a couple of minutes she handed it back. 'Very interesting,' was the only thing she could think of to say. Then, looking at the clock on the dashboard, she reset her watch to the local time of five thirty-two.

'How much longer before we get to the hotel, Luke? I'm so thirsty.' And tired, she thought. It had been a long journey. She had left home at six-thirty to check in for her flight from Heathrow at nine.

'Not long, about ten minutes now,' Luke supplied.

Using her knuckles to rub her eyes, gritty with fatigue, she rested her head against the back of the seat, longing for a shower and a comfortable bed. She had not slept much the previous night. Then her flight had been full to capacity and she had been unlucky enough to be seated next to a mother with two squabbling young children, so trying to recoup her lost sleep had been impossible.

Luke announced, 'Here we are!' And he jerked the car up the steep uneven driveway towards Ledera Resort. They stopped at a security checkpoint. Luke said something, and the bar was lifted. The car pulled up to a small wooden hut and stopped, allowing Kathryn to alight. As she did so, a small girl appeared below a sign reading 'Office'.

'Miss de Moubray?' the girl enquired.

'Yes, that's me.'

'Hi, I'm Rosemary, welcome to Ledera.' The girl smiled warmly. Her tiny face, the colour of creamy coffee, was dominated by huge green eyes; wide and startled, they gave her face a look of permanent surprise. Painfully thin, her stick-like limbs poked out of stained cotton shorts and a baggy tee-shirt. She looked like an undernourished child with an adult face.

Lifting Kathryn's bag out of the boot, Luke set it down

on the ground. She was about to pay him when Rosemary stepped in. 'The transfer from the airport is complimentary, Miss de Moubray.' And she handed Luke an envelope, saying, 'I think you'll find that in order.'

'I'm sure you know the fare from Hewanerra to Ledera, Missy Chastenat.'

A knowing look passed between the two St Lucians, and Kathryn was aware that it was *not* 250 EC.

'We'll get your bags taken care of, Miss de Moubray. I'm sure you're tired after such a long journey, so if you'll follow me, I've got a really nice room ready for you.' Rosemary began to walk along a small stone pathway chatting to Kathryn who followed a few steps behind.

'Our restaurant, the Dasheene, is open till nine-thirty for dinner and there's a complimentary cocktail on your first night.' Then, as if sensing her fatigue, Rosemary added, 'You can have a light supper in your room if you don't want to go to the restaurant; I can arrange that for you, no problem.'

'I'm very tired, all I want to do is shower, relax a little, then go to bed. I think that the Dasheene, and the cocktail, may have to wait until tomorrow night.'

'That's fine, if you change your mind you know where I am.' Rosemary's lilting voice, soft and melodic, rose on every vowel.

'Your accent is beautiful, are you from St Lucia?' Kathryn asked.

'Yes, I was born in Vieux Fort, not far from here. I'm French Creole, but I've spent a lot of time in Canada where my father lives. I suppose it's rubbed off a bit.' Both women turned as Luke ran back up the path to join them.

'Missy, thought you might like my card, never know you might want to do some sightseeing.'

Kathryn hesitated. 'I thought I might hire a car and kind of cruise around myself.'

Sensing her caution, Luke rolled his eyes. 'Not a good idea, no way, not on your own.'

Rosemary glared at Luke. 'Don't take any notice of him, this area is quite safe. I drive all the time on my own, so do most of my friends, and lots of tourists.' Rosemary snatched the card out of his hand. 'We'll call you if we need you.'

Placing his index finger on the side of his broad nose, Luke moved close to Kathryn – so close she could smell his breath. It was pleasantly spicy, like a mild Indian curry. 'Remember Luke Vernan knows everybody and everything in St Lucia. I can show you very good time.'

'Thanks, Luke, but I'm sure I can have a good time on my own,' she said, walking past him to where Rosemary was opening a tall louvred door.

'You'd have a better time with me!' Kathryn heard him shout as she stepped into the room.

'Don't let the men here bother you, they all try it on, but most of them are harmless. If you've got any problems, come see me.' With a spark of envy, Rosemary was thinking that a woman as attractive as Miss de Moubray was going to be hounded by men wherever she went.

Kathryn barely heard her, she was too busy looking at the view. It was breathtaking. The entire west side of the suite was exposed to a tropical valley, densely packed with lush vegetation and dominated by huge twin pitons. Wrapped now in the unique Caribbean twilight, the tropical trees soared majestically into a pale indigo sky streaked with amber.

'This is absolutely spectacular,' Kathryn said, wishing for an instant that Jack was with her to share the stunning vista. A cool breeze stirred the abundant bougainvillaea blossom overhanging the terrace, and a natural stone waterfall trickled into a sparkling plunge pool.

'The hotel has been used by film crews on many occasions, it's very unusual in that it's exposed to the elements.'

'*Unusual* is an understatement, it's quite beautiful,' Kathryn murmured, engrossed in watching the end of what she suspected had been a magnificent sunset. The final remnants, a few wispy tangerine tapers, glowed for several minutes across a darkening horizon before being swallowed up by the sea. Somewhere deep in the valley, a dog barked. Then all was still, save for the nocturnal whistle of tree frogs.

Rosemary's voice, brisk and businesslike, broke the spell. 'I hope you'll find everything to your satisfaction. As you now know, we have natural ventilation, so there are no fans. I must warn you it gets cool up here at one thousand feet above sea level, so be sure and use the blanket provided. We have no television and no telephone. If you want to use the latter please come to my office. There's a room safe in your wardrobe, the key should be inside. I think you'll find every other essential; if not, you know where to find me.' She handed over a large key in the shape of a dove.

Taking it from the girl's tiny birdlike hand, Kathryn noticed her fingernails were very long and painted white.

'I hope you're going to be happy here with us, Miss de Moubray.'

'How could I fail to be otherwise?' Kathryn replied.

It was the water pounding on the wooden roof that woke her. Propping herself up into a sitting position, she first adjusted her eyes to the dark then, pulling the mosquito net to one side, Kathryn fumbled to find the light switch. It was raining hard. She peered past a wall of water; a single palm tree, bent almost double, flashed across her vision. It was at that moment that she heard the wind, a low growl at first, rising to what sounded like an agonized howl. At least she assumed it was the wind; then, unsure, she supposed the sound could be that of a wild animal.

'It's hurricane season in the Caribbean, so be careful.' Rod had given her a final warning which now came back to niggle her. She wanted to pee, but was afraid to get out of bed. An overweight lizard, the size of a small mouse, crawled up one of the bedposts, stopping before it reached the top. Her skin began to crawl, and a thud on the stone wall behind the bed set her heart racing. And as whatever it was began to move, banging against the headboard inches from where she sat, Kathryn grew rigid with fear. When something brushed against her bare shoulder, she screamed, and out of the corner of her eye she saw a huge bat suspended across the back of the mosquito net. Still screaming, she ran into the bathroom and with shaking hands managed to lock herself in. Trembling uncontrollably, she sat on the toilet, her legs tucked tightly against her chest, her head on her knees. Already she was questioning her motives for being in a strange island, in search of an ageing Nazi who could even prove to be dangerous. '*If* you even find him,' she whispered. Yet she knew the compulsion to trace her grandfather was strong enough to see her through. It was like an obsessive passion that transcends all reason.

Kathryn stayed where she was until dawn. When she stepped gingerly back into the bedroom, she was relieved to see the bat had gone. She padded quietly across the slatted wooden floor; the rain had stopped and the valley, still wet after the storm, was the deepest emerald green she had ever seen. The air was very still, and the sea in the far distance held a dark glacial sheen. There was no sound save her own breathing, and the recent rain dripping from the palm leaves. She watched the sun rise over the twin pitons, the light changing subtly from white, to yellow, to gold. Almost afraid to move, Kathryn felt if she reached out to touch the beauty, like a dream, it would fade.

'Good morning, Miss de Moubray, sleep well?'

Kathryn was eating a slice of mango, she swallowed before replying. 'Give or take a bat or two, I slept fine, thanks, Rosemary. You've got one hundred and two wall tiles, two of which are chipped, and forty-six floor tiles in the bathroom. I counted them all in my self-imposed exile from the nocturnal wanderings of creatures and things that actually go bump in the night.'

'You *didn't* sleep well then...' Rosemary looked dismayed.

'After about four-thirty, I didn't sleep at all. The problem is, I'm not used to sharing my bed with any animal other than the human variety, but I suppose I'll get used to it. I'm sure the bats are as lovable as anything else, if you treat them right. I'll invite him in tonight and tell you how I get on.'

'I'm really sorry. I know it can get a little wild at night, but most people enjoy the getting-back-to-nature feel; some even find it very romantic, almost like camping without the tent.'

'I think I'd have settled for a huge tarpaulin last night; anyway, like I said, I'm sure I'll get used to it. Just tell the rest of your guests that if they hear screaming in the night, I'm not making mad passionate love or being murdered.'

Rosemary gave Kathryn a very odd look before saying, 'Enjoy your breakfast, Miss de Moubray, and have a nice day.'

Kathryn watched her walk down the stone steps leading from the restaurant before finishing her cup of coffee and leaving the same way.

The hire car arrived at nine prompt, unusual for the West Indies. It was a bright red Mitsubishi jeep.

The young man from Avis stood next to the car, openly admiring Kathryn. He patted the bonnet. 'Brand new, miss. Only got her last week.' Then, 'Sign here,' he pointed to the hire document. 'You want it for one week, right?'

She nodded, inadvertently affording the young man a glimpse of the ample cleavage beneath her scoop-neck short cotton dress when she bent briefly over the car bonnet. He stared with big eyes, tempted to ask what she was doing tomorrow night. But he valued his job too much and confined himself to, 'She's all yours, five-wheel drive, goes like a dream. Have yourself a good time in St Lucia.'

After the rep had backed away to his waiting colleague, a dreamy smile plastered on his face, Kathryn climbed into the jeep and inspected the interior. It was basic but, like the rep said, brand new. Rosemary had advised her to take the scenic route to Castries, informing her that the journey would take about an hour and a half. Unsure of her exact plans, she decided to sneak back up to her room before setting out, and take her suitcase with her.

When, almost three hours later, Kathryn finally arrived in the capital of St Lucia she was feeling hot, exhausted and disgruntled and had lost count of the amount of times she had cursed Rosemary for failing to tell her that part of the scenic road from Soufrière to Canaries was still under construction to widen it from a one-car track to a two-car track. In any civilized country it would have been deemed dangerous and closed. The only other time she could recall undertaking such a hazardous journey was on the road from Madrid to Malaga. She had been with Tony; heady with the first rush of new love and marriage, the hairpin bends and dizzying heights had seemed like an adventure. But today's trek had been a nightmare that Kathryn did not want to repeat in a hurry, and for most of the journey she had been considering checking out of the Ledera Hotel into somewhere closer to town.

After several abortive attempts she eventually found her destination: the Victoria Hospital. The cool shade of the reception area came as a welcome relief from the sweltering midday heat.

'Can I help?' The voice came from a young girl.

'Yes, I've come to see the registrar. It's about my maid; she's due to come into hospital next week to have a minor operation,' Kathryn improvised quickly. 'But unfortunately her father who lives in America has tragically died and

125

she's had to fly there for the funeral, so she won't be able to have her op as planned.'

The girl, a bored expression sitting comfortably on her face, pointed with a long finger to a door on her right. 'Through there, third door on the left.'

With a hurried thanks, Kathryn rushed past the desk, hoping to catch the registrar alone. She was lucky, the small room was empty. As she rapped on a glass partition, planning her tactics, she was transported straight back to her eighteen-month stint as an investigative reporter for *Newsweek* magazine. She was pleased to see the face of a young man appear, in her experience men were always easier to bribe. Rory Williams, her colleague at the time, had never ceased to be amazed at how easily she was able to gather information, and had often joked that with her looks, his attitude, and a vagina, he would be worth a fortune.

She smiled sweetly.

'Good afternoon,' the man grunted.

'My name is Susan Maynard, I'm English, and I represent a charity called "Get A Life", dealing with cancer victims. We've lodged an appeal to raise money for a new vaccine, which is being developed in the West Indies by—' she used her own GP's name, '—Dr Raymond Sawyer.'

The registrar, who wore the same bored expression as the receptionist, did not reply. Undaunted Kathryn ploughed on. 'My job is to collate data on cancer victims living in this part of the hemisphere; you know the sort of thing: age, occupation, lifestyle, diet, etc. I need facts and figures. I thought you might be able to help.'

'All our medical records are confidential.' His tone was as surly as his face.

'I understand that, but perhaps you could just tell me if there've been many cancer patients in, say, the last year.'

He shook his head, a stubborn set to his jaw.

'OK, how about if I ask you about just one patient; an old man in his eighties, suffering from cancer. I think he may have come here for treatment.'

He seemed to be thinking. 'White man?'

'Yes.'

'We have a lot of patients, I can't remember.'

'How many Caucasian men in their eighties suffering from cancer can there be living in St Lucia?'

The registrar said nothing to this. So, ignoring his sullen expression, Kathryn pushed her head through the dirty glass window that separated them. At the same time she slid two one-hundred dollar bills across the counter. 'Perhaps this will help you to remember.'

He regarded her in silence out of hooded eyes.

'Listen, I desperately need to contact this person. It's a matter of life and death.' She placed a further three one-hundred-dollar bills on top of the others. This time Kathryn could smell his greed as he gazed at the notes in awe: it was probably more money than he earned in a month. Encouraged, she whispered, 'Go on, take it, no one will ever know.'

Kathryn had to stifle a triumphant smile when his big hand closed over the money. Then, looking furtively from side to side, he slid it into his back pocket, saying, 'I'll be right back.'

The sound of a door opening on the far side of the room

averted her attention. She swore under her breath as she glimpsed first a wheelchair, then the wasted legs of an old woman – a large brown envelope lying in her lap. She was being pushed by a nurse whose white uniform was spotted with blood, with a dark stain on her starched white collar.

'Have you seen the registrar?' the nurse asked.

'He's slipped out, he told me to wait, but he did say he might be a long time.'

The nurse seemed to be contemplating whether she should stay or not. '. . . I'll come back later. If I know any-thing about Winston, you could be in fer a long wait.' Turning the wheelchair around she bent down to speak to the patient, who was muttering something under her breath. Whatever she said made the old lady smile.

The nurse shouted over her shoulder, 'Tell Winston, Staff Nurse Weekes will be back later. An tell him if I find out he's bin liming again, I'll personally tan his hide.'

The old woman cackled at this, shouting something Kath-ryn did not understand as she was negotiated in her wheel-chair through a battered swing door.

'I think this is what you want.' Kathryn jumped as she heard a sharp hiss in her left ear. And her heart leapt when she saw a manilla file in the registrar's hands.

'Go to the bathroom, read it, and get it back to me as soon as possible.' She went to take the file from him, but he held on tight. 'I want it back in five minutes, understand?'

There was no mistaking the intent. 'I understand, and thank you.'

She was pointed in the direction the nurse had taken. 'The bathroom is that way, a few doors down on yer left.'

The stench of urine, mixed with insect repellant, greeted

her on entering the long narrow lavatory. There were three stalls. Going into the nearest one, she sat down on the broken toilet lid. A mosquito landed on her arm but she successfully swatted it, leaving a trail of blood across her bare flesh. Then, with the file open on her lap, she began to read.

Name: Hans Van Beukering.
Date: 29th April 1996 (*Three months previously,* Kathryn noted.)
Date of birth: 21st November 1911.
Place of birth: Amsterdam, Netherlands.
Nationality: Dutch.
Male: Caucasian.
Occupation: Cocoa Planter.
Religion: Roman Catholic.
Address: East Winds House, Anse La Raye, Canaries.

Turning the page, pulse racing, she flicked through a set of X-rays; a brief medical history; a diagnosis of bone cancer; suggested treatment, including chemotherapy. There was a list of drugs and dosages, and the consultant who had examined Hans Van Beukering had signed the form. Before closing the file, Kathryn pulled a pen and notepad out of her bag; she scribbled down the patient's address and the date of admission. Then, squinting to decipher the signatures at the bottom of the form, she was only able to read one of them: *Dr Charles Gibling.*

Chapter Seven

'I'm not at liberty to discuss my patients with anyone, Miss Maynard.' Dr Charles Gibling had a clipped upper-crust English accent, clearly undiluted by his years in the Caribbean. Kathryn suspected that it was deliberate. A thatch of prematurely white hair, in stark contrast to his olive skin and dark brown eyes, framed his lumpen face. He had beautiful hands with long artistic fingers which constantly stroked his neatly trimmed grey moustache. A deep scar, running from his right ear down his neck, disappeared into the collar of his shirt, so she could not see where it ended. It was obvious from his rigid body language and unyielding look that he was determined not to divulge any information.

'I understand, doctor, but what if the circumstances were . . . how shall I say, extraordinary?'

'They would have to be life-and-death exceptional, and even then . . .' He stopped speaking and rearranged his hair.

Kathryn took a letter from her bag and handed it to him. 'This is the reason I'm here. As you can see, it was posted from St Lucia. It was sent by my grandfather to my mother, his daughter, who has subsequently been killed in a tragic accident. There's no address on the letter, and I have no way of informing him of his daughter's death. I think he should know, don't you?'

The doctor looked at the letter, uncomprehending,

because it was all in German. With infuriating indifference, he folded it up before handing it back. 'A letter in German, posted from St Lucia; it means nothing to me.'

'It says that the writer is dying of cancer and has not got long to live. It tells of his love for his daughter, Freda, and of his involvement in World War Two. The man who wrote this letter was an SS officer in Hitler's Third Reich. He's a wanted Nazi, a war criminal.' She waited for the impact of her words to sink in before adding, 'The man is Klaus Von Trellenberg, and I have reason to believe that he is posing as Hans Van Beukering, a Dutchman living on the Island.'

Dr Gibling's owl-shaped eyes at last widened in surprise. 'Have you any proof of this accusation?'

She decided to bluff. 'Yes, I have documents from the Washington Archives and the Berlin Document Centre. I also have an eye-witness account.'

Dr Gibling stood up. He was much smaller than she had first assumed: a long torso above short stumpy legs that now began to pace the narrow strip of floor between his desk and the window. Gibling was worried, yet disguised it well. This woman was the second person in less than forty-eight hours to enquire about Van Beukering. He considered mentioning the man who had questioned him yesterday then dismissed it. The mere memory made Dr Gibling scowl. His first day back in the surgery after two months in South America, and he'd been interrogated by someone calling himself 'Karl Matz', who looked like he'd just jumped out of the imagination of Elmore Leonard or Quentin Tarantino.

He had found the entire episode intolerable and had

remained tight-lipped, until the man had eventually lost patience and stormed out threatening to return. But this girl was different, she put him in mind of his daughter-in-law Sandra, whom he loved as if she was his own.

Kathryn observed the doctor in silence, her head switching from side to side in time with his movements. After about two minutes he seemed to come to a decision. He stopped pacing in front of her.

'I examined a man called Van Beukering in January. I diagnosed bone cancer, and recommended treatment in America. Here in St Lucia, we do not have the equipment to treat this particular, very malignant form of cancer. He refused all conventional treatment, asking only for strong medication to kill the pain. I prescribed morphine. To be honest, I would be very surprised if he's still alive. As far as I'm concerned the man was Dutch. I know nothing more, and do not wish to be involved further.' The doctor looked uncomfortable when he returned to his seat.

'Will you tell me where I can find this man, Dr Gibling? Please, it's very important I speak to him before he dies.'

The doctor took a long time to reply. 'I'm not sure I can do that. I need time to think about it.'

'How much time? I haven't got a lot; nor, by the sound of it, has your patient.'

'I have my reputation to consider, it's a small island, smaller than an English village. If I do give you the address, I must have your word you will not mention my name.'

'You have my word, Dr Gibling.'

'How do I know I can trust you?'

'You don't and there's very little I can say to reassure

you, except that my word is my bond and I've never gone back on it yet.'

The doctor held her steady gaze for a long moment. 'Where are you staying?'

She hesitated. '. . . I'm staying at the Ledera Hotel in Soufrière, but I intend to check out; it's a bit remote for my taste.'

'Stay at Windjammer Landing, you'll like it there,' he said, beginning to write the address on a prescription slip. He handed it to her with a sigh. 'I don't think you'll have any trouble getting in at this time of year.'

Kathryn read the address before standing up. 'Is this place far from here?'

The doctor stood up also. 'No, about twenty minutes' drive. Take the coast road north, you'll see it signposted. It's on the seaside. I'll call you there later.'

'Thanks very much, Dr Gibling. I'll look forward to hearing from you, and I promise not to breathe a word of this to anyone.'

He walked her to the door. 'He was alive before I went to South America nearly nine weeks ago. I prescribed a three-month supply of morphine. I haven't heard from him since, and I can't vouch he'll still be alive today.'

The last remnants of daylight were fading into dusky shadows criss-crossing her path when Kathryn walked towards the reception of the Windjammer Landing Hotel, where she had already rung ahead and booked a room – at the same time calling the Ledera to check out.

The main building was set high on a peninsula, with long sweeping views to a half-moon shaped beach and the sea. The reception was almost a carbon copy of the Casa de Carmone Hotel near Seville, where she and Tony had stayed on their honeymoon. Hand-painted tiles lined the walls and floor, and assorted coins were lying at the bottom of an old stone fountain. Kathryn gazed past a wall of white and yellow hibiscus down to a narrow pathway winding through lush tropical gardens. The automatic footlights and tiny pea-lights strung through the trees were beginning to come on. It looked like an exotic fairy grotto.

A beautiful young girl smiled in greeting, her face framed by a mass of braided hair. 'Good evening, can I help?'

'Yes, I've got a reservation; de Moubray.'

The girl consulted her computer, the brightly coloured beads bound into the ends of her hair swishing across the starched collar of her crisp pastel blue uniform.

'That's fine, Miss de Moubray, your room is ready. Do you have any bags?' Kathryn pointed to the jeep parked in the entrance. 'Just one.'

The girl signalled to a bellman who was leaning against the wall a few feet away. The tall gangling youth moved slowly to life, sauntering towards the desk.

'Wayne, take Miss de Moubray to Room 504.' The receptionist handed him a key. He dangled it from his little finger and headed for Kathryn's jeep.

She followed Wayne out of the building, waiting while he lifted her suitcase out of the boot. 'I'll park it up fer you, miss, the key will be in reception.'

'Thanks, Wayne.' Saying his name produced a wide smile, revealing one broken front tooth, and a gold-capped one. Kathryn supposed he was saving up for another gold cap.

He placed her bag in the back of a nearby buggy, helped her in, then jumped in the driving seat. 'Windjammer de best on St Lucia,' he announced, turning the ignition and pressing his foot down.

The vehicle sprang to life, its striped overhead canopy flapping as it slowly mounted the hillside. In his soft St Lucian drawl, Wayne chatted about the Island. Kathryn was only half listening; she was thinking how great it would be if this was a real holiday, if she was checking in with someone she loved. She imagined long lazy days spent reading, and beachcombing: the most important decisions of the day being whether to wear the black bikini or the floral one, and what wine to have at supper. When was the last time she had done that? she asked herself. *Not for a long time*, she sighed, *far too long*.

The buggy ground to a halt outside a whitewashed cottage. It was dripping with bougainvillaea, the tiny lavender flowers illuminated by twinkling lights hidden between a traveller's palm and an oleander bush.

'Here it is, your home for a few days,' Wayne told her, jumping out.

Kathryn strolled up to the front door, where Chalice vine partially obscured the number hand-painted on to a ceramic tile set into the wall: 504. Wayne opened the door for her, flicked a switch, and the inside was bathed in a pale yellow glow. It was a huge space, furnished with an assortment of rattan sofas, pastel and white cushions, and pine furniture finished in a pale lime wash. There were wooden louvred doors on three sides of the room, all closed. Wayne opened one set, leading her into a small bedroom. A four-poster stood in the centre, draped in a mosquito net, the gauzy fabric fluttering under the overhead fan. The bedspread was turned down to reveal white cotton sheets, and a scarlet frangipani flower lying across the crisp lace pillowcase.

'There's a minibar in de living room, and a list of all de amenities and services. We have two restaurants, and the pool's in dat direction.'

Wayne had pointed to the right, but Kathryn had no idea where he meant. Eager to get rid of the young man, she said her thanks, adding, 'I'm sure I'll find my way around tomorrow.'

His farewell smile was much too keen, and she anticipated what was coming: 'Perhaps you might like *me* to show you around?'

With speed and ease Kathryn responded, 'My boyfriend's arriving tomorrow; but thanks anyway, Wayne.'

'Ah was tinkin dat a girl as pretty as you could not be all on her own. Ah was right.' He grinned sheepishly, finally departing.

Kathryn took a half bottle of champagne from the minibar, poured herself a glass and strolled on to the terrace. She was tired but not sleepy; sipping the champagne, she watched a lizard crawl along the top of the terrace wall and disappear into a clump of jasmine. Like a snake in the grass, she thought; it was running and hiding exactly like Von Trellenberg. Changing identities, changing places, changing names. Van Beukering and Von Trellenberg were one and the same, of that she was certain. She finished her drink, stepping back into the living room to replenish. The second tasted better than the first, and Kathryn began to relax a little. She opened her suitcase, pulling out a sarong that she had bought eight years before in Barbados. Peeling off her clothes, she wrapped the silky garment around her naked body, knotting it across her breasts, chuckling at the bright yellow printed parrot-beak poking out of her cleavage. Slipping out on to the terrace again, she breathed deeply – holding the scent of jasmine in her nostrils for a few seconds before lying down full length on the chaise. She looked into a sky liberally spattered with stars, trying to imagine what her grandfather would look like; what on earth she would say to him if she did find him; how he would react to her. Did he even know she existed? The questions rattled around her brain, and she felt a slight quiver of fear. *No getting cold feet, girl; not now, not this close. Can't afford to get scared and screw up.*

As she sipped the last few drops of champagne, she willed herself to stay in control no matter what happened. With this resolve, she stood up, padding barefoot back inside. She was hungry, and about to call room service when the telephone rang. As she picked it up, she hoped it was Dr Gibling – but was disappointed to hear a woman's voice. A wrong number. Not replacing the receiver, she dialled room service, ordered a club sandwich and French fries, and then headed for the bathroom – where the domed ceiling reminded her of a Moorish palace.

When she stepped out of the shower, she heard the ringing, it sounded like the doorbell. Anticipating room service, her mouth watering, she grabbed a towel and ran into the living room. It was the telephone: her heart skipped a beat when she recognized Gibling's clipped voice.

'Miss de Moubray, Dr Gibling. How are you?'

'Evening, doctor, I'm fine, thanks, this hotel is wonderful.'

'I thought you might like it. I'm sorry to call you so late, but I'm going to my clinic at the hospital early tomorrow morning, and I wanted to speak to you.'

She looked at her watch, it was ten past nine, not that late. 'No problem, I haven't been here long.'

There was a long pause during which she sensed that the doctor was still grappling with his professional integrity.

Kathryn decided a little charm would not come amiss. 'Dr Gibling, I really do appreciate you sparing your time like this. I'd like to ask you to join me for lunch or dinner, here at the hotel; the restaurant looks very nice.'

'That's very kind of you, I'd be delighted . . .' There was another pause and Kathryn waited patiently until eventually the doctor spoke again. 'After you left my surgery today, I had a call from Van Beukering's housekeeper. She asked me to renew his prescription. I suggested it would be advisable for me to see him, assess his condition. She responded by telling me most emphatically that he flatly refused to see anyone, and that he was very sick. I must say this did prompt me to come to a decision.'

Kathryn held her breath, expelling it when he said, 'You can find Van Beukering at Montplasier Plantation near Blanchard in the Micoud Quarter, about three miles from Quilese Forest Reserve. The house is an old banana plantation, and very remote. I must warn you, it's a long and hazardous ride. You're unfamiliar with the island, so it might be wise to hire a driver.'

Kathryn was scribbling the address on the hotel notepaper when she answered, 'Thanks for the advice. And I reiterate what I said earlier, I won't mention your name to another living soul.'

'If what his housekeeper says is true, that's not going to make much difference one way or the other,' sighed Gibling. 'Please call me after you've been up to Montplaisier. I'd like to know how the old man is, and what happens. Take care, Miss de Moubray.'

'I will. And thanks again, doctor.'

The man did not smile often, he'd had little to smile about in his life so far. But he was smiling now, not the wide full-of-warmth-and-love kind, nor the I'm-happy-to-see-you or amused kind either. This was the self-satisfied expression of having got what he wanted. He hit a switch and removed a set of earphones from his head, punching out the telephone digits and speaking after four rings. 'We've got him! The doctor called the girl; he gave her the address. With your permission I'm going in.'

The voice on the other end responded with a straightforward command. 'Wait until I get official clearance. You know the procedure.'

The smile slipped. 'How long? The motherfucker might slip through the net.'

Mark growled, 'Over my dead body. Sit tight, I'll be back to you as soon as possible. He won't get away this time, not if it's got anything to do with me.'

Mark Grossman rang off. He then called Abe Zucker, his superior, who in turn spoke to the chief of police in St Lucia.

An hour later Abe called Mark back. 'It's on for tomorrow, you're reserved on the eight-thirty flight to Puerto Rico, then onward to St Lucia. Make sure you keep the local cops happy, Mark. I don't want a screw-up like last year in San José. That was some heap of shit for me, man.' Abe grunted at the memory then said, 'Good luck.'

Mark immediately tried Adam Krantz at home and got straight to the point. 'I just had word we've located the fox. So if you still want a vacation in the West Indies you're on.'

Adam's heart was thundering loud in his own ears. 'Wild horses wouldn't stop me! When?'

'Tomorrow morning. We leave for Puerto Rico at eight-thirty. I'll meet you at the American check-in desk at JFK about an hour before departure.'

'I'll be there and, by the way, Mark, *thanks*.'

Chapter Eight

Dr Gibling was right about the road to Montplasier Plantation. It *was* hazardous. It wound through dense jungle, and at times became so narrow that it was less than the width of her jeep. She had not heeded the doctor's advice about taking a driver, preferring to be alone. But after getting lost several times, and almost careering into a deep gully, she belatedly conceded the wisdom of his words.

It had been raining earlier and the air smelt damp. As the jeep bumped over coiling branches strewn across the pitted track, Kathryn strained to see through a canopy of banana leaves which were thrashing the windscreen like giant windscreen wipers. She was forced to stop every few feet, peering through a crack in the leaves to where high clouds scudded across a steel-coloured sky streaked with tangled veins of bright blue.

Suddenly the road bent sharply to the left and widened. Cautiously she inched forward into a clearing. Here the vegetation had been savagely cut back, leaving rotting cocoa stumps lining both sides of the road. A lone egret stood regally on top of a solitary mango tree, a white sentinel guarding his even rows of charred troops.

Kathryn was convinced she was seeing things when a long pointed ear loomed up in front of her. It was closely followed by another, slightly bigger, ear; then the whole face of a donkey appeared, lips drawn back across a rusted bit. The animal hee-hawed showing big square teeth, yellowed with age. She ground the jeep to a sharp halt, tyres spinning in the sodden earth.

Jumping out of the vehicle, her feet slipping on the muddied track, she peered round the bonnet. And there, indeed, was a donkey – attached to a cart so antiquated she wondered how it was still in one piece. A tiny man no bigger than a child sat on top straight-backed, a huge grin on his troll-like face.

'Is this the way to Montplasier?' she shouted.

The troll nodded, 'Jus come from there, up the hill – first gap.'

'Thanks,' she yelled, just before being startled by a loud crack. The sound broke the still air and the donkey flinched as the severed end of a bamboo cane landed viciously across its bent back. The animal ambled into life, when she heard the second whip lash. Kathryn wanted to wrestle the bamboo from the old man's hand and beat *him* with it. She felt sorry for the pathetic animal and wondered how much abuse it'd had to endure every day of its miserable life. She scowled at the old man as she watched his wizened head bobbing up and down to the rhythm of the donkey's laboured gait. He reminded Kathryn of a voodoo doll she had once seen in a film set on Haiti.

A few minutes later, she saw the house. Flanked on either side by twin avenues of royal palms, it sat comfortably on the brow of a hill overlooking a steep sloping valley. A two-storey building with bright pink shutters the exact colour of candy floss, it was clearly etched against the jungle green. The main house had been built originally in 1768 by Jean-Louis Montplasier, a French banana planter whose family hailed from Martinique. He had designed it in the French colonial style, with wide sweeping terraces to catch the prevailing breeze, and slanted wooden roofs for heavy rains.

She drove through an open set of wrought-iron gates, tall and crumbling, and choked with Mexican creeper. The jeep bounced across countless pitted holes before swinging right into a wide clearing, scattering several cockerels and disturbing a sleeping Doberman who struggled to his feet to run alongside the car, regarding Kathryn out of wary eyes.

She ground to a halt in front of four wide stone steps. They led up to a set of tall double doors, pink paint peeling from the tightly closed shutters. Kathryn supposed that the house had been very elegant once. She decided it still was, in a faded sort of way: like the structure of a deeply beautiful face that the ravages of time cannot erode. The Doberman sat guard on the bottom step, his eyes never leaving the car. Kathryn was not afraid of dogs, but there was something in this particular dog's eyes that made her reluctant to step out.

She hit the horn hard; the beast leapt up, barking loudly. Seconds later, he was joined by two others of the same breed. And by a tiny ball of fluff, the colour of bitter chocolate, which had white paws and brilliant blue eyes. They all surrounded the jeep, barking. One young dog, its front paws splayed across the driver's window, snarled at Kathryn – lips curling back to bare its sharp white teeth and dark pink gums.

'Pele, *viens ici, viens!*'

At the sound of the command the dog stopped barking and ran towards the owner of the voice; the others followed, gathering pack-like at their master's feet. He patted each one in turn, saying their names in a soothing way. He then issued a sharp 'Stay!', before walking a few feet to the parked car.

The man was naked apart from a pair of torn baggy jeans held together with a knotted rope whose two frayed ends hung in front of his flies. He wasn't young, and his skin – resembling brown velvet – was stretched tautly across muscles hardened by long hours of manual work. Kathryn could not help staring at his navel; it was huge and much darker than the rest of his torso, protruding from his flat stomach like a charred cork.

'Can I help you?' The man had an unusual accent.

'I'm looking for Mr Van Beukering. I believe he lives here?'

'Who wants him?' Craning his long neck, the speaker had pushed his face into the car.

Slightly shaken, yet deliberately polite, Kathryn began to repeat her query. 'I'm looking for Mr Van Beuker—'

She stopped speaking as another voice, this time a female one, demanded, 'Qui est-ce, Pierre?' The woman walked to the bottom step and exchanged a few words in French. Kathryn caught a reference to 'le maître', that was all. This woman was unusually tall; Kathryn reckoned about six foot, with most of her height in her long spindle-shaped legs. As she came closer, Kathryn realized she was older than she had looked at first glance, her skin, a shade lighter than Pierre's, was equally smooth. Presumably she was the housekeeper Dr Gibling had mentioned.

As Kathryn opened the car door, one of the dogs started to growl. She hesitated, glancing first at the dog, then the man for reassurance. When he nodded – 'It's OK' – and held the dog's collar, she jumped down and looked towards the woman who was staring with blatant curiosity shining from her pale green eyes.

'What do you want?' The housekeeper had the same accent as the man and her voice, as deep as his, was deliberately hostile.

'It wouldn't be possible to talk in the shade, would it?' Kathryn asked in a voice calmer than she felt.

An uneasy glance passed between the other two. Eventually Pierre nodded and the housekeeper crooked her finger saying, 'Come.'

Kathryn followed the tall woman up the steps, through the double doors and into a large high-ceilinged hall. In front of them was a wide sweeping staircase that had once been very grand, but which now looked desolate with the wood chipped and several of its carved posts missing: a tired relic of a bygone era. The hall was empty except for one large early French Empire chair covered in what had once been a dark green tapestry fabric; it had faded, the stuffing spilling out of two worn patches.

The housekeeper's bare feet made little sound on the wooden floor, nor did Kathryn's soft-soled sandals. From the hall they entered a large rectangular room. It was covered in a thin film of dust and furnished with eighteenth- and nineteenth-century French and English antiques. Some pieces were heavily carved, others gilded, all were ornate. They were stacked untidily around the perimeter of the room in no particular order, making it resemble an auction house. The walls were painted a dirty dishwater grey, a darker version had been used for the ceiling and the six sets of tall louvred doors that lined one wall. They were all tightly shut, save one, which the housekeeper walked through and on to a long covered terrace.

'It's cool here, we catch the prevailing breeze, please . . .' With a wave, she indicated a tall wicker chair.

Kathryn sat down, dwarfed by the high wing-back. Her companion sat opposite on the edge of a long low chaise. It was covered in a gold and blue pineapple print, but most of the pineapples had faded, only the dark green stalks remained as a scant reminder of how it had once looked.

'My name is Simone Belizaire; the man you saw outside is my brother Pierre. And you are?'

'Kathryn . . .' she paused, considering, 'Kathryn de Moubray.' This produced a perceptible lifting of a pair of arched brows which had been plucked to fine ebony lines.

'So Kathryn, you come here for what purpose?'

'I'm looking for a man called Hans Van Beukering.'

'And what makes you think you'll find him here?'

'I was led to believe he lives here.'

Sliding down the back of the chair like a cat, Simone ran the tip of a tapered index finger across her domed brow where tiny pearls of sweat had gathered. 'Who led you to believe such a thing?'

'I'm sorry, I can't tell you that, suffice to say that the source is reliable.'

Simone reached towards a small table, the veins on the back of her hand were raised and dark blue. She picked up a half-smoked cheroot from a dirty ashtray; she lit it, her eyes tethered to Kathryn's. 'Why do you want to see this man?'

'He's my grandfather.'

A pure white cat, with two black paws and a black patch over one eye, brushed against Kathryn's bare legs startling her. Simone leapt forward to scoop it into her arms. It struggled a little at first, but she held it very tight to her chest, cooing in French. 'Natasha, *ici avec Maman.*' Pressing her face into the thick fur she squeezed the plump body hard. The animal began to squirm and with a disgusted grunt Simone flung it violently to the floor. The cat shrieked, running through the open door as if a pack of wild dogs were on its tail.

A man's voice drifted out on to the terrace. 'I swear Natasha hates you, Simone.' This was followed by soft footfalls and the rustle of fabric. The figure that appeared next was tall and pitifully thin, clad in a long Indian cotton kaftan, the rich burgundy folds intricately embroidered in gold and silver. A scent of musk wafted in his wake as he arrived with a speed that belied his age and condition, not stopping until he was behind the visitor's chair.

Kathryn's heart was hammering hard, so hard she thought it might burst, and she could feel a wild fluttering in her stomach like a pack of scared birds trying desperately to get out. She could smell him, he made the small hairs on the back of her neck stand on end, and she knew before he walked round to face her that this was Klaus Von Trellenberg.

He was smiling warmly, but his eyes were cold, their steely blue undimmed by age. Bending forward, he lifted her hand, his lips barely touching the smooth skin above her knuckles. His balding pate, pink and shiny, was dotted with big liver spots. The marks of death, her grandmother had always said. Several strands of straggly grey hair fell from a long ponytail, untidily tied with a strip of plaited brown and red leather.

'You must be Kathryn.' Before she could find her voice, he continued. 'You're the image of your mother, she was a great beauty, same flawless skin and patrician nose.' Klaus leaned very close, his voice conspiratorial. 'When she was a young girl the Kaiser himself courted her.' Then, snapping his fingers sharply in Simone's direction he said, 'Have we no social graces in this house, why did you not inform me we have a guest?' As he glared at Simone, his smile slipped, and without it he was instantly older; his skin, hanging in folds, looked too big for his sunken face.

Simone made no retort nor did she move. Instead, mesmerized, she stared silently at Kathryn.

When Klaus turned to face his granddaughter once more, he said, 'It's so wonderful to see you, Kathryn. It gives an old man such enormous pleasure, you have no idea quite how much.' His voice, both powerful and distinct, did not sound like that of a dying man, and bore only the merest trace of his guttural mother tongue. The accent, to someone not familiar, could easily have been mistaken for that of a cultured Englishman.

With a queasy feeling in her stomach akin to seasickness, and for want of something better to say, Kathryn stammered, 'You speak perfect English.'

'I was taught by an old Etonian, he and I shared a house in Chile for a while. He was a fugitive, from something or other; he did tell me, but I've forgotten. Age my dear, scavenger of the senses.' He let out a loud sigh.

'In the time I spent with him, I learnt every vowel sound, every nuance and colloquialism, even the great ironic sense of humour that the British are so famed for. By the time he was finished with me, I could have worn his old school tie. I wanted to change my identity, and it was very convenient to become English for a while. I was in, how shall I say?' He waved a hand dramatically and Kathryn noticed he had a finger missing. 'In *transit*.' He laughed without mirth.

'I even adopted an English name, James Taylor. Very British, don't you think?'

Any preconceptions Kathryn might have had of her grandfather had been swept aside in less than five minutes. Not even in her wildest dreams could she have imagined this eccentric character with his slightly camp gestures and theatrical presence, topped by an arrogance evident in his sharp demand to the sullen Simone. And she suspected his overtly flamboyant charm masked an underlying menace. Physically, he reminded her of a thinner Sir John Gielgud as she had last seen him on the West End stage – in *Best of Friends*.

'I'm so sorry, in all the excitement I've forgotten my manners. Would you like some refreshment?' But before she could reply he said, 'Simone, get Pierre to bring some of my best wine, this is a celebration.' As Klaus beamed in Kathryn's direction, the years slipped away and she could see what a handsome man he must have been.

'It's not every day a man gets the opportunity to meet the granddaughter he didn't know he had until a few weeks ago.'

149

Simone slipped silently from sight – like a thief stealing away into the night, Kathryn thought. Klaus arranged himself on the chaise where the housekeeper had been sitting and fussed with the folds of his gown. When satisfied, he patted a place next to him.

'Come, Kathryn, sit with me for a while, it will give an old man much pleasure.' He watched her stiffen, a trapped expression plundering her eyes of their cool beauty. *Like a frightened animal about to bolt*, the old man mused. She was entitled to her fear, even her suppressed hostility he understood. When she walked to the edge of the terrace, putting space between them, he knew it was to conceal her reluctance to be close to him.

'The photographs your mother sent do not do you justice. You are far more beautiful. She is very proud of you and I can understand why.'

'Was she?' The cold retort hurt Kathryn in the saying.

'What do you mean *was*?' Klaus asked sharply.

'She's dead; my mother died in a car accident a few weeks ago. That's the reason I'm here; I was showing an estate agent around her house when I found a photograph of your family taken during the war. You were dressed in the uniform of . . .' She could not bring herself to say the words 'Nazi', or 'SS', knowing that their very utterance conjured up visions of his hideous past. But when Klaus didn't speak, she stumbled on. 'Aunt Ingrid told me about you, then I received a letter you sent to my mother. I didn't know what to do at first, it was such a shock.' Her voice petered out.

At that moment, Pierre walked on to the terrace with a bottle of chilled white wine on a tray, and two glasses.

Klaus was muttering to himself. 'Sorry, so sorry, such a crime to outlive your children. I pray to God I go soon.'

'Your wine, sir.' The insolent body language was in sharp contrast to the subservience in Pierre's deep voice.

A long silence hung in the air as Klaus stared at the ground, shoulders bent. Deserted by his extravagant dignity, he looked defeated, and very old.

'Your wine, sir.' Pierre tried again, searching both faces.

Klaus shook his head sharply as if waking from a dream, and pulling himself up straight, he spoke as if nothing had happened. 'Of course, the wine.' He took the tray from Pierre, dismissing him with an impatient flick of his hand.

The glass that Kathryn was handed felt cool in her warm palm; she took a sip and, staring straight ahead, began to speak. 'When I first found out you were my grandfather I was profoundly shocked; more than that, I was frightened. It rocked my safe little world, I suppose. I got a colleague of mine to research your background in the Washington Archives. I know your complete war record and exactly who you are.' Kathryn had been practising the little speech since dawn that morning, and was pleased she had delivered it so smoothly. A voice in her head said, *You're doing fine, just keep calm.*

'Are you afraid of me, Kathryn?'

She pondered his question for a few seconds, determined to be honest. 'A little, I must admit, but it's more fear of the unknown than of you, if you know what I mean?'

Klaus Von Trellenberg knew a lot about fear but said nothing, his expression bland.

Kathryn continued. 'I felt compelled to meet you, out of a kind of morbid curiosity. I wanted to know what sort of person you are. I had no idea when I left London if I would even find you, let alone what I would say to you if I did. But I suppose I wanted to understand you, understand why.'

'How *did* you find me? Was it Dr Gibling?'

'Let's just say I'm a very good investigative journalist.'

Her adept way of avoiding the question caused him to smile. 'Understand *what*, Kathryn? Will the knowing about something that you could *never* understand make you feel better?'

By way of an answer, she posed the question uppermost in her mind; there was no delicate way to ask so she decided to be blunt, the words tumbled out of her mouth.

'Your record says you were an *Oberführer*, a high-ranking officer, you carried out orders from the likes of Himmler and Reinhard Heydrich. Being connected to those two hellhounds is enough to convict you without any of the other stuff. But I want to hear the truth from you. I need to know in order to exorcize the demons that have haunted me ever since I discovered you were my grandfather. I've had some terrible nightmares: in one of them I'm an inmate in a concentration camp, and you are represented by a hideous masked head.' The memory alone caused her to shudder.

'I've suppressed such a mixture of emotions over the last few weeks, all of it negative and ultimately destructive. Now, I need to confront this thing for my own sanity. Does that make sense to you?'

Klaus fastened her with a riveting stare, eyes as hard as steel. Then in extreme contrast to his expression, he said very gently, 'Yes, it makes a lot of sense. You are a beautiful young woman who has suddenly been plunged into the dark world of the unknown. But you must understand that what you are asking of me is very painful; so much so, I'm not even sure I can comply. You want me to rake the ashes of my past, that is something I have never dared to do before. Because, you see, Kathryn, I'm afraid also, afraid that it can only lead to a path littered with bitterness and self-destruction. I'm not certain I can do it even now, so close to the end.'

In a small voice she pleaded, 'Please try for me.'

Closing his eyes, Klaus tried to think of a way to tell this lovely young woman about his life. He had no desire to taint her, as he himself had been tainted. When he opened his eyes again and began to speak, his tone was resigned, devoid of emotion, making his listener hold her breath.

'I was born an aristocrat, brought up to be a good German, to believe in God and country. I'm not sure in which order. My father, a powerful industrialist, was also a Fascist. He admired Adolf Hitler. He was a visionary man, he saw a new Germany under Nazi power: a bulwark against the prevailing evil of Bolshevism. I grew up as part of his affluent privileged family and I adored my father. When Germany went to war, I was still – at twenty-nine – a young man. I was the archetypal Aryan: tall, blond and ardent. My father and grandfather encouraged me to join the SS, and I in my questionable wisdom thought it the most élite and exciting force in the world. Later, I have to admit much later, after my father's death, I began to question Hitler's tyrannical quest for absolute power. His megalomania increased as it became ever more obvious the war was lost. Many good men were opposed to his obsessive genocide schemes, most of them lost their lives because of it. In November 1942 I did try to voice my resistance, but it was useless.'

His mind drifted back to his arrest and imprisonment and he berated himself as he had hundreds of times in the past for not committing suicide then. At least he would have gone to an honourable death.

'By early 1943 I was resigned to the Führer's insanity, and like many others I had become totally disillusioned, wanting no more part of something I had long ceased to believe in. But it was too late: I was caught up in the chaos, so I did what was asked of me, I did my duty. I wanted to live, I wanted to see my family again, to make love to my wife, to hold my children in my arms. I make no excuse; nor do I ask for forgiveness. You ask me, am I guilty of war crimes? I am guilty of doing what I had to do in circumstances beyond my control. I am guilty of greed, lust for life, weakness and, worst of all, cowardice. But it is not for you to judge me, Kathryn, God will do that.'

There was no hint of anguish in his monologue, just a great sadness, for Klaus Von Trellenberg truly believed he had paid a high price for his part in World War Two. Forced to lead the desolate life of a fugitive, his constant running and hiding had meant an existence bereft of love and all the things that mattered to him. There'd been too many long empty nights lying awake in some foreign bed, when nightmares had stolen his sleep. Countless times he had longed to hold his wife, to hold her so close he could smell her hair, feel her warm breath, enter her body, and hear her telling him she loved him. The laughter of his children had stayed with him for a long time, until one night even that had faded to nothing, and however hard he tried to imagine them at play, he had never heard their joyous sound again. All his happy memories had eventually left him one by one: the rarefied air of a Balkan winter's night; the strains of Bach or Beethoven drifting through a Berlin salon; the noisy camaraderie of a Munich beer cellar. All gone; part of another world, another life that was no more.

'Did you, do you, have any regrets?' Kathryn searched the glassy eyes harnessed to hers.

'Regrets?' He said the word as if it was the most despicable he had ever uttered. 'My entire life since the onset of the war, has been a torrent of regret and shame. Shame for my part in the war machine, and regret that our descendants have to live with the moral devastation the Nazi regime perpetrated. History does not forgive me, nor will it forget. I was only thirty-four years old when I fled Germany. I didn't even speak to my wife before I left and until I spoke with Freda a few months ago I had no idea what had happened to her. My beautiful, gentle Luize.'

He stopped speaking abruptly, his face began to crumble; embarrassed, he covered it with his hands, talking through his fingers. 'Can you imagine how it was for a man like me? A man who adored his family, lived for them, and in all honesty would have died for them.' Taking a deep breath he let his hands drop, and composing himself with supreme effort, continued, 'For the first few years of exile, I was convinced I would be able to return to my homeland to the bosom of my family and that life would return to how it was before the war. It was the only thing that kept me going. My God, had I known that I would never see my dear ones again, I would have stayed or taken them with me.' His voice faltered momentarily.

'I thought many times about returning to Germany – to face probable death, I knew. But my courage always failed me, and I grew to hate my own weakness as much as the life I was forced to lead. I tried not to think of the past and, with the passage of time, inevitably, it became ever more distant – as if none of it had ever happened. Eventually Germany and the war were places I inhabited only in my dreams.'

With great difficulty, Klaus struggled to his feet. Kathryn wanted to help him, but something held her back.

Her voice was filled with contempt when she asked, 'What about all the innocent people who died in the camps? Do you have no remorse for them and their families? Is your sympathy only for yourself?' Searching his enigmatic eyes for a response, she was pleased to see a flash of pain.

Klaus sighed wearily, unwilling to be drawn on a subject he had successfully repressed.

'Kathryn, please . . .' He took a step towards her.

She stood her ground. 'Answer me, have you no conscience?'

'For God's sake, I did what I had to do; sometimes it's circumstances that dictate our actions, not morals.'

'That depends on the person,' she returned.

He was angry now, his voice rose. 'You dare to stand in judgement, self-righteous outrage shining from your eyes; but you have no idea, *you* have never been put to the test.'

She was forced to agree with him, but said nothing.

Then as quickly as it had come his anger subsided. 'I'm dying, Kathryn; yet it seems strange because I've been dead for what feels like a lifetime. The light went out a long time ago.

'It returned for a while when I thought I would see your mother again, my beautiful Freda. I can't start to tell you the excitement I felt when I saw the newspaper article about your father's work with the cancer vaccine and the photograph of Freda standing next to her husband. It was an old photo taken not long after they married, but I recognized her immediately, even after almost fifty years. And the joy I felt when she answered my letter was indescribable.'

In his mind Klaus returned to the day ten weeks before when he had first heard from his elder daughter. He had read and reread her letter hundreds of times, ravenously, greedily, poring over every word until he knew it off by heart. She had enclosed three photographs in her second letter; he recalled how he'd stroked them lovingly, kissing a snap of Freda and Kathryn taken amidst a profusion of English roses in the garden of Fallowfields. Freda had written on the back of the photograph, 'This is your granddaughter, Kathryn, at sixteen'. Klaus had thought her beautiful, he found her even more beautiful in the flesh.

His granddaughter had forced him to confront his tortured past and now at the end of it all, he had nothing to say. His hand moved as if to touch her. But she stood motionless, like a sculpture set in stone, the only movement a slight tremor of her lower lip. He longed to take her in his arms, to feel her youth warm his tired old bones, and to touch her with all the affection of a doting grandfather. She was of his blood, and he wanted to talk to her of family, of her future. The need consumed him. *Just for a moment to feel truly whole again.* Slowly and with great tenderness, Klaus lifted a wayward strand of hair off her face, his fingertip tracing the line of her jaw.

An odd sensation of unreality gripped Kathryn; she felt as if she was sleepwalking whilst awake. It was scary, and the urge to run out of the house was overpowering. Instead she took a long step away from the hand of her grandfather.

Klaus spoke to God in his head. *Have I not suffered enough; am I not to be afforded one last scrap of affection? Is this the final act of retribution: you send my beautiful grandchild to me, then deny me one moment of tenderness. Are my crimes so appalling?* He sighed; it seemed he was not to be forgiven.

Then Klaus began to cough, a thick rasping noise coming from the back of his throat. He clawed at his gown, pulling a pillbox out of a side pocket. Extracting two tablets, he popped them on to the tip of his tongue, washing them down with wine. He refilled his glass to the brim, drinking half, and managed to raise it with some of his earlier animation. 'No more talk of the past, what's done is done. Now we must drink to the future; *your* future, Kathryn. We have plans to make.'

She made no attempt to drink. 'What plans?'

'First, I want you to promise not to discuss what I am about to tell you with another soul.'

'You have my word,' she answered solemnly, thinking that the whole bizarre scene was becoming more like a bad Hollywood movie by the minute. If Klaus were not so serious, she would be laughing, albeit hysterically.

'It's a long story, but I'll try to make it brief . . . My father Ernst was a great lover of music, and a generous patron of the arts. From as young as five he took me to the theatre, the *Deutsche Staatsoper*, and to wonderful concerts. I can, if I try hard, still hear the music now. Afterwards on warm evenings we would walk down the *Unter den Linden*.'

Kathryn had heard of the famous and beautiful *Unter den Linden* in Berlin, though she had never been there.

Klaus stared into the middle distance. In his mind's eye he was a child again, running in front of his parents, round and round the trunks of the linden trees. 'It was one of the most majestic avenues in Europe. It ran from the former Royal Palace to the Brandenberg Tor, nearly a mile in length, and so named because it was lined with linden trees.' He paused. 'Hitler chopped them all down, so they couldn't shield snipers, and invading troops. Thank God, my father didn't live to see that.'

Considering the devastation of Germany at the close of the war, Kathryn thought the trees in the *Unter den Linden* were the last thing his father would have been worried about. But before she could say anything, Simone had appeared at the open doorway – a look of terror on her face.

'*Vite! Vite! Klaus, mon ami*, you must go, they are here for you!'

Klaus pulled himself up erect. At six foot three, he towered above Kathryn whose wine glass had begun to shake, a few drops staining the front of her white cotton dress. Klaus stood very close to her. Taking her hand, he said, 'It's time, Kathryn. I can't keep running and hiding. I'm too old, and I'm very tired.'

Tightening his grip, he bent forward. Brushing his lips

across her cheek then resting them against her ear, he whispered, '*Schlafen mit Geistern.*'

She had no time to ask what he meant, because a moment later four men burst on to the terrace. Two were in police uniform, the others in plain clothes. One of them, a huge figure, approached Klaus.

'Are you Klaus Von Trellenberg?'

'I am,' Klaus replied with cold detachment.

'Klaus Von Trellenberg, you are under arrest. I must warn you that anything you say will be taken down and may be used in evidence against you.'

Mesmerized, Kathryn watched Klaus hold out his wasted arms to be handcuffed. His face seemed to have shrunk in the last few minutes, and a ghost of a smile now flitted across it.

Holding her breath, Kathryn mouthed the words, 'It wasn't me.'

Klaus nodded his comprehension before being led across the terrace. Turning in the doorway, he smiled in her direction, and for the first time in years it reached his eyes. Startling in its brilliance and ablaze with a strange fervour, the look in those eyes would have been interpreted by some as fear or even insanity, but Kathryn knew it was immense relief.

Chapter Nine

The sun, a glowing orb of orange and pink, was half hidden behind a tangled mass of barbed wire rising six feet above the tall prison walls. The dramatic mix of texture and colour reminded Adam of a Lelio Orsi oil painting his mother had recently acquired.

A moment later the sun had dropped out of sight and the Royal Gaol Castries, flanked on either side by two large commercial buildings, changed from starkly surreal to austere and foreboding. Adam shivered and turned to listen to what Mark was saying.

'This prison was built by the British in 1824, originally to house eighty-six inmates. It hasn't been extended since and apparently now houses, at the last count, four hundred and sixty-two.'

'Slight overcrowding problem,' Adam said, rapping three times on the huge prison entrance, his knuckles touching fifty years of dark green paint peeling from the perimeter of a foot-square trapdoor. A few seconds later the door slid open, and a set of black eyes appeared behind a four-bar grille.

'We have an appointment with Dr Henry Spooner.' Mark showed the eyes his credentials. 'We're from the Horowitz Centre.'

A sharp 'Wait,' then the door slammed shut with a muted

click. Mark and Adam duly waited until they heard a shuf-
fling noise, followed by the sound of the door opening. The
eyes appeared first, then the face of a prison guard dressed
in a sky blue short-sleeved shirt and grey trousers. 'Come,'
he said, opening the door wide to allow them to pass under
a stone portal.

As Mark and Adam slid through, their feet slipped on
the recently swilled, uneven stone-flagged floor. They were
in a room about twelve feet square, decorated in a stagnant
shade of green. The paintwork was pitted in places with
tiny holes resembling machine-gun fire.

'Wait here; Dr Spooner is with someone, but he won't
be long.' The guard turned and, with his back to them, he
began writing something on a piece of dirty foolscap paper
on top of a makeshift desk constructed of untreated ply-
wood. Adam noticed a blackboard on the opposite wall, he
stepped up to take a closer look. It was a chart recording
the movements of inmates, it was untidily filled in with
white chalk.

MALE PENAL	324
MALE REMAND	86
ON LOAN TO THE COURT	3
CONDEMNED	9
ESCAPEES	1
VICTORIA HOSPITAL	2
MENTAL HOSPITAL	1

Adam suddenly felt cold, although it was stifling hot in the
airless room. He joined Mark, who was standing a few feet
away by an identical door to the one through which they
had entered the prison. The grille was open and Mark was

peering with avid interest on to an enclosed yard where a dozen inmates were doubled up under heavy planks of wood. They were all dressed in blue collarless V-necked shirts and knee-length denim shorts. A single voice belonging to a guard with a disfigured face rose above the noise of the work. Long fingers of smoke from a nearby fire coiled around the surrounding cell block. As Mark watched one of the prisoners limp painfully up a set of worn stone steps to disappear into the darkness within, he thanked God it wasn't his fate.

'You must be the men from the Horowitz Centre.'

Adam and Mark turned simultaneously at the sound of a booming voice.

'Dr Henry Spooner, Chief Officer of HMP Castries, pleased to make your acquaintance.' Dr Spooner beamed, he seemed genuinely pleased to see them. The three men shook hands, formally introducing themselves.

Mark apologized, 'Sorry we're late, but the Liat flight from Puerto Rico was delayed.'

'So, what's new?' Spooner guffawed, then very politely said, 'Gentlemen, please follow me; we can talk privately in my office.'

They followed the doctor up an open-tread stairway into a rectangular room decorated in the same green as the one below, but it had less cracks and looked as if it had been painted more recently. There were two desks facing each other a few feet apart below an overhead paddle fan which made an irritating clicking noise with every revolution. Three barred windows lined one wall; they were all dirty and fitted with opaque glass and horizontal shutters. Dr Spooner stood proudly behind one of the desks, immaculate in khaki drill uniform, silver buttons and HMP crowns gleaming on each shoulder. His trousers were complete with knife-edge creases, and he wore massive black shoes polished to such a high gloss he could see his face in them.

'Gentlemen, please take a seat.' Spooner had impeccable manners and spoke English with only a slight West Indian intonation. He made Adam think of all the British colonial types he had read about in novels, or seen depicted on film.

They all sat down: Dr Spooner behind his desk; Adam and Mark facing him. Rubbing the dark stubble on his pointed chin, then clasping both hands together, Spooner spoke first.

'As you know, we successfully arrested Klaus Von Trellenberg yesterday afternoon. He was charged with illegal immigration and brought here on remand.'

Adam couldn't contain himself. 'When can we see him?'

Dr Spooner's expression altered subtly. Instinctively, Adam sensed that something was wrong.

'I'm afraid that won't be possible. Von Trellenberg is dead; he died a few hours ago. We're waiting for the coroner's report to confirm a heart attack, but I think it's almost positive.'

Adam felt a crushing sensation in his head, then a rush of adrenaline. '*What* did you just say?' He could not believe what he had heard.

'I said that Klaus Von Trellenberg died of a heart attack – approximately five hours ago,' the doctor repeated politely.

'I can't believe it! I just can't believe it!' Adam reiterated, staring over Spooner's head to a picture of Queen Elizabeth in her coronation robes. 'The son-of-a-bitch has escaped

164

me again . . . He's been living with cancer for months, and a few hours before I get to him, he goes and snuffs it. Twelve years, twelve long years, and the fucking bastard dies on me now!' He brought his bunched fist down on top of the prison officer's desk, sending papers flying.

Henry Spooner gave him a disapproving look before retrieving a file from the linoleum-covered floor. 'I would appreciate a little more respect in my office if you don't mind, Mr Krantz.'

Adam seemed not to hear. He simply glared back with such ferocity, it was as if Von Trellenberg's death was all Spooner's fault.

Mark was contrite. 'This news is a crushing disappointment for him.'

Spreading his hands wide, Dr Spooner shrugged. 'I'm sorry for your sake that the German is dead, but it means little to me. He had committed no real crime here on St Lucia apart from illegal immigration.' He pointed towards the window. 'I've got nine condemned men in there, who between them have murdered a total of sixteen people – men, women and children.'

Adam's voice sank to a low whisper, yet was nonetheless hostile. 'So how many people do you think Von Trellenberg murdered? How many? *Go on*, take a guess. Ten thousand? Maybe a hundred thousand? Answer me, doctor, how many innocent people do you think that monster sent to their deaths?'

In a dispassionate tone, Dr Spooner said, 'I have no idea, Mr Krantz, nor do I care. Klaus Von Trellenberg, I believe, was a Nazi – wanted for war crimes. I'm not an insensitive man, but you must appreciate that something

165

that happened fifty years ago in Europe has no bearing on what I have to do here today.'

Adam raised his voice. 'Does the fact that it happened fifty years ago lessen the evil, absolve the crime? For God's sake, man!'

Mark could see from the tight set of Spooner's mouth that he was beginning to lose patience. Pulling Adam up roughly, he led him by the arm to the far side of the room. 'Cool it, Adam. There's nothing we can do about it now, it's not this guy Spooner's fault. Von Trellenberg's dead, for Christ's sake, it's *over*.'

Adam blinked back tears of frustration. 'But I feel so *defeated*.' He slapped his stomach with the flat of his hand. 'Totally empty inside, like someone just sucked the guts outta me. What a fucking waste.' He dropped his head into his hands.

'I'm sorry, Adam, I really am, but believe me the anger will go away. Think about it positively, at least now you can put Von Trellenberg behind you and get on with your life.'

'Right at this moment, that doesn't help.'

The sound of Dr Spooner loudly clearing his throat demanded their attention. Mark walked back to the desk but Adam stayed where he was, fighting the turbulence of bitter disappointment and the savage desire to kill. The last time he had felt remotely like this was when he was fourteen years old and had found his pet dog murdered, a sign of David daubed on the animal's back. Up until that point, he had been casually unaware of being Jewish. His mother was not Jewish, and his father was a reformed Jew with very liberal ideals. He could only remember him going to worship on highly religious ceremonies, and then only occasionally. Benjamin Krantz had believed in God without fanaticism or hypocrisy. And his work with the Horowitz, Adam had learnt since his death, had had more to do with simple revenge and the desire to recover his art collection, than religion.

Spooner's voice interrupted his thoughts, returning him to the grim reality of Von Trellenberg's death. 'There were three other people with the German when we made the arrest. Two are St Lucians of French Creole descent: a brother and sister, Simone and Pierre Belizaire. They've been living up at Montplasier since 1978, the year that a Mr Anton Van Beukering bought the plantation. Apparently this Van Beukering went away on business a lot, and after one of his trips he returned with the man we now know is Von Trellenberg. He introduced him as his brother, *Han*s.

'Two years later Anton Van Beukering died, and Von Trellenberg took over the plantation. Simone was his mistress for a while; during that time he told her he was wanted by the Dutch police for a fraud he'd committed in Holland. Apparently she believed him. She also cooked, cleaned and warmed his bed, while Pierre tended to odd jobs. They were both paid a minimum wage, but had all their food and keep. We've interrogated them both intensively and their stories are consistent. The drugs found on the premises – cocaine, morphine and a little marijuana – according to Simone, were for medical use, prescribed by Dr Charles Gibling who partially substantiates her story. He *did* prescribe morphine. Initially we charged them all with possession – cocaine isn't used for medicinal purposes and we needed a charge in order to remand them for questioning. Obviously we can't keep them locked up for ever and as soon as they get access to a half-decent lawyer, they'll be out before you can say "Jack Robinson".'

Dr Spooner took a cigarette from a battered pack.

'Anyone else?' he offered. Adam ignored him, and Mark refused. He lit the cigarette; leaning back in his chair, he blew smoke into the air.

Wafting smoke out of his eyes, Mark said, 'You mentioned *three* other people, who was the third?'

'I'm getting to that.'

Aware of the irritation in Dr Spooner's voice, Mark gave Adam a warning nod.

'There was a young woman; Caucasian, very attractive. At first she claimed to be a tourist who'd stumbled upon the plantation by accident. But Simone, after further questioning, told us that this woman had arrived about an hour before the arrest. Pierre substantiated that story. She's on remand at Tapion Women's Prison so if you guys want to question her, you'd better be quick; I can't detain her for much longer. Apparently she's a relative of Von Trellenberg's.'

At this, Adam's ears pricked up. 'Did I hear you say, *a relative?*'

The chief deliberately paused for a few moments to give his next words more impact.

'Yes, she's English, her name is Kathryn de Moubray. Von Trellenberg was her maternal grandfather.'

Kathryn felt light-headed with a mixture of fatigue, outrage and fear. Repeated self-assurances that a British subject who's done nothing wrong cannot be kept in prison without representation seemed to be less and less viable as hour after hour slowly passed. Now, the panic that had been gnawing at the edge of her consciousness since her arrest was threatening to gobble up all reason.

Her wristwatch had been taken from her, along with all her other possessions, late yesterday afternoon when she had been admitted to prison. Snatches of light from a small barred window had kept her informed of night and day, and she reckoned she had been locked up for at least twenty hours. Her throat was dry, her tongue felt swollen and too big for her mouth, and her head throbbed relentlessly as she ran and reran the events of the previous day: a living nightmare that she knew with absolute certainty would remain with her for the rest of her life. Her grandfather's impassioned expression when he was arrested; her own disbelief and outrage when minutes later she had been arrested along with Simone and Pierre; and the organized chaos in the local police station where they were all charged with possession of drugs.

The shock had acted like an anaesthetic to help her through the first few hours of incarceration in the cramped cell shared with three other women, one of whom had knifed her lover. Another had been charged with theft and grievous bodily harm, and the third was a beautiful young mulatto girl who had not spoken a word.

Now, scanning the filthy cell, Kathryn let her gaze rest on the upturned face of her one remaining cell-mate. The two other women had been mysteriously taken away in the middle of the night and the silent young girl, who could not be more than thirteen or fourteen, was her sole companion. The bleak squalor only served to enhance the girl's sultry beauty. Her torn dress exposed long limbs like those of a young filly, brown and smooth, and her bold eyes were as black as the darkest night. They never left the cell door, as if she was expecting someone to come for her at any moment. Without diverting her stare, the girl suddenly spoke for the first time.

'Why are you here?'

Kathryn was momentarily startled; she had tried to make conversation several times, and had been met with mute defiance. 'It's an awful mistake, I've been falsely accused,' she croaked.

Unblinking, the girl still stared straight ahead. 'That's what they all say. That's what my father always said.' The words, uttered in the voice of a world-weary woman who had long since ceased to hope, seemed strangely incongruous when spoken by this fragile child.

'And you?' Kathryn asked hesitantly, a little afraid of what she might hear.

All at once the girl's face changed; it held a rapturous look. 'I killed my father.'

Unable to contain a gasp of shock, Kathryn gaped in disbelief. The girl seemed not to notice. She began to laugh, a strange hollow sound. Then she repeated, almost as if to convince herself, '*I killed my father.*' The strange laughter came again, causing Kathryn to shudder. It only subsided when the cell door swung open and the harsh voice of a female warder was heard.

'Kathryn de Moubray, come with me.'

Kathryn's body ached and it hurt to move. Her legs buckled when she tried to stand, and she stumbled. Taking a deep breath, she exerted every scrap of strength to stand straight, and walked awkwardly out of the cell.

'Where am I going?' she asked warily when the guard turned left, and she noticed they were heading in the opposite direction to the way she had come in. The guard did not reply. This menacing silence deepened Kathryn's unease. She stopped walking. 'I don't intend to take another step until you tell me where I'm going. I have a right to know. I demand to see a lawyer this instant or I'm going to—'

The words stuck in her throat as she felt the force of the blow deep in her pelvic area. Doubling up, she tried to call out as a violent pain shot through her stomach.

In the most malevolent voice Kathryn had ever heard off-screen, the woman said, 'Shut the fuck up, and follow me.' It left no doubt in Kathryn's mind that if she didn't do as she was told, she would be hit again. Too stunned to be angry, or to utter another word, she gripped her stomach and followed in silence, willing herself not to panic. A few moments later, they stopped outside a narrow door. It was different from the cell doors, painted red instead of green, and it was smaller, more like an office door.

This reassured Kathryn a little; she anticipated seeing a lawyer, or the benign face of someone from the British Consulate who would tell her the visit to hell was over.

The warder rapped twice and a muffled voice from within shouted, 'Come in.' The door opened inwards, and Kathryn could not see the occupant of the room until she had stepped right inside. With a sinking heart, she turned to face the man who had arrested her grandfather at Montplasier.

'So, we meet again, Miss de Moubray.'

Terrified by the sound of the key turning in the lock, she turned her attention to the closed door, her heart pounding harder and harder. Still staring at the closed exit, she said, 'I want to see a lawyer. I'm a British subject, I've committed no crime, you cannot detain me without legal representation.'

'All in good time, Miss de Moubray. I have a few questions to ask you first, then I promise you can see a lawyer. Please sit, you'll be much more comfortable.' He indicated a chair a few feet from where he sat.

Kathryn sank into it, grateful to rest her shaking limbs. 'Look, I've told the police everything I know. I'm totally innocent, and there's been a terrible mistake. I was in the wrong place at the wrong time, that's all I'm guilty of. You can't keep me here.' Pressing two fingers to her lips to stop them quivering, she blinked rapidly, trying hard not to cry.

'We can keep you here as long as we like; remember you're not in Britain now. Now, I'm not a patient man and I get very angry when people mess with me. You were in the house of a wanted Nazi war criminal, your grandfather, so don't act the innocent "little girl" stuff. I think you were trying to help him escape.'

'Oh, for God's sake, I'm telling the truth! You're right, Von Trellenberg is my grandfather, but I'd never met him until yesterday. I know nothing about him; you must believe me.'

Her interrogator rose and began pacing around her chair like a huge predatory beast stalking its prey. He continued to pace, saying nothing, the only sound his heavy footfalls and equally heavy breathing. Round and round he went, his face a mask of silent intent, till eventually he stopped in front of her. There was something in his eyes that she had only seen once before, an expression of indescribable contempt. Suddenly Kathryn felt very afraid, more afraid than she had ever felt in her entire life. She began to rise, but he pushed her back down. Clamping his hand over her mouth, he thrust his face close to hers.

'Your grandfather sent innocent Jews to their deaths, not *pleasant* deaths either.' Her teeth were pressing against his palm, which covered part of her nose. Her eyes widened, and she struggled to breathe as he pushed his face closer, his broad nose almost touching hers. His proximity made her want to retch; she recoiled, cracking the back of her head against the stone wall. Aware of the urge to pee, she tried in vain to cross her legs, but the man pressed harder and Kathryn was convinced she was going to suffocate. *Please God, don't let me die. Not now, not here, in this hellhole of a place.* She didn't appeal to God often, but she fervently hoped He could hear her now.

'Do you know how many innocent people your mother-fucking grandfather sent to the gas chambers?'

She squeezed her eyes so tightly shut her head buzzed and she saw stars. She felt his spittle spray her face as, shaking her head from side to side, she tried in vain to push him away, a silent scream exploding in her head.

'The son-of-a-bitch was responsible for—'

'That's enough, Uri!' It was Mark Grossman, his deep voice quaking with undisguised rage. This was the third time he had found Uri in a similar situation, and he had just decided it would be the last.

The man called Uri backed off, but his dark eyes did not leave Kathryn's face for a second.

A lone tear rolled down her cheek, chased by another. *Shit*, she was crying and knew it would have no effect on this monster. Under his savage scrutiny, she wiped her face with the back of her hand, convinced he was relishing her fear. Pulling herself up straight, she held her head high, determined not to give him the satisfaction of seeing her break.

Kathryn had neither seen nor heard Mark Grossman enter the cell. She turned a tear-stained face towards him, her eyes losing some of their fear when he spoke.

'Miss de Moubray, my name is Mark Grossman. I'm from the Horowitz Centre in New York. I'm in charge of the investigation and capture of Klaus Von Trellenberg.' He handed her his credentials. 'I would like to have a few words with you.'

Blinking to clear her vision, she read, 'Mark Grossman, Head of Intelligence. Horowitz Centre, 1146 First Ave, NYC.'

With a perceptible lift of his eyes, Mark looked at Uri and indicated the door. Uri left reluctantly, muttering something in Hebrew under his breath.

After he had gone, Kathryn became aware of another man in the room who had been obscured by Uri's massive frame. He was leaning against the wall at the back of the office, his face shadowed, and remained silent.

'I'm sorry about Uri, I'm afraid he's not known for his charm,' Mark commented ironically, privately reaffirming his decision to get rid of the Israeli. He hated violence of any kind, and felt strongly about the reputation of the organization. They were not a James Bond type outfit, nor a secret service employing spy-masters, and certainly not sadists who enjoyed torture.

After first handing Kathryn a handkerchief, he began to read to her from an admission form. 'You are Kathryn de Moubray of 26 Penzance Place, London?'

'That's correct.'

'You are Klaus Von Trellenberg's granddaughter?'

'Correct,' she nodded.

'Would you mind telling me how you came to be with Klaus Von Trellenberg at Montplasier Plantation yesterday afternoon.'

'I refuse to talk to you further without a lawyer present.'

Mark exchanged a glance with the man at the back of the room and then, wearing the guise of a kindly big brother or trustworthy friend, said softly, 'I promise you, Miss de Moubray, if you answer a few simple questions for us, you will be free to leave.'

'You *promise*?'

He nodded. 'You have committed no crime; we are not the police, nor do we intend to harm you. I apologize again for Uri; he's been fighting all his life, he knows only violence.'

Reassured a little, Kathryn began to speak, her voice stronger than she felt. 'My mother was German, a Von Trellenberg. She met and married my father, Richard de Moubray, at the close of the war. He's a doctor, a consultant surgeon. They divorced in 1972 when I was ten. I lived with my mother until I left home at eighteen to go to university. I knew very little of her past; she was always reluctant to talk about it. I now know why.

'My mother recently had a fatal car accident, and it was this tragic event that led me to her father – Von Trellenberg. My mother's sister Ingrid told me about him. Then

175

later the same day, I was showing an estate agent around my mother's house with a view to selling, when I stumbled upon a box of memorabilia. It contained the usual stuff, letters, photographs . . . I found an old photo of Klaus in SS uniform – the picture had been taken when he was a similar age to me, and I noticed that there was a distinct resemblance. But I was determined to forget all about it and would not have pursued it further but for a letter to my mother that was forwarded to me. It was from her father, and it had a St Lucia postmark. For whatever reason, I then felt compelled to try and trace him.' Her eyes swivelled briefly from Mark to the other man, but she could not see his face.

'And how did you go about that?' Mark urged.

'I came over here myself and bribed a hospital registrar for information, then persuaded Von Trellenberg's doctor to tell me where he was living under the pseudonym of Hans Van Beukering. I then drove out to the address he gave me – Montplasier Plantation.'

During the entire conversation Adam had been studying Kathryn intently. She held herself very erect, shoulders straight. Her eyes, huge and swollen, were red-rimmed; the dark charcoal irises looked almost black against the stark whiteness of her face. A face of extraordinary beauty, Adam had to admit, incandescent and glowing like a beacon in the greyness of the barren room. Yet there was no mistaking the striking resemblance she bore to her grandfather . . .

'As I already told your hired thug, I met Klaus for the first time yesterday afternoon,' Kathryn was continuing. 'He wasn't remotely how I expected.' She stopped for a moment, remembering her grandfather's sadness when he had discussed his wasted life. 'He was just a weary old man who'd had enough of life.'

'What *did* you expect, Miss de Moubray?' This time it was the observer at the back of the room who spoke, but still unable to get a clear view of Adam Krantz, she directed her reply to Mark.

'I suppose I expected him to be more of the stereotype Germanic Nazi: you know, arrogant, tyrannical even. Instead he was more like an ageing thespian, eccentric and camp. It was quite bizarre.'

'I hope you're not trying to convince us that this monster had become a mild-mannered, doting grandfatherly figure, full of amusing anecdotes and social graces. Save it, please.'

It was Adam again, and Kathryn – aware of his underlying tone of aggression – chose her next words carefully.

'I'm not trying to convince you of anything. I'm merely telling you the truth. I think he was a man consumed by bitter regret.'

Finding it impossible to remain impartial in her presence any longer, Adam walked out of the shadows into full view.

'*Regret*, you say?'

There was a cruel set to his mouth, yet for some reason Kathryn did not think this was a brutal man.

'How can you say that about someone responsible for the transportation of thousands of innocent people to certain death? How can you talk so lightly about regret? Von Trellenberg was once a despicable murderer, guilty of genocide in the first degree. Whatever he later became is irrelevant.'

Willing herself to stay calm, Kathryn stood up. Taking

three steps forward, she confronted Adam. She noticed his amber-coloured eyes were unevenly flecked with gold, and that he had a dark mole on his left cheek. Improbable observations to make at a time like this, she thought, yet felt oddly drawn to him.

'I was born in 1962. I had nothing to do with the war, it's not my fault if this Nazi was my mother's father. I never knew him; I hardly knew my own mother. His crimes were hideous, I agree. I can't forgive them, nor do I offer any excuse. But they have nothing whatsoever to do with me. I'm a television producer from London. I have a life of my own. I'm guilty of nothing, except being born his granddaughter.' *That's the legacy he's left me with*, she thought with bitter irony.

Kathryn was shaking, but she felt calmer than she had done since her arrest. 'Talking of brutality, I wonder how many crimes your savage inquisitor Mr Uri has committed in the name of whatever cause he kills for? And you dare to treat *me* as if I'm some kind of terrible criminal. I'm thrown into prison on a trumped-up drugs charge, forced to spend the night with three dangerous females, including a girl who's murdered her own father. I think this whole thing is outrageous and I intend to take it up with—'

Adam cut her off in mid-sentence. 'You seem to forget, Miss de Moubray, that you were in the home of a dangerous Nazi war criminal, who also happened to be your grandfather. The house was stashed to the goddamn rafters with narcotics. What are we supposed to do? Offer you tea and cake, and treat you like some innocent bystander? Give me a fucking break!'

Mark stepped in between them, cautioning Adam with a look which said, *don't antagonize her further*. To Kathryn, he said, 'I'm sorry, Miss de Moubray, just one more question then you can go. Did Klaus tell you anything that might lead us to other Nazis in hiding, or mention any names?'

Kathryn shook her head vigorously and sighed heavily; she just wanted to get the hell out of it, and even considered feigning illness. She had once done a fairly impressive retching scene in a play at school, and was sure it would not be difficult to repeat under the circumstances.

'We discussed nothing like that, there wasn't time. I was with him, at the most, an hour – before your men broke in and arrested us all.'

'In that time did he tell you anything unusual?' It was Adam again.

Kathryn pointed to Mark. 'He said one more question.'

Adam persisted, stepping closer to her again as he spoke. 'Did he mention anything about Nazi loot?'

Planting her feet about a foot apart, she looked directly at Mark, 'I refuse to say any more until I see a lawyer. I'm the one who should be asking the questions – like who is going to pay for all this violation of my rights as a British citizen?'

Mark bridged the few feet that separated him from Adam; they exchanged a few whispered words, then Adam left the room and Mark faced her. 'The charges against you are dropped.'

Kathryn raised her eyebrows in an exaggerated parody of disbelief, and Mark felt obliged to substantiate his statement. 'Dr Henry Spooner, the chief prison officer, has given me the authority to release you after questioning. You are free to go, Miss de Moubray. Thank you for your cooperation.'

This time Kathryn's pale face was instantly transformed by genuine relief. She could feel it stealing over her whole body when she walked past Mark, almost bumping into Adam who was coming back through the door, closely followed by a plain-clothes policewoman. Adam blatantly ignored Kathryn as the policewoman escorted her outside and to the prison entrance. Once there, she handed over a large cardboard box, saying 'Check that all is there.'

The box contained Kathryn's possessions. A tan leather shoulder bag, her passport, money, credit cards, a powder compact, lipstick and comb, wristwatch and, ironically, the hotel notepaper bearing the address of Montplasier Plantation. Screwing it into a tiny ball, she dropped it into the empty box. When the door of Tapion Women's Prison slammed shut behind her with a dull thud, the sound – like sweet music – rang in her ears.

It had been raining for eighteen hours, the hard and unrelenting slanting rain indigenous to the Caribbean. Kathryn walked through ankle-deep puddles, her face lifted skyward, her mouth wide open to let the rain pour in. Water had never tasted so good. The raindrops bounced off her forehead, and on to her extended palms. Above her, the low cloud strung itself like a huge grey sheet across the view, yet she doubted the sky – the colour of dirty granite – would ever look this beautiful again. And with every step she thanked God her terrible ordeal was over.

Not daring to glance backwards, she increased her pace,

breaking into a sprint after a few minutes. She ran on, faster and faster, oblivious to the pounding rain, or the curious stares of sheltering onlookers. It was if she were running for her life. She had covered more than a mile before the pain in her chest became unbearable and she was forced to stop. Breathless, she staggered into the sanctuary of a darkened shop doorway. Panting heavily, she was only vaguely aware of her surroundings and she jumped when someone spoke. 'Bad storm coming.' Facing Kathryn was a young boy, about sixteen. Like her, he was soaked to the skin. 'Storm coming from the Grenadines, maybe a hurricane,' he said. A huge smile, dazzling white in the dimness, encompassed the entire bottom half of his big face. 'You wanna go dancing, tomorrow night? Big party at the Star Trex Disco, ah got two tickets.'

Kathryn began to shiver, but still managed to return his smile, 'Sorry, I can't; I'm going home.'

The hotel receptionist and a young couple at the desk all gave Kathryn strange looks when she collected her key. Blithely unaware of the attention her rain-soaked body was attracting she walked through the hotel grounds to her cottage. She felt lighter than air, invisible almost, and she had to keep pinching her arm to convince herself she was real. In the taxi coming back to the hotel, she had felt slightly hysterical and had laughed out loud for no particular reason, startling herself and the driver – who had shot her furtive glances in the rear-view mirror for the remainder of the journey. Kathryn wanted to tell him she wasn't mad: just glad to be alive and out of hell. Now she picked a sprig of jasmine and inhaled the fragrant scent, mouthing a silent prayer: *I promise never again to take anything for granted.*

There were two messages waiting for her when she entered her room: one was from Dr Gibling; and to her surprise the other was from Adam Krantz. He'd left a number, asking her to call him as soon as possible. She had no intention of returning his call, but she did call the doctor, who said he needed to see her urgently. They arranged to meet at the hotel in an hour.

Kathryn was beginning to think that something must have happened to Gibling, when he finally walked into the Sunset Bar twenty minutes late. He wore the harassed look that was common to most doctors, and apologized before sitting down. 'Sorry I'm late, but I've just come from the mortuary. I had to identify the body, sign the death certificate and arrange for a burial. I'm afraid Simone and her brother Pierre are in custody; the police got in touch with me since Von Trellenberg was my patient.'

Kathryn looked confused. 'I don't understand. Von Trellenberg is *dead*?'

The doctor sat down next to her. 'I'm sorry, I thought you knew. It was in the morning newspaper. He was arrested yesterday, and died in prison in the early hours of this morning. He had a heart attack.' The waiter was a welcome diversion. Dr Gibling ordered Scotch on the rocks, Kathryn ordered a second rum punch.

'I had no idea he was dead. They didn't tell me, the bastards didn't *tell* me!'

Dr Gibling looked at her closely. 'Are you all right, my dear? You've suddenly gone very pale.'

'I *feel* pale, in fact I feel sick.'

'Who didn't tell you?'

'The men who interrogated me in Tapion Prison, the men from the Horowitz Centre.'

It was the doctor's turn to look confused. 'I'm sorry, Miss de Moubray; I think I've missed a piece of the plot.'

Her rum punch arrived and Kathryn took three big gulps, then said, 'Yesterday I went to Montplasier, I met Klaus Von Trellenberg. As I told you before, he is, sorry *was*, my maternal grandfather. I spoke to him for a while, before we were all arrested: Klaus, myself, Simone and Pierre. We were taken to the local police station, and charged with possessing drugs. I was sent to Tapion Prison, I had no idea what was happening to the others, I didn't see them again. Today I was questioned.' Her mind drifted back to Uri. 'I'll rephrase that, *interrogated*, by three men from a Jewish organization – a group of Zionist fanatics at best, or sadistic monsters at worst.'

Dr Gibling clicked his tongue, saying, 'Well, well, you can't say life in St Lucia is boring.'

Kathryn finished her drink, rolling an ice cube around her mouth before commenting, 'Oh yeah, I can't remember the last time I had this much fun.'

The doctor grinned – it was the first time she had seen even a glimmer of a smile crack his sombre face – then with typical understatement he replied dryly, 'I *can* think of better places than Tapion to spend the night.' He clinked her empty glass. 'Put it all down to experience, my dear.'

When Kathryn jumped out of the hired jeep at Hewanerra Airport, she noticed the concourse was very quiet. She dropped the keys and hire documents at the Avis desk then, after picking up her ticket, she checked in for the two-thirty flight to Miami.

'There's no direct flight to London on Thursdays,' the concierge at the hotel had informed her last night. 'If you leave tomorrow, you'll have a six-hour stopover in Miami before your connection to London.' Kathryn had returned with, 'I don't care if I've got to go via Timbuktu, just get me out of St Lucia as soon as possible.'

With plenty of time to spare now, she browsed in the bookstores, idly glancing along the row of titles – a bell ringing in her head when she read the title of a James Herbert novel *The Ghosts of Sleath*. *Ghosts* or *Geister*, that's what her grandfather had whispered to her. *Schlafen mit Geistern*, he'd said. She'd thought it odd at the time, but now back in the real world it seemed even more bizarre. *Sleeping with ghosts, sleeping with ghosts* . . . she repeated the sentence in her mind, wondering what on earth it could mean. Probably the ramblings of an unbalanced mind? *It's a bloody wonder I'm still sane*. The thought brought a secret smile, and a recollection of something Jack had said recently after they'd made love. 'I'm crazy for you, Kathryn, I've never felt like this before. I can only describe it as madness. But if this is how it feels to go insane, I don't mind, because I've never felt better in my entire life.' With a jolt she realized it was the first time she'd thought about Jack since her arrival in St Lucia four days ago. It felt like four months.

She bought the *Herald Tribune*, it was all they had that was less than a week old, and the local rag carrying the Von Trellenberg story on the front page. So engrossed was she in reading the report that she didn't notice Adam Krantz walking across the concourse and she flinched at the sound of his voice.

'So we meet again, twice in twenty-four hours. People will start to talk.' Adam's intention was to break the ice in a light-hearted manner, but his delivery was wrong and it came out sounding sarcastic.

Kathryn lowered the newspaper half an inch, exposing only her eyes. Von Trellenberg eyes, Adam registered.

'I've got nothing to say to you.' Her tone was adamant.

Gently, Adam pulled the newspaper down. 'But I have to you. I've tried to call you at the hotel several times. Did you get my messages?' When she didn't reply he went on, 'I've just come from Windjammer, they told me you were leaving for Miami and I wanted to talk to you before you leave.' He smiled, a first time for her. It was one of those make-you-go-weak-at-the-knees, heart-stopping types of smiles, that turn mere actors into movie stars.

Kathryn focused on a deep dimple in his chin, trying to think straight. Still she didn't respond.

Adam tried again, urging softly, 'I've been looking for Klaus Von Trellenberg for almost twelve years, it's one hell of a long time, I'm sure you can spare me ten minutes of yours.'

There was a long pause before Kathryn said, 'OK, ten minutes, I'll time you.'

He dropped his head to one side slightly, saying, 'Right, let's go. I could use a beer, do you want a drink?'

She nodded. 'A beer would be great.'

They walked towards the bar, side by side, neither of them spoke until they were perched on two red vinyl bar stools holding bottles of Piton beer. Adam drank half of his bottle, wiping his mouth with the back of his hand, while she tried to sip from hers without spilling it as he started to speak.

'Next March my father Benjamin will have been dead thirteen years. Before he died, he told me a story about his father Joseph and Klaus Von Trellenberg. Before the war Joseph Krantz was a successful banker, he was a lover of the arts, and a renowned philanthropist. The family had a large house in Berlin where they led a life befitting their wealth and privilege. My grandmother, an actress and great beauty, was also a Gentile. There were three Krantz children, two sons and a daughter. In the mid-thirties my grandmother became terrified by the widespread anti-Semitism and tried to persuade her husband to leave Germany. But Joseph had friends in high places and believed, like so many others, that he would survive. In desperation my grandmother left for Paris, and later America with my father Benjamin. Joseph was supposed to follow with the other two children, but never turned up. He was an avid collector of Impressionist and Expressionist art, and by the late thirties owned an impressive and priceless range of nearly two hundred paintings – including Renoir, Degas, Nolde and Bonnard, to name but a few. My father, a fine art dealer, later spent most of his life trying to trace this collection. I'm also a dealer, specializing in French Impressionists.' He drained the last of his beer, eyes gleaming. 'I'm now the sole heir to the Krantz art collection.'

There was an intensity about him that Kathryn found unnerving. Quietly she asked, 'Where does Von Trellenberg fit in?'

'He stole my grandfather's art collection, of that I'm positive. He also robbed him of his life.'

Kathryn dropped her bottle and watched it leave a snail-like trail of beer across the dirty floor. *My God, this is going from bad to worse*, she told herself. Aloud she asked, 'What proof have you that it was Von Trellenberg?'

Kathryn's question irked Adam, and he was unable to stop the anger creeping into his reply. 'Do you really think I'd have spent twelve years hunting the son-of-a-bitch without conclusive evidence?'

'Only a question?' she said in a small voice.

Instantly he regretted his hastiness. 'Heh listen, I'm kinda strung out at the moment, all this stuff has left me feeling like shit.'

'You and me both.'

As Kathryn lowered her eyes, there was a fragility about her that appealed to Adam's better nature, his tone softened. 'Look, I'm sorry to be so blunt, but the truth can't be sidetracked or ignored. When I was a kid my dad always told me that if I didn't tell the truth it would come after me, *haunt me*, appearing when I least expected. I believed him then, I still do.'

Her silent unflinching stare said much more than words. Adam felt uneasy, and he was afraid she might do something rash. 'I don't blame *you* for what your grandfather did; you weren't even born. Von Trellenberg is dead and right now I'm not even questioning his ethics or his actions, I simply want what's mine. Are you absolutely certain he didn't say anything to you about his life before the war? I know you told us everything in Tapion, but perhaps you weren't thinking straight at the time and forgot something?'

Kathryn was about to mention the 'sleeping with ghosts' thing, when Adam slapped his stomach with the flat of his hand. 'You see, Miss de Moubray, I've got this gut instinct and it's never let me down yet. I think you're hiding something.' He ignored the negative shaking of her head. 'I believe the old bastard knew he was dying, and got in touch with your mother to impart long-buried secrets, all that deathbed confessional shit. But your mother died, so you went in her place. Did you and your granddaddy have a cosy chat about where he'd hidden my art collection? Was that why you were at Montplasier?'

Kathryn wasn't sure if it was his look of contempt or the animosity in his voice that made angry tears spring to her eyes. She willed herself not to cry: *not again, not here in the airport, not in front of this Adam Krantz who had every right to hate her*.

Visibly shaken, she stood up, and supported herself by holding on to the bar top. It was wet and her fingers slipped. 'I'm really sorry about Von Trellenberg, about everything he did to your family, about being his granddaughter. Believe me, that makes me more sorry than I can put into words right now. But I can't help you; if I could, I would.' She stepped to one side, and glancing up at the departure screen said, 'My flight is boarding, goodbye, Mr Krantz.'

As Kathryn began to walk away, Adam stayed where he was. He waited until she was halfway across the concourse before he stood up. Standing very still, he watched her hand her passport to an immigration officer, his eyes boring into her back until she was out of sight.

Chapter Ten

Nazi War Criminal Klaus Von Trellenberg has been
found on the Island of St Lucia in the West Indies.

The eighty-two-year-old German was arrested two
days ago in a remote hideaway in the south of the
Island. Mark Grossman, Head of Intelligence at the
Horowitz Centre in New York, said he had been
hunting Von Trellenberg for sixteen years. Von Trellenberg, an SS officer, was responsible for the transportation of Jews from the occupied territories to the
work and death camps between 1942 and 1945.

Stefan Lang read and reread the news story before studying
the accompanying 1938 photograph of Von Trellenberg in
SS uniform. He was with two other men, one easily rec-
ognizable as Goering. Stefan didn't know who the second
man was. He was relieved to see that the only physical
characteristic he'd inherited from his grandfather was his
obvious height. Von Trellenberg towered above the Reich
Marshal.

With his heart pumping fast, he dropped the newspaper
to pick up the telephone. As he punched out the digits,
Stefan stared into a small mirror hanging on the wall in
front of where he sat on the edge of the narrow bed. But
it was not his own reflection that stared back at him. It
was Von Trellenberg's: piercing eyes, unflinching in their

mocking arrogance; generous mouth, turned up at the corners, poised to burst into sneering laughter.

Pearls of sweat peppered Stefan's brow; he closed his eyes avoiding contact with the mirror. 'Come on, Mother; answer the phone,' he muttered, desperate to speak to her. 'The one time I really need you and you're not there.' He slammed the phone down in frustration.

Stefan sat on the edge of the bed; he was very still, listening to his own breathing, absorbed in thoughts of Von Trellenberg. The media as usual had dramatized the whole issue, with harrowing details of death camps and mass murder. He threw the newspaper across the room in disgust, questioning why the press had to rehash old atrocities; hadn't Nazi history been rammed down everyone's throat enough already? Weren't all governments guilty of terrible crimes? America had dropped nuclear bombs on Japan, killing and mutilating thousands of innocent people; countless men had been tortured and died in the Japanese POW camps. Whichever side you were on, whether victim or perpetrator, nobody won in the end, everyone was a casualty of war. Stefan didn't care much about what had happened fifty years before, but he did care about today, and how his friends would react – the few he had left – and worse, the reaction of the movie business. If this thing got out, he would be ostracized. It was hard enough to get good parts, but having a Nazi war criminal for a grandfather would be the kiss of death in an industry full of Jews.

Stefan had known bits about Von Trellenberg, but had believed his grandfather was dead. His mother's recent revelation of her past life on the eve of his Aunt Freda's funeral had come as a shock. He recalled how she drank four large glasses of sherry before supper, something she rarely did, then he'd helped her upstairs and at her insistence had stayed with her, sitting on the edge of the bed while she talked in depth about the vast Von Trellenberg country mansion in East Germany, and the large town house in Berlin. And of how she had grown up as part of the cream of pre-war German society; surrounded by servants, enjoying lavish parties, picnics, opera and recitals. Then the war had come, and life had changed irrevocably. She saw her father infrequently and the family's country house had been commandeered for war use, so they'd moved to Berlin.

Ingrid had broken down when talking about the close of the war and the death of her parents. Reluctantly, Stefan had taken his weeping mother in his arms, patting her roughly on the back, bitterness robbing his own voice of every shred of compassion. Obsessed with all that had been lost – art treasures and wonderful furniture, sold or destroyed by the Allies, property that should rightfully have been inherited by him – he recalled being consumed with rage. It had caused his gut to ache then, just like it was aching now.

On top of which, there was a dull throbbing in his head and he could feel a nerve in his neck jumping. He knelt by the bedside, pulling out a small plastic bag from his overnight case. Opening it reverently on the bedside table, he was careful not to spill any of the white powder inside. He poured a little on top of the dressing table and, using his Amex card, formed a neat line. Then leaning forward, he snorted very deeply, throwing his head back before lowering it once more to inhale the remaining few grains. The high he knew would be gradual, not like the first time. He would never forget Sam Morgan's party in Beverly Hills; there had been pots of the stuff all over the place, like household sugar. He thought back, racking his brain for the year: 1983. He had been twenty-four, flying with or without dope. The new boy in town who had just completed his first successful movie. *I was hot, man, a regular born-again James Dean.*

Shit, where have all the years gone, and all the directors, and so-called friends? Wiping a fine dusting of cocaine from his nostrils, Stefan licked his fingers before running them through his slicked-back hair. He pulled a few strands on to his brow, then narrowing his deep-set eyes into what he assumed was a mean and moody pose, he stretched his long torso to his full height of six foot two, squeezing his shoulder blades tightly together. He clenched and unclenched his fists at the same time.

A police siren screaming from the street below jolted him back to the reality of New York and his audition in half an hour's time. It was a great part, his agent Danny had said. He hadn't had a decent job in eighteen months, he desperately needed this one. But Stefan was scared, he hated auditions: the waiting in line with a bunch of other hopefuls; the smart-ass casting directors who thought they knew it all. And the uncertainty. Well, he would show them this time. Scared or not, he was determined, he was ready.

He felt much better when he left the shabby motel in Queens. He psyched himself up on the journey uptown, repeating his lines, telling himself he was good – as good as Tom Cruise, or Liam Neeson or any other god-damned actor worth his salt. By the time he stepped off the subway in Soho, Stefan was convinced he would get the part.

He was agitated when he returned to the motel. He was coming down, starting to get the jitters, he needed another line. He drank a beer, and decided to ring his mother again, then call Pam, do some dope and get laid. In that order. As he hit the telephone digits he looked at his watch. It was a Rolex oyster, the only thing he had left that was worth anything; he was pleased he hadn't sold it last week. Then thought about the twelve hundred dollars he owed Arnie, his dealer. He listened to the first ring, calculating the time in England. It was after nine in the evening, his mother must be in now. He heard the line connect, then a strange voice said, 'Hello?'

'Is Mrs Ingrid Lang there?' Stefan asked.

'I'm sorry, she's unavailable. Who is this?'

The female voice on the telephone was unfamiliar yet there was something in its tone that alerted him. He felt the hairs on the back of his neck stand on end.

'It's her son, Stefan.'

There was a short pause before the woman said, 'Your mother is in St Joseph's Hospital.'

'What's happened?' Stefan knew he was shouting, but the strange voice had engendered a rising sense of panic.

'She fell down the stairs. I'm Ruth Simpson, a neighbour. It's lucky you called when you did, I've just come to collect the dog.' Her voice dropped to a whisper, barely audible. 'I popped in to see your mother last night for a chat.' At this point Ruth's composure faltered. 'I found her, at the foot of the stairs.'

'Is she all right?' Stefan asked anxiously, wondering if her fall had anything to do with the news of Klaus Von Trellenberg.

'To be honest, I'm not sure; all they'll say at the hospital is that her condition is stable.'

Stefan glanced at his watch again. 'I'm on my way. I'm in New York at the moment, with a bit of luck I should be there tomorrow morning.'

Stefan hated hospitals. The starkness and the clinical whiteness conjured up a nightmare image he was too terrified to confront. He never wanted to be reminded of that night in 1987, and cursed as the year popped into his mind unbidden. His pace quickened in time with his heart rate, and with each step he strove to dispel his unwanted thoughts.

The featureless corridor seemed endless, eventually he stopped a passing nurse. 'I'm looking for intensive care. Am I heading in the right direction?'

When she turned, her crisply starched skirt crackled. 'It's three doors down on the left.' The nurse was very young, and very pretty in a scrubbed, clean sort of way. He said thank you and walked on quickly.

It was the sight of the repository equipment next to his mother's bed that made him feel sick, sicker than the sight of her deathly pallor or the two tubes hanging from her grotesquely twisted nostrils like long thick snots.

'Can I help you?' The voice belonged to a ward sister who had materialized like an apparition at the foot of the bed.

'I'm Stefan Lang, this is my mother.' The incessant bleep of the ventilator seemed unrealistically loud in his ears.

Not looking at the sister, he whispered, 'Is she going to die?'

'Your mother is seriously ill, but under the circumstances—'

Stefan rounded on the nurse, 'Is she going to *die*? Tell me, I need to know.'

'Your mother is as well as can be expected.' This time it was a man's voice.

Stefan looked into the pink face of a doctor who had joined the sister. In Stefan's opinion he was far too young to be giving a diagnosis. 'Why can you guys never just say it how it is; you know, straight down the line? Why are you all so fucking ambiguous?'

'I would prefer you not to use language like that in front of Sister Reid.'

The sister merely nodded in a condescending way that made Stefan even angrier. The doctor stiffened and picking up the admission form he read out loud, 'Ingrid Lang was admitted at nine-thirty last night suffering from severe cerebral haemorrhaging to the left side of her brain. She was not expected to last the night. As you can see, she is now in a coma. Her condition is stable and she has a slim chance of survival. If she does live she will never recover all of her faculties.'

The doctor looked up. 'Is that clear enough for you?'

Stefan wanted to hit him. The sight of the doctor's patronizing expression sent him on the dreaded journey back again. It was six-fifteen on the evening of the 21st September 1987. He knew the precise time because it was the beginning of the darkness in his life that had never completely gone away. He stared hard at the doctor without seeing him. Stefan was in All Saints Hospital in Santa Monica. The scene was similar, only then the doctor had been much older, weary of death, his face a mask of superficial sympathy when he informed Stefan that his daughter had died in a car crash, and his wife was fighting for her life.

The desire to kill, maim, destroy had been overwhelming. The anger had stayed, it was the only tangible thing in his life. It had kept him alive, helped him to survive when they pulled the plug and his wife Vicki drew her final machine-assisted breath.

Stefan now left his mother's bedside. He crossed the small room, not stopping until he reached the door where he turned and yelled.

'Just keep her alive.'

It was dark when Stefan arrived at his mother's cottage. He tried the front door, but it was locked. Reaching up, he felt for the key where she usually hid it on the ledge under a broken plant pot in the tiny covered porch. It wasn't there and, after a couple of failed attempts to break in, he decided to check into the Pig and Whistle pub in the village a mile away.

He was just about to get into his hire car when a woman appeared in front of him. She was wearing a woollen headscarf knotted tightly under her chin and pulled down very low so that it obscured most of her face.

'I'm Ruth Simpson, I've got the key to your mother's house. I assume you're Stefan?'

He nodded. 'I spoke to you yesterday?'

'That's right, I found your mother.'

Ruth Simpson bit her bottom lip, and Stefan hoped he was not going to be subjected to all the gory details.

'I'm very sorry,' she said simply.

Stefan stepped closer. 'I've just come from the hospital, they say she's as well as can be expected; if she does survive, she'll have you to thank.'

Ruth pressed the key into his hand. Her fingers were ice-cold. 'I doubt she'll be grateful, I rather think she's had enough of life. I can't say I blame her – old age is intolerable and lasts, for some of us, far longer than is humane.'

He could think of no suitable reply, and Ruth started to walk away – a lone figure on the dark path. Without turning around, she called, 'If you need me, you can find me at Barn Acre a few hundred yards down the lane; and by the way, I've got Sasha with me.'

Stefan shouted his thanks before locking his car and using the key to the cottage which Ruth had just given him. He went directly to the kitchen; he needed a drink and knew his mother kept a few bottles of spirits for emergencies. The kitchen looked the same as it had the day when he'd left home seventeen years before. Potted plants, boxes of herbs and flower cuttings lined the windowsills and cluttered the work surfaces. Stefan located the whisky bottle, relieved to find it half full. He poured a large measure into a small tumbler, adding a splash of tap water. Sitting down heavily at the scrubbed pine table, he drank deeply, draining the glass in one gulp. He refilled, not bothering with water, enjoying the warm glow gently caressing his throat and the almost instant relaxation of his taut muscles. He ran a hand across the tabletop, an instant reminder of childhood evenings doubled over this same table, struggling with his homework. Suddenly his mother was sitting opposite, holding a cup of steaming black coffee to her lips, fixing him with a malevolent stare as she bullied him through his school work.

He spoke to the empty space. 'You and me, Mother, alone in this Godforsaken shithole, never any friends invited back. Nobody ever wanted to come, you see, they were all a little afraid of the big Kraut woman in her dark cottage.'

Stefan laughed out loud, scaring himself with the odd detached sound. He lifted the whisky bottle to his mouth, draining the last few drops; then letting his head drop on to the table, he began to cry. Unsure of what to do next, or where to go, he decided to call his cousin, Kathryn. He doubted she knew about his mother's illness, yet was certain wherever she was in the world she would now know about Von Trellenberg. He wondered if his Aunt Freda had ever told Kathryn who her grandfather really was.

The roaring in his head had returned, he felt hot then cold, and needed some dope. As he dialled Kathryn's number, he considered asking her if she knew where he could get his hands on some good stuff, then dismissed the idea when he heard her soft speech on the answering machine. Waiting for the bleep he planned his message, starting to speak – only to change his mind after, 'Hi, Kathryn, it's me . . .' He left the phone off the hook and stumbled away.

'Pull yourself together, man,' he whispered, trying frantically to think of where he could get some dope. Then he remembered hiding some cocaine in the lining of an old suitcase last year. He'd left the case with his mother and had forgotten about it until now. The suitcase contained his late wife's personal effects and several photograph albums she had lovingly collated of their short time together: professional wedding photographs, candid holiday snaps and hundreds of their daughter Laura from a few minutes old right up to her fourth birthday party ten days before her tragic death. Stefan had wanted to burn everything, but his mother had urged him not to, promising to keep the albums safe until he felt able to look at the photographs without pain. She had assured him that the day would come, and he would thank her for not allowing him to destroy the memorabilia.

Stefan was thanking her now, praying that she hadn't moved the case. Bent almost double, he climbed the narrow staircase leading to the attic, where he had to pick his way through the boxes stacked high into the rafters – most of them full of the tattered remnants of an empty life. Lifting a book out of a chest he read the title: it was German. He threw it back into the box with a grunt of disdain. The suitcase was not where he'd put it; he felt his heart drop, then leap a second later, when he spied the case partially hidden by a mountain of old bed linen. Bending to his knees, he pulled it out from under a pile of torn sheets and pillowcases.

The case was locked. Failing to force it open, he began a frantic search for something to break the lock. But he stood up too quickly, banging his head. Rubbing his crown, as he looked up at the offending beam, he saw something glinting in the darkness and hoping it might be an appropriate implement he poked his head high into the rafters. He had to stretch to grasp the corner of a dust sheet suspended across the beams. The sheet came off after a couple of sharp tugs to reveal what he assumed was a painting. He could see some writing on the bottom of the canvas, but it was impossible from his position to see what it read. He scanned the attic for something to stand on and he found an old stool. It wobbled a little at first, then stayed still long enough for Stefan to prise the picture from its resting place. Panting, he propped it in front of his old drum set, standing back to catch his breath.

The big oil painting was set in an ornate gilded frame. Kneeling down, he looked closely at the image of sailing ships in what he assumed to be a fishing port. Stefan knew very little about art, but as he gazed at the artist's signature he experienced a great rush of excitement. Apart from drugs, he had never felt remotely like this since winning three thousand pounds at the Derby. The cocaine momentarily forgotten, he leaned forward to shift the painting a few inches enabling him to read the title next to the signature.

It was then that for the first time in years the cottage was filled with resounding laughter.

'All these years, Mother. Years of scrimping and saving, of doing without, when all the time you were living with a fucking fortune!'

Chapter Eleven

'Would you mind telling me where you acquired this painting?'

Stefan looked at the owner of the voice with obvious distaste. 'It belonged to my mother, she died recently.' He had played an English butler in a forgettable film a few years previously; his accent was perfect – so much so, he could have been educated at Eton.

Michael Gill of Sotheby's had experienced a surge of excitement when he had first looked at the Monet, then the chill of unease. *Le Port d'Honfleur* he knew had been lost during the war.

'Have you any idea where or how your mother acquired it?'

'None, I've been living abroad. I came back for her funeral and was clearing the house. I found this in the attic.'

'Did your mother not have the painting insured; was there no receipt, no record of purchase?'

'None, I'm afraid. I found nothing in her papers appertaining to the painting. Perhaps she didn't know it was valuable.'

Michael Gill looked at the painting again, he traced the artist's initial and looked closely at the canvas. 'It may be a forgery, attributed to Monet. There are quite a few around . . .'

'What makes you say that?'

'Merely a professional opinion. I've been in the fine art department for over twenty years, I'm constantly seeing work attributed to great artists. To be absolutely certain you'd have to leave the painting with us to be properly authenticated, and have its provenance thoroughly researched.'

'If it is the real thing, how much is it worth?' Stefan wanted to know.

'It's impossible to give you a reasonable assessment until we do establish the authenticity and provenance. That is what you came here for, is it not?'

Pompous bastard, Stefan decided, nevertheless fixing a pleasant smile on his face. No point in letting this man get up his nose. He felt good today, running on all cylinders, high octane, dynamic. He wasn't going to let a creep like this Gill guy rattle him.

'Absolutely, but I'd like a second opinion.'

'I'm sure my colleague Sebastian Ashton, who's been with Sotheby's for more years than he dare count, will be delighted to take a look. If you'll excuse me for one moment I'll get him.'

Michael Gill left the room. When he returned a few minutes later with his colleague, Stefan and the Monet were gone.

Later that day, Stefan checked into the Sinclair House Hotel on the Cromwell Road. He'd been to Christie's, and a couple of dealers in the West End, who had all repeated what Michael Gill had told him. What was it with these goddamn arty-farty types; who the hell did they think they were?

He thought of the last man he'd seen in Mayfair, Lycett-Green or Green-Lycett, some double-barrelled job he couldn't remember. Stefan had found him a smart-ass patronizing prick, who'd talked down to him as if he were a delivery boy, and who'd touched the painting like it was red hot.

In the cab coming back to the hotel, Stefan had come to the conclusion that either the painting was merely attributed to Monet, and therefore not worth the sort of money he'd at first assumed. Or, the other more likely alternative, it was the real thing – looted by his grandfather from some wartime Jewish family who had probably perished. If the latter was true, Stefan knew he would have problems going down the conventional routes. Proving the provenance would connect him with Von Trellenberg, and that was the last thing he wanted. Racking his brains for a solution, he let his gaze roam the shabby room with its peeling paint and threadbare carpet. He detested what he saw, and he knew he didn't want to live like this for the remainder of his life. His eyes came to rest on the canvas; if it was the real thing, as he suspected, it could be his passport on to the other side of the street. All he needed was a private sale, or a disreputable dealer – someone a little bent who would not be adverse to handling hot property. How to make such a contact in a city he did not know well, in a closed-shop business that he knew absolutely nothing about? What does anyone do when they have something to sell? Silently he ran the questions through his mind.

Suddenly he snapped his fingers, then rummaged in his pocket for his pen. He wrote the advert in scrawled letters on a scrap of paper. It read, 'Unique opportunity to acquire important Impressionist painting. Owner leaving the country, must have quick uncomplicated sale. Call 0171 589 6892 before 10 a.m. or after six.'

'This sounds interesting,' Gavin Fox said between bites of croissant.

Christopher Fleming did not look up as he announced, 'Get too big for one's boots. Seven letters.'

Gavin grinned, 'Fleming.'

'Be serious, Gavin, I've tried "pompous", but it doesn't fit.'

'Did you hear what I said, Chris?'

With an irritated sigh, Christopher dragged his eyes from the crossword to the face of his boyfriend. 'Why is it every time I pick up a paper you interrupt me?'

Gavin looked petulant. 'Excuse me, I merely thought you might be interested in someone selling an important Impressionist painting privately.'

'Let me see!' Christopher tried to grab the newspaper.

But Gavin was too quick for him, he whipped it out of his grasp, reading aloud, 'Unique opportunity to acquire important Impressionist painting. Owner leaving the country, must have quick uncomplicated sale.' With that, Gavin finally threw the paper at Christopher who was seated at the opposite end of the breakfast table.

Fleming read the ad for himself. 'Mm, does sound interesting. I'll call tomorrow.' He returned to his own newspaper, not looking up as his boyfriend left the room. He was still engrossed in the crossword when Gavin returned ten minutes later.

'It's a Monet,' Gavin announced, gaining an immediate gleam of interest from Christopher.

'What did you say?'

'You heard me, darling,' he said with a tinge of triumph. 'The owner's coming to the gallery to see you tomorrow at ten with the painting.'

Fleming puckered his lips, blowing his partner a kiss.

'What on earth would I do without you?'

'Young boys, probably,' Gavin whispered under his breath, then winking at Fleming said, 'I've no idea, sweetie.'

At nine-thirty the following morning Stefan left his hotel. He walked down the Cromwell Road to a taxi and gave the driver the address: 157 Fulham Road.

During the journey across London he thought about his forthcoming meeting. He'd been disappointed by the response to his advert. He hadn't expected to be inundated, but he had hoped for more than three enquiries. Only one of which, on behalf of a Christopher Fleming, had sounded promising. When the cab stopped at a crossing and Stefan found himself watching an old woman struggle across the road with a pile of shopping bags, his thoughts digressed to his mother. As a young boy, and during his adolescence, they had been very close – too close, a cloying oedipal relationship. He'd longed to escape the overpowering interdependence and had done so at the first opportunity. Yet now having seen her so close to death, he was filled with a sense of loss and searing emptiness. She was all he had in the world to call his own, and he wanted her to live. Only the cab coming to a halt jolted him back to the immediate present.

Stefan jumped out, paid the cabbie then turned to face

the building at number 157. At first glance the shop looked closed down. The windows were dirty, and the dark blue paintwork was chipped. When he rang the bell, there was no reply. On the third ring he was rewarded by a voice on the intercom and was able to announce himself. A few moments later the door was opened by a teenage boy who looked like a young girl without breasts.

'Mr Fleming is expecting you, please come in,' the boy said, pursing his full mouth.

Faggot, Stefan thought, following the neat bottom encased in tight pants down a dimly lit hall into a large showroom. It was painted a grainy yellow, the skirting and cornice picked out in a darker shade. The effect made Stefan think of vomit. Paintings were stacked around the walls in an assortment of frames. All were covered in a thin layer of dust, and Stefan wondered if this man Fleming ever sold anything. He leaned forward to look closely at an oil painting. There were a lot of loops and circles in different shades of vivid red – the colour of blood, Stefan thought, grunting in disgust.

'Do you like the Miró?'

Stefan turned to see a tall, extremely thin man dressed entirely in black, except for a tiny pink rosebud in one lapel and a red Aids ribbon in the other.

Stefan pointed to the painting. 'If you mean *that*, no.'

The man lifted one eyebrow, something Stefan had never seen done before. 'Miró is not to everyone's taste, nor mine to be honest. I prefer the Impressionists, such wonderful use of light, a joy to perceive.' Stepping past Stefan, he pulled a painting out from the pile behind the Miró. 'Now this is *art*.' He held the painting aloft.

Stefan looked at the portrait of a nude by Renoir with obvious disinterest. 'Well, I prefer it to that stuff,' he pointed to the Miró again.

The man in black stared at the painting with a look of pure adulation. 'I only wish it was real.'

Stefan looked blank.

The man laughed, it was a deep, throaty sound – in complete contrast to his high-pitched voice. 'It's a print, old boy. A good one, I might add.' He sighed, 'But merely a print.' He took a step closer to Stefan. 'I forgot to introduce myself. I'm Christopher Fleming. And you are Stefan Lang, I assume.'

Stefan inclined his head, pleased that Fleming had made no attempt to shake his hand.

'I understand you have an important painting to sell, Mr Lang?' Christopher glanced at the wrapped parcel in Stefan's hand. When there was no answer, he said, 'May I see it?'

Stefan made no move. 'First, I need your word that you would be able to sell privately. I've been to several dealers in the last few days who've been unwilling to handle this painting. They've all said the same thing – that they're unsure of the provenance – and would need to have it thoroughly checked out before they'll attempt to sell. I haven't got time for all that shit; I want a quick, easy sale. That's why I advertised. So before I show you the painting, I must ask if you're concerned about the provenance.'

'One question before I reply.' Christopher looked directly into Stefan's eyes. 'Is it stolen?'

Stefan replied honestly. 'The absolute truth is I'm not sure. I found it in my mother's attic. I can't ask her how it came to be there because she's in a coma. My mother is German, she came here in the early seventies. Perhaps she brought it with her. It may have been a gift. Her family were very wealthy before the war, so it could be an heirloom. She obviously had no idea of its true value, or I'm certain she wouldn't have spent her life here working all the hours that God sends, doing home dressmaking until her fingers bled.'

Christopher raised his other eyebrow. 'I know a couple of people who might be interested in purchasing an important Monet discreetly.' He moved his hand from side to side, 'If the painting is good.' He repeated his earlier request. 'May I see it, please?'

As Stefan unwrapped the parcel, Fleming stepped forward to take a close look. When he bent forward, Stefan observed his face – it held a look of pure rapture. He wondered afresh how grown men could get so excited about an old painting.

When Fleming stood up straight, his expression had changed to one of controlled fervour. 'Stunning, quite divine, but very dangerous. This is a very important piece of art.' Fleming touched the painting as if he were caressing a loved one.

'Is it the real thing?' Stefan could not contain his urgency.

Fleming was tempted to lie, say it was a good forgery, and offer him a silly price, but he detected an underlying menace in Stefan and dismissed the idea. 'I'm *almost* certain it is. I believe we're looking at the original *Le Port d'Honfleur* by Claude Monet. It was part of a private German collection, assumed to have been destroyed or confiscated during the war. If you have no proof of ownership, you might be in danger of having that ownership contested.'

'By whom?'

'My dear boy, don't be so naïve. By the descendants of the original owner, if there are any. It's amazing how people crawl out of the woodwork when something as important as this . . .' he tapped the ornate frame, 'turns up.'

Stefan nodded, aware the dealer was only too right.

With his black eyes fixed on the artwork, Fleming said, 'I need to make a few calls, but I think I know just the man who would be interested in owning a painting of this calibre.'

Mrs Peacock knocked twice then entered the dining room. 'There's a Mr Christopher Fleming on the telephone for you.'

Jack McGowan swallowed a piece of fish before replying. 'Tell him I'm having supper, please, Mrs P. I'll call back later, or better still ask him to call me at the office tomorrow.'

When she returned a couple of minutes later, Jack had finished eating. 'This Fleming man said to tell you it's extremely urgent.'

Standing up with an exasperated sigh, Jack threw his napkin on to the table, saying to his companion who was sitting opposite, 'Excuse me, Kathryn, no rest for the wicked.' Then he strode into his study to take the call. He did not like Christopher Fleming and, dispensing with pleasantries, said tersely, 'What do you want, Christopher?

I'm in the middle of supper, couldn't this have waited until tomorrow?'

In direct contrast to Jack's obvious irritation, Fleming kept his voice overtly pleasant. 'How are you, Jack? Long time no see, or speak. I keep reading about you in the press.'

Jack cut him off. 'And I heard that you'd left the country.'

'I did for a while, but I missed old Blighty. I've got a small place on the Fulham Road now. A friend of mine wanted out of London, I wanted back in, so we did a straight swop. My gallery in the US for his over here. I manage to sell a few paintings, just to keep the wolves at bay. The last few years have been tough in the art market, life is such a bitch when one has to work, so bloody boring. You know how it is.'

Jack knew exactly how it was for dealers like Fleming: living on the edge, always just one step, or in his case maybe two steps, ahead of the law. 'I thought the art world had taken an upward turn?'

'It'll never be as bullish as the mid-eighties, but I'm managing to make an honest crust.'

Jack doubted the *honest*, but said nothing.

Christopher continued. 'Robin Weldon said he saw you at Clive Buchanan's party with a beautiful filly, all right for some, old chap.'

Jack hated the old schoolboy routine and had no intention of discussing Kathryn with Fleming. 'Cut the pleasantries, Christopher, I'm a busy man.'

Fleming's tone had changed to brisk when he said, 'OK, to business. The reason I'm calling you is that I've been offered a wonderful painting. A masterpiece. I know it would be of interest to you. It's a Monet, an important Monet, large and quite beautiful.'

The underlying excitement in Christopher's tone was unmistakable to the astute Jack.

'The owner wants a quick and quiet sale. I said I thought I knew a couple of people who might be interested; you sprang to mind instantly.'

Jack was brusque. 'How much?'

'If it went to auction, I would estimate over twenty-five million pounds.'

Restraining a gasp, Jack kept his voice level, careful not to reveal his astonishment. 'So why doesn't the owner want to send it to auction?'

'I'd rather we met to discuss the finer details of the sale. All I will say is that I can get it for considerably less than that. Deals like this come up once in a lifetime. I would strongly advise you to at least consider it.'

'I've considered,' Jack replied quickly. 'When can I see the painting?'

'Give me a few minutes, I'll call you back.'

When Jack returned to the dining room, Kathryn was sipping a glass of claret. She gave him a quizzical look when he sat down, because he was visibly changed. He looked like he'd been running, his face was flushed, and there was an air of suppressed excitement about him that had not been there before.

'Who was it?' she asked casually, watching him fork a piece of Brie on to his plate.

'No one you know,' Jack answered dismissively, then changing the subject said, 'Now, I want to hear *all* about St Lucia.'

Kathryn just pulled a long face.

Jack finished chewing, he pointed his knife in her direction. 'Like that, was it? You'd have been better off joining me in the Far East.'

'You're right, Jack, I wish now I'd taken you up on that offer.' She stopped speaking when Mrs Peacock appeared round the door.

Jack was on his feet before his housekeeper spoke. 'Telephone for me?'

Mrs Peacock nodded. 'It's Mr Fleming again.'

But Jack had already rushed out of the room without his usual apology, leaving Kathryn to ponder over the mysterious Mr Fleming.

'Yes, Christopher?'

'Can you make my gallery at eight tomorrow night? It's 157 Fulham Road.'

'I'll be there.'

Fleming Fine Art Gallery was in darkness when Jack rang the doorbell at five minutes to eight. A moment later a light illuminated a tiny window a few feet above the door. Jack looked up, spotting the top of Christopher Fleming's head as he descended the stairs.

Opening the door wide, Christopher stepped forward greeting Jack with a thin smile. 'Good evening, Jack, please come in.' He stepped aside. 'Good to see you. My, my, you do look well, if I may say so.'

Christopher held out his right hand; the short fat fingers and waxy skin reminded Jack of a surgical prosthesis.

Wearing a paisley bow tie and a long black jacket over straight black jeans exactly the same shade as his hair,

212

Christopher completed the greeting rituals and announced, 'Follow me.' He then led the way in silence up two sets of stairs into a large room that looked as if it had once been a library.

Empty bookshelves lined the walls; there was no furniture except a huge safe in one corner and an ugly reproduction Empire desk in the other. A loosely draped dust sheet covered what Jack assumed was the painting, it stood on an easel in the centre of the room.

'Stand by the door; you'll get a better view,' Christopher suggested.

Jack did as he was bid, taking a couple of steps back. And once Christopher was happy his punter was in the correct viewing position, he swept the dust sheet high into the air with dramatic reverence.

'*Le Port d'Honfleur*, by Monsieur Claude Monet.'

Jack looked at the painting for a long time, feeling an acute rush of adrenaline akin to pain as he absorbed every detail of the work of art. Collecting Impressionists was one of his great passions. It had started at the age of twelve when his mother had bought a cheap Degas print, and he had vowed one day to own the real thing. But Monet was his great love, and this piece was one of the most beautiful examples of the artist's work he had ever seen.

With his eyes fixed on the painting, Jack said, 'I want the truth, Christopher. Is it stolen?'

Fleming considered his reply carefully. 'Not quite.'

Jack, his brows raised, said, 'And what does that mean?'

'Let me rephrase,' Christopher added quickly, aware of the legendary McGowan temper.

'The truth, Fleming; it's really quite easy, you ought to try it some time.'

Laughing nervously, Christopher Fleming patted his hair in place with twitching fingers. 'It's like this. The owner was recommended to me by a friend of a friend. He wishes to avoid the conventional route, i.e. Sotheby's or Christie's. Because,' he paused, '. . . how shall we say? He's a little unsure of the provenance.'

Jack was about to speak, when Christopher held up his hand and continued, 'The owner recently inherited the picture from his mother, who was German and came here after the war. He claims she was from a wealthy family and thinks that she inherited the picture on the death of her own parents, who presumably perished during the war. Anyway, I've done a little research myself, and it seems the painting was once owned by Joseph Krantz, a wealthy German banker who lost his art collection before, during and after the war. This particular Monet was believed destroyed by the Russians at the close of the war, but to be honest no one's absolutely certain. Joseph Krantz was an avid collector, he bought and sold extensively; there's no proof to say that he didn't sell this painting legitimately before the war.'

Jack scrutinized Fleming's simpering face. 'The authenticity? I'll need to have it checked out.'

'Fine by me, there's no doubt it's the real thing.'

'I do hope you're telling me the truth, Christopher. Are there any living heirs to the Krantz collection?'

It was at this point that the other man decided to lie. He had always disliked the arrogant Adam Krantz intensely. He was American and far too rich and successful to be even remotely likeable, and it gave Christopher a perverse pleasure to be selling a painting that he knew Krantz would give his right arm to own.

'No, not to my knowledge, they all perished in the Holocaust.' He raised watery eyes, and added without a shred of emotion, 'God rest their souls.'

Jack fought with his conscience. The deal was dubious, of that he had no doubt, but then so were a lot of deals. His eyes strayed to the Monet again. To own something that exquisite was worth a risk. He made up his mind. 'How much?'

Fleming rubbed his chin, as if pondering. 'As I believe I indicated on the phone, a Monet this rare and quite this perfect would fetch on today's market about twenty-five million pounds.'

'I won't ask again, Christopher, and you know how I loathe playing games, how much?'

'To you, fifteen million. A bargain, I must say.'

'Twelve,' Jack retorted.

'I refuse to haggle over such an astounding work of art; there are other buyers, you're not the only one.'

'Fourteen million, any currency, anywhere in the world,' said Jack.

Fleming returned, 'Done!' He held out his hand, reminding Jack of a Dickensian character, Scrooge's younger brother perhaps, who had just concluded a very satisfactory deal.

'I'm warning you, pal,' Jack said in a light-hearted way, yet Fleming knew he wasn't being light-hearted when he concluded his sentence, 'if there's any trouble on this picture, you're history.'

Chapter Twelve

'I told you Von Trellenberg was my grandfather.' Kathryn's voice was barely audible, her bent head moving from side to side as if in denial. 'My aunt informed me of this, but I got the impression when we last met, that you didn't believe me?'

'I must be honest I was sceptical,' Patricia Gillman admitted.

Kathryn continued. 'He was a Nazi war criminal. I suppose you read about it in the papers, he was captured in St Lucia last week. I was there. I talked to him before his arrest, and subsequent death.'

Dr Gillman covered her surprise with ease. Her reaction, when she'd seen the news, was one she knew many of her peer group shared: that the Horowitz Centre was made up of a bunch of Zionist fanatics, who were reduced to hunting senile and decrepit old men who probably couldn't even recall what they'd done the previous day, let alone what had happened fifty years ago in Nazi Germany.

The doctor listened avidly as Kathryn, without prompting, continued talking about her grandfather. 'Apparently he worked with Reinhard Heydrich who had overall responsibility for the mass murder of Jews. Von Trellenberg was responsible for the emigration of Jews to labour and extermination camps. That monster was my mother's father.'

Dr Gillman noticed Kathryn was under extreme stress; she looked exhausted, her eyes were ringed with dark shadows and she looked like she had not slept for days.

'You mentioned you were in St Lucia?'

Kathryn nodded.

'Would you like to talk about it, Kathryn?'

'Yes, doctor, I do want to talk about it. I've got so much stuff going round and round my head, it's driving me mad.' She took a deep breath, biting the cuticle on her index finger. 'Klaus had been in touch with my mother before her death, I think I told you that last time . . . Well, as a result of that I eventually traced him to St Lucia, and then to a remote plantation house in the south of the Island. Klaus had adopted the identity of a Dutchman called Van Beukering and been living there for eight years. I didn't have long to talk to him before he died.'

Kathryn had no intention of mentioning the fact that she herself had been arrested and sent to prison. She'd had enough therapy in the past to know that suppressing the experience would not help it to diminish; on the contrary, it would probably grow out of all proportion. Yet she had no desire to relive the nightmare, not at the moment. Sitting on the sofa in the opulent comfort of Patricia Gillman's London consulting rooms made recent events seem even more remote. And that was fine by her.

'I'm experiencing great difficulty in coming to terms with the knowledge that I'm the descendant of a Nazi. I can't eat properly, and I wake up in the middle of the night shaking, afraid to go back to sleep in case of another horrific nightmare. I can't concentrate at work, and feel that I'm becoming totally paranoid – you know, losing my grip.'

Kathryn paused and Dr Gillman could see her entire body was shaking. 'I'm scared, doctor, I'm scared I'm going to crack up again. I feel so ashamed. I can't stop thinking about him, and the terrible things he did.'

Patricia Gillman leaned forward, looking directly into Kathryn's eyes. 'I think you are overreacting a little, doing what you always do, Kathryn, taking on board the guilt. You mustn't blame yourself for events that happened long before you were born. It has no relevance whatsoever to your life today. This is the nineties, the war ended fifty years ago, another time, another place. You have to forget this Nazi. He was your grandfather, so what? You didn't choose him, it's not your fault. You did nothing wrong and have nothing to feel guilty about. I advise you to forget the whole thing. It's a shame your aunt felt she had to tell you. Ignorance in this case would have been bliss. Immerse yourself in your work, that's always been good therapy for you, and very soon the entire episode will fade like an old photograph or a hazy recollection from something long past. Believe me, Kathryn, you must forget Von Trellenberg unless you want to become another one of his victims.'

'Yes, I know.'

'Have you spoken to your aunt since you got back from St Lucia?'

'No, I've tried but she must be away. I can't get a reply from the house. But Ingrid believed her father was already dead. She was so calm and detached about it I could have throttled her.' Kathryn repeated Ingrid's words in the same accent, with a harsh Germanic ring.

'He was . . . a highly respected man and a good German, who served his . . . country with loyalty and integrity . . . let him rest in peace. Some *integrity*! Anyone would think he'd been working as a night porter.'

Kathryn wrung her hands so hard they burnt. After a few minutes she rummaged in her bag, pulling out a pack of cigarettes and a disposable lighter.

'When did you start to smoke?' Dr Gillman asked her as she lit a cigarette.

'Just.' She held up her hand as if to ward off what she knew was coming. 'Don't say a word, doctor. I need them right now, OK?'

'Fine,' said Patricia Gillman, fighting the impulse to tell Kathryn that smoking wouldn't help. 'To get back to your grandfather, what can you gain from dwelling on the subject? I doubt he had much choice about his rôle. In Nazi Germany you did what you were told or faced a firing squad.'

Kathryn exhaled smoke. 'Strange, but he was likeable in an odd sort of way.'

'What did you expect, the storm-trooping jack-booted archetypal Nazi that Hollywood has given us for the last fifty years? Believe me, they weren't all like that.'

'I know that, and no, that wasn't what I'd envisioned. I suppose I just thought he would be more aggressive; less, how can I put it accurately?' she searched for the right word. 'Less *appealing*.'

'Did he talk about his past at all?' Patricia asked, making notes on Kathryn's file.

'Not much, a little about his family. Mostly his deep

regret about his life. He did say one thing that I found very weird.'

'What was that?'

Before he was arrested he whispered in my ear, *'Schlafen mit Geistern.'* Kathryn paused and shrugged. 'Roughly translated, it means: *sleeping with ghosts.'*

'Have you any idea what significance it could have?' Dr Gillman asked, coughing and wafting smoke with an exaggerated sweep of her hand.

Kathryn ground her cigarette out in an ashtray that looked as if it had never been used before. 'None whatsoever, Klaus did start to tell me something a few minutes before we were interrupted by the police. It may have had something to do with that. Who knows? Or it may have something to do with Adam Krantz.'

'Who?'

'A man I met in St Lucia, he's an American, a New York art dealer.' Speaking of Adam forced her to think about him. Since returning from St Lucia, she'd tried not to; but his face kept floating into her mind at the most unexpected and sometimes inopportune moments – like the other night when she'd been making love with Jack. She could hear Adam's voice now, impassioned when he talked of his father and grandfather. The recollection brought her back to her own grandfather.

'Adam claims that Klaus stole a priceless art collection from the Krantz family before the war. He's been hunting Von Trellenberg for twelve years. I didn't like him when I first met him, but then the circumstances were not great. Later on, I was drawn to him, sympathized with him, and found myself wanting to help. I sort of thought that if I could help him find the lost art stolen from *his* grandfather, it would help eradicate some of the guilt I feel about my own.'

There was no mistaking the discernible tenderness in Kathryn's voice when she spoke of Adam Krantz, and Dr Gillman studied her with concern. 'The plot thickens. Are you attracted to this man, Adam Krantz?'

Kathryn thought about the question, one she had not even dared confront. 'Well, he's very attractive physically. Muscular, dark-skinned, sensual with a wonderful smile. But of course he would never be attracted to me.'

'Why not? You're extremely beautiful.'

Kathryn blushed. 'It would be impossible with our backgrounds. How could he allow himself to be attracted to the descendant of a *Nazi*?' She spat out the last word.

Patricia Gillman felt a profound sadness steal over her. Kathryn de Moubray had been severely damaged in her life, but she had been coping well, and now this. She asked, 'Have you spoken to your father or Jack about Von Trellenberg?'

'My father's taken Emily to America for medical tests. Apparently he heard about a revolutionary new treatment for MS, some doctor with a clinic in Dallas, according to his secretary. I really don't want to bother him right now, he's got enough on his plate. Jack came back from the Far East a couple of days ago and we had supper last night. I thought about telling him, then changed my mind. What do you think?'

Patricia Gillman considered her reply carefully. Kathryn was a chronic repressive, storing instead of confronting her emotions was her way of dealing with trauma. She had developed the disorder at nine when her father left her; it had then escalated with her mother's lack of communication, and her subsequent marriage failure.

The doctor hadn't met Jack McGowan, but he sounded sympathetic. 'Are you afraid of Jack's reaction?'

Kathryn said 'Yes' without hesitation.

'Why? Because you think he'll blame you, hold you responsible for your grandfather's crimes? Despise *you* because Klaus Von Trellenberg was a Nazi, reject *you* because you're related to him? Is that what you're afraid of, Kathryn?'

Kathryn lit another cigarette, inhaling deeply before she replied. 'I haven't really analysed the reasons. That's what I pay you for.' She grinned and so did the doctor. 'I just know I'm scared to tell him.'

'If you want my advice, I would talk to Jack. Don't be afraid to share this thing with him. What can he possibly do that would be so terrible? He'll be shocked no doubt, he'll most probably be interested, and if I'm not mistaken he will be sympathetic and supportive. Men like Jack love to feel needed, particularly with younger women. I'm positive he will prove to be a great comfort.'

Kathryn looked at her watch, she had ten minutes to get to the office for a meeting. She stood up, holding out her hand. 'Thanks, Dr Gillman, talking to you has made me feel better already; sometimes I don't know what I would do without you.'

Patricia Gillman smiled fondly. 'If you talked more to other people, Kathryn, you could do without me easily.'

Kathryn winked. 'I know that, doc; but just think of all the fun we'd miss.'

*   *   *

Rod Franks faced Kathryn across the boardroom table. They had just concluded a production meeting and he had asked her to stay behind a few minutes.

'You look tired, Kathryn, and distracted. I know you well enough to detect there's something wrong. Would you like to talk about it?' Sensitivity and sympathy were not two of Rod's redeeming characteristics, and she rightly assumed that she must look terrible for him to have noticed.

'I'm tired, that's all, but thanks for asking.'

'You're more than tired, Kathy, it's like you're burdened with something; you know, carrying the world on your shoulders. I noticed it as soon as you got back from the West Indies; I put it down to your Nazi story dying on you – literally.'

'Would you accept women's problems, and leave it at that?'

'OK, I get the message. If you don't want to talk about it I understand, but what I can't tolerate is you bringing your shit to work. I'd appreciate you dumping it at home, at your boyfriend's, in the dry cleaner's; anywhere but here, understood?'

Kathryn stood up, she pushed her notepad and pencil into her briefcase. In a voice that even she noticed sounded strangely detached, as if she were a ventriloquist's dummy with her mouth operated by strings, she said, 'I understand perfectly, Rod. I know I'm not doing a good job at the moment, so I think it best if you accept my resignation.'

A look of dismay creased his face. 'Hey, I don't want you to *resign*, Kathy. You're the best I've got. We've come a long way together. I think you're being hasty. How about,

I'll tolerate the women's problems if you'll think about not resigning?'

Her mind was in a turmoil. She loved her job, loved the business, she didn't really want to leave Trident. She didn't know what she wanted any more. Her world had been turned upside down, and inside out.

'I promise I won't let you down mid-production; I'll finish the Deception job which will take another two weeks, then I'll go.'

'Are you setting up your own company?' For the first time he looked sincerely worried and just to rattle his cage she was tempted to lie and say that she was.

'No, Rod, I'm not.'

'Well, what is it? Come on, Kathryn, we've been friends for a long time, surely you can talk to me. Is it money, has someone offered you more dosh to work for them? If so, whatever you've been offered, I'll raise.'

With a sigh she sat back down. 'It's got nothing to do with money, Rod. In fact I've just come into quite a bit from my mother's estate. I've got a lot on my mind at the moment, that's all. It's something I can't discuss with you, with anyone; let's just say it's a family matter.' A silence fell then Kathryn said, 'What would you say if I asked for a short sabbatical?'

'How short?'

She was tempted to go for a year, but Rod's wary look changed her mind. 'Six months?'

He looked at the back of his hands pondering. Kathryn was a good producer, there were others but few as reliable. He came to a quick decision. 'I don't want to lose you, Kathy, you've got six months to do whatever it is you've got to do. And when you come back, I want you shit-hot, baby, ready to rock and roll.'

'Thanks, Rod, I really appreciate you keeping my job open.'

They both stood up, he scratched his head. 'I must be mad!'

Spontaneously she grabbed his hand, planting a kiss on his cheek. 'You're not mad, you know I'll work even harder when I get back.'

He picked up his pen and, handing it to her, said, 'Can I have that in writing, please?'

The sun glinted off the top of her smooth crown as she walked; she was so light on her feet, it was like she was gliding along on roller skates. He imagined her full breasts jiggling inside the flimsy cotton fabric of her shirt as he followed, admiring her from the back. She's still got a great butt he decided, recalling the first time he had seen it. Kathryn had been thirteen. The peephole from his bedroom to her bathroom had taken him hours of careful planning and secret drilling. With a sly smile twisting the corners of his mouth, Stefan thought back to his adolescent voyeurism. A vision of his cousin stepping out of the bath, soap suds dripping from her budding nipples and sprouting pubis, made his pace quicken. He felt hot, an erection stirring as she turned into the multi-storey car park and out of sight. He hailed a cab, asked the driver to wait, then to follow the dark blue Golf GTI driven by Kathryn.

He got out of the taxi at the end of Penzance Place. Leaning nonchalantly against the bonnet of a parked car, he watched Kathryn take a bag of groceries out of the boot and enter number twenty-six.

He waited a full ten minutes before walking towards her front door to ring the bell, fixing his most beguiling smile firmly on his face.

Kathryn was surprised to see him. '*Stefan*, what are you doing here?'

'Did you get my message? I left it on your machine a few days ago,' he supplied.

She thought back. 'I did have a partial message, but I didn't recognize the voice and thought it was a wrong number; it must have been you.' Kathryn made no attempt to invite him in.

'I'd like to talk to you, Kathryn. I think you know what it's about. Can I come in?'

She hesitated. 'My boyfriend's picking me up in half an hour,' she lied. 'I've got to get ready; can we make it some other time?'

Stefan took a step towards her. 'I want to talk to you about Von Trellenberg. It's important.'

A quick flash of fear entered her eyes, then was gone. But not before Stefan had relished his moment of power. He felt like a lion, and for a short moment he was fourteen again and terrorizing his shy cousin.

'OK, you'd better come in,' she said, holding back the door. She then led him across the hall and into the drawing room. It was cluttered in a warm, cosy sort of way; a home, he thought with a pang of envy. Kathryn had done all right for herself. But then she would, he conceded bitterly, it was easy for a woman. Easy to give some hot-shot guy a great blow job, to lie on her back, smooth thighs parted

226

and with a look of love and promise plastered across her beautiful face. Silently Stefan congratulated himself that even when he'd been desperate for money, his body screaming for dope, he'd never prostituted himself. *I'd probably be asking fifteen million dollars a movie by now, if I'd been prepared to go down on some fag casting director, or get laid by an ageing producer.*

Kathryn broke his train of thought, thinking how handsome Stefan was, and how scary. Even after twenty years she could still see him stealing into the woods near her house. The memory of the day he'd strangled the neighbour's cat had never left her. Kathryn had caught him, and been threatened with the same fate if she told anyone. When she'd tried to run away, Stefan had rammed his hand down her panties, forcing his fingers between her legs, pulling her hair at the same time. When she'd tried to cry out, he'd stopped her with his own mouth pressing hard on her lips, so hard it stung. Then he'd bitten her neck in several places; the marks had taken a week to subside. She recalled how she'd run out of excuses for wearing a polo neck sweater in mid-July.

Stefan sat down on the sofa without being invited. Kathryn stood stiffly in the centre of the room. 'What do you want, Stefan?'

He crossed his long legs, and leaning back he relaxed into the sofa. He'd had a line of cocaine less than an hour before and felt good, in control, just fine and dandy. He was dressed in stone-washed denim jeans, fashionably frayed at the knee, and a pale grey sweatshirt. There was an air about him, cocky, arrogant, and something else she couldn't quite put her finger on.

'Can't a relative call on another relative just to say Hi? I was in London, I thought we could catch up. I looked for you after Freda's funeral but Mother said you'd left. Then I went back to LA, I'm starring in a movie with Julia Roberts later this year.' When he got no reaction to this lie, he concluded that either Kathryn didn't believe him, or that sort of stuff didn't impress. Stefan assumed the latter.

'Stefan, I think I made it very clear to you at my eighteenth birthday party that I never wanted to see you again.'

Stefan stared at her long and hard. She was telling him to take his dirty hands off her; once more he felt the crippling rejection and burning indignation of the occasion when Freda had ordered him out of the house.

'That was a long time ago, we were just kids; we've both grown up a lot since then. I'm a successful actor, you're a producer; we've both been married, lots of water under the bridge. Come on, Kathryn, live and let live.' His disarming smile relaxed her a little, and she sank into a chair a few feet from where he sat.

'OK, Stefan, truce; live and let live. Now let's get on, shall we?'

He paused, aware that Kathryn was highly perceptive and knowing he had to be careful how he approached the subject of Von Trellenberg. He wanted to know how much *she* knew, if anything, about the Monet. 'You know our grandfather was Klaus Von Trellenberg?'

Kathryn didn't want to talk about Klaus, but the desire to get rid of Stefan overcame her reluctance. 'Yes I did, but not until after my mother's death. Your mother told me.'

It was at this point he decided not to reveal that his mother was ill in hospital. The last thing he needed was

228

Cousin Kathryn poking her nose into Ingrid's business, *his* business now.

'Mother's away. She went to visit a friend in Berlin when she found out about her father being still alive, then dying in custody.'

'That figures,' Kathryn said, picturing her Aunt Ingrid and some other German woman swopping secrets and commiserating with each other.

'Did Freda ever talk about her past?' he fished.

Kathryn crossed her legs, pleased she was wearing trousers and not her usual short skirt. 'No, never. Like I said, Ingrid was the first person to tell me. I must admit I did a little research, and found out exactly who Von Trellenberg was, and what he'd done.' Kathryn closed her eyes, trying to shut out the image of her grandfather as she had last seen him, being thrown into the back of a police car in St Lucia.

'I find the entire thing abhorrent, and would rather forget all about it. I've got no desire, I'm sure you feel the same way, to be associated with a Nazi. Most of my friends would be appalled, and I guess your film scripts would dry up pronto if they got wind of it in Hollywood.' Kathryn stood up. 'So if that's all, Stefan, you'll have to excuse me, I've still got to get ready to go out for supper.'

Stefan jumped up, blocking her path to the door. He stood very close to her, his pupils dilated, and she realized he was stoned.

'No, it's not all, Kathryn.'

'Please, Stefan, get out of my way. I've got nothing more to say to you.'

Bitch, fucking stuck-up little bitch. He wanted to throttle

229

her. *Calm down, Stefan, what good would that do . . .*

He listened to the voice of reason in his head. 'The news was a shock to me as well, Kathryn, I found out by reading a report in the *New York Times*. I had no one to talk to.'

'What about your mother? Share it with her, she should be able to answer all your questions. I don't want to talk about Von Trellenberg.' She sighed, tired of the confrontation. 'Now *please*, Stefan, will you leave, before I—'

'Before you what?'

She took a step to one side. 'You're stoned, off your head, what are you on?'

He started to laugh, his laughter had always scared her as a child when it usually preceded some frightening game she was forced to participate in. Like the time he had dressed in a black cloak and taken her to a disused mine shaft, where he had tied her up with rope, making her chant some weird ritual verse he'd concocted.

'Before you *what*, Kathryn?' he repeated, walking out of the room. 'Oh, don't worry, I'm leaving now, so you won't have to call the police.' He opened the front door, then without turning he began to laugh again, shouting over his shoulder, *'Ciao!'*

She shuddered when a second later he finished with, 'For now.'

Chapter Thirteen

'Do I hear one million two hundred thousand? The bid is against you, sir.'

Adam touched the side of his nose. 'One million *three* hundred,' he said.

'I have a bid for one million three hundred thousand; do I hear one million four?' The auctioneer glanced around the packed room; there were no takers. 'Going once, twice, three times.' He brought his hammer down. 'Sold for one million, three hundred thousand dollars.'

Adam smiled as the Pissarro was lifted from the easel and a Renoir drawing took its place. He glanced at the list of items left for sale; there was a Van Gogh he was interested in, but he suspected it would go for well over estimate. Word was out that Harvey Jay Friedman, a keen collector, was prepared to own it at any cost. That was the trouble with most of the very rich collectors thought Adam, their love of investment overruled their love of art; the game became purely one of acquisition, particularly if they knew several other collectors wanted the same piece. He waited until the end of the sale, making notes next to the lot numbers. He was finally leaving the saleroom when he heard someone call his name. He turned to face Bill Kirk, a colleague and friend.

'You were right about the Van Gogh, Adam.'

'Yeah, I'd have liked it myself, but not at that price.'

'Well, you know what they say. If Harvey Jay wants, Harvey Jay gets.' The two men strolled towards the foyer.

'Tell me about it, Bill. Harvey tried for years to buy a Cézanne owned by my father. It was the one painting the old man would never part with. It was a gift from his father to my grandmother and she carried it to America in 1938 rolled up in her suitcase. Harvey even pursued my mother after my father's death, offering her ridiculous sums. Eventually I had to intervene and wound up getting real mad with the megalomaniac son-of-a-bitch. The man's a fanatic.'

Bill smiled. 'That's probably why he's a billionaire.'

Adam grinned. 'The old bastard needs all that money just to get laid. Have you seen some of the women he's been through? Shit, man! I'd rather feel cold and hungry, than feel most of them.'

Bill burst out laughing. 'Come on, that Marilyn Shane he married a few years back was OK. I wouldn't have thrown her out of the sack.'

'I can't remember her, I've lost track, there've been so many. Was she the one with the pneumatic breasts?'

Bill nodded enthusiastically. 'That's the one! She was at a party not long ago with a friend of mine, wearing a dress cut so low you could almost see her navel. She was making a pass at him, coming on real hot. And you wouldn't believe some of the stuff she told him about Jay.' With a licentious glint in his eye, Bill leaned closer, eager to impart a particularly slanderous piece of gossip into Adam's ear, when someone tapped his friend on the shoulder.

Spinning round, Adam encountered a pair of eyes the

palest shade of blue he had ever seen. Momentarily mesmerized by their penetration, he was caught off guard.

'Are you Adam Krantz?'

'Yes I am, do I know you?'

Bill intervened, 'Adam, I'll be in touch.'

Adam glanced briefly in Bill's direction. 'Yeah, Bill, catch you later.' Then giving the third party his full attention, he repeated, 'Do I know you?'

The man patted his sparse hair with quick nervous movements. 'No, I don't think we've met. My name is Michael Gill, I work for Sotheby's in London.' He extended a short extremely white hand covered in fine sand-coloured hair. Adam shook it firmly.

'I believe you know my colleague, Sebastian Ashton?'

Adam nodded. 'Yes, Seb and I go back a long way.'

Gill had never heard his superior called 'Seb', and doubted whether he'd like it. He straightened his tie, it had elephants and palm trees printed on a bright yellow background.

There was a long pause, during which Adam looked at Michael Gill expectantly, eventually he asked, 'Is there something I can help you with?'

Gill coughed, cleared his throat then lowering his voice said, 'I believe your family once owned an important art collection presumed lost during World War Two?'

'That's correct, but . . . ?' Adam was a bit lost.

'I think I may have seen a Monet from your grandfather's collection last week, a man came into Sotheby's trying to sell *Le Port d'Honfleur*.'

Adam held his breath, he could feel a sharp burning deep in his gut. 'Are you *sure*?'

'Absolutely, I know a little about the history of the painting and to be honest I was unsure of the provenance. The man who was trying to sell it seemed highly dubious. I advised him to leave it with us to be authenticated. He wanted a second opinion and I asked him to wait while I consulted Sebastian. When we returned, he'd gone.'

'Who was this man, did he tell you his name?'

'Sorry, nothing, no name, no address; all he did say was that his mother had died and left him the painting. Since I was coming to New York, Sebastian suggested I look out for you at the sale today.' Michael Gill had soon spotted the ponytailed Adam from Sebastian's description. *You can't miss Adam Krantz, long hair, dresses more like a hip American movie star than a highly respected art dealer.*

The rush of excitement Adam had felt at first was slowly ebbing away. 'Are you sure it wasn't a fake?'

'I can't be absolutely sure, but in my humble opinion, and I've only been wrong once in almost twenty-one years,' he placed his hand on his heart, 'I believe it was the real thing.'

'Do you know if this guy has shopped the picture around the trade; if so, he may have told a dealer something—'

Michael Gill intervened, 'Or he may have sold it privately by now, and be on a plane to obscurity.'

Gill patted his hair again and Adam wished he would keep still, the man's nervous movements were beginning to make him feel nervous himself. 'Before I left London yesterday I heard a whisper that a dealer called Christopher Fleming was selling an important Monet.'

Adam knew of him; a shady character, the sort of dealer he detested. He replied grimly, 'I've heard of him. You have to count your fingers after he shakes your hand. Wasn't he involved in that big forgery scam a few years ago?'

'That's the one,' Gill confirmed. 'Fleming's the type who gives our business a bad name, definitely not to be trusted.' As he finished his sentence, he looked over Adam's shoulder, towards a young woman who was gesticulating madly for him to join her. 'I've got to go now; it was nice meeting you.'

Adam followed his eyes. 'Send my regards to Sebastian. Tell him he owes me dinner. And thanks, Michael.'

Consumed with thoughts of the Monet, he watched Gill join his female friend. He turned to leave, muttering under his breath.

Joanne was biting into a sandwich when Adam walked into her office. Between mouthfuls of pastrami, she managed to ask, 'Did you get the Pissarro?'

'Yeah, I got it,' Adam said, passing her desk to his own office. He shrugged out of his black jacket, throwing it across the back of the sofa, and undid the top button on his white shirt.

'How much?'

'One million three,' he shouted.

'A bit more than you wanted to pay,' Joanne commented. Then not waiting for him to reply, she said, 'Johnny Earle will be pleased and you've still got a couple of hundred thousand in there to play with.'

Adam didn't respond. Preoccupied with Michael Gill and the Monet, he remembered his father talking about *Le Port d'Honfleur*. It had hung in his house in Berlin and as a young boy Benjamin had been fascinated by the way the light on the boat sails changed when observed from different angles. That was the genius of Monet's brush strokes. In his mind Adam now addressed his father. *To have the Monet back, Dad. Wouldn't that be something? To hang it here in the gallery where I could see it every day and share it with you . . .*

Joanne, shouting through the open door, brought him back down to earth.

'I've got a few messages for you; one very urgent, sounded like life and death, from your ex.'

'Everything with Jennifer is a big deal, if she breaks a fingernail it's a major disaster.'

Joanne chuckled. 'Anyway I gave you the message.' A moment later she appeared at the doorway. 'You don't look so good, a bit pale, you're not sick are you?'

He rubbed his temples and lied. 'I've got a headache, that's all, it was so damn hot in Sotheby's this morning. And talk about crowded; man, you'd have thought they were giving the pictures away.'

'I've got some really good painkillers,' she said, returning to her desk and rummaging there, finally producing a pack of tablets. Filling a glass with Diet Coke from the can she was drinking herself, Joanne placed both on her boss's desk. 'Our doc gives them to David for his back. Go on, do what Mama Jo says, take them.'

Adam, left with no choice, did so dutifully.

'So did Harvey Jay Friedman the Second, or is it the Third, I can never remember, get the Van Gogh?'

'It's the second, and yeah, he not only bought the Van Gogh, he took away a stunning Gauguin and a most desirable Matisse as well. I'd have loved the Gauguin but it went for well over estimate. Sometimes I wish old Harvey Jay would get what he deserves and give us all a break.'

'I won't presume to ask what that might be,' Joanne said with a wry smile.

'There are several things that jump instantly to mind, one in particular, which I refrain to discuss with a lady present.'

'I can guess. Anyway enough of assholes like Old Man Friedman ... How about something infinitely better, like pastrami on rye?'

He didn't feel hungry, so he lied again. Sometimes he found Joanne's concern mildly irritating, it was like having his mother working for him.

'S'OK, thanks, I grabbed a dog on the street.' He looked at the clock on his desk, trying to calculate the time in England. 'Is it five hours, or four hours back in London? I forget when they change to summer time.'

'Five hours, it's eight-thirty in the morning. You want something to drink? I've got a couple of sodas.'

He didn't reply, hoping she would assume that he'd declined. A moment later Joanne appeared in person. 'I've got to slip out for fifteen minutes to pick up some panty hose, if that's OK.' She swivelled round, exposing a thick ladder running the length of one leg. 'I'm constantly laddering my stockings on that damn desk. You've got to get me a new one. Either that or you,' she pointed an accusing finger at Adam, 'buy the panty hose.' Gathering up her bag, she slung it over one shoulder. 'See you later.'

After Jo had left, Adam looked in his address book for Johnny Earle's number and dialled. A maid answered, informing him that Mr Earle was not available. As he was leaving a congratulatory message, he imagined Johnny striding around his new brownstone, hanging the Pissarro above the imported French fireplace circa 1796, and arranging the fine European antique vases on either side of the mantelpiece. Adam also visualized Anne-Marie Earle, the newly acquired French-born wife, hosting a cocktail party. Standing next to the painting, dressed in some elegant couture extravagance, holding the obligatory glass of vintage champagne and saying something trite like, 'Johnny 'as always 'ad a great appreciation for ze French Impressionists.' The only art Johnny Earle had seen whilst growing up on the streets of the Bronx had been graffiti. Adam doubted whether he would even have known the difference between an Impressionist and an Expressionist, or a Pissarro and a Picasso, until a few years ago.

Still holding the telephone to his ear, he punched out another number.

It was picked up after two rings.

'Hi Douglas! Adam Krantz here, how are you, hope I haven't disturbed you?'

'Hey, man! Well timed. Looks like you just got me out of nappy duty.'

Adam couldn't remember how old Douglas's kids were, or how many he had now, and was pleased when his friend changed the subject. 'I saw that piece about you in *Art World*, interesting article, great photograph. You look younger than ever, how do you do it?'

Adam smiled, 'I stopped having long lunches and reduced the alcohol intake. I only drink at night now.'

'I tried that,' Douglas said. 'It lasted about a month and

then I found I was drinking more between six and ten than if I'd just kept up a steady pace all day.' He chortled and Adam imagined Douglas Fraser's big brown eyes sparking with humour.

'So, what have I done to precipitate this unexpected call, Adam? I assume it's not merely social?'

'You assume correctly, Doug. Do you know a guy called Michael Gill?'

Douglas scratched his head. 'Tall, skinny, ash blond, works for Sotheby's?'

'Yeah, that's the one.'

'I've met him a couple of times, at auctions and a few social events, can't say I know him very well.'

'He approached me this morning in the lobby of our Sotheby's, told me about a guy he'd met in London last week who had a Monet to sell. *Le Port d'Honfleur*, which as you know used to belong to my grandfather.'

Douglas whistled. 'That's one serious picture, what did Gill say about it?'

'Oh, that he was dubious about the provenance, and had asked the guy to leave it with him to be authenticated. The guy must have got pissed 'cause he left with the Monet. Anyway he went on to say that it's rumoured Chris Fleming has a Monet he's trying to sell over there. Is it true, Doug?'

Adam heard Doug sigh. 'News travels fast. That Gill is like an old woman. I simply heard a whisper, and a muted one at that. I didn't call you, Adam, because I wanted to make a few discreet enquiries myself first. I haven't found out anything so far. As you well know, Fleming's a bloody rogue. This painting he claims he's got could well be a fake.

I didn't want to build your hopes up.' Douglas thought back to 1983, when he and Adam had travelled to Switzerland together, convinced they'd found six paintings from the Krantz collection. Douglas would never forget the crushing disappointment on Adam's face, or the dark depression that had lasted for days, after he had found out the paintings rightfully belonged to a French family.

'Have you got Fleming's number?' Adam asked.

'I think I might have, hang on a tick, I'll check.'

As Adam waited, he could hear the faint strains of a baby screaming in the background, then Douglas was back on the line.

'You're in luck. His gallery is 0171 730 9279. I've got no idea where he lives now, he used to be in Eaton Mews South. But he may have moved. You know how it is with spivs like Fleming, constantly changing address, for various reasons. It's a while since I spoke to him; to be honest I try not to, the man gives me the creeps.'

'Thanks, Doug. By the way, how is Claire?'

'As well as can be expected, under the stress of living with four children under ten, not to mention a fifth, coming up to forty-five and suffering a mid-life crisis. And Jennifer?'

'Past tense,' Adam said flatly.

'Sorry to hear that. In my experience female specimens as rare as Jennifer attract far too much attention, always tricky. I'd advise you to acquire a plain Jane no-nonsense type, get her banged up every couple of years, and play around; much more fun. At least you've always got some-one to warm your bed at night.'

'Thanks for the advice, but I'm not looking for another

wife right now. I may be coming across the pond very soon; if so, I'll look you up, I owe you lunch.'

'That would be splendid, Adam. I'd love to see you. Funnily enough your name came up in conversation last week. I'd just bought a set of Lautrec drawings at Christie's, and Peter Savill suggested I get in touch with you, said they were right up your street. I've still got them, I could do a very good deal.'

'When I'm in town, I promise to call. If you've still got the Lautrecs then, we might well have a deal.'

Douglas pushed. 'They might be gone by then, I could do you something now.'

Adam, resigned, said, 'If they go, they go.' Then, 'Nice talking to you, Doug.'

'Same here; I'll look forward to seeing you soon. Take care and a word of warning, watch your back dealing with Fleming.'

'Don't worry, I can handle myself, but thanks anyway.' Adam replaced the telephone, about to dial Chris Fleming's number, when he heard Joanne return. He crossed his office to lock the interconnecting door.

There was no reply from Fleming's gallery. He tried all afternoon without success, finally giving up at six-thirty, New York time. When Adam tried again the following day, his call was answered by Gavin Fox.

'I'd like to speak to Mr Fleming, please.'

'Who may I say is calling?' The voice had an effeminate ring.

'Tell him it's Adam Krantz from New York.'

'May I ask what it's in connection with?'

'No, I want to speak to Fleming, please.'

'Hold the line.' Adam heard the receiver slam down, then the sound of footsteps, then nothing. A few minutes later the same voice came back on the line. 'I'm very sorry, Mr Fleming's in a meeting at the moment. Can I take a message?'

Adam was seething. 'Tell him Adam Krantz is coming to London to collect his painting, *Le Port d'Honfleur*.' Adam put the phone down before the other man could respond.

'I'm going to London, Joanne.'

'How long will you be away this time? I don't want to harp on about my vacation, but if I don't get away soon I'm going to hit you with the divorce lawyer's fees.'

Adam sighed, he was holding a large bound book on Monet. 'This is really important, Joanne.'

'So is my vacation.'

'More important than reacquiring one of the most valuable paintings from the Krantz collection?' Opening the book, he pointed to a photograph showing *Le Port d'Honfleur*. He tapped the image. 'There it is, hanging in my grandfather's house in Berlin before the war. It's the only photograph of it *in situ*.'

Joanne was still looking at the crucial page when Adam explained. 'I think a dealer in London may be selling it. As sole beneficiary of the Krantz estate the painting belongs to me, but proving it is going to be difficult.' He slammed the book shut. 'Of course the dealer could have sold it on by now, or it could be a fake. Whatever, I've got to go see.'

Joanne's voice was wistful. 'Such wonderful brushwork, the awesome use of light and shade, such depth of emotion. I quite understand your need to go.'

242

'I think words are inadequate to describe his genius,' Adam said, meeting her eyes.

She was certain there were tears in his, and to hide her embarrassment, Joanne became brisk. 'When do you leave?'

'Tomorrow night.'

'I don't suppose I'll see you at all tomorrow then, you've got a busy schedule.' She looked in the diary. 'A meeting in the morning with the restorers, then lunch with Tom Meyers about the exhibition next month.' She looked up, 'I assume you want me to cancel cocktails at the Newtons?'

'Goddamn, I'd forgotten about that . . . Yeah, call Henry and apologize, explain I had to go away urgently. I won't make our tennis match on Sunday either, but tell him with the extra time to practise he might just beat me next week.' Adam started to walk towards the door, then turned back as if he'd forgotten something. He slapped the side of his head. 'Geez, I almost forgot, I need you to sort something out for me before you leave tonight, it's urgent.'

'Can't it wait until the morning? Give me a break, Adam; it's almost seven and I promised David . . .'

He dropped a folder on to her desk before she had finished speaking. Joanne looked at the name 'Jetsun Travel', then began to smile as she looked inside and read the heading on the itinerary. 'A week for two in the Bahamas.'

Adam pulled a long face. 'Sorry, Maui was full, anyway like I said it's the rainy season out there. The agent convinced me that Eluthera is beautiful, second honeymoon stuff.'

Joanne was beaming. 'I don't know what to say!'

'Well don't, listen, it's infinitely cheaper than any divorce lawyer's fees in this town.' They both laughed.

Joanne stood up, tapping him on the arm with the travel folder. 'Thanks, Adam, I really appreciate this.'

He winked. 'You're worth it. Like you constantly keep telling me, what would I do without you? In all honesty I'm not sure, but I am damn sure I don't want to find out.'

She flushed blood red and when Adam reached the door, she crossed her fingers on both hands. 'Safe journey and good luck; I'll be here holding a bottle of champagne when you get back with the Monet.'

Suddenly Adam's expression altered, the merriment of a few minutes before replaced by a single-minded look Joanne knew well.

When he spoke, his voice had lost all its joviality. 'If the Monet is there, I'm determined to have it. Whatever it takes.'

Chapter Fourteen

Adam looked at his watch for the third time, convinced she wasn't coming. He ordered a second Scotch and water, while finishing the first.

'Sorry I'm late.'

Adam got up from the bar stool at the sound of Kathryn's voice. He was wearing black trousers and a white cotton shirt unbuttoned at the neck, she could see a dark birthmark resembling a thumbprint below his Adam's apple. He was shorter than she remembered; she was wearing high heels, and they were almost the same height.

By way of apology, Kathryn explained, 'As I was about to leave home, my father called from America. His wife is seriously ill, she's having some revolutionary treatment in Dallas. Anyway, thanks for being patient.'

Adam guessed from the forced formality in her stilted words that she was nervous. 'The Scotch helped pass the time,' he said feeling unexpectedly nervous himself.

'I could use a little help myself. I think a large vodka and tonic might hit the spot, Stolichnaya if they have it.'

Adam ordered the drinks from the bar as the maître d' approached. 'Your table is ready, Mr Krantz.' They were led to a river-view table in the Savoy Grill. Politely Adam waited for Kathryn to be seated, thinking that the dark sienna shade of her dress suited her beige skin tone.

He came straight to the point.

'Thanks for agreeing to see me today, under the circumstances I thought you might take a rain check.'

With a wry smile, she said, 'I considered it, I must admit, but since the surroundings are slightly better than the last time we met, I decided to risk it.'

Making no comment, Adam took a cigarette from a pack of Marlboro Reds. 'Do you smoke?'

She helped herself, saying, 'I did, then I stopped, and started again. Recently.'

He lit her cigarette for her, then lighting his own inhaled deeply, exhaling before he spoke. 'Last week I was told by a guy from Sotheby's that a Monet was being shopped around the market. The painting in question belonged to my grandfather.' Adam took a sip of water. 'To cut a long story sideways, I traced the picture to a dealer in London. I've been to his place in the Fulham Road several times, it's locked up. I can't get a reply either by phone or fax, seems like the bird has flown. Probably sold the Monet, if he ever had it, for a few million bucks to some stinking rich Arab who has it hung in his palace in the Middle East somewhere.' The thought made him feel physically sick.

The maître d' reappeared to take their order. Kathryn had no appetite, she ordered without relish the first thing that caught her eye: fish of the day, which was sea bass, and vegetables.

Adam chose Dover sole. 'I love fish in England, especially when it's served from the corner shop with all that crunchy batter and fat French fries,' he enthused.

They both smiled in unison. Kathryn freshly amazed at how the warmth of Adam's smile transformed his face, like unexpected sunlight on a stark winter landscape. He in turn was moved by the sadness he saw in hers.

As he ground out his cigarette, he felt mildly disconcerted by this insight and said, 'Down to business,' rather more sharply than intended. 'What I didn't tell you in St Lucia was that before the war Ernst Von Trellenberg – Klaus's father – and my grandfather were friends. The Von Trellenbergs came to my grandfather's house in Berlin many times. In 1938 Ernst offered to help Joseph. Confiscation of Jewish property was becoming widespread, and exit visas were almost impossible to obtain. He advised my grandfather to surrender all his property to him, in something called an Aryanization programme.'

Kathryn asked, 'A what?'

'It was some scheme devised by the Nazis to enable them to steal, legally. Jews had to sign their possessions over to an Ayran, can you believe that?' Adam felt his anger rise. 'Why Joseph didn't listen to my grandmother is beyond me; why stay in Germany?'

He lit another cigarette as Kathryn said, 'I assume some people hung on hoping it would pass, we all do that sometimes. No one even in their worst nightmares could have predicted what happened next.'

'Yeah, I suppose, it's just difficult to imagine not wanting to get the hell out.' He inhaled. 'Anyway, Ernst promised to store the paintings – at least those considered "degenerate" – and to save the old masters from the greedy hands of Goering and co. Klaus, in his official capacity as an *Oberführer*, was to arrange for visas and safe passage to America for the entire family. Ernst, I'm sure, intended to keep his word but tragically he died a few weeks later.'

247

Adam stopped speaking, looking at Kathryn with narrowed eyes. As he continued to stare silently, her face blurred into that of Klaus as a young man. Tall, blond, handsome: *the archetypal fucking Aryan*.

Adam didn't recognize his own voice a moment later when he resumed. 'Klaus, unfortunately, did not inherit his father's integrity and my grandfather and four other relations lost their lives in various concentration camps.'

Kathryn felt sick. Sick to the stomach, sick to the back teeth, and every type of sick she could think of, just talking about Klaus Von Trellenberg. The urge to get up and leave was almost overpowering.

'Look, I'm sorry about your family, and about your lost art. I'm sorry about everything connected to Von Trellenberg. It's been hard for me these last few weeks, you know; hard to come to terms with who I am. Have you any idea how it feels to find out in your thirties that your grandfather was a Nazi war criminal?

'Well, it feels like being hit by a twenty-ton articulated truck. I'm recovering, but the pain just won't go away. It kind of sits in my gut like constant hunger. I look like him which is bad enough, but what's really scary is I keep wondering if I've inherited any of his flawed personality.'

From somewhere, Adam found he felt an unexpected wave of sympathy, and found himself realizing how tough it must be for her. He still wondered if she was hiding something. He'd thought so in St Lucia, but he wasn't sure now.

The food arrived, momentarily stemming their conversation. Adam bit into his fish as Kathryn cut a small potato in half, letting it slide down her throat.

'I know it's rough for you, but I've got to go down every avenue. It occurred to me that Von Trellenberg's capture kind of coincides with the Monet turning up, I thought you might have remembered something since we last met? A chance word perhaps? You were under a lot of stress when we interviewed you.'

She looked as if she was about to make a comment about her treatment in Tapion Prison, so he told her, 'By the way Mark Grossman was very sorry about all that rough stuff involving Uri. The man's a barbarian, he's been fighting Arabs for so long he's got no idea how to relate to civilized people. I thought you might like to know that he's no longer involved with the Centre.'

Kathryn preferred to change the subject. 'Is this Monet a very valuable painting?'

'About forty million dollars on the open market.' Adam elaborated. 'My father often talked passionately about *Le Port d'Honfleur*. He always said if there was one painting he would love to recover, it was that one. So in sentimental terms alone, its worth is immeasurable.'

'Were you close, you and your father?' Kathryn asked warily, afraid that he might think she was prying.

He seemed not to mind, and responded with ease. 'Very, I miss him desperately. We were more like brothers than father and son. There was rarely a cross word between us, and he was a wise old bird, my dad. He knew exactly how to handle his strong-willed, high-spirited son! He was only seventeen, the same age as my son now, when he arrived in America with my grandmother as an impoverished German immigrant. But he became an American, a very wealthy one. Yet Ben never lost his priorities, he could have lunch with a Hearst or a Rothschild, then a few hours later play bridge with the storekeeper from his old neighbourhood.' Adam swallowed hard.

He spoke of his father with such obvious affection that it filled Kathryn with envy, and a sense of loss.

'Is *your* father still around?' Adam asked.

'He left home when I was nine and I didn't see much of him after that. He's a consultant surgeon, his life has been devoted to fighting cancer. He's always travelled extensively, and after he remarried, his new wife and I didn't hit it off. I suppose I was very difficult, understandably, and she's intolerant. I'm afraid it doesn't make for happy families. I used to joke with my friends at university when they were writing psychology essays, look no further than my dysfunctional family for material: divorce, bitterness, loneliness, resentment, jealousy, repression and tragedy – all in there. About the only thing missing is murder.' She paused. 'Sorry, I almost forgot. My grandfather has provided that, now we've got the lot.

'The trouble is, I'm the repressive type, and all the years of *storing* take a hell of a lot of sorting out. I've done the therapy trip, which has helped a lot. At least now I try not to blame myself too much, and I'm getting better at not taking on other people's problems.'

'Talking about therapy,' Adam chimed in, 'I went to see a shrink about ten months ago after my wife and I split up. I came out of the office convinced the guy was more fucked up than me, and for that he charges two hundred and twenty bucks an hour.'

She laughed properly for the first time in weeks.

'Is there someone special in your life right now, Kathryn?'

'Sort of.'

'What does that mean?'

'OK, I have someone, but we live separately and do lots of separate things. His name's Jack McGowan. He's a lot older than me, fifty-eight next birthday. We share, how can I put it?' She searched for the right words, 'An ambivalent relationship, which is fine with me.'

Adam made no comment.

'When I first met Jack he was married, but when we met again later, that was over in all but name. So we started to see each other. He's very good to me; you know, supportive emotionally.'

Adam asked, then wondered why he had, 'Are you in love with him?'

Kathryn forked a large piece of bass, thinking about her reply. 'I'm not sure, sometimes I think I am, then there are other times when I know I'm not. I suppose the fact that I question it means no. Let's say I'm in *need* with him.'

It didn't take a degree in psychology to work out that the guy was a surrogate father figure, Adam decided. He found himself thinking that she deserved more, then questioned why he should care.

'And you, Adam; separated, you said?'

'Almost divorced. I keep hanging on, hoping we might get it back together. She blames me for neglecting or failing to see her needs. On reflection she's probably right, but I think that our marriage really started to fall apart because Jennifer got caught up with a crazy bunch. I call them

251

the Armani Angels. Wealthy, privileged, fucked-up people, who think their money gives them the right to live apart from the rest of the world on their own terms, with their own perverse set of rules. Anyway, the inevitable happened, she met someone else. It's really tough on Calvin, our only son, he's just about to embark on the wonderful trip of adulthood. Thank God as kids we're spared the reality of life! Sorry to sound such a hardened cynic, but life sucks sometimes.'

'Have you got a girlfriend?'

'Nobody special. When I fall, I fall hard. If things don't work out with Jennifer, I don't think I'll take that trip again.' He glanced at her empty glass. 'Sorry! With all this talking, I forgot to order wine, what would you like?'

'Nothing for me, thanks, the water's fine.'

Adam ordered a glass of red wine, then cleared his plate. Kathryn had left half of her food. He pointed to her littered plate. 'Not hungry?'

She lied. 'I had a big breakfast.' Then moving her plate to one side, she placed her palms flat on the table, studying her fingernails. 'Adam, I think I should tell you something that my grandfather said. It might be important.'

Adam could barely conceal his interest.

'I've been debating with myself whether or not to mention it since you called me yesterday morning. But I really want to help you if I can. When I met Klaus, albeit briefly, he said something weird just minutes before his arrest. He whispered three German words to me, *Schlafen mit Geistern*. That means "Sleeping with ghosts".'

'Is that all?'

'That's all, I'm afraid.' She sensed his disappointment. 'I

haven't got a clue what it means. I was going to contact my mother's sister Ingrid to see if she can throw some light on the matter, but apparently she's in Germany visiting a friend.'

'The ramblings of senility?' Adam suggested.

'No, I don't think so. Klaus had all his faculties, he was extremely articulate and bright. I didn't think about it at the time, but now I believe he was trying to convey something to me, some sort of message. I had hoped it might mean something to you, the name of a painting perhaps?'

Adam racked his brains. 'Nothing springs instantly to mind, possibly the title of a book, in German, some sort of code?' He gave up as the waiter arrived with the dessert trolley.

Kathryn declined and Adam waved a hand to indicate his own refusal, asking her, 'Would you like coffee?'

'No thanks.'

He ordered a double espresso for himself as Kathryn pushed her chair back saying, 'I've got to go, I'm due in a meeting at two-thirty, it's almost that now.'

Adam rose, 'If you remember anything else, I'm staying at the Berkeley.' He extracted a business card from his inside pocket and scribbled his room number on the back. 'I'll be in London for a few more days, I'm going to fish around the trade a bit more, see what I can dig up on Fleming.'

The name struck a chord in her memory. 'Who's Fleming?'

'Chris Fleming, he's the dealer I've been trying to locate. At best he's an eccentric rogue, at worst a goddamn crook.'

Fleming, Fleming. She ran the name through her head,

positive she had heard it before, then remembered her manners, 'Thanks for lunch, Adam. I enjoyed it very much.'

'You sound surprised!' His face broke into the dazzling, knock-'em-dead smile again.

He could turn a bloody nun on, Kathryn thought, returning his smile with a pretty impressive one herself. 'I am a bit; the last time we met you were . . . how can I put it?'

'Any way you like, remember I'm American.'

She wasn't sure what he meant by that, and choosing her words carefully, said, 'You were *emotionally disturbed*.'

Adam burst out laughing, so loud that several people turned their heads in his direction.

'Did I say something funny?'

'You English are so polite! I acted like a goddamn asshole in St Lucia, not only to you I might add. Mark's still pissed at me.'

'You're right, you were an asshole, but you had good reason to be. You were seriously pissed off.'

'Now you're talking my language, Kathryn. And, look, thanks again for coming.' He hesitated. 'You can call me any time, even if it's just to talk.'

In that split second, Kathryn felt a slight sexual *frisson* pass between them, dismissing it a moment later as ridiculous. Why would Adam Krantz want anything to do with the granddaughter of the man who had caused his family so much pain?

She wished him goodbye and good luck, and left him standing at the table, watching her retreating figure as he had done in St Lucia.

He found himself hoping she would call, then questioned his motives for wanting to speak to her again. *Don't ever forget she's a Von Trellenberg,* he reminded himself, ordering a large Scotch on the rocks, pushing thoughts of Kathryn resolutely out of his mind.

Stefan Lang answered the telephone after the first ring. He was surprised to hear Kathryn. 'Stefan, do you know when your mother's coming home?' Her voice, he noted, was stiff and tinged with disdain. *Kathy, Kathy, Bitch Kathy,* he repeated in his head.

'Why?' he asked.

She suppressed her irritation. 'Why do you think? I want to speak to her. Do you know or not, Stefan?' She waited for him to speak, but she could hear loud rock music in the background and suspected that he was stoned.

Stefan yawned. 'I've got no idea when she's coming back or where she's staying now. If she calls, I'll tell her you asked.'

Kathryn was about to say more when the phone went dead. Shaking with anger, she slammed it down, and was about to pick it up again when it rang. It was Jack.

'Kathryn, I'm home.'

'How was it?'

'Bloody awful flight, we were delayed coming out of Dubai. But we got the contract. Deal done.' Jack was happy. 'Fancy coming over for a quick bite here, or we can slip out to the bistro round the corner?'

Kathryn was tired, and didn't feel like driving over to Hampstead. 'Sorry, Jack, I've had a hard day. I'm wrecked, I'm going to have an early night.'

'We can both have an early night if you like?'

She groaned inwardly. 'I'm *really* tired, Jack, you know dead-on-my-feet tired, I'm trying to get this Deception job finished before my sabbatical. I think Rod's hoping to kill me before I get a chance to enjoy the break.'

Jack still wouldn't take no for an answer. 'It's half six now, I'll send Tom over to pick you up. Mrs P. can prepare a light supper here and Tom can take you home any time you like, you can still be in bed by ten.'

Kathryn felt like screaming. Instead she relented. 'OK, compromise: I'll pop over for a drink, but I don't want anything to eat, and don't moan if I'm lousy company.'

When the chauffeur rang her doorbell half an hour later, she had changed from her business suit into jeans and a shirt. Soon she was sitting in the back of the sleek Bentley – consumed by thoughts of Adam Krantz. She wanted to help him trace his grandfather's lost art, and asked herself why the compulsion was so strong. Was it merely to eradicate the guilt concerning her own grandfather? That was part of it she knew, but it was the other part she was afraid to confront. Dr Gillman had asked her if she was attracted to Adam. Now she asked herself the same question, and was forced to admit she was extremely attracted to him. Helping him would not only give her an excuse to keep in touch, it would also give him a reason to be grateful. A slow smile creased her face: *who knows what could develop out of gratitude?*

When Kathryn arrived, she was told by Mrs Peacock that Jack was changing and would be down in a few minutes. She refused a drink, then remembered something she had forgotten to tell Rod and asked if she could use the telephone. Sitting down behind Jack's desk, she looked at the photograph of his daughter Laraine on her twenty-first birthday. There was no resemblance to the pitifully thin girl she had seen in a paparazzo shot weeks before her death.

As she waited for Rod to reply, Kathryn picked up a pencil and began doodling on a small notepad. It was then that she saw the name 'Fleming' with an address next to it. A bell rang in her head, and it all came back to her now. *There's a Mr Christopher Fleming on the telephone for you.* She'd forgotten what she wanted to say to Rod and, replacing the phone, she stared at Jack's handwriting – jumping like a scared rabbit when a moment later Jack himself appeared at her side.

'Sorry, Kathryn, did I startle you?'

'No, I mean yes.'

'Make up your mind; anyway who did you expect? There's only me and Peacock in the house.'

Jack leaned against the edge of the desk, he was dressed casually in charcoal sports slacks and a pale grey cashmere sweater.

Kathryn stood up and, straying to the window on the far side of the room, she looked out on to the neat front garden. Turning to face him, she asked, 'Have you ever heard of a painting by Claude Monet called *Le Port d'Honfleur?*'

Kathryn observed Jack's reaction with interest. His features were composed in what he and she both knew was a mask of indifference. He replied in his usual ambiguous manner.

'Why, should I have?'

Frowning, Kathryn said, 'It infuriates me, Jack, when

257

you answer a question with a question. Why can't you be like other people and just talk straight.'

'Because, my sweet, I'm not like other people.' He joined her at the window, aware of her rigid body language. He pecked the end of her nose, very curious to know why she had mentioned the Monet.

'Why do you ask, Kathryn?'

'I asked you first; just *tell* me, have you ever heard of the picture? It's a simple enough question, why all the secrecy?'

'OK, I'll tell you on one condition.'

'What?'

'That you tell me why you want to know. If you do, I promise to tell you the truth.'

'For Christ's sake, Jack, have you heard of the painting or not?' She felt her anger rise.

'Yes, I have. Now tell me why you want to know?'

Smoothing her hair back with both hands, she took a deep breath. 'There's something I haven't told you yet, I simply didn't want to talk about it at the time.' She took another deep breath. 'When I was in St Lucia, I was arrested and imprisoned overnight in Tapion Women's Prison. I was interrogated by three men from the Horowitz Centre about my gran—' She stopped abruptly, unable to bring herself to say 'grandfather', finishing instead with 'Klaus Von Trellenberg'.

Jack looked quizzical. 'Why did they question *you*?'

This was the bit she'd been dreading, she felt as if her guts had been tied in a tight knot. 'Klaus Von Trellenberg was my grandfather.' Kathryn waited for his reaction, anticipating repulsion, rejection, horror even. But she saw only shock.

258

Jack had read about the Nazi in the newspapers. He could not have been any more astonished if someone had just told him his eighty-six-year-old mother had run off with a toy boy. In an incredulous voice, he said, 'So *that's* why you went to St Lucia?'

She nodded. 'It's a long story, one I'd rather tell you later if you don't mind.' Kathryn sounded weary, and for once he knew better than to push.

'The men who questioned me wanted to know if he, Klaus that is, had mentioned any other Nazis in hiding, or said anything unusual when I met him. I was terrified; I just wanted to get out of there and eventually, after about an hour, they let me go. When it was all over, I wanted to forget, obliterate it from my mind, that's the reason I didn't confide in you.'

'What a terrible experience! They had no right to interrogate you without a lawyer present. If I'd known sooner, I'd have taken them to the Court of Human Rights. Fanatical zealots all of them!' Jack took her hand in his; he stroked it very gently as she continued.

'I was beginning to forget the entire episode, when I had a call from a man called Adam Krantz. He's the son of Benjamin Krantz, a German Jew who emigrated to America with his mother before the war. To cut a long story short, Adam was one of the men who interrogated me in prison. He's an art dealer, as his father was before him. Apparently his grandfather owned an important art collection before the war; a lot of it was stolen or destroyed. Anyway Adam found out that a dealer in London was selling *Le Port d'Honfleur*, a Monet once owned by his grandfather. He claims it was stolen, and belongs to him.'

Christopher Fleming's snivelling assurances echoed in Jack's head, and he had to muster up every ounce of willpower to keep his rising temper under control.

'During lunch yesterday, Adam mentioned the dealer's name – Fleming. I knew I'd heard the name before, but I didn't know where or when. A few minutes before you came into the room, I was trying to call Rod and I saw the name on your notepad. Then I remembered Peacock interrupting our supper to tell you Christopher Fleming was on the phone; you know, it was just after you got back from the Middle East.'

Adjusting his glasses, Jack played for time. 'Yes, I remember, he called me to say he had a painting for sale, the Monet you've mentioned. Fleming's a crook, he was involved in a forgery scam a while back that caused quite a furore in the art world. But he hired a hot-shot lawyer, probably using the money he'd made, and got off with a fine. He left the country not long afterwards. When he rang here that evening it was the first I'd heard of him for a long time. He offered me the painting and I said I'd get back to him. I then did a little investigative research and discovered that the Monet had in fact belonged to the Krantz family, and had been destroyed by the Russians at the end of the war. I assumed Fleming was up to his old tricks again, trying to sell me a fake, so obviously I didn't return his call.'

Moving closer to her, he asked, 'Now does that answer your question?'

She pecked his cheek. 'Absolutely, have you any idea where Fleming is now?'

He laughed. 'Probably in the South of France spending

the loot he's made from the sale of the "Monet".'

'Many a true word said in jest,' Kathryn commented.

Jack's mind raced; he knew Fleming had left the country, he hoped for good. 'Let's forget Fleming, I'm dying for a large gin and tonic and burning with curiosity about your trip to St Lucia.'

Kathryn tried to smile but it was a weak attempt. She even considered feigning a migraine, an idea quickly abandoned at the thought of the ensuing fuss. She watched Jack cross the room, calling for Peacock to get them a drink. Gritting her teeth, she followed, vowing to stay for only one.

Chapter Fifteen

It was almost nine when Tom dropped her off at home. The chauffeur waited until she had opened the door, before pulling away from the kerb with a wave. Kathryn made a mug of tea, she felt drained from Jack's barrage of questions, and the retelling and the reliving of her time in St Lucia. Jack had wanted her to stay, and had succeeded in making her feel bad because she wanted to go. Cupping her mug of tea in both hands, she sat at her small cluttered desk in the corner of the living room. 'Your life's a mess,' she muttered, placing her mug on top of a pile of unpaid, overdue bills. She called Rod again; he wasn't at home and she left a message asking him to reach her asap.

Kathryn then slid her hand inside the pocket of her jeans, pulling out a crumpled slip. With the flat of her hand, she smoothed the wrinkles out of the paper, then sorted through a drawer to find Adam Krantz's business card. She flipped it over, reading his room number at the Berkeley on the back.

Adam answered the phone after two rings.

'Hi Adam, it's Kathryn.'

'Funny you should call, I was just thinking about you.'

Kathryn felt herself flush. 'Yesterday at lunch you mentioned a man called Fleming.'

'Yeah, Fleming's the dealer I think may have bought the painting from the mystery man who was touting it around town.'

Kathryn said, 'I think I may know where to find Fleming. I think we should talk.'

'Can you come over here?' Adam suggested.

She didn't feel like going out again and asked, 'Have you eaten?'

'Yes, but it was a long time ago.'

'Well, how about you come over here . . . I'll rustle up something.'

There was no hesitation at the other end. 'Where are you, Kathryn?'

She gave him the address, and he announced, 'I'll be there within twenty minutes.'

When Kathryn put down the phone, she felt instantly revitalized. She sprinted like a two-year-old filly into the kitchen, rummaging in her pantry where she found a pack of *linguine* pasta, and a jar of tomato and basil sauce.

The doorbell rang exactly eighteen minutes later. She was smiling when she opened the door. 'Come through,' she said leading her visitor across the hall into the drawing room. She was pleased it was Wednesday, the Portuguese maid had been and the house was comparatively neat.

'Make yourself comfortable,' Kathryn was saying, 'I'll get us a drink, what would you like?'

Adam's eyes roamed the room. 'Scotch on the rocks.'

Her face fell. 'Sorry, no whisky, a little brandy perhaps, and enough gin to ruin a hundred mothers.'

Adam wasn't sure what she meant, and put it down to

not being British. Constantly baffled by the hundreds of weird sayings and colloquialisms, he'd stopped asking people to explain.

'Champagne any good?'

He grinned. 'OK, if you insist.'

She left the room and Adam took the opportunity to look around. The house had a strong female aura and he supposed that was what was missing in his own apartment. He couldn't understand why, since it had been decorated by a raving queen. Lighting a cigarette, he searched for an ashtray amongst the eclectic mix of antiques and quirky *objets d'art*: a juxtaposition of elegant fabrics and eccentric furnishing touches that seemed to work. He admired an amber dowry chest that Kathryn had bought on a trip to Morocco, and an exquisite mother-of-pearl box she had lovingly carried back from India along with the assorted kilm cushions and tapestry throws. He suspected that nothing was there to impress, but to be enjoyed. The room exuded vitality, yet was strangely soothing. It was warm, it was a home, and Adam felt extremely comfortable. A framed photograph caught his eye, he stooped to pick it up from a small side table. It was of Kathryn, she was wearing a simple ankle-length black evening dress. He thought she looked very beautiful with her hair piled high on top of her head. She was smiling into the face of an older man dressed in black tie.

Not making a sound, Kathryn had crept up behind him. 'That's Jack McGowan, chairman of Anglo Gowan. You may have heard of the company?'

Adam shook his head. 'Not much of a corporate man myself: all those stuffed shirts and grey suits playing high finance and crazy mind games. I can't think of anything worse than a board meeting.'

Kathryn agreed but didn't say so. 'That photo was taken a few months ago at a charity do, one of those awful boring dinners where everyone talks incessantly about everyone else.'

'You don't sound very enthusiastic.'

'I'm not,' she said emphatically, handing him a glass of champagne. 'Jack drags me kicking to a lot of social events I could well do without. You know the "A list" round of openings, first nights, book launches, etc. I suppose I'm just too damn lazy. I prefer to stay home in jeans and sweater, read, watch a good movie or entertain friends.'

'I had the same problem with Jennifer. She dragged me along to her fancy parties until eventually I put my foot down, refusing to go to all but a very select few.' He sipped the champagne. 'Mmm, good stuff!' If he'd had to place it, he'd have said it was Krug 1982.

'How long have you lived here, Kathryn?' he asked as she sat down on the sofa.

'Since my husband Tony and I split, almost four years. I've just inherited my mother's house, which I'm selling and I'm thinking about investing in a small Victorian terraced job. I've got my eye on a particularly lovely one in Chelsea.'

'I don't know why you want to move from here. I think this is really great, it's got a good feel.'

'I'm pleased you like it. Jack thinks it's too fussy, but then he likes clean, simple lines; no clutter. It's just as well we live separately. My untidiness would drive him crazy. Tony was fanatically tidy as well.'

She stopped speaking, her mind drifting back to an ugly incident when her ex-husband had screamed at her for not emptying an ashtray. She had retaliated by throwing it at him. Refusing to dwell on the subsequent events of that evening, she concentrated her attention on Adam, who thought by now he'd covered all the small talk necessary to be polite.

'So, tell me about Fleming.'

Kathryn stood up, she crossed to her desk and returned holding a piece of paper which she handed to him. 'Christopher Fleming's address in the country.'

'Where did you get this?'

Reluctant to involve Jack, she said, 'When you mentioned the name 'Fleming', it rang a bell. That's because a few years ago he was involved in a forgery scam, and I remembered that a reporter friend of mine had covered the story. I told him I needed to get in touch with Fleming urgently; I got the address from him this evening.' With a pang of contrition, she consoled herself with the fact that she had only told one lie. 'I thought we might go down there tomorrow?' She looked to him for confirmation.

Adam noted the 'we', but made no comment. He was studying the address in Sussex. 'How long will it take to drive down?'

'Depending on time of day, and traffic, a couple of hours.'

Adam wrinkled his nose. 'Do I smell burning?'

Kathryn jumped up. 'Oh shit, the pasta!' She ran into the kitchen, and was lifting a boiling pan off the gas hob when Adam appeared at the open door.

'Need a hand?'

'I need someone else to cook. I'm hopeless, just as well

I live alone.' She grimaced when Adam rescued another pan. He held the bubbling mass of tomato and basil sauce over the sink.

'We made it, I *think*.' He sounded more hopeful than he felt, knowing that he could grab a club sandwich from room service when he got back to the hotel.

'I hope you don't like your pasta *al dente*?' Kathryn said, using a colander to drain the boiling water off a mountain of angel hair *linguine*.

He plucked a strand into his mouth, smacking his lips together. '*Bellissimo!*'

'Liar,' she said, grinning as she piled pasta into two deep bowls, pouring the sauce on top. Then rummaging in the untidy fridge to produce a hunk of what looked to Adam like mouldy Parmesan cheese, she pointed to a drawer on his right. 'The grater's in there, so do your stuff while I set the table.'

Kathryn left the kitchen clutching a black pepper mill and a basket containing four slices of French bread, the remnants of yesterday's loaf.

Adam, his nose wrinkling, grated the cheese on to a small plate. Balancing the bowls he carried everything into the living room. Kathryn was nowhere to be seen.

'I'm in here!'

He moved towards the sound coming from the other side of the hall. 'Here' was a small dining room, entirely candlelit, the warm light flickering across pale oak walls that to Adam looked original. The panelling was in fact a very good reproduction of the late eighteenth-century period. Gas flames licked three authentic-looking fake logs set in a small grate, and four tall tapered candles in delicate gilded candlesticks stood in the centre of a circular table. This was covered in an emerald green tablecloth finished with a darker green fringed border.

Taking the bowls from his outstretched hands, Kathryn placed them on two cork table mats. Humming an unrecognizable tune, she filled their glasses, putting the champagne bottle back on the table. Adam noticed that he'd been right about the label, it *was* Krug; but a year out with the date, it was 1983.

'Sit and eat,' she said, piling cheese on top of her pasta. Adam sat down, refusing the Parmesan when she passed the plate.

'It's good . . .' he said after a couple of mouthfuls.

'It's food!' she retorted. 'Anything tastes good when you're hungry.'

They both attacked the meal in silence, eating and drinking heartily, not stopping until they had almost finished. Using a chunk of bread to mop up the last few drops of watery sauce from the bottom of his bowl, Adam licked his lips then wiped them on a paper napkin.

'That was delicious, Kathryn.'

She agreed. 'It wasn't too bad considering I can't cook to save my life.' She stood up, beginning to clear the plates. 'No, stay where you are,' she said when he offered to help. 'I'm going to stick them in the dishwasher, and return posthaste with a bottle of good claret. An appreciation of fine wine was the only worthwhile thing Tony taught me,' she finished. She leaned forward. Her face, bathed in the soft glow of candlelight, seemed unreal to him, ghostly almost. The inclination to touch her luminous skin, if only to reassure himself it was not that of an apparition, was overpowering. After she had left the room, Adam breathed deeply, unsure of the emotions she was awakening in him.

When Kathryn returned, she was carrying a bottle of Margaux and two glasses. She poured, then settled back into the chair she had vacated. She felt light-headed and put it down to drinking on a partially empty stomach, afraid to admit that Adam was responsible.

He lit a cigarette, and handed her the open pack. She took one, and he lit hers, saying for want of something better, 'So, you were married; what happened?' She was grinning.

'Well, I think you can guess after tonight.' Sipping her wine, she looked down into the glass. When she looked up again, he noticed her eyes were the same shade as the slate roof on his mother's house after a downpour, and looked like they had been forced into their perfect almond shape by the width of her high cheekbones.

'Is there something wrong, Adam?' Kathryn enquired.

'No, why?'

'It's just that you were staring at me in a strange way.'

Slightly disconcerted by her awareness of his scrutiny, he said, 'You remind me of someone I knew once, that's all.' Adam paused, reluctant to say more, or to admit that she was possessed of an enigmatic sensuality that he found extremely provocative. 'You were telling me about your husband . . .'

'We were incompatible. Tony was, and still is I assume, an anarchist type, with an ego to match his temper. I got tired of feeding that ego; it was a ravenous creature, never satiated. I also got scared of his unpredictable rages, often violent. Tony liked the chase, the actual acquisition bored him very quickly; and the women he chose were usually drop dead gorgeous, as well as empty-headed.

'He was several years older than me, very good-looking in a rugged Steve McQueen sort of way. You know, the macho-man type. I suppose that's what attracted me in the first place, that and his sense of humour, he was very funny. Well, he made *me* laugh, certainly in the beginning. When things began to go wrong, I foolishly got pregnant. I lost my daughter.' Adam noticed she said 'my', and not 'our'.

'I suppose I thought a baby would fill the loneliness, or more simply I wanted something worthwhile to love. She was born prematurely at thirty-four weeks, and lived for three.' Kathryn's voice faded with the awareness that this was the first time she had talked about the loss of her baby to anyone except her father.

'I guess I blamed Tony; we all have to blame someone else for something that's too painful. Anyway after that, I couldn't bear him to touch me. It's weird, but when you stop loving someone, you see them as they really are, and often don't like what you've got. I had a hard time finding myself after we split. For a while, I was a wreck, an emotional bankrupt. After the divorce I reverted back to my maiden name. Doing that helped, and now at long last, I'm getting there.'

Adam sensed her vulnerability, he'd seen it briefly in the prison in Castries, the little-girl-lost quality lingering quietly beneath the protective suit of armour she obviously donned for her everyday life. The sudden urge to climb the wall that surrounded her, get inside her mind, and explore her innermost thoughts caught him off guard.

'After St Lucia I had a beam of instinctive wisdom so

270

powerful I couldn't ignore it. I know that sounds a bit dramatic, a tad corny even, but it's the best way to describe it. I've decided to do something I've wanted to do since I was a little girl. I've got this gut instinct.' Clenching her fist, she placed it next to her stomach.

'Am I allowed to ask what it is?'

'I don't want to talk about it yet, I'm afraid of tempting fate.'

'I know exactly what you mean . . .' Adam's mind drifted back in time to 1983, when he'd heard about several pictures in Switzerland believed to have been part of the Krantz collection. Kathryn saw his expression change, and rightly suspected he was thinking about his lost inheritance.

Throwing her head back, she drained the glass. Then stretching forward to grab the bottle, one of the tiny buttons on the front of her shirt popped open. She made no attempt to fasten it and he could detect the outline of one of her nipples through the side of the gap. Gulping his wine, Adam was powerless to stop wild notions running around his head. He envisioned Kathryn sitting in the same position as she was now, but perfectly still in a Degas pose: hair piled on top of her head as in the photograph of her with Jack, her body completely naked. Thighs slightly apart, this fantasy was of her cupping her breasts in a childlike manner, as if she had just discovered them, her expression innocent yet inviting.

'You understand, Adam, don't you . . .' It was more of a statement than a question.

Adam shook his head to dispel the tempting image. He'd totally forgotten what they'd been talking about. 'Yes, yes I do.' He set his half-empty glass down and, roughly pushing his chair back, stood up. Suddenly eager to leave, if only to quell the turbulence Kathryn had so unexpectedly aroused in him, he announced, 'I've got an early meeting tomorrow morning.' He was deliberately curt, a cover for his rising desire for her.

Surprised by this abrupt turn of events, yet sensing his agitation, she crossed the room to stand next to him. 'Going so soon, Adam, what a shame . . .'

Her nearness was unnerving, Adam muttered, 'Such is life, never enough time.' Then strolling into the hall, he slung his jacket over his shoulder, telling her, 'Thanks for the pasta, and for this.' He patted the side pocket of his jeans, where he'd put Fleming's address.

'My pleasure.' She deliberated about offering to drive him down to Sussex and finally made up her mind with the thought that she who hesitates is lost. 'I can drive you down to Fleming's tomorrow, if you like?'

Considering what her proximity was doing to him now, the thought of sharing the close confines of a car for several hours made Adam decline. 'Thanks for the offer, Kathryn, but this is something I want to do alone.'

Disappointed, but able to cover it with ease, she managed a thin smile. 'I understand, but you'll let me know how you get on?'

He nodded, 'Sure.'

'When do you leave London?'

'The day after tomorrow.'

He shifted from one foot to the other, raking thick fingers through thick hair, uncomfortable, eager to leave. 'Next time I'm in town, or if you're in New York, we must do something . . .' His voice trailed off.

'That would be nice,' she agreed lamely. Then taking a step towards him, she stretched forward to unlock the front door. The movement caused another button to open, revealing a patch of smooth beige-coloured skin.

Adam felt his throat dry up, then his lips and his entire mouth. His fingers itched to undo all the buttons and touch her breasts. *Just once wouldn't hurt*, the voice of lust whispered in his head. He grabbed her hand before it reached the lock. 'Goodnight, Kathryn,' holding it for a long moment; dropping it abruptly when she leaned forward, her lips parting slightly to rest on his cheek.

When her mouth found his, Adam stood riveted to the spot, like a dummy. Still he didn't move as she forced his lips open, finding his tongue. She sucked it into her own mouth greedily and Adam could not stay still a moment longer. His hands moved robot-like up the length of her back, and into her hair. With the tips of his thumbs he slowly caressed her neck, enjoying the smell of her, the softness, the warmth. She felt good, magic, he wanted more. Releasing his tongue, she used hers to lick first his teeth then his lips. Adam opened his mouth wide, devouring her face, her ears, any square inch of flesh he could find. Sweet Jesus, he wanted her, the intensity of his desire was reminiscent of the early years with Jennifer, only more violent.

Pushing her roughly against the wall, he grabbed the collar of her shirt and with both hands forcibly ripped her blouse apart. Several buttons flew into the air, and Adam stared at her large breasts, the dots of her nipples strained against white lace. She balanced against the wall, her arms above her head, her legs spread-eagled, reminding Adam of a crucifix. Without warning he felt a wave of nausea, his desire ebbing away as quickly as it had come.

Her eyes were closed, and when after a couple of minutes she opened them, Adam had backed off from her and was standing a few feet away, hands hanging by his sides. He mumbled, 'I'm sorry about the blouse,' stooping to retrieve the buttons, trying to hide his embarrassment, 'I'll buy you a new one.'

'No, I'll fix it,' she said, pulling her shirt together to cover her breasts, suddenly feeling acutely embarrassed herself – the words *'He doesn't want you'* banging in her head.

When Adam straightened up, he felt more composed. 'That was reckless of me, I kinda got carried away. These things happen sometimes.' Picking his jacket up from the floor, he dusted it off with the flat of his hand. Ashamed of the lust she'd awakened in him, and more than a little afraid of the violent passion she'd stirred, he inwardly apologized – *Sorry, Ben* – to his father, who was probably turning in his grave right now.

A hush descended. Adam stepped towards the door, crushing one of her blouse buttons underfoot, the noise sounded ridiculously loud like a crashing boulder. He was about to walk out when she spoke to him.

'Just tell me one thing before you go, Adam; did you stop because you don't fancy me, or did you stop because of who I am?'

Spinning round to face her, his expression resembled the one he'd worn the first time she'd met him in the prison cell in Castries, a mixture of aggression, and anguish. 'All right, Kathryn, you asked for it. You're a beautiful woman with a great body, I got carried away, that's all. When I was a young kid a big black guy from Brooklyn once said to me, a standing dick has no conscience. I think that about sums it up.'

Kathryn nodded mutely. There was nothing more to say.

She looks so sad, he thought, like a lost soul. He hesitated for a split second, battling with his inner turmoil, every instinct telling him to get the hell out before he lost control again. Finally, opening the door, he muttered goodbye. She didn't reply but he felt the weight of her body push the door shut. As he walked down Penzance Place, he found himself wishing Kathryn's grandfather had been Stalin, Jack the Ripper, Hannibal Lecter: any other monster but Klaus Von Trellenberg.

Chapter Sixteen

Gavin Fox was in the bathroom when he heard the car tyres crunch on the gravel drive in front of the house. He tweeked the curtain to peek out of the narrow window. A tall man was alighting from a white car, and a moment later the doorbell rang. As Gavin descended the stairs, he hoped it was the delivery of a small antique table he was expecting. He could not resist a quick glance at himself in the hall mirror before he opened the door.

'I'm looking for Mr Fleming. I believe he lives here?'

Gavin looked the stranger up and down in approval.

'He lives here sometimes, but he's not here at the moment. Can I help?'

The man stepped forward. 'Where is he?' He thrust his face close to Gavin.

There was something in those eyes that Gavin didn't like. 'I really don't think it's any of your business . . .' He started to push the door shut, feeling a quick thrill of fear as a foot was stuck out, stopping him.

'I've had a long drive, I think you should at least offer me a cup of tea.'

Gavin ignored this, pushing with all his strength against the door. But he wasn't strong enough and a second later the man was in his hall slamming the door shut and saying, 'Don't be alarmed' to his retreating figure.

The telephone was still in Gavin's hand when the stranger ripped the lead out of the wall and snarled, *'Where is Fleming?'*

Gavin whimpered when the man pinned him to the wall and clasped his throat, making the skin below the Adam's apple turn an ugly red.

Gavin knew Christopher had gone to Zurich, but had no idea when he was due back. It was a struggle to speak, he stuttered, 'Not here. Tomorrow, he's coming back tomorrow.'

'What time?'

Gavin picked a time at random. 'About twelve, said he'd be back for lunch.' The man released his grip a little, and Gavin felt his breathing return to normal.

'Good, I'll stay here until he arrives. You and me can have us a little party. And I hope you're right about tomorrow, faggot-face, 'cos I'm going to be very pissed if your cock-sucking boyfriend doesn't come back with my money. I might just break every fucking bone in your body.'

Detective Inspector Sean Edwards had one eye on his computer screen, and the other on Greg Henderson's back. No mean feat considering his desk was located at the far end of the long narrow office, and Henderson was standing close to the door. He strained to hear what Henderson was saying, but the babble of technology mixed with the incessant human banter made it impossible. Why had he wanted to be a policeman when he could have been an accountant like his mother had wanted; he should have listened to her!

Edwards saw his superior's back leave the room. He

concentrated properly on the screen, scanning a list of telephone numbers. Gavin Fox had made one hundred and four calls, in the month preceding his death. Most were to the gallery, to Christopher Fleming, another friend called Roland, and his mother. There were six, to the same number in one day, then a further four the following day. It didn't take Edwards long to trace the number to Anglo Gowan, 24 St James's, London.

'I've reason to believe that you purchased a painting from a Mr Christopher Fleming recently.'

Jack, his face a genial mask, smiled easily and said with just the merest a hint of curiosity, 'Yes that's correct, Inspector Edwards, why?'

'Mr Fleming, you may, or may not know, had a partner called Gavin Fox, they were also lovers. Mr Fox was found dead three days ago at his cottage in Sussex. Fleming has disappeared, he hasn't been seen since he locked up his gallery ten days ago. Mr Fox was murdered, stabbed to death.'

'I see,' Jack commented flatly, then picking up a glass of water from his desk took a sip, replacing the glass carefully on a solid silver place mat. 'Can I offer you refreshment, inspector? Tea, coffee, soft drink. Or a hard drink perhaps?'

Sean Edwards shook his head while extracting a pencil and notepad out of his worn tweed jacket, which was covered in what looked to Jack like dog hair.

'Please take a seat, inspector; you look uncomfortable.' *And untidy*, Jack thought.

The inspector sat down awkwardly on the edge of a chair. He faced Jack across his huge desk and, chewing the end of his pencil, thought how much he detested the Jack McGowans of this world. He'd met a few in his time; powerful, megalomaniac bastards who thought themselves impervious to the law. He suspected this man was no exception. The smooth smile and well-practised charm did not fool Sean, who knew they were part of an essential artifice to disarm the opponent. He also knew that Jack thought him a fool, and it would give him the greatest pleasure, nay joy, to drag him down to the station. As he wrote Jack's name on the top of the statement, he relished that image.

'So tell me, inspector, what's all this got to do with my painting?'

'The sale of the Monet, *Le Port d'Honfleur*, was the last transaction Mr Fleming and Gavin Fox made before Fleming disappeared and Fox was murdered.' Sean Edwards coughed, looking at his notes. 'How much did you pay for the picture, Mr McGowan?'

'I don't think that's any of your business,' Jack countered Edwards' steely gaze, his own not faltering for a second. 'Fleming was aware of my interest in French Impressionist work, particularly in Monet. It's an astonishing picture, quite unique. It was a quick and uncomplicated transaction. All above board, I might add.' Jack added, 'I do hope there's no problem with the painting, inspector?'

From inside his jacket, Edwards produced a Polaroid photograph; he handed it to Jack. 'Is that the picture?'

Jack nodded.

'According to an art expert from Sotheby's it's worth going on twenty-five million pounds. We found the Polaroid in Gavin Fox's cottage; his young assistant told us Mr Fleming had sold the painting to a man fitting your description. Strange to have no bill of sale, no bank deposit of any kind, no record of any financial transaction. How much did you pay for it, Mr McGowan?' Edwards sighed, 'I won't ask again.'

'Fourteen million pounds. And I have got a bill of sale,' Jack added defensively, then reminded himself quickly that he had no reason whatsoever to feel guilty. He used a small key to open a filing cabinet on the right-hand side of his desk, rummaging in the files for a few moments before pulling out a slip of paper. 'Here it is,' he said handing it to the policeman. 'Fleming must have destroyed his copy for some reason.'

Edwards studied it carefully. 'Can I have a copy of this, please?'

Jack took the slip of paper from the inspector's hand, 'Of course.'

'But there's still the matter of the actual money. Have you any idea what happened to the fourteen million pounds?'

Deliberating for a couple of seconds, Jack decided to tell the truth. He surmised correctly that Inspector Edwards was the dog-with-a-bone type of copper, tenacious and bloody-minded. 'Fleming agreed to drop the price if the money could be paid into an account in Switzerland, I can prove that I did in fact transfer nearly fourteen million into a numbered account.'

Making no comment, Edwards turned his attention to an oil painting on the wall opposite the desk. 'What a beautiful sight, not that I profess to know the first thing about art, but that . . .' He whistled. 'How much is something like that worth?'

Hiding his impatience with difficulty, Jack retorted sharply, 'It's a Degas. I bought it five years ago at Sotheby's. I paid four million pounds for it, it's worth a lot more now.'

'That brings me back to the Monet. I wonder why Fleming wanted to be paid abroad, why he kept no receipt, no record of the sale . . . It makes me think that the picture might have been stolen.'

Jack drummed his fingers on the arm of his chair. 'I bought it in good faith, inspector. I paid a price negotiated with a reputable dealer.'

At this Edwards' eyes rose. 'I hope you're not going to insult my intelligence by trying to convince me that you didn't know Christopher Fleming was a crook, not a man known for his integrity.'

'Listen, inspector, I've got no reason to defend my decision to purchase a painting from a known dealer for a sum of money we both agreed. It's called a deal; you know, buy sell, buy sell. I've been doing it since I was twelve.'

'Where is the painting now?'

'It's in a bank vault, until I decide where to hang it.'

'I'd like to see it if you don't mind.'

Jack stood up, his fingertips pressing down so hard on top of his desk that the flesh under the nails turned white. 'I *do* mind, inspector. I'm a very busy man and I can't see what relevance this has to Mr Fox's death.'

Edwards remained impassive, a slight quizzical movement of his straight eyebrows the only indication that he'd heard. 'I am investigating a murder case, and I'd be obliged if you cooperated, Mr McGowan. You know how it is, the police are pedantic bastards at the best of times. Either you produce the painting or I get a warrant to search.'

Jack held up his hand. 'OK, OK, inspector, I really wouldn't want you to have to go to such lengths, all that exhausting pen pushing. I'll arrange to have the painting brought to my office tomorrow morning, if that's convenient?'

Edwards rose, fronds of fine brown hair dropping on to his brow. He made a feeble effort to smile, then stuffed his pad back into his pocket. To Jack, he looked more like an impoverished farmer than a detective inspector from Scotland Yard.

'Tomorrow morning will be fine, Mr McGowan, around ten OK? Meanwhile I'd advise you not to discuss this with anyone, and please don't make any arrangements to leave the country at the moment.'

Aware that the policeman was trying to intimidate him, Jack grinned broadly, steering him towards the door. 'I'm entirely at your disposal; I look forward to showing you the most stunning piece of art you're ever likely to see outside a gallery. Until demain then, Monsieur Poirot, at ten o'clock.'

The spurious smile slipped from the inspector's face in response to this mockery, revealing his own thinly disguised contempt. 'I'll look forward to it,' he snapped, then opening the door himself, he left without saying goodbye.

The following morning Jack was spraying his office with air freshener when Kathryn burst in, unexpected and unannounced. She threw a tabloid newspaper on to his desk, saying, 'Why did you lie to me, Jack?'

The headline ran: GAY SEX SLAYING. Quickly he

scanned the accompanying news item, not speaking: *Gavin Fox, art dealer, has been found bludgeoned to death in his Sussex cottage. Christopher Fleming, Gavin's gay lover and a notorious art dealer, was convicted of a forgery scam seven years ago. Fleming has disappeared after reputedly selling a priceless Monet to Jack McGowan, chairman of Anglo Gowan. Detective Inspector Edwards of New Scotland Yard is heading the investigation, and would like to question anyone* . . . Jack stopped reading to look at the old grainy photograph of Fleming and Gavin, posing in what looked like a holiday snap.

Finally he snarled, 'It didn't take long for that bloody inspector to blab to the press, did it?' He threw the newspaper into the wastebin with a disgusted grunt.

'I asked you a question, Jack,' Kathryn insisted.

'I'm sick of questions! Yesterday I had Inspector Plod hurling them at me with manufactured politeness; and now you, shouting at me in an accusing manner. A few minutes ago, I had the same inspector and his foul-smelling sidekick crawling all over my office. I'm up to *here* with questions,' he indicated an imaginary space above his head.

'You owe me an explanation, Jack.'

'OK Kathryn, calm down. I bought a painting from Fleming. I admit I knew the man was flaky, that was a risk I was willing to take. I didn't want to make a fuss, it was that simple. I swear I didn't know the painting had a dubious provenance.'

'You lied to me, though, you said you never returned Fleming's call, you said—'

Jack slammed a clenched fist down on to the top of his desk, scattering a pile of papers and overturning a silver inkwell. His voice rose to a hoarse roar and he was shaking, red blotches breaking out across his neck and temples.

'What I do with *my* money is *my* business. If I chose not to discuss it with you or anyone else, that is also *my* business.' He pointed a finger in her direction. 'Do you understand?'

He didn't wait for her to reply. 'You don't own me, Kathryn, I'm not answerable to you, or anybody else for that matter. I can't understand what all the fuss is about. If I'd screwed your best friend behind your back, left you at the altar, or lied to you about something important like telling you I'm not married when I am, then you might be entitled to your ridiculous rancour. So I told you a stupid little lie? Big deal! Don't try to tell me that you've never lied before . . . You storm in here, all flashing eyes, looking so virtuous, I could throw up.'

Kathryn recoiled as if stung.

'I'm sorry, Jack, if that's the way I make you feel, I think it's time I left.'

She marched towards the door; a moment later he was running around the desk to stand in her path. He reached out to her with both hands; it was a definite appeal.

'Grow up, Kathryn, avoiding the truth isn't such a heinous crime. I've got to do it virtually every day of my life.'

'Not to me you don't, Jack, at least not any more.'

Later that day when Adam returned to the Berkeley, the pretty receptionist handed him an envelope with his room key. 'Message for you, Mr Krantz. And are you still checking out tomorrow? We have a request for the room.'

Adam was smiling. 'Yes, I'll be leaving tomorrow morning around ten, can you organize a taxi to Heathrow, please.'

She nodded then with a dreamy expression watched him walk across the lobby, trying to remember the name of the American film star this guest reminded her of. Her colleague had suggested Tom Cruise, but she knew it wasn't him.

The lift doors swished open, Adam stepped inside pressing Floor Six. Tearing open the envelope, he scanned the big square handwriting, beginning to read.

Dear Adam,

I hope this letter catches you before you leave for Paris. I wanted to write to you rather than speak, sometimes it's easier to express yourself in the written word, well it is for me. I half expected you to call after you went down to Sussex. And when I didn't hear from you, I assumed you'd drawn a blank. After you left my place the other night I was filled with such self-loathing it was scary, and on that note I want you to know I understand completely why you rejected my advances.

I was shocked this morning, when I found out about the murder of Gavin Fox, and that Jack McGowan had bought the Monet from Fleming. Remember I told you I'd got Fleming's address from a journalist? Well, I lied. I'd seen it written on a notepad at Jack's house. I want you to know that I had no idea he had bought the Monet; I just lied because I didn't want to involve him.

If you need to speak to me about any of this, you know where I am.
Take care,
Kathryn.

Screwing the letter into a tight ball as soon as he reached his room, Adam sat on the edge of the bed. He tried to remember what Kathryn had said about Jack McGowan. He was chairman of a big company, something . . . Gowan. Picking up the phone, he asked the concierge to send up all the daily papers. When the bellman arrived ten minutes later, Adam had remembered the name. He gave the kid a five-dollar tip, then scoured the newspapers, reading the mass coverage quickly. Then he got Anglo Gowan's number from Directory Enquiries, and taking a deep breath, punched it out with such ferocity his fingertips stung.

A receptionist answered. 'Good afternoon, Anglo Gowan.'

'I'd like to speak to Mr McGowan.'

'I'm afraid Mr McGowan's in a meeting, can I put you through to his secretary?'

'Yes please,' Adam said, drumming his fingers in rhythm with a drumming in his temple.

'Fiona Cartwright . . .' Her sharp voice reminded Adam of the Moneypenny character in the Bond movies. He imagined the speaker with severe hair and black-rimmed spectacles. The reality would have surprised him. Fiona was the opposite: small, plump, blonde and very wholesome.

'I'd like to speak to Mr McGowan urgently.'

'He's in a meeting. May I ask what it's concerning, perhaps I can help?'

'I doubt it, I want to speak to him. When will he be

through?' Adam could hear the secretary tutting and papers rustling as she consulted a diary.

'The meeting was due to end twenty minutes ago, but he's got another at three. Can I take your name and number and get him to call you back?'

'Listen, this is very urgent; can't you drag him out for a couple of minutes?'

'No, I cannot,' she retorted indignantly, muttering under her breath something about Americans being extremely rude, then in a distinctly curt tone, 'May I suggest you leave a message.'

Adam had no choice. 'My name is Adam Krantz and I'm staying at the—' he paused, then said, 'On second thoughts, tell Mr McGowan I'm on my way over. I should be at your place in less than half an hour.'

Exasperated, Fiona said, 'I must warn you he may not be able to see you.'

'I think when he knows what it's about, he'll make time.' Adam put the phone down before the bewildered Fiona could reply.

He was waiting in the reception of Anglo Gowan as Jack came out of his boardroom, booming voice resounding down the hall ... 'Lunch with Robert Stigwood on Friday will be fine, set it up, Paul, just the three of us.'

When Jack walked into reception, Fiona caught his eye. She was pointing at Adam's back.

In two long strides, Jack was addressing the back of Adam's head. 'I believe you want to speak to me?'

Adam turned to face him. 'You don't know me, my name is Adam Krantz. I'm a New York art dealer and I believe you've got something that belongs to me.'

Jack raised his eyes. 'I have?'

'I believe you recently bought a painting called *Le Port d'Honfleur* by Claude Monet.'

Jack said, 'I really don't think that's any of your business.'

'I have proof that *Le Port d'Honfleur* was stolen from my grandfather before the war. I am his sole beneficiary. The painting belongs to me.'

Jack could feel a muscle in the side of his cheek jumping uncontrollably, a sure sign that he was getting irate. 'I know nothing about the painting, so if you'll excuse me, Mr . . .'

'Krantz. Adam Krantz, grandson of Joseph Krantz, a German Jew who was forcibly relieved of his art collection by the Nazis.'

Jack recognized the blind passion in Adam's eyes; he'd seen it many times in the mirror in his own, and warned himself to tread carefully. 'Listen, Mr Krantz, I'm very sorry about your grandfather's art collection, but really it's not my problem. I do hope you find your painting . . .'

Jack had tried to step to one side, but Adam barred his way. 'Just answer me one question, Mr McGowan; did you purchase a Monet from that crook Fleming?'

Jack sighed heavily, he knew he was losing patience. 'Like I said earlier, I don't think what I do is any of your business. Now, you really must excuse me, Mr Krantz, I'm a busy man.'

Adam did not move. '*Le Port d'Honfleur* was stolen, and rightfully belongs to me. I intend to have what is mine, whatever it takes.'

Jack resented the threatening note in Adam's voice and

288

replied with one of unmistakable menace in his own. 'A word of warning, Mr Krantz, don't bite off more than you can chew; something might get stuck in your throat, and choke you.'

'Don't fuck with me, McGowan. This thing is very simple: *I want my painting back*. You've bought stolen goods; it's tough I know, but life is like that, you can't win 'em all.'

Jack now pointed a finger at Adam, telling him, 'Get out of my way before I have you forcibly removed.'

Adam stood his ground, holding Jack's angry glare. He recalled something his father had always said: *Don't ever let your opponent read your eyes.*

'Get outta my face, Krantz! And stay out,' Jack growled then, pushing the other man to one side, he strode in the opposite direction. He was seething when he heard Adam's shout.

'See you in court!'

Chapter Seventeen

Nadia liked to look at Paul when he was asleep. There was something profoundly childlike in his even breathing, in the set of his small features, and the few wisps of hair fanning across his unfurrowed brow. They were in her new bed in her recently acquired freehold house in First Street, Knightsbridge.

'*Knightsbridge, Knightsbridge.*' She whispered the word in reverence, thrilling to the sound. Every item in the house was new, Nadia had insisted. She wanted no reminders of where she had been, only reassurances of where she was going.

As long as she lived she was certain she would never forget the day she had moved in; the moment of anticipation when she had placed her key in the front door. Her stomach had ached; not with pain but pleasure as she had looked up at the freshly painted pale pink walls, the bright white shutters and the bobbing heads of the petunias tightly packed into the window boxes at the foot of the four gleaming windows. Paul thought it was like a doll's house, but to Nadia it was the culmination of ten years of long hours, hard work and going without. *You're just like a kid*, Paul had scoffed. *The novelty will wear off. It always does*, he'd added cynically. Well, it hadn't yet, even after two months, and Nadia hoped it never would. She felt a quick surge of pleasure as she shifted her gaze from Paul to the billowing cotton drapes surrounding the four-poster bed – so white, they hurt her eyes if she looked at them long enough. Then, with pride, she moved her eyes to the exquisite Regency bow-fronted dressing table that had arrived yesterday. It held an array of gleaming glass perfume bottles and a tall, frosted glass vase. A rare smile, rare in that it was warm, creased her square face as she glimpsed the ribbon, and the card dangling from a bunch of her favourite white lilies: a gift from Paul.

She continued to smile, thinking about her abortive attempt to arrange the flowers – interrupted by Paul grabbing her from behind, telling her between moans, bites, and kisses how much he loved her, missed her, and did not intend to leave her for as long as a fortnight again. When he'd tried to undress her, she'd raced around the bedroom with him in hot pursuit, both giggling like schoolkids when they'd finally fallen on to the bed together.

With long tapered hands, Nadia stroked the pristine counterpane, her mind drifting from thoughts of Paul to the first night she had spent in this bed, uncovered and naked, her dark chocolate-coloured skin even darker against the snow-white linen. With deliberate precision she had spread her legs wide, stroking herself with long sensuous movements, her reliably agile fingers bringing her body to a quivering orgasm quickly and adeptly. She had then licked her fingertips, enjoying the taste and the scent. She recalled lying very still for a long time afterwards, the only sound her heavy breathing and the muted hum of traffic on Walton Street.

That night, and again tonight, Nadia marvelled at how

far she had come from the one-roomed squalor of her child-hood. She'd lost count of the times she had thanked God for being so generous in giving her a brain as well as beauty: her passport across to the other side of the street. Paul snored softly. Resting her head on one hand, she lay very still observing him, thinking about what he had told her during dinner. She recalled the conversation word for word.

Jack's worried about the Monet he bought from Christopher Fleming, you know the dealer who disappeared and is suspected of murdering his boyfriend. Apparently the picture is dodgy – Fleming hadn't told him about the provenance. It belonged to some Jewish family before the war and was believed destroyed.

At this she had interrupted with her own view. *Do you really believe Jack McGowan didn't know? Come, it's Nadia you're talking to! Jack makes sure he knows the far end of a fart if there's money involved.*

Paul had been forced to agree, and had told her more. *The police are sniffing around, and an American called Adam Krantz has turned up out of the blue with some far-fetched story about his family in Germany during World War Two. Says that he intends to take advice about making a claim as sole heir to the Monet. Jack pooh-poohs it, more or less, and ordered him out of his office. But for all his bluster he must be worried, because I overheard Fiona speaking to the shippers about transporting the painting to Jack's house in Cap Ferrat.*

Paul turned over in his sleep, so she couldn't see his face any more. Inching down the bed, she fitted her body neatly into his back, gently sliding her arms around his thick waist. She glimpsed the bedside clock. It was after twelve, and she had to be in court early in the morning. But sleep was impossible, and after twenty minutes she slipped out of bed and crept downstairs. Humming softly to herself, Nadia made a pot of tea using her sparkling new kettle and china teapot. She added a teaspoonful of honey and a shot of brandy to the cup. Then with her bare feet folded under her body, she snuggled into the sofa, sipping the hot brew, her mind consumed by thoughts of Jack McGowan. Nadia had never forgiven him for getting rid of her weeks before the AFM merger, cheating her out of two hundred and fifty thousand pounds in stock. It was not a lot of money to someone like McGowan, but to her it was a fortune. Considering the phenomenal risks she'd taken to hush up the litigation deal, he should have paid her at least that, if not more, out of his own pocket. She'd been tempted to pull the plug on Jack then, but by implicating Anglo Gowan she would automatically be pointing a finger at the chief executive, and Nadia wasn't ready to lose Paul Rowland yet. She wondered if that time would ever come. She didn't relish the thought. What had started out for her as a casual office affair, had developed – much to her astonishment – into a deep and passionate love. Paul was the father she'd never known; the brother she'd always wanted; and the supportive friend she'd never found time to cultivate.

Finishing her tea, she rested the cup in her lap letting her head drop back. A few wiry strands of densely black hair fanned out across the soft down-filled sofa cushion. Closing her eyes, she allowed herself a secret smile – the movement softened her hard mouth. At last she began to drift into a light sleep, consciousness slowly ebbing away as her mind drifted back to something she had overheard

Jack saying to Paul about her being a black bitch on heat, who was hot to trot with any guy who was well hung.

Nadia's last waking thought was of how kind fate had been in giving her this opportunity to get even with Jack McGowan.

He was in a tunnel but it wasn't dark, it was blindingly bright. He was swimming but not moving, the water was thick, much thicker than normal water. It stuck to his naked body like glue. He knew he had to get out; then, and only then, he would be safe. He could see the end of the tunnel, there were fields and trees, and children playing – he could hear their shouts and laughter. His arms felt heavy as if weighted down and his legs, he realized with a sense of terror, had stopped moving. The children's laughter was getting thinner, their voices fading. It was then he heard another sound, it was faint at first and he thought that he'd imagined it, but it got louder and more insistent as he woke up with a start, fumbling for the telephone.

'Adam Krantz?'

Using one elbow he struggled into a sitting position. 'Yes, I'm Adam Krantz.'

'You don't know me, Mr Krantz; but I know of you. My name is Nadia Foreman, I'm a lawyer. I've got some information that might be of interest to you, concerning a certain painting.'

Adam was wide awake now, his senses alert. 'Information, what sort of information?'

'The only kind worth having, Mr Krantz, the kind you need to win. I don't want to discuss this on the telephone, so if you're interested I suggest we meet.'

There was a short pause.

'Yeah, I'm interested. Where and when?'

'My place this evening at six-thirty, the address is 28 First Street, London SW3.'

Adam swung his legs out of bed. 'I'll be there. But, look, how do you know about me, and where I'm staying?'

He heard her laugh, it was unusually deep, like a man's. 'I'm not a good lawyer for nothing, Mr Krantz.'

Adam looked at the piece of paper in his hand then back at the number on the door, they were the same. He rang the doorbell, glancing up expectantly at the first-floor windows. When there was no reply he tried again. He waited for about five minutes before deciding that the house was empty. Wondering if he had got the time wrong, he began to walk down the street, turning a couple of seconds later when he heard his name.

'Mr Krantz, wait!' Nadia Foreman was out of breath when she caught up with him. 'I'm sorry I'm late, an overseas call I had to take, sod's law – someone always calls when you're just about to walk out the door.'

Adam knew the feeling, he smiled his understanding. 'No problem, I just got here.'

'I'm glad I caught you, please come in.' She opened her front door and led the way down a narrow hall.

Adam watched her slip out of her jacket and then she ran her hands across her hair which was tightly scraped off her face into a thick ponytail, caught in the nape of her neck by a tortoiseshell clip. She had big square shoulders accentuated by a tiny waist, and thin limbs with long narrow ankles. There was an animal quality about her; a big

295

cat, panther-type beauty that Adam found compelling, yet unappealing.

Following her through to the drawing room, as usual he was perplexed by the lack of space most London houses offered, and wondered anew why on earth people were prepared to pay astronomical prices for such pokey properties. Adam sat down on an uncomfortable damask-covered antique chair, coming to the conclusion that he would never understand the English.

'Would you like a drink?' Nadia offered. 'Tea, coffee or something—' She was about to say 'stronger', when he intervened.

'Scotch on the rocks, please.'

Crossing to a console table laden with bottles and glasses, she poured him three fingers of Johnnie Walker. She then poured herself a large gin and, handing him his glass, said, 'Back in a tic, with the rocks.'

Left alone, Adam looked around and felt he was in a showroom, the type set up by property developers to show potential purchasers the ideal home.

Nadia returned carrying an ice bucket. She dropped two cubes into his glass then, filling hers to the brim with tonic, sat down in an identical chair opposite Adam.

He'd downed half of his Scotch when she said, 'Cheers.'

Crushing an ice cube, he swallowed the shattered fragments before returning, 'Yeah, cheers.'

'I'll get straight to the point, Mr Krantz.'

'I'd prefer to be called Adam.'

Nadia smiled, thinking that Adam was not in the least how she'd expected. His voice had the deep intonation of permanent laryngitis, and he looked like a slightly more refined version of Andy Garcia: exactly her sort of man.

'And you can call me Miss Foreman, if you don't mind.'

Adam wasn't sure if she was teasing or not. Then he realized she was. 'OK, Nadia, let's get down to business. Why did you want to see me?'

Her glassy eyes, uncompromising, surveyed him from under heavy lids. 'Please correct me if I'm wrong in any of this.'

He inclined his head, 'Fire away . . .'

'You are Adam Krantz, grandson of Joseph Krantz – a German Jew who before the war owned one of the most important art collections in Europe. A painting from that collection has recently turned up in London through the dubious dealings of one Christopher Fleming. The picture is by Claude Monet, who needs no introduction, and was bought by Jack McGowan, who also needs no introduction. I believe you two have already crossed paths, or swords. Which was it?'

'Both,' Adam replied, noncommittal.

'I'm a litigation lawyer,' she leaned forward, handing him her card. He glanced at it briefly. 'And I'm good at what I do.'

This made Adam grin, warming to her. 'I hate false modesty.'

Nadia returned with an emphatic, 'So do I.' Then, 'I've heard through the grapevine that you intend to make a claim for the painting. Is that true?'

Adam was cautious. 'How do you know all this, and why are you so interested?'

'Suffice to say a good friend told me; in confidence I might add, I'm taking a risk on his trust by contacting you.

Let's just say, I have a vested interest in this case. I'm sorry but I can't tell you any more at this point.'

'You mentioned on the telephone that you had some information for me?'

Nadia set her drink down. 'I have. But first, tell me, have you taken legal advice? And *do* you intend to make a claim?'

Adam thought about his meeting that morning with Charles Walker of McGregor, Smith and Walker, who had advised him that because the sale had taken place in England he might well be able to make a claim to the picture through the English High Court. He'd spent the remainder of the day in his hotel room, reflecting on the advice, finally deciding to seek more. 'The answer to your first question is that I took advice this morning from McGregor, Smith and Walker.'

Nadia nodded her recognition. 'I know them.'

'I was given their name by a colleague here in London and according to Charles Walker, one of the senior partners, I've got a reasonably strong case.'

'"Reasonably strong" is not strong enough. You need watertight. Tell me the evidence.'

'Why should I?'

'Listen, it's up to you. I'm a lawyer, I might be able to help, and I promise not to bill you.'

The final comment produced a wry smile from Adam. 'That makes a change.'

There was something about Nadia he liked, she had a kind of raw upfront feisty approach – the American way, he understood. In direct contrast to the pomposity of the Walker guy he'd met earlier. He made a snap decision born out of gut instinct. It had never failed him before, and

298

looking into Nadia's level gaze he doubted it would now.

'The Monet was part of a huge collection owned by my grandfather Joseph Krantz. He was a wealthy German Jew who built a large banking corporation during the first part of this century. The painting was stolen during the war, along with others, by a Nazi officer called Klaus Von Trellenberg. My grandfather left a will bequeathing all his art to his male heirs; my father's dead, so I'm the sole beneficiary.'

'Is Von Trellenberg the Nazi who was caught recently?' Nadia cut in.

'That's the one; anyway, more about him later. I've got a photograph of the painting *in situ* in my grandfather's house in Berlin, taken before the war. I also have a sworn statement from Marlene Gurtner, the daughter of Eva Gurtner, a housekeeper who used to work for my grandfather. In it she claims that her mother witnessed Von Trellenberg deport the family, and steal the art collection. The painting would achieve more than forty million dollars on the open market, so why did Christopher Fleming sell it for half the value? It was offered to a colleague of mine at Sotheby's by a man who, along with Fleming, has dropped off the face of the earth. Anyway it doesn't make sense for either this mystery man or Fleming to have dealt with the picture so secretly unless of course the provenance was so dubious. Fleming obviously advised his client not to go through the normal channels, and to let him sell it privately and quietly. I believe that's exactly what happened. The pair of them are probably laughing all the way to the bank as we speak.'

Adam had finished his drink, he rested the empty glass on his lap.

She started to rise. 'Another?'

He held up his hand, gesticulating for her to sit down. 'No thanks, I've been drinking too much lately.'

'Join the club,' she said, relaxing her legs and drinking deeply as if to underline her comment. Pointing at him with her glass, Nadia measured her words. 'Jack McGowan is a tough bastard. He hasn't got where he is today without fighting, and being first ahead of the game. And he hates to lose. Jack would rather give something away than lose it. I must warn you that you'll have a hard battle on your hands, but I think you stand a good chance of winning. There'll be a lot of public sympathy on your side. The media will back you, that is if you play your cards right. Jack and the press are arch enemies. I think Jack bought the painting from Fleming aware that the provenance was dodgy. If you can prove that, you have a good case. Jack knows Fleming is a crook, and I know Jack. I used to work for him. I'm positive he wouldn't have been able to resist such a good deal. I also know that he intends to ship the painting out of the country. If he succeeds, you don't stand a chance of seeing the Monet ever again. Unless, of course, Jack McGowan invites you to stay in his house in Cap Ferrat.'

Adam looked shocked. 'How do you know that?'

'Trust me, I know. If you want to validate what I'm saying, ring Aston and Heller. They're the agents for the shippers.'

'Is it possible to stop him?'

Nadia stood up. 'Yes, you hire me to act for you and we issue an interlocutory injunction to stop him taking the painting out of the country.'

Adam hesitated. 'I'll have to think about it.'

'Don't think too long, Adam. If my information's correct, the painting is due to leave England in less than a week.'

Jack was nervous. He couldn't recall having felt like this since he was fourteen, and about to embark on a much longed-for first date with Rebecca Wilson. Rebecca with the long blonde ponytail, and grass-green eyes. Rebecca who went to grammar school and lived in what his mother always referred to as a posh house. Years later Jack had met Rebecca again when he was on his way up, and she was on her way down. Heavily pregnant with her third child, her youthful bloom had fled with poverty and alcohol abuse. Jack recalled enjoying a surge of self-approbation that had compensated fully for the fact that she had dumped him for Tommy Pickering, the local councillor's son.

Two days ago in a drunken desperate mood, he'd penned a handwritten note to Kathryn and had been both surprised and delighted to receive a note back the following day – agreeing to see him. Now in the minutes before her arrival, he practised his lines like an anxious amateur thespian waiting in the wings on first night. Only to forget the entire script when he heard the doorbell, followed by the Peacock's voice, then soft footsteps in the hall.

When Kathryn walked into the room, Jack was leaning against the mantelpiece in a contrived pose. She was dressed casually in a blue trouser suit, and simple white tee-shirt.

'Kathryn, how are you?' He knew he sounded stilted, and willed himself to relax.

'I'm OK, Jack, and you?'

'Fine, just fine, you know me, keep attacking.' Jack was

wearing his contrite hat, it sat awkwardly on his head, and in truth did not suit him. Kathryn wanted to laugh.

'Well, to be totally honest – you know, that quality that seems to escape me from time to time – I've been bloody miserable. Everyone at the office has suffered, even the ever tolerant Fiona is considering handing in her notice. I—' His deep voice, usually so forceful, dropped an octave, it sounded tinny. 'I love you, Kathryn, and I'm damned if I can live without you.'

Then, regaining some of his sense of humour, he pointed to his groin. 'And nor can he, hasn't even raised his ugly head to find out what the weather's like, let alone get up to any naughty business.'

She began to laugh; the sound filled his senses, warming him like a large shot of good Remy Martin.

In that instant, all the anger that had been sitting in her stomach like a lead weight for the past week slipped away, and she felt an enormous wave of relief. 'Come here, Jack McGowan, you old fool.'

She opened her arms, and he fell into them. He filled his nostrils full of her smell, holding her so tight it hurt. She struggled to breathe yet was loath to leave his embrace, it felt safe and secure and comfortable. Then with a start, she realized this was exactly how she'd felt when as a child she'd slipped into her father's side of the bed, cuddling up close to him after a bad dream. Was it so bad to have your father as your lover? The question popped into her head, followed by an image of Dr Gillman.

Kathryn pushed Jack gently away as Mrs Peacock's brown head appeared at the door. 'Excuse me, but there's a gentleman at the door who insists on seeing you.'

Jack scowled, his irritation evident, he spoke over Kathryn's shoulder. 'Who is it for God's sake; I'm not expecting anyone.'

Peacock coughed delicately. 'He says he's here to serve legal papers. I think you should see him . . .'

Angry that his intimate moment with Kathryn had been destroyed, Jack strode across the room, saying, 'I'll sort it out. This won't take long.'

Kathryn stood next to the window. She peeked around the curtains to where a man stood on the doorstep. She could just distinguish the top of a dark red head moving up and down. Moments later, she heard Jack running back inside. He burst into the room, and she knew by the outrage on his face that there was something very wrong.

'I can't believe this!' He was clutching a piece of paper in his right hand. '*This*,' he waved it in the air in time with his shaking voice, '*This* is a writ.'

Kathryn looked blank.

'An injunction to stop me taking my own property out of the country.'

'I don't understand, Jack.'

Throwing the piece of paper on to the sofa in disgust, he willed himself to stay in control, reminding himself that losing his temper would do no good whatsoever.

'That smooth-talking American bastard Adam Krantz has sworn an affidavit to the effect that the Monet I bought, and paid a small fortune for, belongs to him.'

So Adam hadn't left the country. Kathryn now knew how people felt when they said their legs had gone weak. She held on to the arm of the sofa for support; pleased Jack was so distracted he wouldn't notice her distress.

'And that scheming black bitch Nadia Foreman is acting for him. It's obvious she knows I intend to ship the painting to France and has convinced this Krantz guy that he's got a case.' Jack clenched and unclenched his fists. 'If the painting leaves the country, it leaves the jurisdiction of English law.'

'So what happens now?'

'I have to reply with a sworn affidavit that I bought it fair and square from Fleming. Then we go to court and the judge rules.'

'And if he rules in Adam Krantz's favour?' Kathryn held her breath.

Jack hardly heard her, he was pacing the floor, busy making notes in his head to call Paul, and bawl him out about his girlfriend. Then George Powell, a brilliant litigation barrister.

He finally stopped pacing to answer her question. 'I'll have to hand the painting over for safe keeping, until the case is heard in the High Court.'

'Forget it, Edwards, you've got nothing to go on. You're barking up the wrong tree. McGowan's fingerprints were in Fleming's gallery, so what? We know he went there to look at the painting which he then bought, for what we assume was the asking price. You know as well as I do that Fleming would not have parted with the picture before he was sure the money had been transferred.' Chief Inspector Henderson loosened his tie, folding thick arms across a barrel chest.

Sean Edwards began his reply to his superior. 'We know that the money was transferred from McGowan's account in Grand Cayman into an account called Westgarth, in

Credit Suisse, Zurich, and the interest was paid. The Swiss as usual are being totally unresponsive and secretive. We found a letter at the gallery from Credit Suisse in Zurich – saying that since there were no funds in the Westgarth account they intended to close it until further notice. So where is the money?' Edwards frowned, bushy eyebrows meeting at the bridge of his nose to form a thick hedge.

Henderson shrugged. 'Your guess is as good as mine. Fleming withdrew the money and is probably now on some foreign beach with a fourteen-year-old toy boy. He sold the painting, got the money, argued with his boyfriend, killed him ... and did a runner. He was a friend of Dorothy's, so maybe—'

Sean raised the hedge quizzically. 'Who's Dorothy?'

'"A friend of Dorothy" is the terminology for a homosexual, a pouf, faggot, gay, turd burglar, whatever you care to call the nice boys. So maybe Fleming had another boyfriend who killed Gavin in a passionate rage.'

Edwards shook his head emphatically. 'No, I've covered that one. Fleming had lived with Gavin for eight years. They were, according to all their friends and associates, the ideal couple, very much in love.'

Greg Henderson grunted. 'Spare me the bloody details.'

'My hunch is that the Monet was definitely stolen, and Fleming double-crossed the guy who offered it to him in the first place – didn't pay him his share of the money from McGowan. He then does a runner, leaving his boyfriend Gavin to face the music. Michael Gill from Sotheby's has given us an accurate description of the guy who brought the picture in to him originally. Angus is touching up the photofit now, I thought I'd run it in the press next week.'

Henderson nodded his approval as Edwards continued, 'The mystery man gets real mad when he finds out Fleming has done a bunk, and Gavin takes the rap.'

With deliberate impatience, Chief Inspector Henderson glanced at the list of messages on his desk. Without looking up he said, '*Bullshit*. I think that your theory stinks, and if I were you I wouldn't mention it to anyone else. Now listen carefully, Edwards.'

Edwards leaned across the chief's desk. Eager to get rid of him, not only from his office, but from his squad, Greg Henderson made a snap decision. 'I'm taking you off the Fleming case.'

'You can't do that, sir! I've put a lot of hard work into this. I'm following up some serious leads right now, just give me another couple of weeks.'

The telephone rang, the chief inspector picked it up, pressing the hold button whilst saying, 'OK, I'll give you one more week. Unless you can come up with something concrete, you're off the case.'

'I think what we have here is a clear case of *Nemo dat quod non habet*; or to give it its abbreviated version, *Nemo Dat*.'

'Speak in layman's terms, the school I went to wasn't that big on Latin.' Jack's smile was pleasant in stark contrast to his piercing stare.

George Powell had been mildly surprised when Paul Rowland of Anglo Gowan had called last night to inform – or warn – him, he wasn't sure which, that Jack McGowan wanted to consult counsel on an urgent matter of an interlocutory injunction. The name 'Anglo Gowan' was notorious in the City, and Jack McGowan's reputation preceded him. George Powell, naturally inquisitive, had looked forward with relish to their meeting today. Men like McGowan never failed to fascinate him. The twin elements prevalent in their personalities – tenacity and a desire for omnipotence – mirrored his own, and he liked to think that if he had not taken up law and become a leading barrister, he, too, would have headed up a powerful corporation.

George fingered his neat moustache and close beard, which was tri-coloured: dark brown, red and grey. The rest of his once dark hair, now streaked with grey, swept upwards from his high domed forehead.

'*Nemo Dat* is the transfer of title; the exception to the rule deals usually with those cases in which a seller with no right to the goods may nonetheless pass a good title to a third party. In most such cases, the question which arises is which of the two innocent people is to suffer for the fraud of the third. The law has to choose between rigorously upholding the rights of the owner to his property, on the one hand, and protecting the interests of the purchaser who has bought in good faith and for value on the other hand.'

'Well, on the one hand, I bought a Monet from a known dealer for fourteen million pounds. What other hand is there? Surely possession is nine tenths of the law?'

George Powell leaned forward, allowing his barrister's baritone to boom out, his diction perfect. 'I quote Lord Denning: "In the development of our law two principles have striven for mastery. The first is the protection of property, no one can give a better title than he himself possesses." This principle applies to you, Mr McGowan.'

'Does that mean my title is good?'

'Well, the buyer acquires no better title to the goods than the seller had. Fundamentally what it means here is that if Adam Krantz can prove without any question of doubt that he can lay claim to the picture, and that the said picture was stolen and its subsequent sale was made without the owner's authority, then he has a pretty strong case.'

'And what about *my* case? Fourteen million pounds' worth of painting bought from a dealer who's disappeared. Just as well, he wouldn't have lived very long anyway if I'd got my hands on him.'

Powell ignored this, lighting a pipe, smoke billowing into the air.

Jack hadn't finished. 'There's no way I can even claim my money back. The police can't trace the cash. Fleming is probably living it up in Rio by now!'

Puffing hard on his pipe, the barrister sent smoke circling towards a ceiling that was already yellowed with nicotine stains. 'Did you know that the painting was stolen when you purchased it from Mr Fleming?' Jack's defensive body language and cautious pause were not wasted on the barrister. 'I have to know the truth to build a case for you.'

Jack replied honestly. 'No, I didn't know it had been stolen.'

'Did you know Christopher Fleming before this transaction?'

Jack shifted uneasily in the wooden chair; it was high-backed, hard and extremely uncomfortable. It put him in mind of his schooldays, of sitting in the 'Squirm Chair', as the kids referred to it, in the headmaster's study. In fact George Powell's office was not unlike that same room, dowdily clad in dull green paint, dust and clutter.

'Vaguely, I'd bought a couple of paintings from him before.'

'And would you have described Fleming as a man of integrity?'

'No, not particularly, but then I wasn't interviewing him for a job. He had a beautiful painting to sell. I wanted it. We haggled a little on the price and eventually settled at fourteen million: a deal is a deal.'

'This painting is valued at about twenty-five million pounds. In view of the agreed purchase price, did it not at any point occur to you that its recent history might be, how shall we say, *dubious*?'

George Powell's face had become fuzzy. Jack blinked to clear his vision. When that failed he took his glasses off, cleaning each lens with his handkerchief. When he replaced them, he could see the barrister clearly.

'To be honest I was more worried about the authenticity than whether it had been stolen or not. I thought the Monet might be a fake, so I had it checked out by a friend of mine, Phil Murray from Sotheby's. He's an expert in the French Impressionist School.'

Powell looked over Jack's head for a moment, lost in thought. 'Did this friend mention anything about the history, or the provenance of the painting?'

At this point Jack decided to bend the truth, not wishing to disclose that Phil *had* told him both about the Krantz family, and Adam Krantz. He had given Phil Murray five thousand pounds to keep his mouth shut.

'No, he didn't. Don't ask me why, perhaps he didn't know.'

George raised sparse eyebrows, his brown eyes darkening to almost black. 'Are you trying to tell me that a Fine Art expert of Sotheby's calibre, specializing in the Impressionist School, did not know about the provenance of a Monet as important as this one?'

Jack shrugged. 'Ask him if you don't believe me.'

'I didn't say I *didn't believe* you. I merely questioned Mr Murray's knowledge. I do hope he will not look foolish when cross-examined under oath.'

Jack stood up and stretched. His backside ached, and he longed to rub it. 'Do you really think this thing will go all the way to the High Court then?'

'If Krantz wins the injunction, I have little doubt that he will take the case to the High Court. He's going to claim that he has the better title, because by purchasing for half of the actual value, you bought with a lack of good faith.'

Cracking his knuckles one by one, Jack narrowed his eyes. 'What are my chances of winning?'

'I don't know what evidence the other side have got, Mr McGowan. We have to rely on justice to prevail.'

'*Justice?*' Jack snarled. 'I know all about so-called justice! If I have to rely on that, I'm up Shit Creek without my Monet *or* my fourteen million pounds.'

Standing up, Powell pushed out his stomach, placing both hands inside his jacket on his hips. He was very tall, at six foot five a few inches taller than Jack. Now, he moved around his desk to stand close to Jack, who detected a glint of steel enter his eyes. But there was something else, something that Jack recognized instantly. It was what his father had called 'Vulture Eye', the predatory gleam before the kill. Jack suddenly trusted Powell.

'The law has little to do with innocence or guilt; it has everything to do with the presentation of evidence, and the consummate skill of the presenter. Winning is my game. I don't like losing any more than you do, Mr McGowan. And, as you are no doubt aware, such occasions have been rare in my career. You have my word that I will do everything in my power to see that it does not happen this time.'

Chapter Eighteen

The drive to Channing Lodge wound through thickly wooded grounds, overhanging branches laden with water dripped on to the windscreen and bonnet of her car. The incessant swish of the wipers was loud in her ears as the drive widened and swept towards the front of the creeper-clad Queen Anne rectory. The house would have been pretty if her father had not, at Emily's insistence, spent a small fortune on ugly double-glazing and obtrusive half-swag curtains at each window. Stepping out of the car, she saw Richard de Moubray appear at the door.

His face creased in a smile when she walked towards him. 'It's good to see you, Kathy, it's been a long time.'

Kathryn was tempted to remind him it had been at her mother's funeral, which was exactly six weeks and four days ago. He kissed her on the cheek, then taking her by the hand he led her inside. He didn't let go until they entered the large kitchen which in Kathryn's opinion was the best room in the house. It exuded a warmth, in its farmhouse clutter, that the rest of Channing Lodge lacked.

As her father busied himself filling the kettle, Kathryn explored his face in detail. She thought he had aged since the funeral; not in an obvious way, but some of the fire had gone out of his eyes, and his body language was tired. At sixty-five, he was seven years older than Jack, yet the gap seemed more like twenty. But she conceded he was still an attractive man. Abundant grey hair curled boyishly on his collar and across his wide brow, and regular exercise had kept his slim five foot ten inches in good shape.

'Good journey?' Richard asked pleasantly. 'I thought about you in this filthy weather.'

'The traffic was terrible coming out of London, but after that it was fine.' She noticed a letter addressed to Emily de Moubray on the kitchen table. It prompted her to ask, 'How is Emily?'

The slouch of his shoulders, and heavy sigh, said it all.

'Not well I'm afraid, she's not responding to treatment, her deterioration is very rapid. She's resting at the moment, but perhaps will feel well enough to see you later.'

Kathryn did not want to see her particularly, but knew she would have to if only for her father's sake.

'I'm very sorry, Dad.' She wanted to say sorry *for you*, but couldn't get the words out. 'You said on the phone that you wanted to see me. Dad, you knew Von Trellenberg was my grandfather. When did you first find out?'

Richard de Moubray ignored her question, instead he said, 'Tea?'

'Yes please,' Kathryn answered as he lifted the kettle off the top of the Aga, and poured boiling water into a chipped bright canary-coloured teapot. He placed it on a tray, added two cups, a sugar pot and milk jug.

'Shall we go into the drawing room, Kathy? It's a little more comfortable in there.'

She followed him out of the kitchen, through a dark hall, into the drawing room. A large bay window faced a broad sweep of lawn interspersed with a variety of fruit trees and thickly stocked flowerbeds. It was still raining hard. A thick counterpane of grey mist covered the garden that, Kathryn knew, on a good day would be very beautiful. She had only been to Channing Lodge once before, on a dark January afternoon. On that occasion the house and grounds had been covered in a thick blanket of snow.

Sitting down on the sofa, in front of a dying log fire, she absorbed every detail of the room in the time it took her father to pour the tea. The entire house was a testament to the fussy Emily. Chintz upon chintz, and everywhere the inevitable clutter of twee collectibles and Emily's own crudely executed watercolours clashing with the gaudy floral wallpaper. Richard handed her a cup. It was a silly size, too small, and had bright scarlet flower buds around the rim.

'You don't take sugar, Kathryn, do you?' She shook her head, pleased he had remembered.

Settling himself on the opposite sofa, he sipped his tea thoughtfully, clearly contemplating what he was about to say. After a few moments he spoke.

'When I first met your mother in 1945, she was barely nineteen. She was very beautiful in a cool Slavic way. I was only two years older. The war, as you know, had taken its toll of all of us. But at the end, the Germans had a very rough time. I think I fell in love with her courage, more than anything else. I don't know if she ever told you, but she was raped and brutally beaten by two Russian soldiers who left her for dead. She was admitted to the hospital where I was working.'

'No, she never mentioned it,' Kathryn said quietly. 'She never talked about the past.'

'Freda was in a bad way, she'd lost a lot of blood. Personally I thought she would die. When she didn't, she saw me as her saviour, and my naïveté was enough to make for a classic case of mistaking gratitude and sympathy for love. You know the rest. I brought her back to England much to the astonishment, and initial horror, of my friends and family.' For a moment he looked wistful.

'We settled into rural life. She became the perfect doctor's wife, and for the first few years things were fine.' He stopped abruptly.

'Then what, Father. What happened?'

Richard put his cup on the floor; taking a handkerchief from out of his back pocket, he blew his nose noisily. Kathryn sensed he was playing for time, considering how much or little he should disclose.

'It's difficult to discuss, but it was our sex life you see, your mother—' He coughed, his acute embarrassment beginning to embarrass Kathryn.

'Freda found it distasteful.' He dropped his eyes, surveying the back of his hands. 'Perhaps it was me, I don't know, or her past experience. I'm not entirely sure, but believe me I did try. After you were born, she refused to continue lovemaking. At first I put it down to post-natal depression and suggested therapy, but she flatly refused to talk about it and encouraged me to seek gratification elsewhere. I thought in time it would pass. I must admit I pushed her sometimes when I was very frustrated. Then she would consent, but in such a cold mechanical way that I felt like a rapist. I couldn't come to terms with it, and began searching for something more.

'It was at this point I met Emily, and for the first time

315

in my life I felt completely whole. I know you've never liked Emily, but you must understand she's given me such a lot. As you know, your mother became ever more distant and I, for one, found her almost impossible to relate to in her latter years.'

Kathryn cupped her tea in both hands. 'So when did she tell you about her father?'

'About three weeks before her death she rang me here. It was quite early in the morning and I was still in bed. I'd just returned from a trip to America. I was dog-tired, suffering from jet-lag. Emily took the call and when I got up a couple of hours later, she told me that Freda had sounded very anxious. I rang her back immediately, and was surprised when she asked if she could see me as soon as possible. She said it was a matter of great urgency. She offered to drive down here, but as it happened I had to be in London the following day, so we arranged to meet at the Ritz for afternoon tea.

'When we met she was very agitated, she said she needed my help. She then told me about her father, Klaus Von Trellenberg. That he had been a Nazi officer, that she had never believed he was dead, and had recently found out that he was living in the West Indies. She asked me to lend her five thousand pounds. With the money she intended to join him there. He was dying of cancer, and she wanted to be with him for the little time he had left. She had a couple of insurance policies that were due to mature in the next couple of years and she promised to pay me back. I wasn't bothered about the money; I was shocked and concerned for her, and for you. She begged me not to mention it to you. I agreed to lend her the money, and swore I wouldn't breathe a word to anyone.'

Richard got up to throw another log on to the sputtering embers of the fire then, running the flat of his hand down his worn corduroy trousers, he sat back down.

'I kept my word, and I assumed she was going ahead with her plans. I didn't hear from her again; then you rang to tell me she was dead. When I read about Von Trellenberg's capture in the newspapers, I thought I should discuss it all with you, and fully intended to, but I had to dash off to the States with Emily. On my return I read about your boyfriend Jack, and the Monet that was supposedly stolen during the war. I thought it was time to talk.'

Kathryn was aware of a heavy weight being lifted from her shoulders; she felt almost light-headed and she spoke in a voice tinged with compassion. 'I met Von Trellenberg, Father. I went to St Lucia, and found him. It was the most bizarre experience of my life.' A vision of her grandfather sweeping dramatically on to the terrace of the crumbling plantation house entered her head. 'I'll never forget it.'

'What an extraordinary thing to do, Kathryn! Did it never occur to you that you might have been in danger?' Richard's look of horror only confirmed to her how little he knew of his only daughter.

'No, Father; it never occurred to me. I went on gut instinct. An impulse, a compulsion to find my roots. Did it occur to you, the day you left a nine-year-old little girl, that she might be dying inside?'

Her father winced, but it was too late, the floodgate was open: condemnation pouring forth so powerfully, it was impossible to stop.

'Did you never think about me when you spent four years in America? In all that time, apart from birthday and Christmas cards, I had three measly letters, one of them only half a page long. That works out at less than one a year.' She couldn't look at him. 'Just tell me, Dad, did you think about me? Ever? Much? At all? A telephone call would have been enough, five minutes a week of your precious time, even once a month would have made all the difference.'

A hush fell, the crackling of the fire the only sound in the still room. Kathryn gave him a sideways glance, stunned to see tears streaming down his face. In that moment he aged visibly before her very eyes.

'But I did call, many times. I'm sorry your mother didn't tell you, Kathryn. Every time I rang Freda always found an excuse for me not to speak to you. You were out at a friend's, doing homework, horse riding, or whatever. She would tell me what you had been doing in her usual detached manner, and that there was no need to worry about you. Your mother didn't make it easy for me to come to the house, but I can't use that as an excuse. I could have been more forceful and insisted, but I was wrapped up in my work, and Emily. God forgive me, I still am.' He licked a tear from his top lip.

'I'm not a bad man, Kathryn, I'm just a bad father. As we get near the end, our past catches up with us, forcing us to face the grim reaper with honesty. I'm sure that no life is without regrets. I'm sorry, Kathy, truly I am. I know that's not enough, but can you forgive me?'

She felt very weary, and wasn't sure if she could answer him honestly. 'I'm sorry too, Dad, but perhaps we still have time. Never too late to say never.'

318

He seemed ready to brighten a little, but just then his ears heard a faint knocking sound, followed by Emily's voice shouting for him. 'She wants her tea, I'll be back in a little while.'

Kathryn raised her eyes as the knocking increased. 'Yes, go on, Dad, before she brings the house down.'

Richard left the room and Kathryn sat very still. She was filled with an immense sense of relief. She had confronted her father at last, and was secretly pleased she had reduced him to tears. The morning newspaper was neatly folded on the arm of the sofa; she picked it up, smiling at her father's half-finished crossword. She even answered one of the clues, then glanced at a story about crime in inner city Liverpool. She was about to drop the paper, when a black-and-white Photofit caught her eye. Kathryn's hand shook when she recognized the unmistakable face of her cousin Stefan. Her pulse quickened as she read the caption: *The police would like to question this man in connection with the murder of Gavin Fox. If you have seen him, or have any information as to his identity . . .*

Kathryn dropped the paper hurriedly as her father returned, looking harassed. He joined her on the sofa. Lifting her hand he kissed it, then sandwiched it between both of his, resting all three in his lap.

'I've just remembered something else your mother said the day I met her in the Ritz. She said that she intended to bury her father in the family tomb on the Trellenberg country estate in East Germany. I doubted that it still existed and said so. Freda confirmed that it did, and said that it was something her father had always wanted, and she was determined to—'

Before he could finish Kathryn was on her feet shouting, 'That's *it*! Why didn't I think of it before!'

Richard looked puzzled. 'I've obviously said something important, am I to be enlightened?'

'In due course, Dad.' Then inwardly chiding herself for burning the 1936 photograph of the Von Trellenbergs with the name of the Schloss on the back, she asked him, 'Did Mother mention the name of the family house in Germany; did she say it was located at Mühlhausen?'

'No, she didn't say, but I'm sure your Aunt Ingrid could tell you.'

'Oh, she's been away in Berlin. I'm not sure if she's back yet.'

Richard was puzzled by this news. 'But Ingrid hasn't set foot out of Surrey for years . . .'

'Father, I think you've just solved the mystery of sleeping with ghosts.'

Richard looked even more confused. 'I have?'

'I promise to tell all very soon, but first I've got to try and find Ingrid.'

It had stopped raining by the time she reached Coombe Ridge, Aunt Ingrid's cottage. When she climbed out of the car, patches of blue were appearing in the sky like watery ink spots on a billowing white sheet. She looked at her watch, congratulating herself on making good time: Wiltshire to Surrey in less than an hour. Getting no answer on the phone, she'd decided to make the journey on spec, perhaps see if any of the neighbours had heard from Ingrid. She lifted the latch on the wooden gate and walked down the path. Dead rose petals were scattered like rusted jewels across the lawn, and there were weeds popping out of the long grass. Ringing the doorbell, she was filled with an odd sense of foreboding. She waited a couple of minutes before trying again. After the second time, she left the porch to peer in the front window, turning at the sound of a sudden voice.

'You looking for Mrs Lang?'

The owner of the voice was a rotund young lad, about thirteen, who was trying with difficulty to control an exuberant red setter puppy.

'Yes, she's my aunt. Do you know if she's back?'

The dog dragged the boy forward. 'She's still in St Joseph's Hospital in Cranleigh.'

Instantly concerned, Kathryn asked, 'What happened, is she all right?'

'Ruth Simpson from down the road found her, she fell down the stairs an' there was a lot of blood,' the boy explained in wide-eyed, gory relish. With the callous insensitivity of the young, he elaborated, 'Mrs Lang's in a coma. My mum went to see her yesterday, she said the old lady's going to die.'

When she crept into the private room, Kathryn recognized her cousin immediately. Stefan was sitting at Ingrid's bedside, and Kathryn could hear his voice clearly. She held back, reluctant to intrude.

'You're going to be fine, Mother, I promise. Nothing and no one can hurt you now.' He was holding Ingrid's hand. Kathryn watched him stroke her fingers, noting how pale and lifeless they were. Like a waxwork dummy, she thought, listening to Stefan as he continued in the same

321

distinct monotone, almost as if he were talking to himself.

'I'm going to take you away to somewhere warm. You and I will swim together, like we used to when I was small. You'd like that wouldn't you, Ma.' He patted her hand, there was no response.

Kathryn backed out of the room with stealthy footsteps. She fled down the corridor, bumping headlong into a man whose white coat bore a tag saying, 'Dr Andrew Lloyd'.

'Excuse me,' she muttered, as the doctor steadied her with both arms.

The doctor carried on walking, his chest still warm from the pressure of her ample breasts. When he was sure she was out of earshot, he whispered, 'The pleasure was all mine.'

'Mr Lang, Mr Lang . . .' The voice and the hand on his shoulder were both insistent. Stefan tore his eyes away from his mother's face with reluctance.

'Mr Lang, I must ask you to leave now.'

The voice was different, much softer, more concerned than the usual doctor's. Turning his head, Stefan smiled up at it. 'Will she be able to come out of hospital soon?'

'I think you know the answer to that, Mr Lang. Your mother is dead.'

Kathryn called Sean Edwards from Heathrow.

'I have some information in connection with the Gavin Fox murder. I know the man in the Photofit, in the newspaper today. His name is Stefan Lang.'

'Who is this?' Edwards asked irritably, convinced it was another hoax. He'd had three already that week. Scribbling the name 'Lang' on the back of an envelope, he suddenly heard the caller say something that made him sit bolt upright.

'Stefan Lang is the grandson of Klaus Von Trellenberg who stole the Monet in the first place.'

'Please go on, madam.'

'Klaus Von Trellenberg stole the painting from Joseph Krantz before the war. Stefan, his grandson, recently sold it to Fleming. I think you and Stefan could have an interesting chat. You'll find him at Coombe Ridge Cottage, Church Lane, Cranleigh, Surrey.' Kathryn hung up without giving her name.

A moment later she strode across the busy concourse to join a queue snaking towards Immigration. Glancing up at the departure screen she saw that her flight, Lufthansa 278 to Berlin, was boarding at Gate Twenty-two.

Chapter Nineteen

'Jack's going ape-shit, Nadia. Why on earth did you take on this Krantz case? He's blaming me for telling you about it. He doesn't think you could have found out any other way.'

'Listen, Paul, I haven't got time right now to explain. I'm due in court in less than an hour. I'll talk to you about it tonight, anyway you know it's unethical to discuss a case.'

She heard Paul take a deep breath then sigh. '*Make* time, Nadia. Come on, this is *Paul* you're talking to, not one of your clients.'

It was her turn to sigh. 'OK, he's right, you did tell me – inadvertently, I must admit, over dinner last week. Remember you said that Jack was planning to take the Monet out of the country?'

Paul muttered, 'Yes, I remember.'

'Well, I was intrigued. So I did a little mooching around. I found out that Christopher Fleming is not someone you would trust with your grandfather's heirlooms, and that the Krantz family lost their priceless art collection, before and during the war – including Monet's *Le Port d'Honfleur*. The case fascinates me, that's all. It's got nothing to do with you, Paul, so just stay out of it.'

She was doodling on the back of a used envelope drawing

a big head with horns, oversized glasses and a downturned sour mouth. She scribbled 'Jack McGowan' underneath.

Paul, angered by her dismissive attitude, hissed through clenched teeth. 'Try telling Jack that! I don't have to tell *you* what he's like when he's thwarted.'

A vision of Jack McGowan steaming into her office the day she had refused to hush up the litigation deal during the AFM merger entered her head.

'Too right,' she agreed. 'He thrives on his daily fix of submission and displays unreasonable behaviour when opposed or confronted. He demands compliance, then is contemptuous of the compliant. In standing up to him, you gain his ultimate respect.' She wanted to add, *You should try it some time, Paul.* But she bit her tongue, it wasn't the time or the place.

The wisdom of her words defused his temper. 'Well, I'm stuck in the middle here. And I'm worried about you. When Jack's like this, he can get *very* nasty. On that note, I think I should warn you he's hired George Powell to handle the case.'

Nadia whistled. 'Wow, hot stuff!' Then, undaunted, 'I like to be in good company, it brings out the best in me.'

She heard a noise in the background, and waited while Paul spoke to his secretary, then to her. 'Got New York on the line, want to speak to me urgently. I'll call you later. Good luck, and be careful, Nadia.'

'Don't worry. I'm a big girl, I can take care of myself.' Before putting down the phone, she said, 'Off the record, Paul, if Jack asks about me, or the case, just tell him I intend to win.'

A few minutes later Nadia left her office and took a taxi

to the Royal Courts of Justice in the Strand. Adam was already there. He watched her step out of the cab, thinking that she looked like a schoolmistress. She was wearing a simply cut navy blue business suit, and a white shirt with a tie at the neck. In one hand she was holding a bulging briefcase; the black leather was worn, and the stitching had come undone on one of the seams. She held a stack of files in her other hand.

'Good timing! I like prompt clients,' she said smiling.

'And I like prompt lawyers,' he retorted with a lazy grin. Looking at the briefcase he said, 'Can I help?'

'No thanks, I'm used to it.'

They walked side by side. Nadia looked him up and down. He was wearing a suit; and a dark charcoal shirt with a button-down collar and no tie. Black cowboy boots instead of tan, and a black belt with a tarnished pewter buckle. His long hair was greased back into a ponytail.

'You look like you're going to either a rock concert or a funeral, I can't decide which.'

Adam surveyed his suit. 'Believe me, it feels like the latter, you said wear something sombre.'

'By "sombre", I meant not jeans and cowboy boots.'

'You're lucky. I *never* wear suits. And I object to this one; it cost me eighteen hundred bucks.'

'You were robbed,' she said, striding ahead.

'Gee thanks! Is this a special kinda tactic to make your clients feel relaxed?'

Searching his face for signs of tension, she asked, 'You don't feel nervous do you?'

'A bit,' he admitted. 'All this pomp and tradition shit, like it's a bit daunting for a hick Yankee boy like me.'

Nadia's eyebrows shot up. 'Give me a break, Adam. *Hick* is not a word I would use to describe you . . .' He grinned at her and she thought once more how attractive he was – in a sensual, moody kind of way.

'I feel like I'm about to take Holy Communion or get married,' he commented as they passed under two elaborately carved portals fitted with iron gates. 'This place is like a church.'

'It is a bit like that, I agree. But, believe me, whilst it may look like a cathedral it operates more like a casino in terms of dispensing justice.'

Adam whistled as they entered the Great Hall. 'Wow, some building! It's awesome . . .' He was looking down the two hundred and thirty foot length of the vaulted Main Hall. Shafts of sunlight filtered through the handsome windows ornamented with shields that were emblazoned with the arms of all the great Lord Chancellors of England. He followed Nadia through a gateway and up a short flight of stairs to Court Six. She flashed one of her most appealing smiles when she spotted George Powell deep in conversation with Jack McGowan in the corridor outside the courtroom.

'Good morning, George, Jack, good to see you both.'

The first and only time George had met Nadia Foreman, he had disliked her. Now as she stared fixedly in his direction, her body language reeking of arrogance, his initial impression intensified.

Jack, his back ramrod straight, did not move until Nadia was a couple of feet from him. Then, turning swiftly, he regarded her with the sort of benign indifference that heads of state bestow on their subjects during walkabout. A curt nod sufficed, without so much as a glance at Adam.

Nadia nudged Adam as his counsel, Timothy Ward, approached – wearing a black gown and wig.

'Good morning, Nadia, Mr Krantz.'

'Morning, Tim,' Nadia returned. 'I see we've got Po-face Lamont.'

Timothy nodded grimly. 'Afraid so.' Then to Adam, 'There's just one point in your statement I want to check.' The barrister glanced briefly at Adam's affidavit. 'You say you rang the shipping company, Aston and Heller.' He was looking at the copy of the bill of lading.

'That's correct,' Adam said.

'But there's nothing in here to say how you first acquired information of the proposed export of the painting.'

Adam did not look in Nadia's direction when he lied. 'I received an anonymous telephone call.' He inclined his head towards Jack. 'Someone obviously doesn't like him.'

The door to Court Six had opened; the usher to the court appeared. 'We are ready for you now.'

Nadia glanced briefly at Adam, seeing the worry clearly etched on his handsome features. 'It's going to be OK,' she murmured. 'Come on, cheer up, you're not on trial for your life.'

'Feels like it,' he said, falling in step behind her as they trooped into the sombre confines of the courtroom. He sat on the bench behind counsel, instantly reminded of all the English black-and-white courtroom drama movies he'd watched as a child.

'All rise.'

Adam was pulled to his feet by Nadia as Mr Justice Andrew Lamont entered. The judge tilted his head to the court who, in turn, bowed. On lifting his face, Adam studied the judge. He reckoned he was a man of about fifty-eight, his face held the affable air of a kindly country vicar.

'He looks OK,' Adam whispered.

'Don't let his geniality fool you, it's a mask for a will of iron,' Nadia hissed.

'Court is in session. Krantz versus McGowan,' the clerk announced.

A moment later Timothy Ward was on his feet, stating his client's case. 'May it please, my Lord . . .'

Judge Lamont started his Judgement at three fifty-five. Adam felt his heart beating faster and faster when, after less than ten minutes, he came to the conclusion.

'I have listened to the evidence in this case with great interest and I find I preferred without question the evidence of the plaintive Adam Krantz as set out in his affidavit. I found it more balanced and reliable than the version of events set out in the affidavit of Mr Jack McGowan.

'I order that the painting be delivered up to a designated bank vault until such time as the trial of the main issue is heard. Namely whether Adam Krantz has better title than Mr Jack McGowan to Claude Monet's *Le Port d'Honfleur*.'

The judge rose, as did the court.

Chapter Twenty

'Schloss Bischofstell was built by Rupert Heinemann in 1745. The stone used for its construction was taken from the nearby ruins of the castle of Stein, which was destroyed in the Thirty Years War. In 1802 it was taken over by the Prussians and bought by Otto Von Trellenberg in 1815. After the war it was used by various East German state organizations until reunification in 1990.'

Kathryn listened avidly to the young estate agent, Matiers Remarque, who from time to time stole sideways glances at her perfect profile as he sat at the driving wheel. He spoke English with an American accent. When she'd questioned him about this, he'd admitted to misspent time in California.

'The property was leased by the Treuhand – the government organization responsible for property formerly owned by the East German state – to the Priorate, a charitable foundation of the Freemasons. The Priorate commenced extensive modernization and refurbishment work to bring the property up to standard for use as a school, but their lease was cancelled by the Treuhand successor organization in early 1995.'

Looking directly at Matiers, she was about to ask if he knew anything about the Von Trellenberg family when the Mercedes swung sharply to the right. Feeling a little queasy, she fixed her eyes on the road in front, deciding to wait until they got to the house. They were turning off the main E40. The road ahead was clear and Matiers put his foot down, quickly leaving the small town of Erfurt behind, speeding towards Mühlhausen. He started to talk about another large property close to Dresden she might want to see. Feigning interest, she let her thoughts slip back to how easy it had been to trace the Von Trellenberg Schloss.

On arrival in Berlin she had transferred to an internal flight to Leipzig, where she had stayed overnight in a charming, if kitsch, hotel. The following morning the local post office had informed her that there were only two large country estates in the vicinity of Mühlhausen. One had been bombed during the war and never rebuilt, the other was called 'Schloss Bischofstell'. No sooner were the words out of the man's mouth than she remembered that was the name on the back of the photograph she had destroyed at Fallowfields. The postmaster informed her that he knew little of the estate, advising her to go to the local authority in the state capital of Erfurt. The young clerk there had been very helpful, informing her that Schloss Bischofstell was for sale through an agent in Berlin. The clerk wasn't sure which one, but thought that it would be one of the bigger companies; she had given Kathryn the names of three real estate offices. The first one Kathryn called told her the sale of Bischofstell was being handled through a subsidiary of the prestigious English company Knight Frank and Rutley. On making contact with them, and after being transferred to several departments, she was eventually put through to Matiers Remarque. Kathryn told him her

German mother was in the hotel business in England, and wanted to come back to Germany to live. He seemed unconvinced of her value as a potential buyer, but agreed to meet her to view the property.

The car sped through historic towns and villages: their characteristic timber-framed architecture complementing a landscape of steeply wooded hills, lush valleys and winding rivers – all dominated at intervals by ancient castles and monasteries. After almost an hour they passed through the medieval walled town of Mühlhausen, then took a twisting road out of town for about three miles, which seemed to Kathryn to go on for ever. It ended abruptly in a sharp bend leading up to a small hump-backed bridge. When the car mounted the top of the bridge, Matiers told her where they were.

'There it is, Schloss Bischofstell.'

Kathryn felt a great lurch in her stomach as he pointed through a clearing in the trees. Her eyes followed his finger to a vast Baroque house sitting regally on top of a steeply wooded hillside, the late afternoon sun casting a tawny glow on its sandstone walls.

Matiers turned left into a narrow lane, driving slowly towards the vaulted entrance to the estate. 'I called the caretaker so he should be here to let us in.'

Sure enough, when the car slowed to a halt in front of a set of tall iron gates, the aged caretaker was waiting.

The gates swung open after Matiers had handed the man his business card and the Mercedes passed into a central courtyard, where Matiers and Kathryn alighted. They waited for the old man to shut the gates before smiling in unison as he approached them.

'Good afternoon, Herr Schiller.' The caretaker did not return Matiers's greeting. He merely inclined his head, muttering something about it not being a good afternoon for him and handed over a big bunch of keys, staring at Kathryn for a long moment. Then speaking directly to her, he glanced in the direction of a timber-framed garden house.

'I'll be in there if you need me.'

When the caretaker was out of earshot, Matiers hissed in a stage whisper, 'He's an old devil, but reliable.' Then briskly, 'Follow me, Miss de Moubray.'

Falling in step behind the estate agent, Kathryn could not resist smiling as she thought about the similarities between the odd agent from Brinkforth and Sons, and this German version. She came to the conclusion that they were a breed unto themselves, produced from an international mould.

Matiers commented professionally, 'The property has enormous potential for commercial use. With a minimal amount of improvement of course.' Then he strode up a stone staircase leading to a carved oak door.

Kathryn looked up, and recognizing the Von Trellenberg coat of arms above the door, felt her stomach lurch again. They entered the west wing of the house together, their feet echoing on the mosaic floor. There was an imposing oak staircase to the first floor, and high oak panelled doors to left and right, both leading to the central corridors. They went through the left door, passing several classrooms running the length of the building. Halfway down the corridor, Matiers entered one of them.

'As you can see these classrooms would easily convert to bedroom suites.' With a crooked finger he beckoned her to join him at one of the deep windows. 'Come and look at the view.'

They stood side by side, looking out across a wide sweep of lawn running down to a lake. 'It's stocked with trout; I think that's all old man Schiller lives off.' Matiers winked at Kathryn.

'Has the caretaker been here long?' she asked.

'I'm not sure, but I think someone at the office said that he's been here since before the war. His father was the head gardener. Apparently he worked for the Von Trellenbergs.'

Kathryn seized her chance. 'What happened to them?'

Matiers strolled to the other side of the room. 'All dead. Klaus Von Trellenberg was a Nazi, an SS officer wanted for war crimes. He was presumed dead ages ago, but was captured recently and then had a fatal heart attack in prison. You must have read about it in the English press?'

Kathryn shook her head. 'I try not to read the papers . . . full of rubbish.'

He grimaced. 'Yours are the same as ours then!'

They walked back to the entrance hall, up the wide staircase to another long corridor exactly the same as the one on the ground floor. Towards the end, Matiers stopped at a tall panelled door. It was different from the others in that it looked original.

'This room has not been touched, it was the Von Trellenbergs' bedroom. It's supposed to be haunted.'

Hovering nervously on the threshold, Kathryn expected to sense something, but felt only the stillness of an empty room. No chill, no whispering voices, no ghosts.

A sudden noise from the far wall startled them both. Kathryn looked towards the sound made by a bird flapping vainly against the windowpane. She ran to its aid, trying to open the window. The catch was stuck and wouldn't budge. Terrified, the swallow flew up into the rafters, its wings fluttering frantically. Matiers went to help; he glanced gingerly up towards the bird as a large dropping flew past his head to land on the floor a few inches from his feet. Together, they managed to lift the window, standing back to allow the bird to take flight. Still afraid, the creature hesitated, and they had to stand very still until it eventually came down from its perch to fly away to freedom. Kathryn watched it swoop low over the tiled roof of an ancillary building, before heading off down a long avenue of mature oak trees, stopping on the roof of a stone building that looked like an orangery at first glance. A second later she noticed that it had no windows and thought that perhaps it was a folly.

She pointed. 'What's that building?'

Matiers glanced in the direction of her finger. 'Oh, that monstrosity! It's the Von Trellenberg mausoleum. Apparently Ernst Von Trellenberg built it at the turn of the century. He and his father are buried in there. It's ugly don't you think?'

'I don't agree, I think it's delightful. I'd like to take a look if you don't mind.'

'I'd planned to look at the gardens last.' Matiers sounded and looked put out.

The Germanic way, she thought wryly. *Pedantic to the last.* Matiers's rigid body language reminded her of her mother, and she recalled something Freda used to say frequently, *You must not disturb the order.*

Well, someone has to for God's sake, decided Kathryn,

leaving the room, with Matiers following in her wake.

Back outside, a paved pathway led from the courtyard and through coniferous woodland down to the avenue of trees they had seen the bird fly past.

Kathryn was only half listening to the estate agent as he chatted about the grounds; his words were barely audible above her grandfather's whispered entreaty. *Schlafen mit Geistern, schlafen mit Geistern. Had* it been an entreaty? She wasn't sure. Over and over again the sentence reverberated in her head, not stopping until they reached the tomb.

It was a large building about forty foot square. The stone used in the construction was different from that of the house, darker in hue, less mellow. The Trellenberg coat of arms graced the pediment above the entrance. And, high above that, looking like it was about to take flight, sat a German eagle carved in bronze and aged to a patina of dull green. Dead vine covered the entire building like a tattered brown coat, and the once handsome oak doors were warped and pitted with woodworm. Two thick link chains hung across the entrance. Matiers touched one of two padlocks, the rusted lock looked as if it had not been opened for years.

'Who wants to visit the dead?' Kathryn whispered, then turned at the sudden sound of ducks quacking. They paddled out of the lake up on to the bank, stopping a few feet from where she stood. Kathryn wandered around the building looking for another entrance. There wasn't one, and she returned to the front.

Matiers was pointing to his left, giving her his spiel. 'There's a very nice ornamental garden over there. It could be quite beautiful with a little thought and tender loving care. There's also a substantial garden store, two large greenhouses and a vegetable garden which could be made productive again. Do you like gardening, Miss de Moubray?'

Lost in thought, Kathryn didn't hear him. She was staring straight ahead, trying to think of a way to get into the tomb.

Sensing her distraction, Matiers fell silent, speaking only when he felt it absolutely essential. The remainder of the garden tour took less than half an hour, and they were returning past the entrance to the caretaker's house when Schiller came out.

'Your office telephoned, Mr Remarque. I couldn't find you. They said to call back as soon as possible, said it's urgent.'

Matiers inclined his head very politely. 'Excuse me, Miss de Moubray. I'll be right back.'

'Take your time, I'll stroll back to the car. I think I've seen everything I need to see, for now.'

The caretaker didn't move a muscle. He stood very still, eyes unblinking, staring hard at Kathryn again. A spark of recognition entered the staring. She was startled when a moment later he said, 'You're a Von Trellenberg.' It was a statement, not a question.

She was about to deny it when he moved in very close. So close, she could see the whites of his eyes in detail. The pupils were bright, alert, youthful, not like an old man's at all.

'You're the living image of Klaus.'

He's mad, she thought, experiencing a quick tremor of

fear. And she was glad to hear Matiers step out of the cottage.

'It wasn't important at all, Herr Schiller.' He gave a quick look of astonishment, like a schoolteacher to a naughty boy, before starting off at a brisk pace towards the car.

Kathryn held back for a second, looking at the old man who was rooted to the spot, still muttering.

'You're a Von Trellenberg.'

Kathryn insisted on being dropped off in the town of Erfurt. 'It's such a pretty area, I thought I might stay overnight, do some sightseeing tomorrow. Get a feel for the place.'

It was obvious by the look on the estate agent's face that he didn't believe her reasons. But who was he to argue, he had to get back into town for a dinner date, and was late. At her request he stopped the car in front of a small timber-framed pension and Kathryn jumped out, saying, 'I'll be in touch, and thanks.'

She waited until the Mercedes was out of sight before walking into the hotel and asking for a room.

A few minutes later she was being shown into a single room overlooking the street on one side, and a kitchen wall on the other. It was clean and basic, with a low-beamed ceiling and bright red gingham bedspread and drapes. She freshened up then walked down the creaking staircase to the tiny entrance hall.

'I'd like a taxi and a drink please.' A young boy behind the desk smiled. 'In which order?'

Kathryn returned his smile. 'Depends which comes first.'

'In this town it's debatable.' He picked up the telephone. 'I'll call for the taxi, then get you a drink.' As he dialled the number, he asked, 'What would you like?'

Kathryn ordered a vodka and tonic and waited for him to complete the taxi booking and leave for the bar before slipping behind the reception, her eyes alighting on a small brass box. She lifted the lid to see an assortment of paper clips, elastic bands and postage stamps. Hearing footsteps, she quickly popped the box into her shoulder bag before the lad reappeared with a tray bearing her drink. Two seconds later the taxi driver poked his head around the door.

'Taxi?'

The boy said, 'For the lady,' handing her the vodka.

She took a couple of sips then left, jumping into the back of the car. 'Schloss Bischofstell, please.'

Looking out at the gathering shadows of dusk, the taxi driver seemed concerned when he said, 'Are you meeting someone up there? It's getting dark . . .'

'Yes, I'm meeting someone,' she assured him, hoping she'd be able to rouse the caretaker. 'But I need you to wait for me, and bring me back. OK?'

The driver started the car. 'Fine by me: you pay, I stay.'

Herr Schiller was standing next to the gates when the taxi pulled up, illuminating his shock of white hair in its headlights. He showed no sign of surprise when Kathryn jumped out; it was as if he was expecting her.

He just nodded as she walked past him into the courtyard and told him, 'I want to talk to you.'

Silently he led her beyond the courtyard into the low timber-framed cottage she had stood outside earlier. It was surprisingly bright and cheerful inside.

'Do you live here alone?'

He shuffled towards a brick fireplace. The grate was neatly stacked with paper and logs waiting to be lit. 'Yes, my wife died five years ago. I can't offer you much to drink, a beer perhaps?'

She shook her head. 'No thanks, Mr ... ?' She'd forgotten his name.

'Schiller, Erwin Schiller, and you are?'

'Kathryn de Moubray. My mother was Freda Von Trellenberg.'

He began to laugh, and to her surprise the sound was full of youthful gaiety. Between chuckles he managed to say, 'I knew it! As soon as I laid eyes on you. Well, well, Freda's daughter ...' His laughter subsided, but his voice was equally animated. 'Your mother and I used to play together as children. My father was head gardener here, we lived in a grace and favour cottage on the estate. There's only a year between us. Freda was younger than me, or was it the other way round? I can't remember. Anyway Joachim was older, and would have nothing to do with us. And Ingrid was sullen and bad-tempered, always running to her father telling tales. Freda and I used to hide in the woods from Ingy, as we called her. Freda would jump out of the bushes to scare her, and I'd pull her pigtails.' He laughed again. For Kathryn it was like being in the company of a child.

'Oh, we had such fun in those days! The house used to ring with laughter, and what parties! Dignitaries from all walks of life dined here. From the Weimar, the arts, the professions, even—' He dropped his voice to a low whisper, looking over his shoulder, 'Even Hitler came once. I'll never

340

forget that day. It was the talk of the entire district for weeks. I saw him standing over there in that very corner.' He pointed. 'What times . . . Then the war came, and it all changed.' Schiller spat into his fireplace. 'The Russians robbed us of everything, every shred of pride and dignity.'

Kathryn had to stop herself saying that it was Hitler who had started what the Allies had been obliged to finish. Abruptly she changed the subject.

'My mother always talked fondly of this house. She told me of her wonderful childhood here, and how she had longed to come back, but of course that wasn't possible. Unfortunately she died before reunification.'

Schiller coughed, then spat again. 'I'd like to have seen Freda again. That would have been nice; yes, I'd have liked that. I don't get many visitors these days.'

'I'm sure she would have loved to see you, too.' Kathryn's tone was warm and attentive. 'Before my mother died she talked of the family tomb, of how she would love to be buried there with her ancestors.'

Kathryn fished in her bag, pulling out the purloined brass box. She held it in front of the old man's face with a reverent expression on hers.

'These are my mother's ashes. It was her dying wish, to be with her ancestors in Bischofstell.'

Erwin touched the lid of the box with his forefinger. Kathryn prayed he wouldn't try to open it. Quickly she pulled it into her chest.

'I noticed earlier that the tomb entrance is padlocked, do you have a key?' She was dismayed when he shook his head.

'Nobody goes in there. I haven't even been in myself.'

He shuffled from one foot to the other, lost in thought, until suddenly his eyes opened wider as he remembered something. 'There *was* a set of keys for all the padlocks, used to be kept by the old gardener . . .'

Asking her to wait, the caretaker left the cottage. He returned five minutes later carrying a torch and rattling a tin. Kathryn thrilled to the sound of metal on metal.

Schiller looked pleased with himself. 'Found them in the old gardener's shed! Now, let's go see if we can grant dear Freda's last wish before it gets too dark.'

The moon, rising behind the mausoleum, lit the still surface of the lake, making it gleam like a sheet of sheer black ice. The ornamental eagle, ominous in the darkness, looked ready to swoop down on their heads. Yet Kathryn felt no fear, only the heady rush of anticipation as she watched Schiller try his selection of keys. Finally she heard a satisfactory click then his triumphant cry: 'That's the one!'

She breathed a sigh of relief when the restraining chain fell on to the stone step with a dull clang. Stepping forward she asked the old man, 'Would you mind very much, Erwin, may I call you Erwin?'

He seemed delighted by this. 'Of course . . .'

'It's just that I would like to do this alone. You do understand, don't you?'

Handing her the torch, he touched the lid of the brass box, saying in a solemn voice, 'Rest in peace, Freda.' Then he stepped back, swallowed up by the descending darkness.

To Kathryn's surprise, the door of the tomb opened easily, without so much as a creak – the hinges could have been oiled last week. She shone the torch over the walls, patches of mildew casting darker shadows in the dim light. A rat scampered inches from her right foot, making her stifle a scream. Moving forward into the gloom, she heard the sound of her own feet – deafening in the still chamber – crunching dead leaves. A moment later her leg touched something cold. She directed the torch beam on to what looked, at first glance, to be a coffin. Then, moving the light along the surface, Kathryn could see it was a huge lead crate much too big to be a coffin. Unless the body was ten foot tall, and about five hundred pounds. Standing the torch on the floor, she tried to lift the lid. It was too heavy. She picked up the torch again, directing the light all around her. It came to rest on a large crowbar propped up against the far wall. Using this as a lever, she tried the lid again. It moved slightly. Encouraged, she sat on the middle of the crowbar, pushing down with her full weight. The lid opened a small crack. She tried again. This time it fell open with a resounding clang. Shaking with the exertion, she shone the torch inside before her nerve failed her.

The crate looked as if it was full of bales of cloth stacked in neat bundles. She lifted the top one out; it resembled a roll of bedding. Then Kathryn peeled the cloth back to reveal a roll of canvas. With the utmost care she unfurled it and shone the torch on it. It was a portrait in oil of a young girl. Moving the beam of light down the painting, she let it rest in the corner. She felt her pulse quicken when she read the name 'Renoir'.

Her excitement mounting, Kathryn quickly counted the neatly packed canvases remaining in the crate. She calculated that there were at least fifty. Then, even deeper within the tomb, the torch picked out another crate similar to the one she had opened, and beyond that another. Suddenly, she turned sharply at the sound of a voice.

'Are you all right in there?'

Kathryn shouted back at Schiller to reassure him, then she grasped the lid of the open crate with both hands. But it was too heavy to replace. She decided to leave it open and was about to rejoin the caretaker outside, when she spotted something else slipped down the side of the trunk. Slipping her hand inside, she pulled out a leatherbound book. Shining the torch on the cover, she read the gold-embossed lettering. *'My War. 1939–1944.'* She opened it to see the name 'Klaus Von Trellenberg' on the first page, with his date of birth written underneath. She snapped the book shut, stuffing it down the front of her sweater.

Moments later, she was outside in the moonlight again with Erwin. He was holding a length of chain in one hand, the padlock was in the other. She waited, the night masking her emotions as he fed the chain through the padlock, locking it with a resounding click.

Chapter Twenty-one

The message arrived with his scrambled eggs: the envelope neatly propped up against a glass of orange juice on the breakfast tray. Adam took a sip of juice, thinking how fresh it tasted. Then, forking eggs into his mouth, he began to read the fax.

Dear Adam,
  I've found the Krantz art collection. Here in Germany. There are about 150 pieces in all. There's too much to explain in a fax! I'm in a place called Erfurt near Leipzig. Staying at the Hotel Bayerischer Hof. Telephone number is 03601 800. I await your call.
Kathryn de Moubray.

Adam's mouth dropped open as he reread the fax. It had been sent to the gallery in New York. Joanne had forwarded it, with a short note of her own: 'Got back after a great vacation. Thought this wouldn't wait for your return! Good luck!'

Christ, Kathryn! How on earth . . . ? Adam crossed to the small desk in the corner of the room. He was shaking, and there was a whooshing noise in his head like surf rushing over shingles. He found the code for Germany, mouthing a silent prayer as the telephone rang out. At last he heard a man's voice.

'Hotel Bayerischer Hof.'

'Miss de Moubray, please.' Adam tapped his foot impatiently while he waited to be connected, and felt like screaming at the voice which came back and politely spoke to him in accented English.

'I'm sorry, Miss de Moubray is not in her room. May I take a message?'

'Tell her Adam Krantz rang. I'm on my way to Germany and will be in Erfurt later today. By the way, do you have a room for tonight?' He waited while the receptionist consulted the reservation chart.

'Yes, sir. We have a small single, not one of our nicer rooms. Or a deluxe double with a wonderful view. The rate for the single is—'

Adam cut in, 'Give me the deluxe.'

'Will that be for just the one night, sir?'

Adam thought about the paintings, and German bureaucracy. 'I'm not sure at the moment, but I think I'd better make it for at least two.'

The voice was saying, 'We look forward to welcoming you to the Hotel Bayerischer . . .' when Adam hung up.

Adam caught the flight from London to Frankfurt at eleven-fifteen. It was delayed for fifteen minutes and he arrived in Germany at one thirty-five. After clearing Immigration, he hired a six series BMW similar to his own, taking the A5 road towards Kassel.

The traffic was light, and he estimated he could cover the two hundred kilometres to Erfurt in an hour and a half. He probably would have done so, if he had not taken a wrong turning. But he spoke no German and wasted twenty minutes trying to get directions – eventually provided by an American tourist.

On finally entering the town, and checking in at the Hotel Bayerischer Hof, he had no more time to lose. 'I'd like to see Miss de Moubray. Can you call her room, please.'

'No need, I'm here.' Kathryn was standing behind him. 'I saw you arrive from my room. I've been waiting for you.'

The palms of Adam's hands were wet with sweat, and he gripped the handle of his bag tighter to stop it slipping from his grasp. His voice sounded as nervous as he felt. 'I caught the first available flight. In fact I'm still in shock.'

Kathryn gave him a warning look, followed by, 'I think you should freshen up in your room, then we can talk.'

Adam glanced at the receptionist with understanding. He accepted his room key and declined an offer of help with his luggage. Then, mounting the staircase to his left, he inclined his head in Kathryn's direction. She followed. Neither of them spoke until they were safely in the room and Adam had locked the door. She sat at the bottom of the four-poster bed, and Adam leaned against the window facing her.

Framed by the heavily carved wooden posts, draped in red velvet, she appeared very small. Her eyes were darker than he remembered.

'Is it true, Kathryn, what you said in your fax?' There was a buzzing in his ears reminiscent of that experienced when standing on his head as a child.

'Yes, it's true. You remember I mentioned that Klaus had whispered something to me, the day he was arrested in St Lucia?'

Adam recalled the conversation over lunch in the Savoy. 'Something to do with ghosts?'

'That's right. His actual words were *Schlafen mit Geistern*. *Sleeping with ghosts*. I had no idea what it meant until I went to see my father in the country. The same day you went to court for the injunction hearing.'

Adam said, 'By the way L won.' Then he thought how little that seemed to matter in the light of what Kathryn was telling him now.

'I know. Jack told me.' A quick vision of Jack's furious face flashed in front of her eyes, but she concentrated on the matter in hand.

'To cut a long story short, Dad told me that a few weeks before her death my mother asked him to lend her some money to visit her father and pay for him to be buried in the Von Trellenberg tomb in the country Schloss in Mühlhausen. It was at that point I had an idea: suppose Klaus had been trying to impart a clue to me? *Sleeping with ghosts*: the family tomb. It was a long shot, but I drove to Surrey to see my Aunt Ingrid, to find out more. When I arrived at her cottage, I learnt that she was in hospital. Dying. I went straight there – only to be confronted by Stefan, her son. He'd told me she was away in Berlin! And I believe he's the man who was trying to sell the Monet in the first place.'

Adam intervened. 'So *that's* where the Monet came from.'

Kathryn nodded. 'I assume Ingrid had hidden the picture, then Stefan found it ... sold it to Fleming ... who subsequently sold it to Jack.' She didn't add that she suspected Stefan of murdering Gavin Fox: that was one for the police to sort out.

'Anyway, I flew to Berlin. I couldn't remember the name of the Schloss. It was written on the back of a photograph I'd found, but I'd burnt that weeks ago. As it happened, things turned out to be pretty easy. I went to the post office, found out the name of the house. I then went to the local authority in Erfurt who told me the house was for sale, and gave me the addresses of three estate agents. For once, I was grateful to Germanic efficiency! I posed as a potential buyer and made an appointment to view the Schloss.

'We went out there yesterday afternoon and I saw the mausoleum. But it was padlocked, hadn't been opened for years. I had to persuade the old caretaker to let me into the tomb. And let's just say I did so without the aid of either sex or money.'

Adam could not help grinning, even though he was agog to hear the end of the story.

'Anyway . . . there's a crate in there bigger than a coffin. It took all my strength to lift the lid.'

Adam watched her grip the edge of the bed, screwing the bedspread into a tight ball.

'That crate is full of paintings, Adam! Dozens of canvases, all rolled separately in what looks like baby blankets. There's another two crates, slightly smaller, which I assume contain more art. I didn't have a chance to look.' She swallowed, coughing to clear her throat. 'I'm sure Klaus was trying to tell me about the hidden art that day in St Lucia, and I'm certain if we'd had more time together he would have told me everything.'

Breathing deeply, Adam crossed to the window. His arms were rigid, fixed to his sides as he looked down on the street below. He saw people going about their daily business. Two women holding shopping baskets entered a butcher's; a poodle was peeing up the side of a gleaming Mercedes; and a couple of tourists, cameras slung across their bent backs, gazed in a shop window. The normality of the scene seemed completely incongruous when all around him felt unreal. When he turned round, he was fighting back tears. 'Goddamit, Kathryn! I don't know what to say . . .'

In three steps she covered the space between them and found his hand. She squeezed it gently. 'You don't have to say anything.' Then handing him a sheet of foolscap, she added, 'Take a look at that lot.'

The paper was crisp, and yellowed with age, the corners curling. He read the heading, to which an English translation had been appended: '*10th November 1939. Protocol recorded in the residence of the Jew Joseph Maximilian Krantz b. 21/11/1896. Presently in protective custody. The housekeeper Eva Gurtner, Gentile b. 16/7/1902 was present. Criminal investigator Hermann Preuss and* SS *Oberführer Klaus Von Trellenberg officiated.*'

Adam could hear his own heart thumping like a tribal drum in his ears as he read the inventory that followed.

5	DEGAS EDGAR	(*oil on canvas*)
4	MONET CLAUDE	(*oil on canvas*)
8	BONNARD PIERRE	(*oil on canvas*)
12	MATISSE HENRI	(*mixed*)
4	MANET EDOUARD	(*etchings*)
2	NOLDE EMIL	(*oil on canvas*)
16	BRAQUE GEORGES	(*drawings*)
4	RENOIR PIERRE AUGUSTE	(*oil on canvas*)
6	DÜRER ALBRECHT	(*watercolours*)

2	CRANACH LUCAS	(*oil on canvas*)
1	VERMEER JAN	(*oil on canvas*)
4	TOULOUSE-LAUTREC HENRI	(*prints*)
4	REMBRANDT VAN RIJN	(*etchings*)
2	PISSARRO CAMILLE	(*watercolours*)

He felt foolish as his tears dropped on to the foolscap, blurring his vision. Embarrassed, he quickly wiped his tear-stained face with the back of his hand, as he heard Kathryn speaking.

'Come on then, Adam Krantz; let's go check the treasure – see if all your paintings are there, before someone else steals them.'

'Erwin, I'd like to introduce you to Adam Krantz.'

They were standing in the courtyard at Schloss Bischofstell. The caretaker stepped closer to Adam, scratching his head. '*Krantz*, I know that name. You any relation to Joseph Krantz?'

'He was my grandfather.'

'Well, well . . .' the old man said, chuckling. 'What with Freda's daughter, and now you! Your grandfather used to come here often, you know.'

Adam searched the old man's eyes, as surprised as Kathryn had been by their brightness. 'You knew my grandfather?'

'He was a close friend of Ernst Von Trellenberg. I heard my father talk about him sometimes; your grandfather loved the gardens here at Bischofstell. They were a wonderful sight in those days! Lakes and fountains, and tall hedges all cut in different shapes by twelve gardeners. Not counting the two apprentices and me. Mr Krantz would spend hours talking to my father Walther about landscaping, and plants. My father always said that for such a wealthy and powerful man Joseph Krantz had not lost the common touch.'

Encouraged by this, Adam said, 'My grandfather was a Jew. Before the war he owned a large collection of art. As you probably know, Jews had to register all assets over five thousand Deutsche Marks to the government. Often they had those assets confiscated.'

Erwin, who now looked solemn, gave a silent nod.

'Joseph Krantz entrusted his entire art collection to Klaus Von Trellenberg, who was the son of one of his closest friends. The art was packed into crates which Klaus stored in the Von Trellenberg tomb here at Bischofstell. Kathryn found out, that's why she came here.'

Erwin looked at Kathryn, who confirmed what Adam had said.

'I *am* Freda Von Trellenberg's daughter, but I didn't come here to bury her ashes. I came to look for the lost art; it's here, Erwin, in the tomb, where my grandfather hid it more than fifty years ago! I'm really sorry I had to lie to you.'

Erwin looked from one face to the other, then he burst into his infectious laughter. 'Don't be sorry, I haven't had this much fun in years!'

They counted one hundred and eighty-five pictures, packed into three crates. There were eighty-six oils, and thirty-four watercolours, the remainder made up of etchings and drawings.

'I want you to have this.' Adam handed the caretaker a

Cranach drawing he estimated to be worth at least three hundred thousand dollars. 'Sell it and retire.'

His eyes shining, Erwin looked first at Adam then the drawing. A moment later Kathryn was sure that the old man's laughter could be heard for miles around.

On arriving back at the hotel, Adam called David Greenberg his lawyer in New York, then the American Embassy. He took a subsequent call from Greenberg that resulted in a long conversation with a German lawyer based in Berlin. They arranged to meet the following day.

It was almost nine when Adam rang down to the desk to order a bottle of champagne. The best the hotel had to offer was a non-vintage Moët & Chandon, thankfully it was ice-cold. Kathryn was in his room, sitting on a small dressing-table stool. He sat on the edge of the bed.

All day he had been trying to think of a way to thank Kathryn. Words seemed so trite. He had thought about offering her a choice of one of the paintings. Then dismissed it as insensitive, it categorized her relationship to him with that of the caretaker. Eventually he decided the simplest way would be to ask her what she would like, and was about to do so when she spoke first.

'By the way, I found something else in the trunk.'

'You did?'

She fished in her bag, pulling out a leatherbound book. 'This is Klaus Von Trellenberg's diary. It's in German but I read the whole lot last night. It makes interesting reading. My grandfather was a Nazi, there's no denying that. He moved in high circles and, if he hadn't escaped, would have been tried and sentenced for war crimes. But he did lose

353

faith in the regime, and he did try to do something about his disillusionment and horror at what was happening. He was arrested in 1942 for alleged resistance, then imprisoned and acquitted on lack of evidence.' She tapped the leather cover, 'It's all in here. There's a lot of propaganda stuff which I won't bore you with, but there are four passages I've scribbled down in translation and which I'd like you to hear. The first one was written in November 1938.'

Adam wasn't sure he was in the mood for the outpouring of a repentant Nazi, but had no choice as Kathryn began to read aloud.

'I have been with Joseph Krantz today. We talked in depth about his emigration and the dangerous position he finds himself in since the terrible events of Kristallnacht. *The pressure on the Jews is increasing enormously – arrest and anti-Semitic violence is rife in the streets. Joseph has been issued with an order to report all his assets, both business and personal. My father warned him to get out of Germany last year, but he refused to leave his beloved homeland. Yet in spite of all this, he remains in good spirits and is always a wonderful host, articulate and warm. I'm trying to obtain the necessary papers for him to leave Germany, but it's getting increasingly difficult. I hope to have some good news for him later this week.'*

'The next entry relating to Joseph Krantz comes a week later,' Kathryn explained.

'I've had news today that I am to leave Berlin. I have spoken to Joseph, explaining that I will no longer be able to help him. As part of the Aryanization programme, I have advised him to sign all his worldly goods over to my safekeeping. He has my sworn promise that they will not

be confiscated, and will duly be passed on to his male descendants in the event of his death.'

'Now, listen; we go to January 1939,' said Kathryn.

'Today was a sad day for Joseph Krantz and myself. Together we packed up his art collection. Joseph has had three crates specially made, the insides lined with wax paper. All the prints and drawings were removed from their mats, and the paintings from their stretchers and frames. The canvases were rolled individually and wrapped like babies in fine woollen cloth. We prepared the inventory together and it was witnessed by Eva Gurtner, Joseph's housekeeper. I embraced Joseph whom I have known since I was five years old, promising to keep his treasures safe. Before we parted he insisted on giving me a gift of a Monet. I am not a lover of the new Impressionist work, and I tried to refuse. But he insisted, telling me that my Luize had always admired the painting, because Le Port d'Honfleur reminds her of her childhood growing up near the sea at Bremerhaven.'

Adam's mouth fell open. 'Holy Shit! So, it wasn't stolen?' Not looking up, Kathryn carried on as if he hadn't spoken.

'Joseph was right. When I returned home, my wife was thrilled and made me hang the painting there and then. I've stored the crates in the family mausoleum at Schloss Bischofstell next to the body of my father. When all this is over, and I don't think that will be long, I hope Joseph and I will be able to share a bottle of his finest claret together, whilst listening to our favoured Handel.'

She paused for a moment, the diary moving slightly in her shaking hands. The centre of her palms felt wet, and

355

she gripped tighter as she read the last passage. It was dated 15th December 1944.

'Tonight I am leaving Germany, leaving the mayhem and devastation of the wasteland that was once my beloved homeland. As I write, I can think only of my family, but am convinced it will be much worse for them if I stay. I live in hope they will be able to join me very soon.

'I have not forgotten my promise to Joseph Krantz. I have written to Luize explaining everything; I know she will make sure his art collection is returned to the rightful heirs. I have no idea where I will be tomorrow.'

Kathryn felt her voice breaking up, as she read the final sentence.

'I still believe in God, and I hope he can find it in his heart, to forgive me.'

Kathryn closed the book.

Adam was confused. Elated by the discovery of his longed-for art collection, and tormented by a mixture of other emotions. He could feel his father's presence. He'd felt it in the past, but this was stronger than ever before. Ben was talking to him, his voice as clear as a bell rang in his ears: *What an ironic twist of fate, son. After all your years of fruitless searching, it's taken Klaus's granddaughter to reunite you with your past.*

Kathryn stood close to him. 'What are you thinking, Adam?'

Running his hand across his jaw, then biting his bottom lip, he said, 'I was thinking about my father, and your grandfather: ironic, don't you reckon? After the years I hunted Klaus, all the time I spent hating him, at the end of the day he'd tried to *help* my grandfather. And it was

356

you, his granddaughter, who found my art collection. It's too weird. I feel like I'm acting in some Hollywood movie, and any minute the director's going to say, "Cut" and we return to the real world.'

Kathryn clutched the diary close to her chest. 'I know the fact that our grandfathers were friends, and Klaus tried to help, probably doesn't change anything for you, Adam.' She paused, 'But it does for me.'

'I'm not sure of anything right now. For the next few hours, do you think we could forget the past? I don't want to talk about it.' Then he added, 'Or the future.'

'What *do* you want?'

He was smiling when he said, 'I wanna get drunk.' Then, 'Join me?'

As if on cue the champagne arrived. They drank it, and ordered another bottle, both giggling when Kathryn tripped on the bedside rug. She stumbled, losing her balance, and was still giggling when Adam caught her in his arms. He held her tight, and longer than necessary. In that short moment she felt a rush of heat fill her entire body, and her face was flushed scarlet when he eventually dropped his hands. Neither of them moved. Kathryn laughed a little, it was forced and brittle, to cover her nervousness.

He took a single step back to her.

'Adam, I'm scared,' she managed to mumble in a small voice.

He cupped her face in his hands and, kissing her, whispered, 'Snap.'

Then he was eating her, covering her mouth with his, kneading her lips, licking, biting and touching every inch of bare flesh he could find. She gave him more, tearing at

357

her own clothes in frenzy, exposing her nakedness for him to feast upon. Whispering her name over and over, he dropped to his knees in front of her, his hands gently gripping her hips. She stroked the top of his dark head, watching his awed fascination as he gazed at her large breasts rising and falling in motion with her heavy breathing. Kathryn would never forget the look on his face before he fell on her, sucking each nipple hungrily like a child suckling his mother. It felt totally natural, in fact nothing in her entire life had felt this natural.

'I want you, Adam. Inside me, deep inside.' As she uttered these words, she felt as if she had been searching for years and had suddenly found the key to her soul mate's cell.

In silence she helped him undress, touching his stomach where the dark hair curled in his navel, her fingertips tracing a downward route. Then taking his hand, she led him to the bed, skin to skin, body to body.

I've never wanted anything in my entire life as much as this, she thought, when Adam entered her, saying her name.

Two days later, Adam and Kathryn checked into the Hotel Bristol Kempinski in Berlin. The following week was spent in frenzied meetings with lawyers, the German Ministry of the Interior and the German Cultural Foundation. At the weekend they were joined by an associate of Adam's from the Institute for Art Research in New York. He came with Oskar Weiss, a renowned German art historian, to authenticate the Protocol, and the signatures of Von Trellenberg and the accompanying criminal investigator. Oskar, a Jew who had left Germany in 1935 to live in England, took great interest in Von Trellenberg's diary and spent hours poring over it with Kathryn.

On Saturday afternoon, after a long lunch, Kathryn accompanied Adam on a pilgrimage to the street where his father had been born. It was now filled by a block of flats. That night he took her to the Opera at the Staatsoper. Afterwards they walked down the Unter den Linden – Kathryn recalling Klaus's reminiscence of similar evenings spent with his own father. Later they talked long into the night, discussing their hopes, their fears and their joys. Kathryn had never before confided so much to any single person and she decided that Dr Gillman would be proud of her.

Afraid of scaring Adam off, she held back from saying that she now knew what all the fuss was about; why they wrote countless songs and wonderful poetry about this thing called love. It was almost dawn when they eventually slept, slotted into each other's bodies like two spoons.

The ringing of the telephone woke Adam first; still half asleep, Kathryn heard him say, 'Yeah, it's Adam Krantz, put her through.'

Adam was still wondering how on earth Jennifer had tracked him down when she announced without preamble, 'It's Calvin. He's missing, he ran away from school three days ago, and hasn't been seen or heard of since. Hell, Adam, I'm scared!' Kathryn turned in her sleep, one eye open she saw by the look on Adam's face that something was wrong. Suddenly wide awake, she sat up, looking at him quizzically.

Adam was already out of bed. 'I'm on my way. If I can

get a flight this morning, I should be back in New York later today.' There was a pause then he said with more confidence than he felt, 'Don't worry, honey. I'm goddamn sure as hell he'll be all right. If I know anything about Cal he'll be somewhere warm, where he can get his hands on a pizza and beer.'

But when he put the phone down, he was pale. He sat on the edge of the bed, resting his head in his hands, worry evident in his voice when he told Kathryn the news, adding, 'Jennifer's distraught.'

When Kathryn reached out to him, he moved; not deliberately, but even so she felt excluded, aware this was something she couldn't share. 'I'm sorry, Adam,' she was trying to say when he picked up the telephone again. As she slipped out of bed, crossing the space to the bathroom, she heard him speaking to the hotel desk, asking them to book him on the first available New York flight: 'I don't mind which airline.'

When Kathryn closed the bathroom door, she was filled with an overwhelming sense of isolation. It was familiar, yet felt more acute after the closeness she'd shared with Adam over the last week. When she emerged, he was dressed and hurriedly throwing clothes into a suitcase, not looking at her.

They both jumped when the phone rang. Adam took the call. It was the desk, he was reserved on the Lufthansa flight to JKF at eleven-twenty. But it was already after nine and he would have to leave within ten minutes to catch it. As he grabbed his leather jacket and bag, she touched his arm thinking, *I want a little more time with you.* Aloud, she said, 'I'm coming with you to the airport; I'll pick up the first flight to London. There's nothing to keep me in Berlin now.'

He nodded his understanding. 'Come on then, let's go.'

On the journey out to the airport by cab, neither of them spoke much. Adam was preoccupied by Calvin, running all the possibilities of where he could be over and over in his head. Kathryn was preoccupied with thoughts of Adam, imprinting his physical characteristics on her mind. Like being on a quiz programme where the contestant has to memorize lots of objects in a short space of time, then recall them. That's what she wanted to be able to do after he had gone.

As they reached the airport terminal, Adam was staring straight ahead when he said, 'I want you to know, Kathryn, that I've had an amazing time with you.' The sentence had such a final ring, she felt like he'd just plunged a sharp knife deep in her belly. He was out of the car before she could reply, ready to race through the revolving doors. Minutes later, she joined him at his check-in desk. They were both stiff and awkward, like gauche teenagers on a blind date.

'I'll go and get my ticket now.' She looked at the departure screen. 'I might get on the British Airways flight, it leaves at twelve. Plenty of time to buy duty free, I could do with some perfume, and I promised to get my godson one of those Swatch watches with the bleepers. He's been harping on about one for ages.' Her own voice prattling banalities made her want to scream, and she was pleased when he eventually interrupted.

'By the way, Kathryn, I never got round to saying thank you for what you did. It took a lot of intuition, and guts as well. I want to do something for you. You know, like give you something.'

She pointed to his groin. 'I think you just did, all last week.'

It was the first time she had seen him blush, and she felt her own cheeks redden, too. 'Will I see you again, Adam?'

He'd been dreading this, and it showed. 'Right now, I'm not sure. I've got a lot of stuff to sort out with Jennifer, and now this thing with Calvin.'

She said simply, 'I hope he's OK.'

Adam said nothing further and a silent wall seemed to slide between them. But Kathryn couldn't let him go without telling him how she felt; she knew if she didn't say it now, she would never say it. *Love knows no shame, just do it.* She willed herself, and the words came tumbling out: 'Adam, I'm in love with you. That means I'll be there for you, if and when you need me.' She searched his face hopefully. His mouth was taut, yet his eyes communicated his understanding. Lifting her free hand to his lips, he kissed her fingertips first, then the centre of her palm.

'I'll be in touch,' he said, letting her fingers slip slowly from his grip.

Is that all, she wanted to scream at him. *Is that the lot, is that all I get? Damn you, Adam Krantz, damn you!*

She watched him cross the concourse, suddenly seized by a terrible premonition that she would never see him again. She thought at one point that he was going to turn and wave, but she was wrong.

Kathryn began to shake as she felt the cold steal over her body, an all-consuming icy chill that seemed to freeze the very marrow of her bones.

Chapter Twenty-two

Sean Edwards was tired. He was not just exhausted from lack of sleep; he was tired of being a policeman. He'd left an irate Greg Henderson back at the Yard who had now given him just twenty-four hours to come up with some evidence or he was off the Fleming case.

Henderson had dismissed the telephone call regarding Stefan Lang as a hoax, suggesting as usual that his inspector was barking up the wrong tree. Driving down to Surrey, Edwards had gone over and over the evidence or lack of it, coming to the conclusion that he wasn't a good detective and should take the job of sales rep his Uncle Reg had offered him in his small pharmaceutical company. But at least finding the cottage had proved easy. The lane was deserted when he pulled up in front of Coombe Ridge.

A strong wind had picked up in the last half hour and he struggled against it to open his car door. He passed through the open gate, wet leaves swirling up into the air like charred confetti. He noted several patches of weed poking out of the overgrown lawn, choking the roots of a rose bush close to the front door.

The place looks deserted he thought, as he pounded on the front door. He waited for a few moments and when there was no reply, eventually peeped through the letter box. There was no mail on the doormat, not even a circular;

this, he concluded, proved there was either someone living there, or someone calling in to check the house.

He peered through the window into the vacant front room, focusing hard to see through a thin film of grime. There was a newspaper, unevenly folded, lying on a small polished table next to a brightly patterned mug. Next he sauntered around the small property and tried the back door; it was firmly locked. Through the kitchen window he saw there was some crockery in the sink and an unopened carton of milk stood in the centre of a table.

Leaving the window, Jack searched the bin. There was a used McDonald's carton, two beer cans, three Coke cans and yesterday's *Daily Mail*. With a gloved hand he extracted a beer can, a Coke can and the McDonald's. He placed them carefully in a small bag he was carrying, and was about to replace the lid when out of the corner of his eye he saw part of a letter. It had been torn several times, and he had to fish around in the bin for the other pieces. Reassembling most of them, he read part of Gavin Fox's address in Sussex and the first five numerals of his telephone number. Totally engrossed, he failed to hear the soft footsteps behind him and jumped when he felt someone tap him on the shoulder.

'What the fuck are you doing?'

Sean Edwards turned slowly to see a tall man dressed from head to toe in funereal black. He could not recall ever having seen eyes quite like this man's. He'd seen cold eyes before, killer eyes. But these were different: almost as if they were implanted, special effect eyes, like in a horror movie.

He experienced a quick *frisson* of fear; thinking that the Photofit was a good likeness. And in the same moment Edwards wished he hadn't come to the cottage alone.

He took a step back, fumbling in his coat pocket for his credentials, found his wallet and felt marginally better for flashing his ID in front of the man's face. 'I'm Detective Inspector Edwards; I'm looking for a man called Stefan Lang in connection with the murder of Gavin F—'

Stefan's fist entered the inspector's mouth on the final syllable and once again Sean berated himself for not bringing his partner, who had wanted to come with him. He staggered back a few feet in shock, rather than loss of balance. There was a loud ringing in his ears, then a gush of wetness flooded his mouth. He was only vaguely aware of swallowing something that he thought was a tooth, when the next blow rained down.

Stefan was feeling a great surge of power; his whole body was on fire, pulsating, vibrant, more alive than it had felt in years. He raised the hammer. 'I am the power,' he roared like the lion he was.

There was a dull clang in Sean's head as the sledgehammer made contact with his skull. He stumbled, falling to the ground, faintly aware of a dog barking, and the sound of rushing water. He touched the side of his head; it felt soft and mushy and wet, like the mud pies he used to make as a child . . . he thought before he slipped into unconsciousness.

From the moment Kathryn entered Jack's house, he was aware of a subtle change in her. He couldn't put his finger on what it was, yet knew instinctively that something had happened.

There was a contrived outward control about her that didn't fool him for a moment. He sensed that something was bubbling under her calm surface; a boiling cauldron with the lid about to lift off. They were sitting on opposite sofas in his drawing room. He'd been getting ready to go to a business function, and had been surprised by her unexpected call. He was still dressed in his bathrobe, bare feet crossed at the ankles. She was wearing no make-up, and her freshly washed hair had dried naturally in soft waves that framed her face. Jack thought she looked extremely beautiful. He thought about asking her to marry him. 'Do you want a drink, Kathryn?'

She shook her head. 'I can't stop long and anyway you're going out.'

'Only to a boring do; if I'd known you were coming back from your business trip so soon, I'd have cancelled and taken you out instead. Tomorrow night, perhaps?' He looked hopeful, and she felt like shit.

'I haven't been away on a business trip, Jack. I'm sorry I had to lie to you. I've been to Germany, where I found out that the Monet – *Le Port d'Honfleur* – wasn't stolen. It was given to my grandfather Klaus in 1939 by Joseph Krantz.'

As she uttered the words, Kathryn realized it was the first time she had referred to Klaus as her grandfather without feeling shame.

'Apparently they were friends, my grandmother had often admired the painting and it was a gift to her.' Jack showed no surprise, but she was aware that did not mean he wasn't experiencing any.

'What wonderful news! Adam Krantz is going to be pissed off,' Jack sneered. 'And I can't wait to see that bitch Nadia Foreman's face, when she finds out.' The sneer turned into short bitter laughter.

'I don't think it'll make much difference to Adam Krantz now.'

'What makes you say that, Kathryn?'

Instantly her body language changed. It was subtle, but Jack noticed the slight stiffening of her shoulders, and a faint tremor in her left hand. Intuitively he knew that he wasn't going to like what she was about to impart.

'I've been to Schloss Bischofstell, near a place called Mühlhausen in East Germany. It was the ancestral home of the Von Trellenbergs who lived there until the onset of the war. My mother apparently was born there . . .

'I found the Krantz art collection hidden in the Von Trellenberg tomb in the grounds of the estate. It's priceless: a hundred and eighty-five important masterpieces. I also found a diary written by my grandfather. Although it didn't absolve him of blame, it helped to explain a few things, family things. Jack, I—' Kathryn's voice trailed off, she looked down, staring at the back of her hands.

'Have you got something else to say to me?' Jack spoke in a deliberately cool voice, in stark contrast to the way he felt.

'Yes, I have, Jack. I don't want to see you again.'

Still outwardly calm, Jack said, 'Look at me, Kathryn.'

When she did as he bid, he could see she was close to tears. And in that instant he saw his daughter's face resting on Kathryn's shoulder. It looked exactly as it had done when he'd last seen her. Jack recalled his reluctance to look into her open coffin, but his wife had insisted. When he'd seen her expression of serenity, a sense of overwhelming relief had visited him. Laraine had been dressed in a long evening gown, and had looked as she had done on her eighteenth birthday. Jack had marvelled at the skill of the undertaker, and had given him a thousand pounds tip. Now, as Laraine's face faded and Kathryn's reappeared, he longed for that same sense of relief to recur.

'Why, Kathryn?' was all he could find to say. Then, when she hesitated, 'Please, I need to know the truth.'

'I'm in love with another man.' There; she'd said what she'd spent all last night rehearsing. It had proved easier than anticipated. 'I'm sorry, Jack.'

'Don't be, Kathryn,' he heard himself say in an indifferent manner, as if talking to an employee or a distant acquaintance. 'Am I allowed to ask who he is?' She nodded, but he'd already added, 'Or shall I guess. Can I have two clues first?'

'I don't want to play games, Jack. I think you know how much I detest—'

His interruption was swift. 'OK, no games, no clues; just *one* guess.' In that instant the light flickered across his spectacles, illuminating his eyes which were gleaming like two diamond chips. 'Here's a wild guess, in my opinion a rank outsider. But instinct tells me I'm right. Is the new love of your life our arrogant American friend, Mr Adam Krantz?'

The strength and control of her own voice astonished her. 'Yes, that's right. I've fallen in love with Adam Krantz. He's married, and I've got no idea if we even have a future together. But what I've had with him this past week can't be compared to anything I've had before. And, I don't want anyone else. Can you understand?'

'I can understand that you are hopelessly infatuated with an undeniably attractive man, but you should think carefully before making any rash decisions.'

Kathryn had anticipated that Jack would try to talk her round, to manipulate her, in his 'Daddy knows best' sort of way. She didn't blame him. She knew he hated losing. But she stood up, she was weary and eager to go.

'This isn't a decision, Jack, it's an *emotion*. I'm responsible for what I do, but not for the way I feel.' She crossed the space that separated them. 'I want us to be friends.'

'*Friends!*' He spat the word out with such disdain she was momentarily shaken. 'I'm in love with you, Kathryn. I've hardly slept or eaten since you've been away . . . fucking Adam Krantz. I suspected you were up to something by the tone of your voice on the telephone. And Paul told me that Krantz had left a brief message for Nadia before leaving the country, not saying where he was going. I put two and two together. Now, you offer me friendship like it's some sort of prize. Well, I don't need any more friends, Kathryn. Sincere or otherwise. I've got them coming out of my every orifice.'

Kathryn could see an ugly scene developing. She moved cautiously towards the door. 'I'm leaving now, Jack – before either of us says something we might be sorry for.'

He snarled. 'Yes, off you go! Run away, walk out the door, and out of my life just like that. Things are starting to get mean and nasty, so why not leave me to mop up the debris? It's a good trick of yours: stir the shit, then leave before it hits the fan.'

She had promised herself she would not allow him to antagonize her. She was angry now, because he was succeeding.

He grabbed her arm, pulling her roughly towards him.

'Is he a good fuck, Kathryn, is that it? What does he do for you that I don't? Tell me!'

She wrestled her arm free, backing towards the door. She was soft spoken, but Jack heard her last words distinctly.

'He's not my father.'

If it hadn't been for a crash on the M4, Stefan would have caught his flight to Nice. As it was, he arrived at the British Airways check-in desk when the plane he was supposed to be on was already flying over Kent. Stefan tried to remain calm in front of the ground stewardess.

'I'm sorry, Mr Lang, Flight BA 257 to Nice has just left. If you'll wait a minute, I'll check in the office to see if there's any availability on the next flight.'

Stefan thought he detected a slight quiver in the girl's voice, then put it down to his own overwrought nerves, and the fact that he desperately needed a line. As soon as he'd checked in, he would snort all the stuff he had on him. The thought gave him an anticipatory surge of pleasure, as did the idea of Fleming's shocked face when he would open the door of his apartment in Monaco to be greeted by Stefan. Then he felt his heart race as he recalled the moment of glory when he'd taken Gavin out. No more cocksucking for him, Stefan grinned. He'd missed Fleming once, in Zurich, but the concierge, after a little coaxing, had recalled making flight arrangements for Mr Fleming to go to Nice, and onward to Monaco. He was still smiling, when a man appeared in the position the ground stewardess had vacated. He was in plain clothes.

'Are you Mr Stefan Lang?'

There was something about the man that sent alarm bells

pealing in Stefan's ears. He said 'Yes' in a tentative way, planning to make a run for the escalator.

'Mr Lang, I'm Detective Bob Landesman. I'd like to ask you a few questions about the murder of Gavin Fox, and Detective Inspector Sean Edwards.'

Stefan immediately spun round, only to face another man blocking his path. There was an explosion in his head, followed by a drumming in his ears.

'You were seen leaving Gavin Fox's house. And at Coombe Ridge Cottage, we've found the murder weapon. It's covered in prints. Careless of you, Mr Lang.' Inspector Landesman took a step closer to Stefan. 'You're nicked.'

Jennifer was waiting for Adam when he arrived at JFK. She looked tired, but not distraught. Her first words were, 'Cal's OK, he's at your mother's.'

Adam let out a long sigh. 'Thank God! I can't tell you what's gone through my mind since you called this morning. Holy shit! I've had him in a car crash, mugged by some fruitcake, and lying dead in a gutter . . . Thank God!' he repeated. Then, 'Where the fuck *has* he been?'

Jennifer wished Adam wouldn't swear. She'd managed to stop him for a while, but he'd obviously slipped back into his old ways without her. 'I'll tell you everything in the car, your mother is expecting us for supper.'

Neither of them spoke until they were on Interstate 95, heading for Connecticut. Jennifer broke the silence. 'Calvin has spent the last few days in a motel with a girl. They smoked a little dope, and got a little bit crazy, from what I can gather.' Adam couldn't resist a smile, then composed his face when Jennifer said, 'I blame myself for all of this, and as you can imagine I've been through hell these last few days.'

He tensed when she put her foot down, moving into the outside lane to overtake. 'Slow down, Jennifer, you're driving too fast!' he snapped.

She ignored him, accelerating more, as she said, 'I've left Jordan, we had a terrible row last weekend. He and Cal argued. Jordan got very drunk and turned nasty. When I defended Cal, Jordan went berserk. I thought he was going to kill me.'

Adam experienced the strongest urge to say, *I warned you that bastard Tanner was no good.* But he resisted.

'He didn't hurt you or Cal, did he?'

Adam's obvious concern encouraged her, and she expanded the truth. 'He slapped me around a little, but nothing serious. I was more concerned about Calvin, who ran out of the house. I found him hitching a lift into the nearest town. He was in pretty bad shape emotionally.'

Jennifer pretended to stifle a sob, yet made sure it was loud enough for Adam to hear. He heard, yet felt nothing. She swivelled her eyes in his direction; his face was an impregnable mask.

They continued the drive in silence. He considered telling her about the discovery of the Krantz art, then decided he would save it for when he saw his mother.

It was dark when Jennifer zoomed up the long drive to Charlwood Lodge, the house Adam's parents had made their retirement home, bringing Helen Krantz rushing to the front door. 'Adam, darling?'

Embracing his mother, he whispered in her ear, 'How are you?'

'Fine, just fine, all the better for seeing you.' She pinched his arm, and nodded when Jennifer asked if Cal was there. 'Turned up this morning, looking for all the world like a lost soul,' she said.

The photograph had been taken five years ago, on vacation in the Florida Keys. Adam had chartered a boat for a few days' deep-sea fishing. Calvin was beaming with pride, as he displayed a prize marlin he had landed. Next to him, Jennifer was laughing and looking directly into the camera, her long hair billowing back from her tanned face. She looked beautiful, Adam observed, but there was more: she looked very much in love.

He put the frame back on the dressing table, and padded in his bare feet towards the bed. Jennifer had been given the large guest suite next door. It felt strange, to be back in this room. It had been decorated since he'd slept there last, but still held echoes of his childhood: good memories, happy times. He'd been lucky, raised in the bosom of a secure and loving family, protected and cared for by both parents. This brought him full circle to Calvin, and their conversation earlier. They had talked long after an over-excited Helen and Jennifer had gone to bed – both women were overwhelmed by the news that for almost sixty years the Krantz art collection had been safely wrapped up, like a baby, and that now Adam had recovered it.

But Adam's man-to-man talk with his son had caught him off guard, leaving him forced to conclude that Calvin was no longer a child.

He sighed, cut the light, and closed his eyes. A moment later they shot open when he felt Jennifer slip into bed next to him. Before he could speak, she had straddled him, her naked body writhing against his, whispering, 'I've missed you baby.' When he didn't respond, she rolled over and lowering her head, she took him in her mouth. Adam felt the familiar surge of desire as, skilfully, she aroused him. With both hands, Jennifer then fed him inside, making soft mewing sounds as she moved up and down, then muttering over and over, 'God, I've missed you, Adam; missed you fucking me.' As her pace quickened towards orgasm, her breathing reminded him of a panting dog. She fell on to his chest and, lying very still, she listened to his heartbeat slow down, his breathing change depth, and felt his erection slowly die. 'Did you come, Adam?' When he didn't reply, she asked again, more urgently, 'Did you?'

Pushing her to one side, he sat up, and switching on the light, said flatly, 'No, I didn't.'

Feeling hurt, she spoke in a little girl voice. 'Why not? Did Jenny do something wrong?'

Adam didn't even want to talk about it. 'No, I'm just overwrought, it's been one hell of a week.' Turning back to her, he planted a soft kiss on her cheek.

With a perceptive start, she realized it was the sort of indifferent peck given to a sister or good friend. Aware that Adam was an extremely sensitive man, Jennifer knew it would take more than a few bouts of lovemaking to win him back. But she was determined to have him. Her determination fuelled her confidence, convincing her she could restore their relationship to the way it was before.

For his part, Adam found it irksome that Jennifer assumed she could just walk back into his life as if nothing had happened: Jordan beats up on her, she gets mad, runs

374

back to him. One fuck, and suddenly it's, *I never stopped loving you, Adam*. And everything was supposed to be hunky dory. He flinched when she stroked his back, saying, 'We were so happy once, remember how it was? It could be like that again. We all make mistakes, Adam, I'm prepared to admit I've been a fool. I want us to be together again, a family, like we used to be. I know that's what Calvin wants as well.' She snuggled up close, resting in the crook of his arm. 'I promise to try really hard, if you will, even if it's just for Calvin's sake. Let's start afresh, lots of people do, let's forget the past.'

Adam stared up at the ceiling where a shaft of moonlight, shining through a fan light opposite the bed, cast a silvery glow shaped like an elongated bony finger. As a child he'd been terrified of such effects. Not afraid any more, he stared at the ghostly claw pointing at him. Yet all he could see was Kathryn: her eyes, taking on a smoky navy blue hue when she was excited. He saw her pushing her hair off her face, as she did when she laughed, and biting her bottom lip when nervous. Then her expression changed, to one of awe. He'd noticed it the first time he'd made love to her in Erfurt, and again on many subsequent occasions. It was an expression he'd only ever seen on Jennifer's face once, when she'd first held Calvin. But Kathryn looked like that whenever she touched him, as if he was the most beautiful thing she'd ever encountered. Finally, he saw her the way she'd looked that morning, when he'd left her. Like a little girl, abandoned by her parents in some strange and terrifying place. With a pang of regret, Adam wondered if he would always imagine her looking like that. With a deep sigh, he said, 'Yeah, Jen, let's forget the past.'

Epilogue

'Two minutes, one minute, on air.'

The camera panned to the neat head, and skilfully padded shoulders of Shelly McGuire.

'Tonight, I am delighted to welcome from London . . . Kathryn de Moubray, ex TV producer, who has written a wonderful book. I read it in less than two days, I just couldn't put it down.'

Kathryn groaned inwardly, wishing the whole media circus was over. Three more live interviews, a signing to do for Doubleday on Fifth Avenue tomorrow, then Cape Cod and a much needed rest.

McGuire beamed into the camera. '*Sleeping With Ghosts* has been on the New York and London bestseller lists for eighteen weeks now, and film rights have recently been optioned.' She turned to her star guest. 'I believe this is your first book, Kathryn. And it's based on a true story?'

Kathryn had been asked the same question eighteen times during the past week. The smile fixed on her face was wearing thin, and she hoped it looked more sincere than it felt.

'Yes, I decided to write it after having lived it. I thought it was a good story, and would make fascinating reading.' She refrained from telling the whole truth: that writing the book had been cathartic in helping her through an illness that she had feared at one point would take her life.

'It seems millions of people feel the same way. Your grandfather was Klaus Von Trellenberg – the Nazi who was captured in St Lucia two years ago. You were there when it happened, would you like to talk about how you found him?'

Kathryn stiffened. 'I can't give too much of the story away, my publishers will kill me.'

Feeling her guest withdraw, Shelly digressed. 'I'm sure you can tell the viewers about Adam Krantz, the New Yorker whom the main character is based on. I understand that he's donated most of the art to the museum founded in his father's name?'

'That's right. The Krantz Foundation is currently exhibiting a selection of some of the works we found in Germany, and of other paintings that were stolen or confiscated as being "degenerate" during World War Two. The exhibition will run for eight weeks.'

Shelly looked at the second timer. There was a minute and a half left. 'The ending in the book isn't true to life is it, Kathryn? You don't have to give the story away, just say yes or no.'

'No, the ending is not true.'

'Well, I'm afraid we're running out of time. I wish you even more success with the book, Kathryn, and look forward to the movie. Any ideas on who will play you?'

Kathryn laughed. 'None whatsoever, I just hope they make a good job of it.'

'It was great meeting you, I hope you enjoy the rest of your stay in New York, and thanks for appearing on McGuire Live.' Shelly beamed as Kathryn reciprocated.

Off air, she turned to her guest. 'I meant what I said about enjoying your book, I read it in forty-eight hours. I know you couldn't say on air, but would you mind telling me what actually happened?'

Kathryn was smiling now, but not like before. This time it filled her face, reaching her eyes, making them shine like polished steel.

'As you know, at the end of the book Kathryn dies of cancer, leaving a daughter by her lover. In real life, I recovered and got my man.'

'Thanks so much for telling me,' Shelly gushed. 'And now, will you inscribe my book?' She handed Kathryn a copy of *Sleeping With Ghosts*, and a pen.

Kathryn wrote in her big flowery hand:

> 'It was great being on your show, Shelly.
> Best wishes, Kathryn Krantz.'